trick

of the

spotlight

BOOK ONE

IN A SERIES OF FALLING STARS BY

m.l.east

First edition 5/5/2020
Revised 11/11/2020
Edited by Marjorie Argent, Ava Gu
Cover photography by Erik McLean
Cover design by M.L. East

ISBN 979-8-6571-8607-9
ASIN B08863XVXD

M.L. East
34ST.ML@gmail.com
linktr.ee/ML34ST
@ML34ST

♥ ♡ ♥ ♡ ♥

For my forever friend, who has read every version
and variation ever written of this book many times over.
I could not—and would not—have done this without you.
Thank you for sharing this delicious little secret with me.
Cheers to many more years, you absolute gift of a human.

♡ ♥ ♡ ♥ ♡

just a note...

This series will explore topics of sensitive nature. For readers who wish to inform themselves of what elements will feature in this book, both a *general guide* and a *comprehensive list* are available at the following link:

Views expressed within the narrative do not reflect those of the author, but she welcomes feedback on how to better engage with difficult topics in an inoffensive manner.

Thank you for your understanding.

Contents.

Smoke and mirrors.   1

Eggshells.   7

Idol eyes.   11

Aftermath.   24

DigitAlive.   29

High-strung.   36

Backstage.   42

Minchi.   48

Lucky me.   55

Delusion.   64

Maize.   71

Unreal.   76

Held.   80

Unwelcome.   83

Suite dreams.   87

Soup or salad?   98

Wrecker.   106

Harmony.   113

Dissonance.   120

Grandkid.   125

Tangerine.   133

Mocha.   137

Red light. 142

Yellow light. 149

Green light. 155

Triggered. 161

Gallery. 170

Presence. 175

Merlot. 181

Palette. 187

Fresh start. 194

Blindside. 202

Wake-up call. 210

H. 213

Denial. 217

Triple-edged. 221

Painkiller. 228

Take no prisoners. 235

No return. 241

Pressurized. 244

Breaking point. 252

No foul. 259

Insidious. 263

4-letter word. 269

Written off. 275

Centrifugal. 279

Reality check. 283

5 stages. 287

Final straw. 290

Cast.

Glossary.

Acknowledgment.

...and a hint

This series is set primarily in Seoul, South Korea, following a cast comprised of multicultural individuals. As such, this book will contain some romanized Korean and Japanese vocabulary, as well as terms and slang commonly used within the K-Pop community.

Please note –

Definitions and translations can be found in a *glossary* located at the back of the book, along with any relevant cultural context.

Smoke and mirrors.

I hadn't thought straight all week.

"We're gonna be fine, Kit. Totally fine. *More* than fine. Everything's gonna be *great*." My nerves were catchy, so neither of us could sit down, but thankfully, my manager was kind enough not to pace. We both just floated around the dressing room like it was an art gallery too modern for our taste. "Just gotta do like we rehearsed, and everything is sure to go smoothly…"

Dear, dear Ilsung—the walking pep talk responsible for every advance in my career. Any other day, he could soothe away the panic, but today, his hair was mussed and his bubbles had gone flat, because we both knew that this talk show appearance could make or break me. The entire country routinely devoured Tick Tock Talk live, and highlight reels went out to most of Asia and a huge chunk of Westerners. Stans and antis alike would be watching my every move, hanging on my every word. Even the slightest slip-up could start a firestorm on Twitter, and I'd be out of work for six months. A slightly bigger slip-up could get me canceled entirely.

Needless to say, I was second-guessing everything… especially the darn shoes. Were stilettos really the best we could come up with? Sure, I wouldn't have to walk far on camera, and sure, I'd be sitting for most of the duration of the show, but I just knew I was gonna make some all-too-GIFable gaffe, like tripping or twisting my ankle. In this world of red carpets, flashing lights, and high stages, *shoes*—which had been so inoffensive before—had become my nemesis. Every now and then, I almost missed my days of flip-flops and grass-stained sneakers. But, no. I wasn't going to trip. It wasn't in the script.

Ilsung was right. We'd practiced so much. Every detail was accounted for, right down to which way I would cross my legs on the couch. For Pete's sake, we even ran a full dress rehearsal in our studio, and I'd fielded every question perfectly according to script.

There was a knock and we both pretended not to jump.

A small bowing figure mumbled something to the effect of "They're ready for you" through a crack in the door before fleeing back down the hall. I could've vomited but I shook a laugh loose instead and we hurried to follow him.

"Past the studio door, there's a red curtain," another faceless voice told me. He gestured far more than necessary and spoke mostly to Ilsung, but I tried not to take offense. Nobody ever believed I could really understand Korean. "Wait quietly behind it. When they call you out, we'll open the curtain, and then you're on."

Ilsung held up a fist with a twitchy grin. "You can do it, Kit. Fighting!" I shouldn't have giggled but he looked almost green. And then, he was ushered away and I stepped through the massive soundproof door into the shadowy horde of staff and security.

The backstage gloom had the airless, sterile feel of a crypt, or a bunker, or maybe a bank vault. A bank vault made sense. For one hour every weekend, this studio sealed in around a select few of Korea's national treasures. Every top model, actor, and K-Pop artist had at one point stood in the cherry-red glow of this curtain, feeling the spotlight scorch through it. Someday, I'd be strong in stilettos, secure in my career, and unfazed by the neon screaming 'ON AIR.'

But not today.

"Ladies and gentlemen, I'm sure you've all heard her story… She's the idol who puts the 'global' in KJ Global Entertainment."

Bull.

KJ had plenty of other non-Korean artists—talents from China, Japan, Vietnam, Malaysia, Singapore, Thailand, et cetera—and what did it matter where I came from anyway? I was here now and I wasn't planning on leaving *ever*. Besides, the 'global' wasn't meant to signify that we fancied ourselves a diverse crowd. It stemmed simply from the fact that we marketed globally, much the same as most other Korean entertainment agencies.

"The girl who chased her dreams halfway around the planet!"

Another misrepresentation. I definitely didn't come here chasing dreams. I was too poor to care about dreams when I got scooped up on some producer's whim.

"Lately, it seems like everyone is talking about her. And you know what that means! It's time for a Tick Tock Talk!"

The curtain whipped open and for a moment, I grinned blindly into bright screaming nothingness. Then someone nudged me forward, and I stepped out into the glare.

"Ladies and gentlemen, please get on your feet and welcome our very own American dream—Kit Allister!"

Oof. Cringy.

But I smiled and waved to the audience. Everyone I saw was animated with applause, looking full of good intentions—no glares, no hostility. None *yet* anyway.

"Hello, hello, hello!" Charmingly bad English, but he switched back to Korean soon enough. "Such a joy to finally meet you, Kit-shi! My name is Choi Sangchul and I'll be your host this evening here on Tick Tock Talk!"

"Thank you very much for having me! I'm so excited to be here!"

"How kind of you to say so! Come sit down, Kit-shi! You've got quite the story to tell!"

I settled onto the couch, crossed my legs, and folded my hands… Exactly the pose I'd practiced with Ilsung. I was to move as little as possible. Smile. Sit pretty. Look innocuous. Likable.

"I'm sure you've all heard about the amazing Kit Allister and the wild journey she's been on over this last year, but let's hear it from the girl herself! Where are you from, Kit-shi?"

Bumfunk, Ohio.

"I'm from New York City!"

Barely lived there a year.

"Everyone, did you hear that? New York City! The Big Apple! Our girl here ditched the capital of the world to come live in Seoul! Watch out world, we're on the rise!" The audience gave a hearty cheer. "So Kit-shi, what's it like in your hometown? I've never been!"

"They also call it the city that never sleeps!" Probably because everyone's working three jobs to make rent. "It's a very dynamic place to live, but personally, I've come to prefer Seoul."

"And what were you doing with your life before stardom?"

Well, let's see. I scrounged by on minimum wage, lived with eight roommates, and I dropped out of nursing school. So yeah, life was super glamorous. "I worked as a barista at a quaint little coffee shop in Brooklyn!" Why did no one ever question how I survived on that? Why did no one ever wonder if that was all I'd aspired to?

"How *stylish!* Do you ever miss it? Do you still make yourself trendy coffee drinks now that you live here in Seoul?"

No. I can't afford anything but instant. "Of course! My favorite drink is a traditional macchiato with a sprinkle of brown sugar!"

"So you've got an espresso machine at home? Ahh, the idol life!"

I nodded and smiled and swallowed the vomit. Indeed. The giant fabrication that was my idol life. "Latte art is actually sort of a hobby of mine. I love to share my efforts with my Instagram followers."

"Ah, yes! I noticed you're up to fourteen million followers! Congratulations, Kit-shi! What other sorts of things do you post?"

'Selfies' taken by a professional photographer. 'Candids' in agency-owned outfits. Fruit salads at bougie cafés I've never been to. Lots and lots of subtle product placement. Oh, and pictures of a small white dog named Bitna that never has been and never will be my pet.

"Oh, it's very casual! Just my everyday life at KJ!"

"Well, well, well! If you'd all like a sneak peek into the life of an idol, go check out the Kitstagram! Who knows? You might spot a few juicy hints in there about what it's like behind the scenes at the nation's top entertainment agency!"

Ooh. Red flag. Shut that down. "Oh, no. I assure you there's nothing juicy going on! If anything, my life might seem a little boring on Instagram!"

"Is that right? Your life sure doesn't seem boring on Twitter!"

Dammit.

Choi Sangchul was deviating from the script.

I put on my most innocent face. "Really? That's news to me!"

"Well, we'll talk about that later. First, let's hear more about how you became an idol! It's been a little over a year since you debuted with KJ, correct? How exactly did that come about?"

My coffee shop had an open mic night, and a friend badgered me into performing the one K-Pop song I knew by the one K-Pop group I cared about. Someone uploaded it to YouTube, and for some reason, it went viral. A few days later, a flowery email from a KJ talent scout popped into my inbox. I was obscenely under-qualified, but also strapped for cash, so I ignored all the fine print and accepted the offer.

But as usual, the truth was too boring for television.

"Joining KJ was my dream! So when I heard that they were accepting new trainees, I spent all my savings on a ticket to Seoul! And well, the rest is history!"

"Such an inspiration! I think we can all learn from Kit-shi's example! Take a risk, everyone! Chase your dreams!"

"I'm so grateful to the staff at KJ for taking such good care of me since then. I couldn't have made it this far without my team's help."

That was the truth. Being a novelty got my foot in the door, but once that shine wore off, keeping my name on the charts required a herculean effort. My career would have dried right up if not for my loyal team training my voice, pushing my body, fixing my Korean, picking out every outfit, perfecting my hair and makeup…

"Kit-shi, I think you're leaving out something of a major detail… Wasn't there a very specific reason why you wanted to join up with KJ in particular? You know, a very specific five-man reason?"

Oh, them?

The one K-Pop group I cared about?

The one subject legitimately unsafe for me to discuss on air?

We should've planned for this. There was next to no gossip to be had about me, but leave it to Sangchul to sniff out that one drop of blood in the water. My eyes found Ilsung standing near Camera Three. He was tugging on his hair. I'd told him a million times to stop doing that. He had really nice thick hair for someone his age and he was going to damage it.

"Ahh, you want to hear about my love for Vortex…"

"*Yes*. Yes. I want to hear *all* about it."

Eggshells

Vortex.

Mahn Jaeyoon. Kim Mino. Bae Namgi. Kasugai Ryo. Oh Saichi. To the untrained eye, they were just five pretty boys churning out meaningless pop music, but to any K-Pop fan, they were the pinnacle of the genre. There had never been a group as huge as them, and there never would be again.

"Tell us how you first heard about them!"

"One morning, around two years ago," I was finishing up a night shift at a twenty-four-hour gas station when "I heard Vortex's debut song 'Delusion' play on the news."

"Vortex. *Vortex*. Korea's pride and joy! Our boys playing on the morning news in New York City! They don't call it the debut heard around the world for nothing, folks!"

"And that was just their debut! It seems like every day they break a new record, top another chart—! The world tour they're planning is *unbelievable!* DigitAlive is going to knock the world's socks off!"

Sangchul let out a whistle and threw some oddly suggestive look at the camera. "Quite a fan, aren't you?"

"Oh. Um, I'm just so proud to be at the same agency as them."

"*Mmhmm.* Sure, Kit-shi. Anyway, tell us what happened next!"

"Well, I really liked 'Delusion' so I listened to it over and over until I knew it by heart, but of course, I didn't understand the lyrics. I looked up lots of English translations but they were all a little dissatisfying, so I decided to teach myself Korean."

"Sure! We've all been there! Why, just last week I too learned a whole language because of one song I liked." That was some thick sarcasm. The audience snickered.

"I had spare time," I lied. It was a welcome break from my other studies. A little splash of something I was actually good at. Something I actually enjoyed.

"And?"

"And in the meantime, I sang along to 'Delusion' so many times that I guess I accidentally learned how to sing too."

"Ladies and gentlemen, can you even believe your ears? Isn't she just brilliant? And to think she had all that innate talent just waiting inside of her and Vortex dragged it out!"

Nope. *Definitely* not innately talented. As a kid in Ohio, I used to pity whoever sat in the pew in front of me at church. My voice could make your hair stand up, and not in a good way. By the time I finally got good at singing, all my roommates in Brooklyn were sick to death of 'Delusion' and had it memorized as well as I did. I always caught them unwillingly singing it while they did their dishes.

"Think about it, folks. No wonder our girl Kit-shi topped so many charts in her first year! She had KJ's best, *Oh Saichi*, as her vocal coach!"

Oh Saichi.

My heart took a swing at my ribs and knocked the air out of me because even his name conjured magic, echoes of a voice like liquid starlight. The man of movements like quicksilver. Vortex's Oh Saichi.

Half-Japanese, half-Korean, one hundred percent a god onstage. And to call him KJ's best was almost an insult. He was Korea's best choreographer. Asia's best dancer. The Milky Way's best vocalist. Vortex had every explosive element needed to dominate the world stage, but Saichi was the spark that ignited them.

"He didn't actually coach me." Sangchul's soundbites would ruin me if I gave them the chance. "I just mimic him a bit."

"Of course, of course. And I assume you learned to dance by mimicking him as well? Is that how you got so good?"

"Well, can anyone sit still when a Vortex song comes on? I *had* to dance! Plus, Saichi-sunbaenim's choreography is so intense that I can't resist giving it a try when I see it! He's a *genius*."

There was a thick drip of silence. Oops?

"Quite the Saichi fan as well, aren't we?"

"Ah. Um." Hashtags and red flags were brewing in his grin. Shut them down, Kit. "I just have a lot of respect for his work. That's all."

He leaned in and spoke conspiratorially, as if his pin mic couldn't pick up every whisper. "Is he your Vortex bias?"

"Oh gosh, no. I don't have a bias! I like all the members equally!" Every other Vortexan out there was allowed a bias and a bias wrecker, but I, for reasons unknown, was not permitted to show favoritism. My team and I could never figure out what first provoked #Kitchi, but at present, Twitter *loved* to spin it the wrong way every time I so much as mentioned Saichi's name. I now had strict orders from my publicist to speak in stiff honorifics with almost icy impartiality. Saichi was no longer my idol. He was my respected Sunbaenim.

"So you're *not* dating him then?"

I was safely sitting and I still fell off my heels. "Of course not! I've never even met him! Why would anyone think—"

"Ahh, about that... You see, we all find that a bit hard to believe! You've been under the same roof for a year and you've never even bumped into him in the hall? Or met in the cafeteria?"

When exactly was Sangchul planning on returning to the script? What kind of interview was this? Who—except me, obviously—even cared if I'd ever met Saichi or not?

"No, KJ is actually a very big agency." I was impressed with how level my voice was. "There are multiple buildings throughout the city and I think Vortex usually operates out of the headquarters, so we're not often 'under the same roof,' so to speak."

"Alright, point taken. But what about outside of work? Haven't you ever been out to drinks with your beloved sunbaes? They must've invited you out when they heard your story!"

"Oh no, *never!* Male and female artists are not to mingle outside of work. KJ has a strict code of conduct, you know!"

"Ha! We all know anything goes for an idol outside the public eye. If idols want to mingle, they will mingle." He gave a brazen wink and sent the audience into giggles. "And if you ask me, it'd be pretty easy to avoid detection if you *'mingle'* within the company, wouldn't it?"

I shook my head. "I think it's much easier to follow the rules."

"Huh. They don't call you KJ's Miss Perfect for nothing."

Darn right. Not a single scandal to my name. My team knew from the get-go that I was an easy target for negative press as an American, so I'd been coached on avoiding scandal from the second I got off the plane. A lot of blood, sweat, and tears polished me into the cleanest idol on the market and I wasn't about to let this jerk Sangchul destroy my reputation with his stupid off-script questions.

"But a word of warning, Kit-shi: the truth will always come out on Tick Tock Talk! And I've got a feeling there's more to you and Saichi-shi than meets the eye… You see, a little blue bird has been tweeting at me that he's *your* fan as well."

What?

Dammit, I flinched. He got me and he knew it. I rushed to recover. "Oh, that's silly! I'm just another rookie at KJ! I bet he doesn't even know my name!"

"I'll take that bet! I have proof!"

"What?"

"If I can prove that he's a big fan, you have to promise you'll blow the camera a kiss. Because *I* bet he's watching this very second!"

"How can you possibly prove—"

"For starters, let's get firsthand testimony! Why don't we ask someone who knows Saichi-shi very well? I'm sure *he* can tell us what's going on behind the scenes, no problem!"

Wait, what? I looked to Ilsung and saw panic. A surprise guest? Who, Saichi's manager? They didn't brief us on any of this! Seriously, what happened to the script?!

"Ladies and gentlemen, I give you Vortex's Kasugai Ryo!"

Idol eyes.

Kasugai Ryo in an enclosed space with me? Nope. My heart was not ready for any kind of direct Vortex exposure today. It took me weeks to mentally prepare for every concert, and a concert involved sharing only very dilute air with Vortex, viewing only from a healthy distance. This was *way* too close for comfort and *way* too sudden. Even with two hands clapped over my chest, I couldn't slow the internal stampede. I did however bump my pin mic, and that was my reminder that I really, *really* shouldn't give in to the urge to scream. This wasn't a concert. This was a television show. National television. *Live* television. Holy crap, Kit Allister, keep your cool.

I got up, but I didn't run. My shoes wouldn't allow it.

The audience was beyond consolation and beyond a safe decibel level, but a minuscule fraction of me remained dubious. Was I being pranked? They couldn't bring out one of the nation's top artists on the fly like this, right?!

Apparently, they could.

Kasugai Ryo came out flashing dental perfection and a fresh gloss to his burgundy lowlights. Steel loops jingled on his leather pants as he swaggered across the stage and a new tattoo peeked out from the deep V-neck of a shirt far too tight for his build.

Good *god*. The real thing. The real Kasugai Ryo. *Vortex*.

"Easy there, girls…" He raised a hand to dull the screaming, but that's not how fangirls work, and he knew that. The studio audience approached full stadium volume and the hysteria made him grin.

Then suddenly, I was looking a Vortex member straight in the eye. He wasn't looking into a camera lens, or out into a rioting crater of fans. Kasugai Ryo was looking directly at me and only me.

"We meet at last, Kit."

His English was distractingly immaculate, and then he thrust his hand at me. I almost didn't understand what he wanted. A *handshake?* I couldn't touch Vortex! I also couldn't leave him hanging though?! Either way, Vortexans would burn me at the stake!

He smiled. I was starstruck. Shell-shocked. Freaking stupefied. But thank god for Ilsung, dodging cameras up and down the edge of the stage, whisper screaming, *"Live, Kit! You're live!"*

I meant to keep Ryo at a straight-armed distance, but the second his hand wrapped around mine, he wrenched me closer. I don't know what he was trying to accomplish, but he clearly overestimated my stiletto skills. I smashed straight into his chest. And I wasn't at all grateful that he caught me. I would've rather had him swipe me off like a bug on a windshield. Instead, I had to hang there in his arms while the screaming pressed in around us and out from inside of me. He laughed and I was close enough to taste his cinnamon gum.

"Well, nice to meet you too. Is this how Americans are greeting each other these days?"

"Sorry" barely fit through the grit of my teeth. Sorry that *you* yanked on my arm on live television, Ryo!

Finally, he set me back on my feet, but not before flashing another grin at the shrieking fangirls. He'd definitely just used me for fanservice, and *I* was the one who would take crap for it on Twitter. Out on a limb, I tottered over to the edge of the stage and squealed, "You guys, Kasugai Ryo is trying to give me a heart attack!"

It was a relief to let out the inner Vortexan, and a relief when my fellow fangirls issued piercing approval. Camaraderie successfully reestablished? I was forgiven, right? I caught Ilsung's eye. He was nodding, shrugging, gnawing his thumbnail. Anything goes when the script was evidently trash from the beginning.

"Welcome back to the show, Ryo-shi!"

Kasugai Ryo.

Brilliant rap artist who ditched the Tokyo underground scene to join up with Vortex. Dark, sharp, talented, and topping every chart wasn't enough for him. Rumor had it he was studying incognito at one of Seoul's top universities. See, why couldn't I have a rumor like that? Why did *my* rumor have to be that I was secretly dating the world's favorite idol?

"I have to say that was quite the… handshake? What's the consensus, Tick Tock Talkers? All of a sudden, I'm starting to think that *these* two are the couple to watch!"

Dammit!

"We're not dating." Ryo laughed and, for just one second, I was grateful. But then he caught my hand again. And lifted it *to his lips*. On live national television! The son of a gun! "But we *could…*"

Our eyes met and he smirked, with the exact same vindictive glint in his eye as Sangchul. He obviously didn't like me and wanted to screw me over. And why? What had I ever done to either of them? Why did they both want my career to go up in flames tonight? Was this a game for them? Some kind of sport?

I tugged my fingers free.

"What a funny joke! Everyone, isn't he a funny guy?"

Ryo shrugged it off and went to sit down. The bland decorations on the table bored him, so with a thud, he put two huge combat boots on display instead. "This is late-night, right? Got anything to drink?"

Sangchul burst into pleased laughter. "Of course not, Ryo-shi, you scoundrel! We didn't bring you out here to drink! We want to ask you a few questions."

"Oh?"

"About your leader, Oh Saichi."

"Oh. Saichi."

I heard a slap. Ilsung had facepalmed. Because of the bad joke? No, he was waving me forward. I was a guest, and yet I was lingering at the far end of the stage, just a few steps from melting into obscurity.

"Don't let Hyung hear you calling him our leader." Ryo brushed his hair down into his eyes and imitated a sweeter silkier voice, "No one leads or follows in Vortex…"

"Just between us, he *is* the leader though, right?"

"Without a doubt." Ryo turned caustic eyes on me. "Are you gonna sit down or what? You scared of me or something?"

Sangchul tutted. "Now, now, Ryo-shi. I'm sure she's just a little nervous. She's a very big fan of yours, you know! Are you familiar with Kit-shi and her story?"

"More or less. I know she joined up with KJ because of Vortex if that's what you're asking… Her and a hundred other prospective talents, that is. I'm flattered, I guess?"

Finally, someone who didn't sugarcoat things. Someone who spoke out what I wished *I* could say. Unembarrassed to emphatically nod, I eased down onto the couch beside him.

He went on, still eyeing me. "Those fan-turned-idol kids don't often make it this far though, so there I will give credit where it is due. Definitely never thought Vortex would share charts and screen time with a former Vortexan."

"Once a Vortexan always a Vortexan," I corrected him. "There's no such thing as a 'former' Vortexan."

I kept looking away, hoping that when I looked back he'd be done staring at me, but he seemed to be weighing out some kind of judgment. Even Sangchul felt awkward and called out to him, but Ryo leaned closer and murmured something none of us understood. Japanese, I assume?

"I beg your pardon?"

"I said, do you speak Japanese?"

"What? No? Why?"

"Just curious."

Sangchul laughed. "I don't know if you can tell by looking at her, Ryo-shi, but our friend Kit Allister is actually an American!"

"I know, bud. But Americans are a diverse bunch, and she's got a very familiar accent that really doesn't match her face…" As much as I wished I was watching the show and not participating in it, I really didn't like being talked about like I wasn't a sentient being sitting right in front of them.

"Hmm, it looks like this truly is your first time meeting Kit-shi."

"It is."

"You've never seen her maybe hanging around your leader?"

Ryo's eyebrows suddenly rammed together. Not in confusion; in irritation. But thankfully, he turned that look on Sangchul, not me. "And why would she be hanging around Hyung?"

"You see, there have been some rumors that they're dating…"

"*Ha!*"

"So you deny the rumors, Ryo-shi? They're *not* dating?"

I relished seeing Sangchul deflate, but there was more in the works. I caught the little ruffle in the staff beyond the camera. Ryo didn't, but only because he was busy rolling his eyes.

"I know you want me to drop some vague loopholey hint, Sangchul-shi, old friend, but I'm gonna go ahead and give this one a hard no. Besides, Hyung's private life is just that: *private*. I wouldn't rat out my homeboy either way, so don't bother asking me this stuff."

"That last bit sounded a little like a loophole to me…"

"Yeah? What evidence you got that Hyung is—?"

The screens behind us flashed and we both turned to see a full wall of tweets, each one sporting #Kitchi and blurry photos of dark lumps bejeweled with lightsticks. My eyes snagged on one in English.

Zade loves Mino @vortexwhortex

so they're mutual fans? I ship the shit out of this #Kitchi5ever

"What are we looking at here?" Ryo grumbled.

As if he'd clicked himself, one of the images blew up and it was not even a little bit blurry. It was undeniably Saichi. Glowing in the light of some pyrotechnic excitement with a pink lightstick clasped under his chin. The longer I looked at it, the more Kit Allister goods I saw, and the less I believed what I was seeing.

Some weak-sounding noise broke free of my throat and Ryo actually elbowed me. "Okay. So maybe he's a little bit of a fan—"

"A *little* bit? He's clearly Head Kit-Kat."

My idol was my fan. Oh Saichi was my fan? Vortex's Oh Saichi. My idol. My fan. *Baffling…* "Hm? Head what? The candy?"

"Kit-shi, do you really not know what your fans call themselves?"

Ryo roared over top of him, "It doesn't mean they're dating!"

"Oooh, an aggressive denial!" Sangchul was practically singing. "If they're not already dating, maybe they should start! Look! *Look!*" Another image popped up and the angle and lighting were laughably identical, but this time, it was me decked out in Saichi gear waving a Vortex lightstick. I had a mask on, but I'd be hard-pressed to argue that it wasn't me in the picture. "Is this adorable or what? Ladies and gentlemen, I ship it. Do you?"

Ryo groaned in transparent annoyance. There was definite conflict in the audience. Some halfhearted cheers, some mutinous muttering, some giggling. Ilsung frantically waved his arms over Camera Four trying to capture my eyes. "*Deny it!*" he urged, but I was having some real breathing issues.

"I too am in aggressive denial!" Dammit, what just came out of my mouth?! Seriously A+ Korean right there. "Um, I mean, idols can't date! We're not dating! No one has to ship anything they don't want to ship! I don't even know him—"

"You sound a little flustered, Kit-shi! I thought you said you were unbiased! I thought you said you just respect your sunbae, but in this picture, you're clearly very, *very* biased!"

Crap.

Luckily, Ryo was consistently on my side, if being on my side meant keeping Saichi unembroiled in this. "Yeah, yeah, what's the big deal if she's got a bias? Kit-shi, just admit to it. The more you try to hide that you like him, the more suspicious it gets."

My eyes found Ilsung texting someone with gusto, probably my publicist who was probably watching this live and getting more disgusted by the second. "I just—"

"*Hellooo!*" The studio door at the top of the stands exploded open and in came Bae Namgi at a gallop, a tidal wave of fangirl hysteria chasing him down through their ranks.

"What in the—? Ladies and gentlemen, it would appear that Vortex's Bae Namgi has decided to pay us a visit?!"

The hulking cameras whirled like pinwheels trying to catch him in their sights, but the studio was Namgi's pinball machine. I could only imagine the kind of nauseating footage was going out live to the nation as Namgi headbutted the boom mic, vaulted into a green screen, and mowed down Ilsung twice with unsolicited hugs. It was only a matter of time before his trajectory crossed the stage, so Sangchul and I took to our feet to brace for impact. Behind us, Ryo was hoarse with laughter. The most he did to subdue Namgi was frisbee a pillow at him.

"Hello Kittie! Hello everyone! Hello Ryo-chan! Hello Sangchulie! Why wasn't I invited? I saw you guys on TV in the dressing room and I was like, what the heck, everybody's having a party without Namgi? And a party with Kittie? *The* Kittie? The real hecking thing?! Hi there! My name is Bae Namgi! Super nice to meet you!"

Ryo coughed out, "Pretty sure she knows your name, Nam-san."

Namgi, the human manifestation of sunshine. Dog's best friend. Vortex's manic middle child. Loud, bright, clumsy, goofy, and maybe a little dumb sometimes, but loving him comes just as naturally as laughing at him.

But what the hell was he doing here?!

With him bouncing circles around me, I was too swept up in his mayhem to get nervous about meeting yet another Vortex member. The Vortexans in the audience were the same; the atmosphere read like a puppy had tumbled through with a stolen shoe. I also may or may not have greeted him with the gooey gush I'd use on said puppy. "Hello Namgi-sunbaenim! What a pleasant surprise to—"

"*Sunbaenim?!* Yuck, yuck, *yuck!* Call me something cute, Kittie! We're friends now, aren't we?"

Namgi, love you dearly but that did not help the whole 'this is our first time meeting' narrative! "Namgi-shi…?"

"*Ewww*, whyyy? Don't be so stiff! Just call me Oppa!"

"W-what?" That word had never left my mouth before. I cringed just *thinking* it. And to call Vortex's Bae Namgi—

He ran up and down the stage and started clapping and stomping in time to the chant, "Op-pa, Op-pa, Op-pa!" and soon the entire audience had joined in. Truly exemplary Namgi behavior. Barge in on a program he wasn't even invited on and just hijack the whole thing... This particular brand of nonsense made him a staple of variety television in Korea. The man bottled the chaos of an atom bomb, and regardless of whether that suited the style of your show, if the programming sparked his fancy, he'd find a way on camera. Most producers embraced this and actively courted his incursions, but some never even saw it coming. Every true Vortexan had watched the YouTube clip of him strolling in on a morning news segment half-pajamaed because they were covering the Dalgona coffee trend and he wanted to try a sip. He made the poor flustered news anchor spoon it into his mouth, and then he was put off when it tasted like actual coffee, and "not like whipped cream at all!"

Sangchul had snapped out of his shock and was eating up the anarchy. "You can do it, Kit-shi! We all wanna hear it! Call your oppa!" Ilsung covered his face with his hands. This was his worst nightmare. The combination of Sangchul and Namgi was volatile. If there was still some semblance of a script out there, it was as good as kindling now. Namgi had probably never read a script in his life.

I sighed and stretched out a hand. "Nice to meet you, Oppa."

"Oh *wow*, a real American handshake! From the American idol!"

That got me.

Namgi was thrilled that he'd made me laugh, his smile almost too big for his face. There was some serious wattage going on there... Enough to blind a person. I was still recovering when he latched on and gave me a full bodyshake, as opposed to a mere handshake. "You're like, *really* pretty in person!"

"Uhh, you too." Oops. But he *was* pretty, with blonde curtains flopping on his cheeks—like puppy ears, of course—and pale turquoise contacts that lit his eyes with a Tahitian glow. Kind of beautiful when he sat still for longer than a second.

"Thank you! Gosh, you're just as great as I thought you'd be!"

"Nam-san," Ryo called. "Come sit." Namgi took a running leap at the couch and Ryo narrowly avoided death.

Sangchul smelled a scoop. "Do tell us, what's this Nam-san business? Does it have anything to do with the Namsan Tower? Is it because Namgi-shi is tall?"

Ryo snorted. But Namgi rushed to explain, nosing his way to Ryo's pin mic. "Noo! He calls me Nam-san and I call him Ryo-chan! It's Japanese! Like him!"

"Is that right?"

One of the staff crept up to equip Namgi with his own pin mic, but Namgi tickled him mercilessly throughout the process, all the while chattering on like his mouth, brain, and body shared no connection, "Ryo-chan has *lots* of nicknames for me. Sometimes he just calls me Bae! That's a thing in English, you know!" He waved at me. "Right? You guys use that, right? It's like baby, right? Gosh, Kittie, if you don't like Oppa, how about you call me Bae?"

"But that's your last name! It'd be rude—"

"It's not rude in Japanese? Call me Bae-chan!"

"But I don't speak Japanese!"

"Neither do I! Ryo-chan doesn't mind!"

"I don't think I should—"

"What about Nam-ah? When he's in a super good lovey-dovey mood, he calls me Nam-ah. Isn't that the friggin' *cutest?* Ack!"

"I can't call you that! It's too intimate!"

"Our Leader calls me Namgi-ya! How's that?"

Ryo clapped his hands. "Focus. Tick Tock Talk."

Namgi stuck out his tongue and I was pelted with the inner echoes of my own words. Wow. I got caught up in his banter way too easily. He was way too good at television. I tried to check Ilsung's face, but Sangchul was already launching his next round of interrogation. "So Namgi-shi, what on earth are you doing here?"

"Ryo-chan looked like he was having fun on the TV. And I've been wanting to meet Kittie *so bad* for like, *so long*. She's *so hecking cool*. Do you know that, Kittie? You are *so* cool."

"Um, thanks."

He looked ready to say more but then he cocked his head, burst into giggles, and channeled a mess of botched whispers into Ryo's ear. I was a little thrown when badass Ryo giggled along, but that shouldn't have surprised me. Namgi could make anyone crack. The mic caught him murmuring, "I thought the same thing earlier."

Sangchul cleared his throat with practiced theatricality. "Are you two going to let us all in on the secret?"

"Heck yeah?" Namgi started bobbing on the couch, subjecting Ryo to unwanted turbulence. "So like, Kittie has an accent, and it's totally hilarious because it's not even the *right* accent! She's an American but she sounds even more Japanese than Ryo-chan does! Kittie, you *just* said you don't speak Japanese, but like, you *do* though."

"What do you mean I have an accent...?" But everyone always praised my Korean! Oh *god*. Were they just being polite all this time? I looked first to Ilsung, then Sangchul, then out into the audience. Not a single reaction.

Ryo had on a mocking grin when our eyes met. "Let's play a little game, Kit-shi." Namgi squealed and clapped at the prospect, and then Ryo switched suddenly to English. "Say the word 'promise' in Korean for us."

"What? Um, *yakusoku*."

"*Yakoosokoo!*" Namgi echoed me but much more like a rooster, and they both disintegrated into laughter. Was it some kind of Vortex inside joke?

"What?"

Ryo's grip on his composure was loosening. "Kit-shi, don't you hear it? That's not Korean! It's *yaksok!*"

Was I really saying it that different? Was it *that* funny? I felt a bit like a zoo animal, but that was semi-normal. On a slow day, my party trick for these shows was speaking English, but I guess I had another one up my sleeve all this time. Namgi fought through the giggles to whisper more.

"Ah, yeah. That's another one." Again, Ryo switched to English to avoid giving me the answer. "Now say 'picture' in Korean."

"*Shashin?*"

"Yup, nope. That's Japanese, Kit-shi. I would know."

Dismayed and a little betrayed even, I turned and asked Ilsung, "It's not *shashin?*" He pointed to another 'ON AIR' sign, clasping his hands in an unspoken plea for forgiveness.

Namgi was inconsolable. "Kittie, it's *sajin*, silly!"

"I think you both know why she talks like that!" I could *hear* the irritating waggle of Sangchul's eyebrows, and I felt the couch move as it turned into a full-body wiggle. "We've all been thinking it!"

Namgi hacked a few times and got his voice back. "Oh, for sure! She talks just like Leader! Kittie, did you learn from him or something? Don't you know that he's *super* bad at Korean?"

"She *did* learn from him! She admitted it earlier!" Sangchul was looking at his producer like they'd won the lottery. As far as television ratings went, they had. This was going to blow up online...

Ryo scoffed. "Why'd you learn from *him* of all people? If you want a model of assimilation, shouldn't you be listening to *my* Korean?"

"Why didn't anyone correct me?"

Namgi patted my arm and I froze at the intimacy. "Because it's cute, Kittie! And don't worry! Your Korean is still miles better than Leader! And totally understandable! Don't ever change!"

"You've obviously been listening to Saichi-shi very closely for a while now," Sangchul hinted. "Maybe even spending a little too much time with him?"

I put my foot down. "No, I'm just a very big fan of his work. I had no idea I was picking up his speaking habits as well."

"Why don't we ask television's favorite loose-lipped idol? Namgi-shi, are any Vortex members currently dating anyone?

Namgi burst into hectic laughter. "Oh, everybody knows the answer to *that!* Leader and Minmin have been dating each other for like, *ever*, right?!"

Oh my god.

The audience roared their endorsement and I covered my face for calm. My OTP: Oh Saichi and Kim Mino. Otherwise known as Minchi. The two of them were always all over each other during Vortex concerts and they were officially the most adorable, shippable thing to happen to this planet.

"This is why I love you, Nam-ah."

"Aww, I love you too, Ryo-chan!"

"Are *you* two dating too?"

"Oh, gosh no. We're *married*."

"I wasn't aware!"

"Nam-ah."

"And we're pregnant! With twins!"

"*Nam-ah*."

"We're naming them after Minchi."

"No, we are *not!*"

Finally, I caught my breath. This diversion was comfortable for me. Easy to laugh and enjoy their interaction, as if this couch was in my living room and there was a glass screen between us. Easy to pretend that my career wasn't burning up before my eyes.

Sangchul still wore the same blinking bewilderment I'd felt a moment ago. Namgi could sweep anyone up into his sky castles, even professional talk show hosts. Sangchul looked to the cue cards for the first time because he needed a reminder of what the hell we were supposed to be talking about. I wished he'd just get back to the script, but clearly, that was never meant to be.

"Namgi-shi, what I meant to ask was what have you heard about Saichi-shi and Kit-shi? Has he ever mentioned her to you?"

"Oooh, heck yes. He never shuts up about her! He's like, always listening to her music too. Plus, even when he's super-duper busy, he still goes to like, *all* her concerts. Like last weekend—"

"Nam-ah, that's a private hobby of his and you shouldn't—"

"Why? It's not like he's trying to keep it a secret!"

"Now we're Tick Tock Talking! How sweet that Saichi-shi goes to all his girlfriend's concerts! Such a devoted boyfriend!"

Okay, Kit. You do not have time to lose your mind over the fact that he's your fan right now. You can process that later. Right now you have to put out Sangchul's dumpster fire conspiracy theory.

"Just because he happens to come to my concerts doesn't mean he's my boyfriend! I wouldn't even call us coworkers! He's miles above me on the KJ ladder! And, and again, we've never even met!"

Namgi giggled. "You two *should* meet. It'd be *so cute*."

Ryo snapped disciplinary fingers at him and then turned to Sangchul. "Listen, I'm warning you, old friend. You're gonna have to quit with the scandalmongering. Take it from me, our Leader is a focused and driven professional who would never do anything that could endanger Vortex's reputation—"

"But they're so obviously perfect for each other!"

"Nam-ah, c'mon. I need a snack. And as for you, Sangchul-shi, next time prepare some better Tick Tock Talking points. I don't have time to sit around talking about utter B.S." And with that, Ryo flicked his mic off his shirt like it was a bothersome spider and he sauntered right out of a live broadcast, whistling for Namgi to follow him. Sangchul and I were shocked motionless.

Fortunately, Sangchul recovered quickly and laughed it off. "Alright, folks! We'll be right back after a short commercial break! Stick around because our girl Kit most definitely lost her bet, so she's gotta blow a kiss to all you viewers at home!"

Aftermath

As soon as the lights dimmed and the cameras shut off, the studio blizzarded with activity. Sangchul tramped off muttering about his insufficient paycheck, security flooded out to dam up the fangirls, and I was snatched up and ushered backstage where I almost broke down in tears watching 'ON AIR' extinguish.

My team and I had held our breath all year, praying for this kind of opportunity. It was a long, arduous year of mornings that began at night, and nights that ended in the early morning. Dancing until it was as easy as breathing, and then turning every breath into part of a melody. Barely eating, barely sleeping, barely a second to myself.

As difficult as my journey had been, things were about to get even crazier because, for better or worse, Vortex got entangled in what was supposed to be my big break today. Maybe it was bound to happen because my K-Pop story had revolved around them from the very beginning, but I'd always dreamed our paths would cross under far better circumstances. Instead, I'd managed to drag down Saichi and piss off Ryo without even trying. My fellow Vortexans were probably vilifying me on Twitter right now.

The studio door felt much heavier on the way out.

"Hey."

The weight of the door suddenly left my hands and I almost fell into Ryo again. We both rushed to speak, me in despair, him in annoyance, but our voices overlapped in a "sorry." He held up a hand, just like he had to scold the shrieking fangirls.

"Don't apologize. Sangchul was playing with fire tonight. And no offense, but it's one thing to mess with a rookie like you; it's quite another to implicate Hyung. You screw with Vortex you're gonna face the full wrath of KJ, and popular or no, this show will go right the hell under if we withdraw our support."

"Still, I should've been more careful with my words."

He laughed. "Or with your accent. But whatever. Just be more careful from now on. And listen, I'm sorry about how things went tonight, so our staff is putting together a little present for you. I'm sure you're familiar with our latest tour? DigitAlive?"

"Of course! The whole human race is buzzing about it!"

He snorted a little and I couldn't tell if that was scorn or pride. "Yeah, yeah. Do you already have tickets or…?"

"I missed out this time. Tickets sold out in *milliseconds*."

"Well, no worries. Tell your manager to cancel whatever you've got going tomorrow night. I'll arrange front-row, ground seats in the VIP section. Sound good?"

Tomorrow. But tomorrow they were playing the KSPO Dome! That was practically their home stage! It was even renovated in their honor to look like a massive vortex! I'd always wanted to catch them in concert there, but even long before the DigitAlive frenzy, any Dome performance was next to impossible to attend because of the limited seating.

Ryo waved a hand in front of my eyes. "I said, sound good?"

"Good?! That's way better than good! We're talking front-row seats! I'll get to—!" His eyebrows ticked up. Crap. I went on sheepishly, "See Vortex up-close…"

"You're pretty close right now?"

"Sorry…"

"I'm starting to believe you're actually a fan."

My face bunched up before I could stop it. What did *that* mean?

"Why would you doubt—"

"Anyway, I'm getting you a ticket, so do me a favor and keep it low-key, got it? Come, have fun, enjoy the concert, but for the love of god, keep your head down. Maybe don't wear a bunch of Saichi fan gear this time? Prove to me that you can handle the incognito life and maybe there'll be more tickets in it for you down the road, yeah?"

"I'll do whatever it takes to stay under the radar. I *promise*."

He laughed again. "*Yaksok*, Kit-shi. It's *yaksok*."

"Right. That."

"Alright. I'll hold you to it. No more scandals. No more #Kitchi." He brushed his jacket back and unholstered a DigitAlive lightstick from his belt. I fought back surprised laughter and accepted it with suitable reverence, but he didn't immediately let go. "Deal?"

I shook the lightstick up and down. "Deal."

"See ya tomorrow night then. Or rather, I hope I *don't* see you, if you know what I mean." I watched him until he was gone and then I couldn't help squealing. Okay, today sucked a little, but Ryo was right. It wasn't entirely my fault. On the bright side, I still got to meet two Vortex members! *And* now I was gonna see all five in concert from the front row at the freaking Dome!

My dressing room was my safe zone, so the first thing I did was kick off my stupid stilettos. Ilsung arrived soon after me, mid-quarrel with my publicist on speakerphone. I had her aggravated anti-Vortex rants memorized word for word, so I tuned them out and played with the lightstick, trying not to giggle when Ilsung made faces at me.

–*Ilsung-shi, am I free tomorrow night?*

–*Perhaps. Why?*

–*I may have just procured tickets to DigitAlive.*

–*PLEEEAAASSEEE can I go?*

–*You know what? Yes. Absolutely. You are allowed to be supportive of other artists. I don't care what anybody says. What's more, you deserve a break after all the stress of TiToTa.*

–*THANK YOU!*

–*Did you just coin a new nickname for Tick Tock Talk?*

"Ilsung-shi, I can hear you typing! I know you're not listening! This is a serious issue—"

"Yes, yes. Very serious."

It got a lot harder for both of us not to laugh when an envelope labeled only 'V.I.P.' slipped ominously under the door. 'My ticket has arrived,' I mouthed to Ilsung and I paraded over to the door in barefoot triumph. Bless his soul, he joined me in my impromptu jig.

I was still crouching on the ground with the ticket clutched in my fingers when my dressing room door swung open and I found myself studying a pair of black heels so shiny they looked milk-white.

"Good evening," a woman's voice purred in English. I frogged awkwardly backward and surged to my feet so fast that my head spun. I recognized her from the news.

Lee Kyungsoon. Hair like a shampoo commercial, smile like a toothpaste commercial, perfectly tailored pencil skirt, and signature long red nails the exact shade of the KJ logo.

She was KJ Global Entertainment's president and CEO, the woman who brought Vortex into the world, and she was also something like my boss's boss's boss. Until today, I was never important enough to even breathe the same air as her, but now she knew my name?! I was moved to say the least. To offset my rude bare feet, I sank into a deep forty-five-degree bow.

Behind me, Ilsung snuffed out his phone call in seconds.

"You're moving up in the world, Kit," she elected to continue in Korean, perhaps out of courtesy for Ilsung. "Congratulations on joining KJ's circle of elites."

What could I say to that? Thank you? You're my hero? I was relieved when Ilsung spoke for me, "We are most grateful to you for allowing a surprise joint appearance with Vortex."

"I imagine you are, manager-shi." Her eyes hadn't so much as flickered from my face. The heat of them made me sweat. "However, I hope you both realize that this changes everything. The two of you can expect to be held to a much higher standard going forward."

"I can assure you that our Kit-shi conducts herself with

impressive decorum for someone who was not raised here in Korea. She has studied and trained very hard—"

I felt immense pressure not to fidget, not to draw attention to my bare feet, but right near my toes, my stilettos sat in a spiky mass of awkward angles looking like a bird with a broken wing. With every ounce of subtlety I possessed, I nudged them under the couch.

"I'm aware." Kyungsoon waved a dismissive hand, impeccable nails catching the light. "Don't forget that Kit was *my* pick, you funny thing. Besides, I would have withdrawn her visa ages ago if her conduct had ever offended me."

I was her pick?!

"So you're not upset by tonight's rather unfortunate proceedings?"

Her teeth flashed the bluish white of winter, stark against her scarlet lips. "The Kit-Saichi narrative? Please. I've been cultivating it. It's *grand* publicity, don't you think?"

The president herself didn't give a crap about #Kitchi? Dang. Now Ilsung was speechless as well. I wished my publicist was still on the phone to hear her say that.

"Regardless, I'll be keeping a very close eye on you both from now on." She smirked. "Many would kill to be in your shoes, Kit. Don't squander the opportunity I've given you." The way she'd said shoes… She'd noticed the discarded heels for *sure*.

"Yes, ma'am." I bowed again. With another wave, she turned and clicked elegantly out of the room, much better in stilettos than me.

"Kit, you know she came all the way here from headquarters," Ilsung whispered. "I think she likes you." I burst into dubious laughter. But, as intimidating as Kyungsoon was, I deeply admired her and her work, and I also owed every part of my current life to her, so yeah, I liked her too.

Digit-Alive

The dome dimmed and thousands let out one long wriggling scream. A beat began, pulsing, intense, knocking things free inside my chest. The screaming was unbearable, but the beat was louder.

Any moment now.

Any moment now, they might appear.

We all grew fevered together, one massive roaring hive mind.

Vortex, Vortex, *Vortex*.

A deafening explosion bleached the air of sound, darkness, color. I squinted through sprays of sparks to find five silhouettes of spangled neon blazing from the stage like LED comets. When they fell back to Earth, their feet bit at tongues of fire to the hitching thump of their latest single, "it's all over now." *Saichi*. There he was in the center. Each beat lanced out from the soles of his feet and burst into fireworks on all sides. Overhead, grids of lasers seared us all into a cage, and then…

Saichi's voice slid into a solo.

A hologram fifty times his size flickered into existence and the dome fell silent, stunned, as his voice climbed through the chaos, swelling, soaring over top of us. His fingers lifted and brushed the ceiling of the dome. Thousands hypnotized into crystal-clear silence.

Then his voice plummeted into another explosion and massive screens strobed to life behind him, all five members now larger than life and snapping, sliding, spinning, surging through the dark.

From there on, the night was one long blur of delirium.

"Boo!" During the intermission, adorable mini meanie Kim Mino was the first to bubble back up out of the stage, absolutely *radiant* in head to toe pastel. He hopped down the stairs like a cotton candy sparrow, basking in the sound of his name in a thousand mouths.

"I'm supposed to plug my new movie but knowing you guys, you've all already seen it, haven't you?" Screams to the affirmative. "And you all heard about that award the other day too, right? Dunno why my managers always make me brag about this shit. You guys already *know* I'm the best actor on the planet. Tell ya what, I'm running out of shelf space for all these darn awards. They gotta start making 'em smaller or something."

Cocky as ever, but he had a right to be cocky. Over the brief course of his rising stardom, he'd already rocked the box offices with his ragtag romcoms, sci-fi thrillers, paranormal mysteries, and tragic dramas. I never had much of a taste for film, but I'd crossed into bizarre genres to witness each of his multifaceted characters glint with every bittersweet truth of life. You'd never expect it from his loudmouth brat persona, but maybe he was an old soul or something with a million past lives to draw from. I thought the same whenever I listened to his music. Once in a blue moon, he'd get needled into contributing something creative to Vortex's discography, and he always wrote the most wrenching lyrics and captivating melodies I'd ever heard.

Namgi's blonde head gophered out of the stage. He shushed us and clearly meant to sneak up on Mino, but it took him two steps to get tangled in his tracksuit and half-tumble down the stairs.

"Nice try, Babo Namgi."

A bodiless voice boomed over the speakers, "Mino, I don't care what you call him in your spare time, but in front of fans, you are to refer to him by his legal name: Bae Namgi. *Bae* Namgi."

Namgi and Mino both bust into belly laughs. "Oh my fucking god, don't you hate it when he does that? Mute your damn mic, Jae! And stop eavesdropping!"

"*Language!*" the voice thundered. Mino's random English obscenities always brought a smile to my face. He'd fit in well with my old Brooklyn friends.

Mahn Jaeyoon appeared at the top of the stairs with all the command of the royalty he was. Cameras swung to magnify him on the screens and Mino hurried to reintroduce him, "Ladies and fangirls, Vortex's motherhenning maknae! KJ's King Jae!"

Namgi joined in, "Seoul's fashion plate!"

"Dishing out his latest line! Vogue for us, baby Jae!"

Jaeyoon was unimpressed.

Tinted glasses slid down his nose to allow full access to dark serious eyes, then he tapped a ringed finger to his lips. *Amazing* how well that worked. No one in the dome dared to make another sound. Satisfied, his black brows unknitted, and we all heard the thud of his boots as he glided down the stairs, a long jacket swirling behind him. Like part of a chessboard, he was split in black and white, boots, pant legs, jacket wings all opposing each other, perfectly complementing the pattern in his hair.

This was Vortex's edgy fashion icon in all his glory. He arranged himself on the bottom stairs and lifted his rings, summoning a waiting staff member with a tray. His scarf cascaded just so, jacket falling artfully open, pop lettering showcased on a shirt half tucked in. He was always like that—always acutely aware of himself, always on display. Every passing moment was a magazine spread.

As he selected a tea, he continued his earlier lecture, "I would have preferred to finish my break in solitude, but I learned my lesson last time. You two are incapable of behaving yourselves without supervision. Now, shall we discuss the small mishap in the first act?"

Mino giggled and the silence began to rumble, then Namgi made a face and it ruptured into pandemonium. Jaeyoon gave an ancient sigh and seemed to take comfort in merely holding his tea.

"Babo, he's talking about you, ya mishap."

"Ohh? Really? Huh!" Namgi's expression was incriminating.

"*Bae Namgi*. His name is Bae Namgi."

"Delusion," Mino barked on, "is our debut single. The debut heard around the world. That's what they call it."

"Yeah…"

"It's our pride and joy. Our number one hit to this day."

"Yeah…"

"We've rehearsed and performed it *hundreds* of times."

"Yeah…"

"So what in the *name* went wrong during the second chorus? You got like three steps behind and then never caught up! You almost knocked Satch's block off with your spin!" By that point, we were all laughing. Mino ribbing Namgi in the emcee section was an almost indispensable part of a Vortex concert. And I *adored* Mino's little nickname for Saichi. "Where's your respect for Jae's creative vision? For Satch's choreography?"

"Oh *gosh*, I have *such* respect. I just, you know, saw a friend in the audience! So like, sorryyy. Got a little distracted!"

"A friend, hah? Real or imaginary?"

"*Rude*, Minmin." Namgi's eyes swung in my direction and my stomach lurched. Was I that friend? Holy crap! To my alarm, Mino's eyes followed his and I swear to actual god: our eyes met.

Jaeyoon sighed again. "Mino, let's be courteous to each other. What strategies can we come up with to prevent this from happening again in the future? Creative vision aside, at the very least, we want to avoid injuries to ourselves and others, correct?"

That was Jaeyoon language for 'don't worry me like that' and Namgi knew it. "Aww, mama hen. So right. So right."

The dome filled with palpable affection. After all, at the core of Jaeyoon's moodiness and eccentricity was a fretting heart that belonged only to his fellow members. He made their success his life's mission. Not only did he design each member's look, but he was also Vortex's executive producer—the mastermind behind every pyrotechnic, heart-slamming, mind-blowing concert. DigitAlive itself was forged in his inner bonfire of creative passion.

"I've got a strategy. It's what I've been telling you all along! If you lose your feet, you just gotta take a quick peek at Satch and then you'll be set! Our leader is *never* off, Babo."

"I'm not the leader."

My eyes shot to the top of the stairs. I opened my mouth to scream but the dome got so loud that I couldn't be sure if any sound made it out of my throat.

Saichi.

Aglow in all white, silver hair in a dazzling metallic mess, ethereal in the spotlight. He floated down the stairs with disregard for gravity, then shuffled over to Mino, giving him a little push.

"Hiya Satch. How's my favorite human doing?" Mino tickled Saichi's side and he squirmed away in snuffly laughter. It didn't take Mino long to snag him and spin him toward the cameras. "Guys. Seriously. I can't even stand it. Look at this man. Look at how fucking cute he is." We were.

"Minnn…"

Namgi informed us all, "Our leader is *blushing*." We knew.

"I'm not blushing," he protested. "And I'm not the leader!"

Mino plastered himself to Saichi's back, his sharp little chin bumping over Saichi's shoulder. Giggling, he pointed at the nearest screen. "You are. See? And you're pouting too."

"Am not. That's just how my face is and you know it!"

"Oh yeah?"

The two were rapidly melting into their own little Minchi world and they were taking every last one of us with them. I couldn't look away from Mino's finger battling Saichi's lower lip, trying to tuck it where he thought it belonged, and I was having trouble remembering to breathe. How was it legal to be so cute?

"Too cute," Mino echoed my thoughts. "Be careful, Satch. You're getting to be a little *too cute*. I might—" His fingers pinched Saichi's chin instead. Oh god, oh god, oh god. They'd been teasing us for *years*. Was this it?! Was today the day?! Was Minchi finally going to kiss?!

Ryo spat a laugh down the stairs. "Get a room, you two!"

"Pshh. Why have a room when we can have a whole dome?"

Jaeyoon rolled his eyes spectacularly over top of a loud and long sip of tea. "Ryo-hyung is right. That's plenty for tonight. We still have our little gifts to pass out before the second half."

"But he's so *cute*, Jae."

He strolled up behind Minchi and his ringed fingers ruffled their hair into twin messes. "Mhm. You're both pretty cute," he muttered, a fond smile on his face. "But don't lead our leader on, Mino."

"*Never.*"

Ryo waved a small stack of CDs as he came down the stairs. "That's right, everybody! We've got presents! This is our new single! Not yet released! Five lucky audience members get an advance copy with our signatures on it!"

Namgi reanimated from his foray into Minchi world and snatched a CD off the top. "Do it. Do it like we talked about!" He squashed it to Ryo's face. "Kiss it, Ryo-chan!"

There was a round of good-natured groans but all five passed around the CDs and pressed them to their lips. The dome began to rumble with unrest.

"Indirect kiss comin' atcha!" Cackling, Namgi frisbeed his CD out into the crowd. I heard a riot break out, but then Mino tugged Saichi close again. He held up the CD like a shield between them and the camera, but from my angle, I saw very clearly how they both kissed the CD together... Yeah, I wanted that one. *Badly.*

Mino deserted Saichi and came prowling in my direction.

Lord above, I'd never ask for anything else. Just that CD.

The fans around me lit up in ear-splitting screams as his eyes panned through us. The footlights gave his dark gaze a wicked sort of glitter, but the incandescent mop of cotton candy on his head was the closest thing to a unicorn mane I'd ever seen in person.

Right in front of me, he came to a sudden stop and sank into a crouch at the edge of the stage. He looked me straight in the eye, waved, and tossed the CD at me.

A CD with Minchi's lips on it...

I think I almost passed out.

And I almost dropped it.

But, but, but—

Wait, but didn't he know how incredibly risky it was to do that?! The whole dome probably just saw that! Even just the fans in my direct vicinity were enough to start a Twitter trend, and judging by the way they were clawing at the ropes of the VIP section, Mino might've just really screwed me over!

He didn't care. I heard him laugh as he walked away. Agh, but also, I now had a CD I would treasure for life, so maybe I didn't care either? If I'd salvaged the Tick Tock Talk disaster, I could salvage this too, right? I *really* didn't want to think about this crap right now!

Ryo cleared his throat with poignant irritation.

Oops… Please don't be mad, Ryo? At least it wasn't a Kitchi interaction? That was sort of splitting hairs, but our deal wasn't technically broken, right? Did he actually see what happened or was I being paranoid?

I couldn't tell. He called out into the crowd, "Alright everybody, it's almost time for the second half! Don't forget to download the DigitAlive app and have it open!"

The audience was still screaming for Minchi as they filed off the stage. No kiss. For now. But Mino did grab Saichi's butt the whole way up the stairs. Celebrate the little victories, I guess.

High-strung.

On the app, I was shocked to see a live feed of their dressing room as they changed costumes. A muscly, shirtless Ryo passed casually in front of the camera and he'd gotten *another* tattoo? In the background, Namgi fell over putting on his pants and Jaeyoon had to help him zip his jacket. And Mino spanked Saichi. We were losing our collective mind when the feed cut out.

Countless notifications bubbled up on my screen: 'So-and-so just ordered three t-shirts,' 'What's-her-face just sent a fan message to Kasugai Ryo,' 'Rando Fanboy just commented on Rando Fangirl's video,' and so on. Thousands of fans playing Vortex trivia, coloring cover art, brushing up on lyrics, browsing through concert goods…

Then I found the news feed. Everyone was adding videos and photos from their seats. Fans who hadn't gotten tickets were interacting from all over, tweeting out every post.

Oh.

Three trends immediately jumped out at me. #LetMinchiKiss, #MysteryGirl, and best of all: #KitAllisterIsHere. Oh *god*.

–Mino just handed a CD straight to some girl! Who's the mystery girl?

    –Mystery Girl is Kit Allister!

    –KIT?! WHAT?!

–That looked like Kit Allister just now…

    –That section is roped off. I'd bet good money that it's Kit.

        –Omg I want an autograph I hope she sticks around

    –She was wearing SO MUCH Vortex gear lmao

–Are they dating? What the fuck. I shipped her with Saichi, not Mino.

    –Did she learn nothing from Tick Tock Talk?

    –Saichi and Mino belong to each other, not to Kit Allister

        –Psycho pervert

          –Shut up homophobe

    –Leave Vortex alone, Kit

        –She's a fan. So are you. So am I. It's fine.

–Cancel Kit

        –gurl do NOT start a war with the Kit-Kats

–I ship any Kit x Vortex!

–Kit's still letting her Vortexan flag fly! Yasss girl! Get it!

    –Isn't it sort of not fair that she gets the CD? She's a KJ artist too. She could probably get it some other way.

    –And why does she get her own section? Think of all the fans that couldn't get tickets tonight. She stole their space.

Things were getting out of hand. If I waited around until the end of the concert, I might get mobbed by Vortexans. And that wasn't fair! I just wanted to enjoy the concert like all the other fans. I didn't want to miss the second half!

Fans in the nearest section were pointing at me. They waved. Yikes. I smiled and waved back. They didn't look hostile…? There was a camera flash. Dammit. Another raised their phone, but the lights suddenly dimmed. There was a collective buzz and we all looked down at our phones.

'Ready for the second half? What song should we do next? Vote now!' The poll blew up in seconds. A Delusion remix was chosen. Then more polls. *'Pick a color palette for the lights!' 'Choose your favorite outfit!'*

'Does Ryo get to wear a shirt?' Of course not. 'Drag and drop your bias to your seat! Ready? Go!'

Wait, what?

The dome detonated when spotlights flared up to show five tiny figures far above us on five tiny platforms.

Oh my god. How could I leave now?

They plunged toward us in a rain of glitter and the whole dome became a giant claw machine with thousands fighting for the joystick. Lightsticks sparkled to life everywhere they went, a neon spiderweb forming across the crowd.

I was too stupefied by it all to even try vying for Saichi. How was he dancing on that tiny wobbly thing?! Mid-rap, Ryo zipped past over my head, and then all too soon, our phones flashed, 'Game over,' and the remix wound down into something more familiar. As the platforms linked up, the five of them spun in and around each other in the signature Vortex move and my heart swelled. *So* satisfying. We'd been watching for that move all night.

Our phones vibrated again.

'Should Minchi kiss?'

I have never clicked faster. Every camera zeroed in on Saichi and Mino side by side. Mino flashed us all a catty grin. He pulled at Saichi's collar, then put a hand on his cheek…

No way.

For real?! Finally?!

Saichi blinked, unassuming.

"C'mere, Satch."

My ears rang with tens of thousands of voices inflating my own. Saichi was trying not to laugh. Mino leaned in. Jaeyoon shook his head behind them and ducked out of the picture. Closer, closer, closer. Mino was milking it! The little brat was dragging it out! I had to gasp for air to scream more.

And then!

The dome fell *pitch black*. Right when their lips were about to touch! Denied *again?* Where was the democracy in that? What about our vote?! How *cruel*.

The audience ignited the darkness with protests. Mino laughed over the uproar and Saichi made some sort of 'hmf' sound and we were left to speculate based on that alone. But dammit, did they kiss or not?! Now I definitely couldn't leave. They wouldn't put it up as a poll if they didn't mean to honor it at *some* point, right?

Before we could protest more, the dome flashed back to life and silver streamers infested the air. It was a song we'd never heard before and it whipped us back up into a frenzy. Namgi deprived Ryo of a shirt, as promised, and Mino danced the entire song with a dirty smirk on his face.

I told myself I'd leave when the encores started. I was already here and already screwed, so I might as well enjoy myself until the very last second, right? I got to play with the LEDs on their costumes, and vote on the order of their solos, and I even helped paint the giant screens behind them with sparkling neon designs. When they played their latest single—the one I now had on Minchi-kissed CD—a digital drum set popped up on our screens. Every time we all got the beat right, pyrotechnics lining the stage rewarded us with fireworks and we earned points to buy concert goods. I won myself a poster because it turns out I'm pretty okay at drums. And also pretty okay at ignoring a storm of texts from Ilsung. I thought I saw one that said, *'I'm sending a car.'*

The first encore came.

I knew I should leave. But then the stage turned into a playground of augmented reality. Through the lenses of our phones, their bodies glowed and left trippy streams wherever they danced. Namgi kept shooting lasers from his fingers, and Ryo burst into flames during the rap.

—I sent a map of the venue. Don't take the main exits. Use the staff exit. The closest one is 18F. The car is waiting outside.
—Never mind. Near the VIP section, there's a recessed trap door that leads under the stage. Go down the stairs and wait under there. I'll make sure the concert staff comes to find you once the crowds die down.

Wasn't that a little much? I'd been to plenty of Vortex concerts and never gotten caught afterward. Plus, after Sangchul nailed me with that picture on Twitter, it became blatantly obvious to my team and me how insufficient a mere mask was. This time, our strategy for anonymity was keeping my hair tucked in my hat. Super itchy, and it had failed anyway thanks to Mino, but still, I didn't need some ridiculous trap door to escape. All I had to do was take my hair back down and change my mask.

Then the second encore came. A bit resentful but resigned to following directives, I gathered my bag and started scanning for the trap door. It was impossible to see anything through all the fog and strobe lights, but I thought I spotted the glint of a handle.

I ducked under the VIP ropes and got ready to run for it. As soon as something distracted that bunch of girls over there—

The fangirling around me intensified. I froze.

Saichi.

Baggy white clothes swelling like sails, Saichi blew across the stage on the wings of a sweet breezy solo. He hadn't been on this side of the stage for the whole concert, but now he was finally heading our way. If I stayed just a little longer, I could see him closer than I'd ever seen him before.

Just a little longer. I couldn't leave now.

Lighter than air, he drifted along the edge of the stage, toes dipping in the footlights. Waves and smiles to everyone, but his eyes seemed to be searching through the dark at his feet. The closer he got, the brighter more blinding he was, and the less I could see of anything else. He grew from a lit window to a whole dazzling winterscape of snow on a cloudless day. But unlike snow, or the moon, or a flashing mirror, the spotlight on him was redundant. He could light his own way. He had the sparkle of a star.

And then our eyes connected.

For a second, he was still, and then a smile burst across his face. Like a curtain fell between us and the rest of the dome, the lights, the screaming, even the other voices of Vortex blurred into a dim hum.

Time stopped, and so did my heart for maybe three entire beats. Then he plopped down onto the edge of the stage and began to sing again, feet swinging beneath him.

Oh Saichi was singing right to me. My heart could stay stopped. I could die happy now. Nothing else mattered.

On the other side of the stage, Mino burst into laughter and started scolding him. Thanks to him, the entire dome's attention swung our way, but Saichi didn't care. He kept waving until I waved back. And then Mino came to fetch him, hauling him up and towing him away *by his belt loops*.

I didn't fully process just how much trouble I was in until Mino turned around and winked, wiggling a pinkie and a thumb. 'Call me,' he mouthed, and everyone around me disintegrated into shrieks.

Oh *no*. Oh *god* no.

I was *screwed*.

But how could I complain?!

It was the final encore and I still hadn't made it to the trap door, but Vortex was going to leave soon, and I was just trying not to cry. Soon, they'd be touring the world. Who knew when I'd get to see them live again? Maybe not for *years!* I needed to see them until the very last second tonight. God, to think I got to sit on the same couch as Ryo and Namgi. And I shook their hands. And I got a CD from Mino. And Saichi *sang to me*. What had I ever done to deserve so much happiness?

The final beat dimmed into an echo and I burst into tears as the five of them sunk through the fog into the belly of the stage.

Then I made a mad dash for the trap door.

Backstage.

There. It was fine. I got to see the whole concert *and* I escaped the crowds. They were all still screaming their goodbyes as the trap door thudded shut behind me.

Safely under the stage, I pulled out my phone to study the map Ilsung sent me. It had been a while since my last time performing here, but I was more or less familiar with the dome's backstage. I just had to figure out how to get back there from wherever I was…

It didn't seem like this door was meant to be used for this particular stage assembly. All I could feel were steel pipes in every direction. I was thumbing around for my phone's flashlight when someone called, "I'm here for your mics!"

"Ah, thank you."

"*Man*, what a rush!"

Oh my god.

Vortex.

They were under here too. Just on the other side of a partition by the sound of it. I knew those voices. It was Minchi. I clambered over a few pipes to get closer because logic suggested that I ask them for help, but *hell no?!* Call out to two world-famous superstar pop gods?! I was barely even an idol compared to them. And while my little problem of getting caught here was their fault, it wasn't their problem.

So I just followed them instead, trying very hard not to feel creepy. The staff member carrying their mics kept their feet wet in a rippling pool of light, guiding them over the bumpy tracks of wires. The only other light to go by was the spectral glow of Saichi.

"Earth to Satch."

"Sorry…"

"Starstruck?"

"A little."

"You could've just gone on Tick Tock Talk."

"I don't like that show."

"You don't like *any* show."

Holy crap. Were they talking about me?! Kill me, oh my god. Smite me right here. I actually tried to cover my ears but then I almost tripped in the dark.

"I didn't know she'd be here. Why didn't you tell me sooner?"

"Didn't notice at first, but then Babo spotted her. Ryo told him to stay away from the VIP section, so of course, he went to investigate."

"So Ryo invited her?"

"Probably. *He* was willing to go on Tick Tock Talk."

"Um, Ryo told me she's not really a Vortex fan. He said it's a publicity stunt. Do you think—"

"Oh, whatever, Satch. If that's true, she's one hell of an actor. Maybe I should give her one of my awards."

"I would've tried a little harder if I knew she was watching…"

"Pshh, tonight was *perfect*. Except for maybe one fucking little annoying detail… Am I right, sound guy? Am I right? Which one of your buddies in the lights department fucking blacked us out? Hah?"

"Sorry, sir. I don't know anything about that."

"You guys got some kinda problem with Minchi?"

"No, sir."

They turned a corner and it was abruptly dark. I immediately drove my shin into a steel bar and my phone flew from my hands. Dammit, I'd be under here all night trying to find it!

"Minchi kisses whenever they damn well *please*. Right, Satch?"

"Get your mouth off my face."

What?! Oh god, did they just…? I stuffed my hands in my mouth to stifle a scream.

"You taste salty. You need a shower."

"Min, get off. It's not my fault the lights went out."

"Either way I'm pissed. Everybody on Twitter is gonna think we just copped out! As if I don't have the balls to do it! I'd do it any day!"

"The hashtag is *let* Minchi kiss. I think they all know that it's not really up to us whether we ever do it or not."

"It *should* be up to us?! The higher-ups can suck a sour dick. Like, if we're willing to tongue each other for their pocket change, then they should be *grateful* and let it happen. Bunch of goddamn assholes."

They were moving again. Their voices began to fade and I was left alone with my heart shaking me from the inside out. There were still tears on my face from the encore and I just heard Minchi complaining about how they couldn't kiss onstage? Good god, this was *so wrong*. To have private access to them right after a concert—!

Thank goodness Ilsung texted me right then and my phone lit up a few feet away.

–Kit. Are you safe???

> –Yeah, sorry. I'm under the stage
> –Vortex paid me a little extra attention during the concert and it blew up on the DigitAlive app
> –And then everything got tweeted out so…

–App? Vortex was encouraging the audience to use their phones during the concert? How bizarre…

> –It was a very digital show lol

–Well, if they were going to make every aspect of their concert so accessible to Twitter then I wish they'd been more discreet about you being there.
–I'm in touch with security. I should be able to get you out soon.

> –Thanks Ilsung-shi

With the light of my phone, I picked my way around the bend and toward the light of a door. If Ilsung was talking to security, then I could just present myself to the nearest staff member and I'd be home free. As soon as I made it through the door, the air pressure eased off—the electricity, the heat, the buzz of the concert faded and I was suddenly among the heroes who made this their normal working day. They scurried past in labeled shirts toting knots of tech and didn't bother with a first glance, let alone a second, at the random fan-looking chick who had just found her way backstage.

"*Hey*. You can't be back here!"

There it was. I was actually a little bothered by how long it took. What if I *was* a fan after Vortex? I pulled down my mask as the burly guard charged for me. "Sorry, actually I'm—"

He stopped up short and stuck a finger to the Bluetooth in his ear. "This is Baek. Call off the search. I've got her."

Semi-amazing how quickly he managed to amass a horde of beefy men in dark suits and dark glasses, and fully alarming how quickly they began to fight over me. A clean, young, capable sort pushed through the circle and sank into a crisp bow.

"Good evening, Kit-nim. I am the chief of Vortex's personal security. Kasugai Ryo-nim has instructed me to escort you off the premises. We have readied a car—"

I frowned. "Ryo-nim? Not my manager?"

Again a flurry of voices, the suits pressing in ever closer.

"Chief Woojin, I have updated orders from Mino-nim—"

"I have spoken with upper management—"

"I have been in touch with her manager—"

"*Hey!*"

Silence in an instant.

"Scram!"

The sea of suits parted impossibly fast. I almost got mowed down in the stampede as the hallway emptied of them. And then it was just me and the wiry shape of Kim Mino leaning on the wall.

"Hiya."

Oh *god*. Kim Mino fresh off the stage.

His final encore outfit clung to his body, a glossy medley of silk that gave him the look of a stained-glass mosaic. Still a sweaty gleam to his skin, cotton candy hair muted, damp. I could *not*.

"Nice to meet you, Kit. *Finally*, am I right?

In that rolling catlike slink of his, with that quirky catlike smirk of his, he strolled up and stuck out a stubby hand. "Shake?" But I wasn't a dog. I was a short-circuiting fangirl who could only manage to stare at his hand.

He clicked his tongue and snatched my hand from my side, jerking it around in a limp awkward wiggle. I opened my mouth but the first idiotic thing that came to mind fell right out, "Did you just kiss Saichi under the stage?" I clamped my mouth shut again.

"What? No? Oh. I mean, his cheek? How'd you know that?"

"Um, um, I guessed?"

He snorted. "Lucky guess. So you got any plans after this or…?" I couldn't get over the fact Kim Mino was *touching my hand* fresh off the stage. He'd just been out there bathed in the adulation of thousands, and now I was alone with him, having a conversation. Well, not really. I wasn't exactly holding up my end. "Hah? You listening? Hello? I asked a question."

C'mon, Kit. Use your words.

"S-sorry."

"*Plans? Yakusoku?*" I laughed. He'd been watching very closely yesterday. He grinned when I shook my head. "Knew you'd understand *that*. But cool. Come with me then." Then he tugged on my hand and turned to go. I *could not*. I dug my heels in and my sneakers screeched on the floor.

"'The hell? Come *on*."

Think, Kit. Use your words *and* your brain. "Um, I can't. I gotta go home. My manager has a car waiting and—"

"Sounds boring. *I* say you get in *our* car and come out with us."

"Out? Out where?"

"Out to drinks."

"*Drinks?!*"

"Yah, alcohol? Liquor? Soju? Beer? Ever heard of it?"

"W-wait, what? *Why?*"

He turned and looked me square in the face. "Because you said you're free," he snapped. "And you're making me late right now, so how about you quit grilling me and make those feet walk!"

My mouth fell open. What sass!

"Um, that sounds great and all, but KJ Global Entertainment's code of conduct says—"

He snorted, and if anything, he moved us faster down the hall to my doom. "*Jesus*. You really do care about that shit, huh? You some kinda goody-two-shoes idol or what?" Did he just say Jesus in English? That was a new addition to his arsenal.

Finally, he stopped… at a door labeled 'Oh Saichi.'

With a sticky note pasted over it that said 'Minchi.'

Mino waved an arm at the door. "I give you the Minchi dressing room. Wanna meet our mutual favorite human?"

I couldn't breathe.

Mino expected me to just barge into Saichi's dressing room right after a concert?! He was so much more than just my favorite person. He was the man who changed the course of my life! The most perfect existence, the most talented artist, the most beautiful being to ever walk this planet, and I was just gonna meet him without any mental prep whatsoever?

"I am *not* going in there."

"What? Why not?"

"I *can't*."

"You nerrrvous?"

"Of course I'm nervous!"

"You should be. This man will eat you alive, baby girl."

"No, I'm *serious!* I can't go in there and I'm sorry but I definitely can't go out to drinks with you either! I could get in a lot of trouble and Vortexans are already keeping a very close eye on me, so really, it was very nice to meet you, and please tell Saichi-sunbaenim that he did a really incredible job tonight, and I hope you both have fun with the drinks thing, but I'm going to just—"

The door swung open and my idol—the man I dream about whether I'm awake or sleeping, the man who occupies every room of my heart—was standing right there.

And he was only wearing a towel.

So I screamed right in his face.

Minchi

"*Kit?!*"

He covered his mouth, I covered my eyes, and Mino covered Saichi's... real estate. The second the towel slipped, he lunged lightning-fast and clapped his hands around Saichi's hips. "Jesus *fuck*, Satch, ya fucking idiot! Both of you, quit fucking screaming!"

"B-but—"

I didn't really notice that I fell. But when I peeked through my fingers, they were a lot taller now and my butt hurt. 'Jesus... fuck?' Who taught Mino *that* English? He was laughing at us both even as Saichi swatted at him and worked frantically to tighten his towel.

Then Saichi turned to me framed in light, and my eyes caught on a pearl earring of water as it slipped from his hair onto his shoulder. Not silver. His hair was chrome as it dried. He smiled through the metallic strands. And he bent a little, held out a hand to me.

"Um, are you okay?"

His real voice... For the first time, I wasn't hearing his voice through a speaker. I was hearing organic *him*. No digital walls between us. Just air, space, light. I actually thought I was floating a moment but no, he was pulling me to my feet. And then there was even less air between us. I had to gasp for it.

Neither of us could move. Time waited while the moment soaked into our skin, fingers knotted through that small open window between us. And I was spellbound in the amber galaxy of his eyes as he whispered, "Hi, my name's Saichi."

Mino's loud snort was incongruous with the enlightenment I'd just achieved. My heart jangled violently back to life and beat the breath right out of my lungs. I think my body bruised from the inside.

"Where'd you come from?"

"America…?"

His fingers squeezed. "And you're really here right now?"

Not sure but "I think so."

"That's amazing… Min, how'd you do it?"

"Satch, for Chrissake, let go of the lady and go put some damn clothes on! We *get* it. You're hot. But ya can't walk around in a towel!"

Saichi's face clouded over and he retreated back into the room. "Tell me where you hid my clothes and I will!" Saichi's bare back, oh god, oh god. Mino took advantage of me covering my eyes again to yank me through the door after him.

Minchi's dressing room is where chaos spends its spare time. Carnage from a violent pillow war littered the floor, along with what I could only assume was the aftermath of an aborted fifty-two pickup *and* a Jenga demolition? Retro pixels blinked out a Pac-Man high score on the oversized television, filling the room with syrupy musical nausea. But what really caught my eye was the circus of art parading from the mini-fridge onto the nearby wall—mustachioed strawberries, a lightbulb sundae, the Sphynx as Pegasus, daisies in roller skates, all rendered in the vivid cream of oil pastels.

Mino dug a bundle of clothes out of the couch cushions and chucked it at Saichi's pout.

"Min, these aren't even mine!"

"They're from Jae. Apparently, after the holey t-shirt incident, you and I aren't allowed to wear our civvies to Sevens anymore."

Saichi trudged into the other room, and even after the door closed, we could hear his mutinous muttering. Mino noticed my fascination with the art gallery. "He's mad talented, right? I kept trying to stump him but that guy can draw literally *anything*. The banana hot dog is my favorite. Pretty sure that one could go for billions."

"Saichi-sunbaenim made all these?"

"Yup, he can't help himself. Always up to something artsy-fartsy. Me, I like games, in case you can't tell. Also, drop the sunbaenim. I hate that formal shit, and so does Satch."

"Oh, um, my apologies."

"So here's my plan. If you get in one of the company cars, Ryo's gonna make sure you get sent home." Which was entirely fine by me. "So we're gonna smuggle you into the Vortex car!" What, in the trunk?! "Here, you can wear the outfit Jae vetoed."

"All this to go get a drink! Listen, it's nothing personal but I don't even drink! And to consort with a Vortex member after hours—"

"No, no, no. Not just a drink, not just after hours. After*party*. And not just any afterparty. *The* Vortex afterparty. Also, it's pretty fucking big deal I'm inviting you so yeah, you kinda gotta come."

"Min, stop! Kit doesn't wanna come to our dumb party!" Saichi reappeared in the doorway. Yikes. He looked so delicious that I was uncomfortable in my own brain. Black studded jeans, leather jacket, tight tank top… What the heck? He was way easier to handle when he wore his usual baggy clothes.

"Satch, how dare you diss on our dumb party!"

"I think you're out of time to shower. Jaeyoon is about three texts away from a stern call, so you better hurry."

"I wonder what weird bullshit outfit he's got picked out for me. Kit, tell Satch you're definitely gonna come, yeah?" Mino started to pull his pretty mosaic shirt up. I yelled something incoherent and covered my eyes again. "What? Don't you wanna see me naked too?"

"*Min!*"

"No! Both of you keep your clothes on in front of me! The concert just ended like five minutes ago so I'm very sensitive right now! Change in the other room or I'm outta here! I cannot handle—"

"*Sensitive*, huh?"

I glared through my fingers as Saichi herded him and that dirty cat grin of his into the other room. "Min, ew. Don't bother her."

I heard them giggling behind the door and my fangirl mind speculated. Especially when I heard a thump and a crash. I broke my own fourth wall to scold myself in the mirror, but I was distracted by the mane of sticky notes on my reflection.

Who's my favorite person?

You are!!!

I ♡ U Satch!

You got this! Fighting!

Minchi 5ever xoxox

Oh my god, Minchi just gave me a cavity. I also felt a little like I was peeping through someone else's love letters, so I jumped a guilty mile when my phone started buzzing my purse with all the panic of a very stressed Ilsung.

"Kit! Are you okay?! My men just notified me you're not in the trap room! Did you find your way backstage somehow? Did you make it to the car safely? You're alive, right?! This *is* Kit, right?!"

"I'm fine, Ilsung-shi! Sorry to worry you!"

Mino popped up behind me in the mirror. And oof, Jaeyoon seriously knew how to make Minchi into snacks. All black made the pink and blue hair look all the more fantastical. I shook my head clean.

"Vortex's security found me and—"

Mino put a finger on my lips and I ceased to breathe. 'Manager?' he mouthed. Saichi slapped Mino's hand away and patted my hair in apology. Something flipped in my stomach and started sizzling.

Mino whispered, "You're on your way home!"

"I'm on my way home?"

"Oh, thank *goodness!* How very hospitable of them to—" I confess I didn't hear a word he said after that because Mino sat Saichi up on the makeup counter and he just started *decorating* him, dropping chains over his head, mussing his hair, fixing his jacket collar, sliding a big steel ring up his finger... No wonder Minchi managed to charm the whole world. It wasn't an act or a stunt. They were as obscenely adorable behind the scenes as they were in the public eye.

"Kit? *Kit?*"

"Yes, absolutely!"

"See, I just knew you'd love the idea! Definitely a 'two birds with one stone' sort of strategy! He's a clever man, that Mahn Jaeyoon!" Oh crap, what did I just agree to?! "Anyhow, rest up! I'll be in touch with more details tomorrow!" That was gonna be a fun conversation.

"Good night, Ilsung-shi!" As soon as the line went dead, I turned to Minchi and bobbed a frantic apology bow. "Really, I should go home. I told him I was going home. I gotta go home."

Mino laughed. "What's the big deal? You'll go home at *some* point. Come to the party!"

"Min, stop pressuring her."

"C'mon, Satch. You want her to come, don't you?"

"Yeah, but…"

"Well then." Mino grinned, tossed his hair, and metamorphosed his entire vibe to say, "We'd like to speak to your manager, Kit," in the most white-lady voice I'd ever heard. I laughed, but only after living out a few unpleasant flashbacks to my coffeeshop days. "I bet I can convince him to let you come. We'll call it networking or—"

I dodged with "Your American accent is better than mine."

He was successfully distracted. "Dunno if you're aware, Miss Kit, but I was in a Hollywood movie. So yeah, I speak fluent American, god dammit piss-hell-shit-fuck."

Got me again. I was a sucker for Mino's brand of code-switches. The laughs didn't land well with Saichi though. Every English word Mino spoke pulled Saichi's bottom lip farther out of his mouth. "Believe me, I saw it in theaters… along with the rest of the entire country. That movie roped in a lot of new Vortexans in America."

"Yeah, yeah. But you were Satch-baited though, weren't ya?"

"Uh—"

Saichi was about to protest, but he stilled when Mino poked an earring through his ear, then another. And Mino just went on talking to me like this was all so, so normal, "Everybody knows you're a massive fan of Vortex, so it'd just be stupid to throw this chance away. Come hang out with us. Get to know the men behind the magic and love on your bias a little."

Dear god. Tempting. "But my manager—"

"You got a crush on your manager or something?"

"No?!"

"Then quit bringing him up. It ain't his business. This is your private life." Beaming, he dug a finger in some pink lip balm and swiped it across Saichi's pout. "Now you're ready, sexy boy."

"I just don't think I should—"

"It's not about what you *should* do, baby girl. It's about what you're *gonna* do 'cuz you *wanna*. I mean, whatever, you do you, but we're gonna go, so if you wanna come, get changed. I'll let the security goon posse know what's up. Sound good? C'mon, Satch."

He shoved a bundle of clothes into my hands and then he was gone. Saichi turned and smiled at me. "To be honest, I don't really wanna go either. I kinda wish I could stay here with you and talk about your new album. They didn't really let you say anything about it on Tick Tock Talk and the host was so rude—"

"Satch, we're now two texts away from a stern call! Nah, wait, fuck, it's one now! Come on!"

Saichi broke into stutters. "Anyway, um, really happy to finally meet you in person. I hope we can maybe meet again someday—"

"I'll see you there."

Oh, okay, mouth. If you say so. I guess we're going then? Yeah. Absolutely. If Saichi's eyes were going to fill with stars like that, there was no going back on it now.

"Satch, incoming stern call!"

With a breathless "Okay! See you!" he raced away.

Oh my *god*. I just met Oh Saichi. In the Minchi dressing room. Right after DigitAlive. I think I fell into a twilight zone when I went down that trap door.

This was not me. Parties were not me. Breaking rules, telling lies, sneaking around, all of it was so not me. I was KJ's Miss Perfect. And I couldn't stop thinking about what President Kyungsoon said about 'higher standards' and keeping a closer eye on me.

But maybe just this once I could get away with it? Just poke my nose in, pay my respects, thank them for extending the invitation, and then hop a cab home before things got messy. No problem, right?

Any amount of trouble was worth it to spend a little tiny bit more time with that angel man and his starry eyes.

I startled when there was a crisp knock at the door. If I got caught in here—! "Allister Kit-nim? Chief of Vortex security here. My men are waiting outside to escort you whenever you're ready."

Ah. Right. The goon posse.

I tried very hard not to think about the fact that I was putting on Saichi's clothes, tucking my hair into his hat, putting on his mask that had at one point touched his face, and soon I was suited up and ready to go. I looked nothing like him, but at the very least I didn't look like whatever Kit Allister was plastered all over Twitter right now.

"Alright. Let's go."

Lucky me.

Screams engulfed us in sharp rolling echoes as soon as my little entourage set foot outside. I felt a little guilty for deceiving my fellow Vortexans, but at least the Saichi disguise was working. I wondered if they realized it was strange that I didn't stop to wave to them or pose for photos or even show them my face. Normally, Vortex members wouldn't come out enclosed in an exoskeleton of broad-shouldered suits, or get into the passenger seat at the front of the car, or have their head dunked into the door like a suspect under arrest…

"Oh, hello there. I don't often get company up here." The woman beside me wore her suit with pristine pride, the KJ logo prominent on her sleeve, over her heart, and perched on the brim of her cap. Smiling, she lifted a dove-white glove in something of a serene salute and set me oddly at ease. "A pleasure to make your acquaintance, Miss Kit Allister. I suppose you're coming with us?"

"Hyejin-shi! What's the hold-up? Let's get this show on the road!" Ryo's voice buzzed through the privacy screen behind us.

"Yes, sir." The car began to wade forward through details of security, gates, and yellow tape that bloomed open around us.

I kept my voice below the unruly racket of Vortex and kept my face angled away from the window. "May I ask where we're going?"

I saw the eye flicker but her voice remained cheery. "We're headed for Lucky Sevens, Miss Kit." At my lack of recognition, she continued. "Currently Gangnam's most popular club, a favorite among KJ artists, and the running host of every Vortex post-concert gathering to date."

"Club? A nightclub?" God save me.

"Yes, ma'am."

"So Vortex is allowed to go to clubs…"

A wry smile. "Yes, ma'am. Vortex goes just about wherever they please. But Lucky Sevens is a rather unique club in that we've elected to oversee the security there. There are rumors that someone in the upper echelons of KJ owns the club, but at the very least, we have so many artists who frequent Sevens on a regular basis that we consider it in our best interest to keep the premises airtight."

"Even from the tabloids?"

"From *any* unsavory characters. We're proud of the fact that there has never been a Sevens scandal. Especially during Vortex events, no one of an unverified identity enters the club, and we keep the building well-isolated from the media."

Comforting, but strange. A safe zone where idols could let loose? That sounded both too good to be true, and also like the sort of wild party I wanted absolutely nothing to do with, scandal-free or not.

"So this afterparty is almost like a company-sponsored event?" Twisting it that way made me feel a bit better about betraying Ilsung.

"In some senses, yes, I suppose so."

"Um, do you think my manager knows about Lucky Sevens?"

Another brief pause. Probably another eye flicker. Her voice turned softer, "Park Ilsung-shi is your manager, correct? Mino-nim informed tonight's staff about your reservations. Ilsung-shi is not to be notified of your whereabouts."

She was watching for my reaction, so I turned away. I knew I was doing something I shouldn't, but the fact that people were going to lie to Ilsung really drove it all home. I'd never lied to Ilsung about anything before. Because if you follow all the rules, what was there to lie about?

"I'll be dropping Vortex off out front and then I'm going to pull around back to the VIP entrance. But Miss Kit, I could just as easily take you home if that's what you would prefer."

"Um, I promised Saichi-sunbaenim that I'd go but… will you be around to take me home if I don't like it?" My voice came out smaller than I intended. "I've never actually been to a club before."

"Of course I will." Now there was *definitely* pity in her voice. Without even taking her eyes off the road, she drew a card from her inner pocket and passed it to me. "I'll wait outside the VIP entrance for an hour. If you need a ride home later in the night, call me and I'll come immediately."

I glanced at the card. 'Shin Hyejin – Chauffeur of Bae Namgi.' Namgi's laughter was the loudest element of the unruly racket behind us as Vortex toppled out of the car. Driving him around required exactly this sort of calm, composed person. I liked her. "Thank you, Hyejin-shi. That makes me feel much better."

"Please think nothing of it."

Next thing I knew, we were in an alley and she was opening my door with a sisterly concern on her face. "Excuse me if I am out of line, but please take care tonight and be safe. Don't hesitate to call me if you need anything."

Her white glove waved off my thanks and then gestured to the immense set of doors before us, three now-familiar letters were stenciled there in ruby paint. V.I.P. Ugh.

Actually, thank god Hyejin dropped me off at the VIP entrance because I would've turned tail and run home immediately if I'd walked into the sheer mass of people filling up the first floor. Up here, I was safely removed from the smoke, lasers, and strobe lights, but the Vortex music was still loud enough to punch me in the diaphragm. It was like I'd walked into a continuation of DigitAlive.

Looking out over the railing, I completely despaired. I didn't fit in on either floor. Down there was too loud, a foggy pit full of way, *way* too many strangers' writhing bodies, all of them intoxicated. And up here, glitzy clusters of bored socialites lounged around swirling cocktails and wine. I even recognized a few celebrities. No, more than just a few; I recognized *all* of them. Everybody who was anybody was up on this floor... and then there was me: the VIP sore thumb dressed like an incognito Saichi in a Pac-Man shirt with two holes in it.

I *really* wanted to leave. There was no way I'd even be able to find Saichi, much less spend any time with him. I'd be searching all night and I'd be uncomfortable the whole time...

Jaeyoon.

I saw Jaeyoon.

He decorated the railing on the other side of the mezzanine, studying the strobing colors that dangled over the dance floor. A dark satin suit clung to his build—three buttons undone, collar messily open, chains glinting on his collarbone.

As I looked on, a swarm of wriggling miniskirts swamped in around him and he waved them off like gnats without so much as a grimace. Yeah, no way. I couldn't go over there. That aura wasn't approachable...

His eyes connected with mine over a sip of wine and my knees locked clear across the club. He batted a hand, calling me over. Yikes. I felt a good fifty sets of eyes land on me, but the heaviest were his. My limbs seemed to completely forget proper walking technique.

"Hello, Sunbaenim. Nice to finally meet you."

His lips quirked. "That shirt again... Is this Mino's idea of a joke?"

"Um, he gave it to me as a disguise."

He popped the hat off my head and frisbeed it out over the crowd. "No need for disguise now." He'd smeared mesmerizing purple shadows on his eyelids that flashed when he looked me up and down. "If I knew you were coming to Sevens tonight, I would've arranged something for you from my line. Also, I would've spoken to you directly about the collaboration. What are your feelings on it?"

Collaboration?! "I beg your pardon?"

"Ilsung-shi hasn't been in touch with you yet?" Ah, right! That whole chunk of conversation I missed on the phone with Ilsung... "That's fine. Here's my pitch: I think we can agree the last forty-eight hours have brought you under a lot of scrutiny. Now that you've publicly engaged with Vortex for the first time, you're unfortunately facing some negative press, and I find it unfair to the level of professionalism you've shown thus far, so I'd like to help you harness this narrative. I've actually been speaking to my team for some time about soliciting a composition from you, and now seems like the perfect time to strike."

"You mean I would write a song for Vortex?!" I couldn't believe my ears. For a moment, I swear gravity lost interest in me. I was about to float right off the surface of the planet.

"The possibilities are endless really. Whether you simply write a song for us or join us in a recording, any joint project would easily drown out the negative publicity and establish a healthier relationship between our brands going forward."

"Anything," I blurted. "I'll do *anything* for Vortex. My only concern would be whether I can live up to your standards."

He held up his trademark rings. "Then rest assured on that front. I'm familiar with your work and I have no doubt you'll do well. Although, now that I see you in person…" His fingers slipped into my hair and tucked it back behind my ear. My gasp multiplied and fizzed its way across the room, but his hand lingered there, warm except for the chilly kiss of a ring on my ear. "I think maybe our collaborations don't have to be limited to music."

What? Wait, wait, wait. *What?!* The club lit his huge dark eyes in sad fairy colors. My heart was jackhammering but I couldn't look away. Until I did. And for some unfathomable reason, I looked down.

At his lips.

Why, why, *why* did I do that?

"What do you mean?"

Those were some really full lips…

"I just think it's a shame to see you dressed like this. I'd love the chance to design a look for you some time in the future, if you'd permit me."

"Um, gladly." Damn my voice for cracking. Damn my eyes for looking at his lips. Damn my mind for making stupid assumptions! "It would be an honor, of course."

His hand dropped away and his eyes returned to the lights overhead, smiling now. Wine slipped past his lips and left a faint burgundy stain. Dammit, Kit! Stop looking!

"Wonderful. I'll keep that in mind. I hope you enjoy yourself tonight. Your drinks are on us, of course. Let me know if anyone gives you trouble. And I do mean *anyone*. That includes Vortex members."

"Th-thank you." Speaking made me even more lightheaded. "Um, would you happen to know where Mino is? I mean Mino-shi, eh, Mino-nim, *sunbaenim*—" Crap!

"Don't hurt yourself. Shi works." At least I won a rare Jaeyoon laugh. He waved a hand at the far wall where a laughing circle of women huddled a velvet curtain. "Last I saw, he was headed up to the Vortex suite, but I'm pretty sure he's indisposed at the moment."

"Can you let him know I enjoyed myself but I had to duck out?"

"Leaving so soon?"

"Well, I'm not dressed for the occasion after all."

"I could fix that." I felt his eyes again, but I'd stopped looking.

"Oh, no, it's okay. I um, I just have a busy day tomorrow and—"

"If you're looking to leave, then I'd advise you turn and run right about now. You've been sighted."

Namgi was his own siren. His wail punctuated every bounce up the stairs and then I spotted him, hurtling toward me like a torpedo of noise. I just barely managed to brace myself on the railing before he barreled into my side.

"*Kittieee!* Oh my *gosh*, I am *so* happy you're here! This is so crazy! I saw you at the concert but like, I didn't know you were gonna come to Sevens! Who invited you? Like dang, I didn't think we were *allowed* to invite you or I totally would've! Are you wearing boy clothes or are you going for like, an urban look? Either way, you are *rocking* it. So friggin' gutsy! And like, wanna know something super funny? That shirt looks *just* like this one Minmin's had since we were kids! C'mon, we gotta go show him! He will *lose* it! But I just gotta grab Ryo-chan a drink first! Want something to drink? What do you drink? I'll get one for you! Because like, welcome to our party!"

"Uhh…"

Namgi was *everywhere*, patting my head, grabbing my hands, hugging me, dancing me around—! He snatched me away from Jaeyoon before I could even catch my breath, but I did catch his eyes as I was danced away. He was asking if I wanted help. I shrugged.

"Ah." Namgi let go and looked down at his hands. "Wait, didn't I already get Ryo-chan a drink? Where'd it go? Crap! I just got so excited when I saw you up here! Are you having fun?"

"Um, I was actually about to head out…"

"*Already?!* But I just found you! I've been wanting to hang out with you so bad! Ryo-chan like, ruined our chance to hang out on Tick Tock Talk, so can't I get like, *one* dance before you go? C'mon, lemme buy you a drink! Just stay for a little itty bit longer!"

"Um…" There was no sense of reality in those blue puppy eyes. They had their own world with its own rules and I was stuck there now. "Maybe just for a little while longer…" Sorry, Ilsung.

"*Yes!* C'mon, pretty lady, let's go! I gotta get another drink for Ryo-chan! Oops, careful on the stairs, Kittie!"

Right. Ryo. *Crap.* Would he be mad that I was here? He was *definitely* gonna be mad about the Kitchi moment during the concert, but that really wasn't entirely my fault. He'd understand, right?

Namgi's blonde head took on every color of the club as we went down the stairs, but the hand on my elbow was what really drew attention. Much more attention than I wanted…

"So what's your drink of choice, Kittie?"

"Um, is there a menu?"

"*No?*" He burst into cackles. "Sooo cute! You're such a sheltered idol, Kittie!" I don't usually like being laughed at but somehow or another Namgi charmed me into laughing with him.

"Do they sell juice here, Sunbaenim?"

"*Hey!* I thought we talked about this! I'm your *oppa!* Don't make me start the chant again! I will get this whole club in on it!"

"Right. Sorry… Sorry, Oppa."

"*Yesss!* Now we're talking! Gosh, are you ever *cute!* Okay, now a drink! I wanna buy you a drink! C'mon!" He looked eager to plunge into the mob around the bar, but they all scattered when they saw who he was. Again, I felt intense scrutiny from my surroundings.

"Oppa, shouldn't we not be holding hands?"

"But if I let go, I might lose you!" He hurt my eyes when he laughed. He was so *sparkly*. I wished I could get a closer look at the galactic sapphires he was wearing as color contacts.

"But all the people are looking…?"

"Pshh, it's fine! What happens at Sevens stays at Sevens! Want me to ask the bartender to write down a menu for you? He'd totally do it if I asked! Him and I are tight!"

"No, no, it's fine! You can just pick something for me, okay?"

"Heck, I only know five drinks, Kittie! But it's fine, I've got a great idea!" Oh god. "Stay here!" He danced up to the bar and flailed his arms at the staff. I didn't like the gigantic sweeping gestures he was making. Was he ordering an entire vat of alcohol? The bartenders looked shocked and more than a little concerned…

When he waved me over, I was relieved to see there were only four drinks on the counter—a tumbler of amber on ice, something slushy full of fruit and flowers, a frothy beer, and a tall glass with a lot of leaves in it. But four was still four too many for me.

"Uhh…"

"They're gonna deliver yours upstairs! Can you help me carry these up to the boys?"

"Oh! Up to the Vortex suite?"

"Yeah!" He pointed at the beer and the leaf drink. "Those two are Minchi's. You're a Minchi fan, right? Tell 'em you won't hand over their drinks until they kiss!"

"Is *that* how to make them kiss?"

"Been trying for years! Hasn't worked quite yet, but if *you* do it…?"

I was staggered. Vortex didn't have a private party room; they had a private *floor*, and it was obnoxiously opulent. We're talking marble floors, glass chandeliers, and tasseled rugs. It was also completely empty. I was so in awe that I may have spilled a leaf on the weird spiral staircase, but soon I was following Namgi's chatter and Mino's whine down a hall.

"Aw man! Where's Ryo-chan? I brought him his favorite drink!"

"Babo, I swear to god, no more drinks. Ryo does *not* need any more and neither do we! See the button? We push the button when we want drinks. We have a *waiter*—"

"What?! Ryo-chan told me not to play with that button!"

"And he's right. We don't *play* with the button. Want drink, push button. Don't want drink, don't push button!"

Another short set of stairs led up into a curtained room. And they wobbled under my feet. Just *why?* Weren't normal stairs hard enough? Was this a funhouse or something?

"But I like ordering at the bar!"

"Yeah, and now Ryo is *hammered* because you keep plopping drinks in front of him! So knock it off!"

"But I *like* hammered Ryo-chan!"

I already didn't have the courage to push through the curtain. But then I heard two giggles that were way too feminine to be Vortex. Vortex alone with girls in their private suite. I didn't need to see that. I didn't need to *be* that. How did I get here? Namgi had apparently forgotten about me, so I was good to just leave, right?

"Sit still, Babo! You're shaking the room!"

"That's the whole *point* of this room though!"

More giggles as the stairs warped under my feet.

"You're gonna wake up Satch!"

"Nothing wakes him up!" Too late. The curtain whipped open and Namgi waved me in. "What's taking you so long? C'mon! Everybody's gonna be so excited to see you! Especially Leader, he's *such* a fan. Oh my gosh, and seriously, show Minmin your shirt!"

Losing the battle not to spill, I was hauled through the curtain into a giant glass birdcage suspended over the dance floor. That was plenty shocking enough, but I was not at all prepared for the state Minchi was in.

Delusion.

Mino had sequined women under either arm. Another straddled his lap playing with his hair, his precious unicorn hair. My gasp was only worth an eyebrow lift to her before she leaned in to kiss his jaw.

"Look, Minmin! I found a Kittie!"

"Oh hey!" Namgi sounded a million miles away, but Mino's voice came very clear. I never knew tunnel hearing was a thing. "I was starting to think you weren't coming! That guy thought the same, obviously." The nightmare tunnel blew itself apart to show me Saichi. He was sprawled out on the other side of the couch with graffiti all over his bare stomach. He slept with his mouth wide open and his shoes waiting neatly in a pair on the floor.

A giggle. A whisper. "What is she wearing?"

"Minmin, doesn't this look just like your old favorite shirt?"

"It *is* my shirt, you moron. I gave it to her."

I thought this was Saichi's shirt…?

"Whaaat? No fair! When did you two get to be such good buddies?! Why wasn't I in on it? Ugh, whatever, *bye* then, Minmin." He patted everyone on the head on his way out, murmuring ducks and geese. "Bye girls, bye Kittie! I'm gonna go find Ryo-chan and hammer him some more! Yeet!"

More giggles from the gaggle. "Someone tell him that doesn't mean what he thinks it means."

The snide one riding Mino flipped me the bird. "Someone tell this freak to put her *own* clothes on before she comes out on the town. What're you staring at, bitch? Go get dressed!"

"Shh, that's Kit Allister."

Okay.

Not okay.

Not my scene. I set down Minchi's drinks and turned to leave. There was a growl. Mino stood up and the woman slid off him.

"Out. Y'all are being rude."

"*Oppaaa*, she's the one being rude?!"

"You know the rules. No catfights in the birdcage."

"But *I* didn't say anything? Can I stay?"

"Nah. All of you, out. Idols only."

"That's not a rule! And rule number two is we *share*. Why does Kit get you to herself just because she's an idol? I could be an idol too! I'd make a way better idol than *her*. *Oppaaa—?!*"

"Shh! Rule three, don't bother Saichi-oppa…"

Finally, I found my voice. "This is *not* what I came for, but thank you anyway for inviting me, Mino-shi. Have a good night." That sounded strong. Good job, Kit.

"Hang on, wait!"

'Never meet your heroes,' said some snarky smart-ass in my head. Why was I even surprised? It wasn't like I actually knew him. I was just a fan and we'd only just met tonight. It could just as well have been Saichi with the glittery women and weird harem rules…

Three pairs of stilettos stomped the funhouse stairs behind me and I was bucked into the air and thrown down the stairs. My eyes burned but I swore it was just because my hands and knees hit solid marble and not because I was actually bothered by a bunch of jerks trying to humiliate me. I got up and was *totally* fine and ready to move on and be the bigger person.

But then I got a drink dumped on me and that was the final straw.

"That's for ruining our night, Bitch Allister!"

"Are you insane?! This isn't even my shirt!" I don't know what I thought I'd do if I caught them, but I chased them all the way to the spiral staircase, all three shrieking and laughing and skittering around in their stupid twinkly stilettos.

Mino grabbed my arm before I reached the stairs. "Hey, my bad. I swear they were super nice girls before *you* showed up. I dunno what that was all about—"

I didn't even know what to say to him. "No, my bad for crashing your little party. Also, if that's what you invited me here for, you've got the wrong idea. I don't look at Vortex like that, and I never wanted to *see* Vortex like that. I'm just a fan."

"Aw. So you're a soft stan, huh?"

"Uhh…"

"You don't wanna fuck us."

"Oh my god, *no!*" How could he laugh after saying something so embarrassing?! "I'm um, I just, I'll see myself out—"

He had my arm again. "Girl, nuh-uh. One, don't go home mad. Two, you can't go back down there looking like *that*." He pointed at the massive cherry blossom of alcohol flowering down my front and I realized that Pac-Man and I were winning a white t-shirt contest.

"*Kill me…*" slipped out. I could change back into my fan gear, but I'd still ruined someone else's shirt.

"Nah, that'd be a waste of a *dayum* good woman."

"Stop looking at me!"

"Bathroom first on the left down that hall."

I wasn't planning on going back up into the birdcage but as I stormed past the stairs, I heard Saichi wail, "Min, you *jerk!* She's gonna hate us now!" and I knew I couldn't leave quite yet. I also physically could not leave because a parade of tuxedos bearing tray after tray of drinks was marching up the spiral stairs, filing like ants up out of the floor. Lead Ant with four different glasses of wine turned a stiff smile on me that read 'You are a *monster…*'

"Miss Kit, where would you like your drinks?"

My jaw dropped. "What do you mean *my* drinks?"

Mino was at my side in seconds, drawn to the commotion of the infantry. "Holy shit...? Yo, waiter, what are all these drinks for? Nobody's even up here!"

Another ant spoke up, "Um, actually Namgi-nim—"

"Fuck me, is he running experiments again?"

"He ordered one of everything for the young lady."

"Jesus *fuck*... Put 'em in the birdcage, I guess?"

As they marched past, Mino pulled me into their ranks and let them sweep us up the stairs. I was getting a little tired of him towing me everywhere. It was only cute when he did it to Saichi.

On the other side of the curtain, Saichi was adorably bedheaded, bleary-eyed, and bewildered watching waiters thunk ice buckets on the floor and cover the table with every size, shape, and color of alcohol. But then he spotted me, and he woke right up.

"Kit! You stayed!" Already worth it.

He leapt up a little too quickly and rammed his knee into the table, slopping drinks left and right. Three waiters produced handkerchiefs but screw the spillage, that was my idol's *knee*. That was Oh Saichi's much-needed knee that made that terrible sound.

Examine. Ice. Elevate affected extremity.

I could see through the hole in his jeans that he wasn't bleeding, but it would probably bruise, so I eased him back down onto the couch and lifted his legs up beside him, wedging a pillow under his knee. Our eyes met as I turned back to him with a handkerchief of champagne bucket ice and only then did I realize what I was doing.

"Um." I pointed to his knee. "This is very important. Please be careful with yourself."

Mino snorted. "Kit, don't you think you're overreacting a tad? Didn't you like, fall down a flight of stairs a minute ago?"

"Kit fell down the stairs?"

"That was different. This is *Oh Saichi*. This knee is irreplaceable!" I eased the ice onto his knee. "Sunbaenim, we're going to leave this on for about twenty minutes, okay? I want you to rest—"

His fingers slipped over top of mine and I froze, caught between fire and ice. Heat startled its way up my arm even as goosebumps pricked my skin. His eyes were waiting to meet mine.

"Please don't call me that? It feels distant."

As the final waiter filed out, the empty quiet of the birdcage slowed its swing to a ponderous sway and I couldn't seem to find words in his eyes. "What did I…?"

"I understand being respectful is important in society, but I don't really like honorifics, and I'm not exactly good at them either so… could you maybe be a tiny bit less formal with me?"

"Oh. Then, Saichi… nim?"

Mino's burst of laughter reminded me that we weren't alone. "You're *so* weird. What is he, your god? Your customer? Patient?"

"Teacher! And respected sunbae! I learned everything I know from him! And, and yes, he's my patient right now! I was almost a nurse, you know." I blurted that out just as another paperweight to hold down my argument, but I regretted it immediately when Minchi exchanged a look of surprise.

A dirty smirk crossed Mino's face. "A nurse, huh? Hot."

"I thought you made coffee," Saichi murmured, intrigued. Could he maybe stop speaking in that soft tickly tone of voice?

"Um, that too." I snatched up the damp folds of Pac-Man again. "I'm really sorry I ruined your shirt. I'll have it dry-cleaned, but if it can't be salvaged, I swear to you, I will find its exact replacement—"

Both were successfully distracted and effervesced into happy laughs. "Oh, don't worry about that, Kit. Jaeyoon *loves* stains."

"Satch, if you give him that shirt, you know he'll throw it out."

"Yeah, but first, he'll get the stain out. Then we just have to fish it out of the trash again." They laughed again. This shirt was evidently some kind of running joke between Minchi and Jaeyoon. Amazing that they'd let me wear something so precious.

"Now that you mention it, yeah, that guy *absolutely* washes his garbage before throwing it away. So Kit, any idea why Babo bought you the entire bar? This is a lot even for him."

"Well, he wanted to buy me a drink, but I couldn't think of any drink names in Korean, and he didn't know many either, so… I guess he ordered me a little bit of everything?"

This time Minchi's laughs were contagious. It must've cost Namgi a fortune, and so many drinks would go down the drain, so why were we all laughing? The magic of Bae Namgi.

"Welp, I guess you're gonna learn *all* the drinks now. Get comfy and pick your poison, girlie. We've got work to do."

"Maybe some kind of juice or tea or…?"

"Mm, I'm gonna say the only tea here is probably a Long Island." Long Island… New York? What? "Ya really wanna start that strong?"

"Is there anything nonalcoholic?"

"Nah, nah, nah. None of that virgin bullshit!"

Why was *that* coming up?! "What's wrong with virginity?"

Mino had relocated his leaf drink and he promptly spat half a plant across the cage. "Not *that* kind of virgin, dummy!"

Saichi's fingers brushed my skin again and I stopped to listen. "Kit, do you not drink? Or maybe you're not comfortable drinking with us? You don't have to feel obligated to drink any of this if you don't want to. Namgi-ya did this on his own."

"But I don't want Sunb—, um, Oppa's money to go to waste."

Saichi shook his head. "He has plenty of money."

Mino caught up. "Hah? Hang on, Kit, you don't drink *ever?*"

"Um, not recreationally. I've had wine at church?" I can't usually tell when I sound like a bumpkin, but I caught it that time.

"Oooh, church… You a Christian? Ryo's Christian. Scary stuff."

"*Min,*" Saichi warned, but Mino was pressing a tiny glass into my hands. It was cute. There wasn't much in there. How bad could it be? Maybe this was exactly what I needed. After all, alcohol was liquid courage, right? And you could drown your sorrows in it? I had a *lot* of sorrows right now, and I definitely wasn't feeling brave enough to hang out with Minchi much longer. But heck, maybe if I downed enough of these, we'd come out of this on friendly terms, and bonus, I might forget the uncomfortable scene I'd walked in on earlier.

"Just down it. You'll feel better, I guarantee it."

One swallow and I choked until my eyes streamed. Courage apparently burned the whole way down. *That* was what people went to clubs and bars for? *That* was what people bonded over?

I had to croak to speak, "What was that, acid?!"

Mino giggled. "This isn't that kinda club." Saichi smacked his leg. "I think that was tequila? Dunno, but whatever it was, you needed it. Now how about a margarita? Or a cosmo?"

"But alcohol's gross…"

"Alcohol *is* gross. But I swear at least some of these are yummy. And they get yummier as the night goes on. Here, try this one." Actual clouds of glitter rolled inside the tall glass he passed to me. "This'll be sweet, and it's pretty, just like you."

"Min, *stop flirting with Kit.*"

Thank you, Saichi. "Is glitter even safe to drink?"

"I mean, even water is unsafe to drink sometimes—"

One sip of fruity sugar and I was convinced. It still had a thorny aftertaste but "Not completely terrible."

"Atta girl. Now we're gettin' recreational!"

Maize

Alcohol always used to scare me because I thought it would make me lose control or forget who I was, but drunk me was just a kid on a merry-go-round. Colors and lights streamed past too fast for my eyes to catch, laughter looping around my head, and all the worries of the world whirled away out of reach. Time lurched and lunged and sunk and spun but it never stopped being funny.

And then, halfway through the Long Island Iced Tea, Saichi curled an arm around my shoulders and I decided I wanted to keep that there as long as possible. Preferably forever.

I didn't feel out of place anymore. There was nowhere else in the world I wanted to be. To heck with going home. I had my own happy little bubble of body heat with an *Oh Saichi* in it.

Mino emptied Saichi's melty ice pack and then he crawled back to his place at our feet, cute as a pet, and put his chin on my knees. "So, now that you're nice and drunk, I've got some questions for ya. First off, you got a boyfriend?"

How devious. I laughed. Saichi choked. "Of course not! I'm KJ's!"

"So? So are we."

"Min! Don't even *think* about it!"

"Oh hush, sourpuss. Would you chill? I'm just curious!"

"You are not 'just curious' and you know it! Back off!" Saichi's arm tightened. I wished he'd hold me with both arms.

"Fuuuck, you are in *such* a bad mood tonight. Thanks to *me* your idol is here partying with us, you big dumb fanboy! You're welcome? Cheer the fuck up!"

I still fundamentally disagreed with that reality. My idol my fan. That was a load of nonsense. But either way, Saichi steamed right over into a cute red mess. "If you acknowledge that I'm a fan of her then why are you still flirting with her? Stop thinking of her like that!"

"Jeez*uz*, why can't you soft stans let hard stans have their fun?"

Goodness gracious, Kim Mino. I grabbed another shot of courage. Gotta keep this merry-go-round merry. He wasn't actually flirting with me, was he? Nah, he wasn't after me. Nahhh.

"Min, what does that even mean?"

I planned to cork Mino's mouth with a beer bottle if he started telling Saichi what that meant, but Mino was busy with the giggles. "You drink *fast* for a rookie."

"Should I be drinking slower?"

"Man, you really *don't* drink, do you?"

"Nope. I grew up dirt poor in a small town. One dive bar, no clubs. We all just wandered around cornfields for fun."

Whoa.

I said that out loud? After my little nurse slip-up earlier, I'd been so careful to watch my mouth, but now I was spouting secrets again? If I pretended like that admission wasn't a big deal, would they just go with it? No, Saichi had that same curious light to his eyes again. He knew too much about my public profile.

Fortunately, his voice didn't come off accusatory. Just interested. "I've never been in a cornfield before. I've been in rice paddies though? I used to chase medaka around them as a kid."

"What's a medaka?"

"Japanese rice fish. What's a cornfield like?"

"Well, corn gets really tall, so it's easy to get lost in it. In the fall, we mow it down in patterns and make huge mazes."

"What? Really? I wanna go in a cornfield maze!" He poked Mino with his foot. Mino pulled his sock off. "Hey Min? Do we have cornfields here in Korea?"

"Probably? I've never heard of us making mazes though." Mino was nursing a new glass and he spoke in burbles into the rim, "I don't think you have any idea how *huge* America is, Satch. They have a shit ton of space to do all kinds of stupid stuff with."

Saichi jerked. "N-no tickling." He yanked his feet up and turned his whole body to face me. His full attention was difficult to handle. Especially when he leaned a little closer and peered through his eyelashes at me. "Tell me more…"

"About corn?"

Mino snorted.

"About you. I didn't know you grew up in a small town. I always thought you were from New York. What else don't I know?"

"Uh…" If InstaKit is your only reference, a *lot*.

"Do you still want to be a nurse someday?"

"Um, no, actually I dropped out."

Another embarrassing secret. Alcohol was black magic and Saichi's eyes were amber magic and they were both luring my lies out into open air. But it was a little freeing? Since landing in Korea, the goal of my team was to fake it until I made it, and lately, the line between me and InstaKit blurred a little more every day. But even as my life changed around me, I didn't feel like I was changing with it. I was still the same lame church-girl bumpkin from Ohio, just carrying a lot more secrets now.

"You gave it up to come here?" Mino asked.

"Um, not exactly. Things just… didn't work out. It's a long story."

Mino read that I was uncomfortable and decided not to allow it. "Sometimes life's like that. Satch's childhood dream was to open his own pastry shop. Obviously that didn't work out."

"That's *adorable*."

"I know, right? Can't you just see him all covered in flour with that dumbass hat on?" I could.

Saichi pouted. "I still might do it someday."

"Anyway, if you ask me, you don't gotta be all cagey about

whatever got fucked up in the past because look where you are now! That stuff *had* to go wrong or you wouldn't be here with us."

"Maybe, but I'm still embarrassed that I dropped out."

Saichi shook his head. "Don't be. I dropped out of high school, so you made it a lot further than me. Sometimes you just have to stop and recognize when something's not right for you. I knew I wasn't book smart and I couldn't fit in, so I left to find something else to do."

Mino scoffed. "You're only bad at books because you're bad at Korean. And you doodle too much when people are talking."

That made Saichi laugh. "Ahh yeah, I ruined a lot of textbooks…"

"Kit, you can't ever leave this guy alone with a pen, a pencil, a marker, *anything*. Look what happens when he runs out of paper." Mino pushed Saichi down and yanked his shirt up, baring the graffiti I'd glimpsed earlier. Even drunk, I didn't have the guts to look closer. I covered my eyes.

"I thought *you* did that to him."

"Nah, he ran out of pages in his sketchbook and then ran out of napkins and I told him to stop vandalizing the menu so—"

"Min, please stop showing Kit my stomach."

"Shouldn't you open an art gallery or something? I don't know anything about art, but even just the stuff you drew in your dressing room… I feel like the world should see it."

"See, Satch? Told you! And Jae said the same."

Saichi sat up and Mino rolled off. The amber in his eyes looked a little harder, a little darker, and his voice lost its tone when he told us, "No, the world sees enough of me. They don't need my art too."

Maybe he had a point. I was nowhere near as famous as he was, but even at this stage, I felt like I no longer had any ownership of myself. He deserved *something* he could keep to himself, and shame on me for prying.

"Then I feel all the more lucky to have seen it. I think you're very talented, Saichi-sun… nim? Shi?" Mino laughed but I ignored him. "And Mino-shi is right. I'm glad you dropped out because you don't need books. You're a *genius* at singing, dancing, choreo—"

"I'm not a genius. I have to practice a lot."

Mino laughed again. "Liar."

His eyes were much softer again when he reached out and patted my hand. "And I'm glad *you* dropped out because even though I'm sure you would've made a wonderful nurse, my life would be much worse without your music in it."

"Oh."

Wow.

"Heavy, Satch. That was a tad heavy."

"Sorry."

"No, no, it wasn't heavy. I feel light—"

"Time for another beer down the Satch hatch."

Right then, Jaeyoon poked his head through the curtain and surveyed the situation—shoes and deflated jackets strewn in all directions, my purse spitting coins and cosmetics across the rug, and a table honeycombed with half-empty glasses.

Oh, and there were two men hanging off of me.

He was not pleased.

Unreal

"This." Jaeyoon stirred the air with a ringed finger. "I do not approve of… this." Mino's head popped up off my lap and Saichi put on a sloppy smile.

"Hmm? This what, Jaeyoon?"

"Hyung, get off of her please. I'm calling Kit-shi a ride home."

I actually saw Mino's feathers ruffle. "*Haaah?* What for?"

"For her safety."

Mino barely found his feet. For some reason, he pushed up his sleeves before setting off on a clumsy warpath across the room. Didn't only old cartoons do that? When it came down to it, he was so much shorter than Jaeyoon that he just looked like a kid throwing a tantrum. "Her safety, hah? You think I'm dangerous, Jae?"

"Not remotely. But you don't know how to conduct yourself around women and you're clearly exercising a bad influence on our leader right now as well. I'm calling a taxi. Let go of my arm."

"*No.*"

"Do not poke me."

"Do not call taxis for no reason."

"I just went through my reasons. You're testing my patience."

"Well, I'm annoyed with you!"

"The feeling is mutual. You're wrinkling my shirt. Let go."

"Shirt. *Shirt*. That shirt. Look."

It was the most transparent misdirection ever, again almost cartoon-like, but it actually worked. All the derision gone from his face, Jaeyoon looked at Pac-Man like a lost lover. "Is it… *stained?*"

"It sure is. Daquiri red! I bet you can't get *that* out, Jae."

"How dare you? I can and will, and when I do, I'm trashing that shirt once and for all—"

"Kit!" Saichi whispered. "Let's run!"

I grinned. "Okay!"

He grabbed my hand and pulled me up. All the alcohol pooling in my head spun and flushed to my feet. I would've hit the deck if it weren't for Saichi's hand. Jaeyoon cursed as we jetted past but Mino chucked Pac-Man in his face and crowed with victory.

"Go, go, go! I'll hold him off! Go on without meee!" The birdcage earthquaked and the stairs cracked like a whip beneath our feet, but Saichi had great sea legs and as soon as our bare feet hit the icy marble, we were as good as gone.

"Kit, this way!"

Chased by shouts of disbelief, we tumbled down a long carpeted hall, door after identical door scrolling past like an old film strip. Saichi selected one at random and we hurled ourselves into an actual black hole. When the door thumped shut, there was an absence of *everything*. Padded walls ate my laugh the second it left my mouth.

"What is this? An isolation cell in a club…?"

"I think this is one of the karaoke rooms." Saichi puffed for air. He kept choking on giggles. The sound of him was a constant relief.

"Where the heck is the light switch?"

I followed the wall and ran into a couch. A little farther and I hit a corner, then another, and then I bounced off of Saichi. I felt the world start to tip but his hands clamped around my shoulders.

"Are you a switch?" he asked and I thought I saw a grin.

"I dunno, maybe?"

"How do I turn you on?"

"*Saichi!*"

He gasped. "I didn't mean—!" We both broke down laughing. The dark was warmer this close to him, and maybe a little too intimate. Just to be safe, I took a step back, but my legs hit solid couch.

"Wha—!"

I grabbed for anything and found his shirt.

"Mmf."

"Oww…"

"Sorry, Kit! Did I land on you?"

"No, it's just my head hit something hard."

A wisp of hot breath flitted past my ear as he pushed himself up and slid something from under my head. It lit up electric blue, searing my eyes with the sudden glow of his face. An iPad? In the pressing dark, he felt all the more ridiculously close, and his body was warmer by the second. I still couldn't get up. Especially not with his knee between my legs.

"Huh." Saichi peered at the screen and then smiled. Behind him, a television blazed to life and a familiar intro filled the room.

'just hold me by Kit Allister,' the screen read. Oh, absolutely *not*.

"No, no, no, turn it off, turn it off!" I wriggled for the iPad, but he laughed and frisbeed it across the couch.

"Why? I love this song. You wrote this one yourself, right?"

"Yes, b-but it's embarrassing!"

"*Why?*" Warm fingers wrapped around my wrists and pulled me to my feet, lifted me up into his orbit, a pull far firmer than gravity. Like I'd never known motion of my own, my body melted into the liquid momentum of him. Because he was *dancing*, guiding me through my own vocals with his hips. I was dancing with Oh Saichi. I'd always wanted—

"Sing it to me? Please?"

"Heck no!"

"Then I will."

His gaze held a velvet flux of azure and violet and his voice smelled like a citrus cocktail as he sang, "*It was too soon so I turned away…*" The lyrics filled his chest, tingling under my fingers. I almost pressed my ear to him, but I couldn't pull away from his eyes.

He knew my debut song.

The song *I wrote…* from a place of fear and failure and grief where I was sure my career was over before it could begin.

Fifteen different songwriters wrote two dozen songs for my debut. Each and every one was miles above my range with lyrics full of quick, complicated twists and turns. At the time, I was too embarrassed to ask anyone to transpose the songs down a few keys, and I didn't want them to compromise their beautiful lyrics just because my Korean was subpar. So needless to say, I mangled every song they threw at me and lost all faith in my way forward. Talentless hack. Karaoke copycat. Vortex cover act. That was all I ever was.

Desperate, I wrote a song for myself, to tell my story. It was husky, vulnerable, and raw. When Ilsung heard it, he took it and ran with it, bless his soul. He put his job on the line and stood up for me in front of an award-winning producer. A few weeks later, 'just hold me' topped the charts.

"Now it's too late to ask you to stay…"

And now I was here with Oh Saichi and he was holding me, dancing with me, singing my own song to me.

"Already over and it never began. I never got my chance—"

Singing with him was a dream I never dared delude myself with. And yet, we had strayed so far from reality that maybe I could.

Our voices braided octaves between us, *"To say just hold me…"* His eyes asked me hesitant questions I couldn't think to answer, and then my lips felt the scorch of his breath.

Wait.

Was he…?

This couldn't be happening.

My mouth had never touched anyone else's before. I didn't know it would be such a momentous thing. I didn't know someone else's lips could make every other thing in the world seem unimportant. Life had been muted underwater until I broke above the surface into sound and color and sun. Like a sun kiss, his lips were nothing but warmth at first, too soft to really feel. But then he pulled sweetly at my bottom lip and a wet flicker made my breath catch.

"Saichi…"

His name threw sparks through the dark that caught in his eyes. We ignited to motion. Our bodies hit the wall like gravity had changed axis, but the acoustic foam caught us like a bed and my mind ran rampant. The sudden heat, the texture of open mouths, the buzz of a low groan… it was too much. My blood sparkled beneath his fingers as they slid from my hair, down my neck, onto my chest.

And then he froze. Too soon, the moment was broken.

"I'm sorry. I got carried away," he breathed.

He stumbled back through the outro of my song and I was in shock, out of breath, frostbitten and scalded all over.

No.

Come back.

My voice had gone to hide somewhere deep in my chest so I reached for him, ready to grab his clothes and yank him back to me. I wanted more. I caught the hem of his shirt, bared a daisy drawn low between his hips. There was this choking urge to push him down like Mino had, to pull his shirt up and trace my fingers along every curling line. His eyes still held a shimmering tinder. If I called his name again—

"Hyung?" A knock from behind me. "Are you in there?"

"Yeah?" he answered right away, and then slapped a hand over his mouth. "Oops."

"Open the door. I'm taking Kit-shi home."

Home? No. Not yet. We weren't done yet. There was so much more I wanted. I wanted to stay. I wanted more Saichi. More time. More touch. Another kiss. When he looked to me, I shook my head violently.

"She's not in here." His shirt slipped from my fingers. The door sealed behind him as he left. "Sorry, I needed a little nap." His voice was muffled now. I didn't like it.

"*Hyung.*" Jaeyoon groaned affectionately, their presence fading. "You always nap at the worst times. How did you lose Kit-shi?"

He left so quickly. In the new silence, I wasn't sure if he'd ever been here with me at all. Did he leave to fool Jaeyoon or did he leave because I did something wrong? It all ended so fast. Why did he stop? Then again, why did he start? Why did he show me everything I never knew I was missing? Why'd he give me what I knew I couldn't have? Dammit. I needed more drinks. I had new sorrows to drown.

"There you are. Hey, *you*. I thought I sent you the fuck home."

I pretended not to see or hear him and tried to retreat back into the karaoke room, but he slammed his fist against the door.

"Oh! Ryo! Hi!"

"Shi."

"Huh?"

"If you're not gonna call me sunbaenim like you damn well should then you could at least call me Ryo-*shi*. I worked my ass off to get fluent. You could certainly try a little harder."

He was exactly as angry as I'd thought he might be. And he was right. I'd been tripping over 'sunbaenim' all night. It was pathetic.

"Sorry! I was surprised—"

"Surprised, my ass. The little fuck-ups aren't cute anymore, Kit. You fucked up *big* tonight. We had a *deal*. No more fucking Kitchi."

I really wished I was sober for this conversation.

"I know, I'm sorry—"

"You think 'sorry' fixes things?! I welcome you into our dome and you implicate Mino, you implicate Hyung, and now you have the gall to show your face at our afterparty? And still wearing your stupid fake fan getup no less. You're so fucking shameless it makes me physically sick."

Again, he was right, but what the hell did he mean by "Fake fan?"

"You're no fan. You're a parasite." He grabbed my wrist. He was suddenly very close. Every nerve in me electrified. Some primal impulse flared through the bottom of my stomach.

Danger.

Fight? Flight?

I scoffed at the thought, but my body ignored me and went feverish with adrenaline. And then my back slammed against the wall, not padded this time. My instincts were right. He wrenched both wrists over my head. Predator attacking. Fight? Flight? I turned my face away, but he wasn't interested in my lips.

He was *biting* me.

"Ryo…?"

"*Shi*, dammit," he hissed and I inhaled a cloud of cinnamon. "Have some fucking respect!"

"Why are you…?"

He spoke a rocky mutter against my neck, "What? Aren't you happy? Isn't this what you came up here for? To fuck a member?"

"*What?*"

Movement caught my eye at the mouth of the hall. I turned my head just in time to be blinded by the flash of a camera. I was too shocked to even cover my face.

Unwelcome

So my career was over.

I couldn't recover from a scandal this huge. Everything I'd done to keep my name clean—a whole year chasing perfection uphill, upstream, against the wind, through hell and high water—all gone down the drain. The incidents with Tick Tock Talk and DigitAlive weren't my fault, but this... this was preventable. I was the one who made one bad decision after another tonight. Coming to a club, getting drunk, making out with Saichi... and predictably, it all blew up in my face. My fans would be shocked. Ilsung would be heartbroken. Kyungsoon would be disappointed and she'd throw me out of the agency and I'd have to fly back to America in shame.

And then what?

There was nothing for me there.

My life was over in the flash of a camera.

"Ugh, not only do reek of alcohol, you actually taste like it too. How drunk *are* you?" My knees gave out when Ryo finally let me go. "Oh come on, get off the filthy floor. Where the fuck are your shoes?"

I couldn't speak. I touched my throat because it burned, and I was alarmed to feel Kasugai Ryo's cinnamon spit still sizzling on my skin. Why would he do that to me?

The paparazzi still stood there with his phone, waiting, as if we might continue. I started to crawl toward him. I could probably take him. I'd get that phone and smash it. 'KJ's Miss Perfect destroys civilian's personal property' was a much more forgiving headline than 'KIT ALLISTER'S FORBIDDEN RENDEZVOUS WITH VORTEX'S KASUGAI RYO.'

Ryo stepped around me and held out his hand to the guy. "Thanks, Daewon. You can head on back down to the party now. Your drinks are on my tab for the rest of the year."

Wait.

What the hell?!

To my disbelief, the man handed his phone right over and waved. "No problem, Hyung. See you around."

"W-wait, *what?!* Why would he give it to you? You know him?!"

The entire hallway went red around Ryo's smile. He swiped through a few before holding a picture out for me to see. It was very clearly me with a man kissing my neck. I grabbed for it but drunk me was so damn slow. He tucked it safely into his pocket and started strolling away, waving. "Scandalous stuff, huh? Gotcha good, Kit."

"Where are you going?! Delete that!"

"Hell no."

"Why not?!"

"I'm done playing nice. You're *finished*."

"Ryo-shi, you just… staged a scandal?"

"Yup. You fucked with Vortex for the last time tonight."

I couldn't believe my ears. "Aren't you taking this a little far? What happened at the concert wasn't that bad! And I'm the one who will take crap for it anyway? Saichi-shi and Mino-shi aren't going to suffer any negative press!" And I didn't ask them to come over to the VIP section and make a scene!

"It wasn't that bad?! It's gonna headline every goddamn tabloid in the country tomorrow! Or at least, it *would* have." He patted his pocket with another smile. "*This* will make a far better story."

"Aren't you worried people will recognize you?"

"No? My face isn't in the picture."

I spat a laugh. "I'd recognize you anywhere. From any angle, from any distance, in any lighting, in any outfit. Every fan would."

He rolled his eyes. "Fine, I'll have it edited then."

"People have tried to edit me into scandals before. It didn't work. They got called out on it."

"Are you seriously trying to drive a bargain with me right now? You think you've got *anything* on me? I could be fucking naked in this picture and you'd still be the one the tabloids shit on, just like you said. It's *you* that has everything to lose, and you know it. Once the president sees this, you'll be out on your ass before you can even book a ticket home."

"Yeah, I get it," I snapped. "You're unbelievable."

He shrugged. "Your career is over. See you never."

Whether I had everything to lose or nothing to lose was just a matter of time. Both were places of desperation. And if he was going to act like an animal, so was I.

I lunged, trying to tackle him maybe? But I might as well have thrown myself at a brick wall. Still, I gained one moment of surprise so I rammed my fingers into his jeans and yanked, I guess trying to rip his pocket open, but I don't honestly know why I thought that would go well. I was drunk and again, I had everything to lose.

"You think you can just attack me?!"

"Why not? You attacked me!"

He had the audacity to laugh at me. "I'm twice your size!"

"So that gives you the right to bite me?"

"No, that's what happens when you stick your nose where it doesn't belong. You're in *my* territory fucking with *my* group."

"I'm sorry for existing? You don't have to ruin my life just because you think I'm trying to step on your toes! I'm just a fan, okay? Believe it or not, I *like* you and I like Vortex, and all I want—" He grabbed my chin and jerked my face up, sawing off the words. I think I bit my tongue, but I was too angry to feel it.

"Just fuck off in general," he growled. "Quit leeching off us and get your own damn career. Better yet, go back to your own fucking country and leave us the hell alone!"

And then he was gone.

The anger ballooned out and left me dizzy and boneless on the floor with that hot crawling need to vomit. Even long after he and his pocket of disaster disappeared, my heart remained hellbent on demolishing my ribs.

Go back to my country? Korea wasn't technically his country either! Why did I have to take xenophobia from a fellow expat? Besides, I couldn't go back. America didn't want me. Hell, I didn't want me right now either. This was what I got for coming to a club, for crossing over the fangirl line and trying to be friends with my idols. I knew better than this.

I had to get out of here. I had to get home. I was going to be sick. I tried to crawl, but nope, I wasn't gonna make it home. I needed a bathroom *now*. My stomach was turning inside out.

The birdcage was deserted and still a total mess, but I did manage to find my purse… *after* I'd emptied my stomach into an ice bucket and cried in self-loathing for a few minutes.

I couldn't call Ilsung. Not only had I lied to him, I'd ruined both of our careers in one night. I was also too embarrassed to call Hyejin even though she'd specifically offered me a safe ride home.

Then I found the CD.

The cover art was a masterpiece. Vortex was picture-perfect gorgeous and I had nothing but love for every one of them, but little two-dimensional Ryo put on a disdainful smirk when I looked closer.

'*Open me!*' was scrawled across Jaeyoon's leg and Saichi's lip gloss was still smudged over the title. I pressed it to my cheek and felt it stick. I wished he'd somehow magically appear.

Inside, I found five priceless autographs scribbled on the inner jacket along with the message, '*Thanks for coming, Kit!*' And there was a phone number. Oh, sweet Jesus. The lip gloss was magic after all. '*Call me!*' I could see Mino jiggling a pinkie and a thumb at me onstage. Mino, come help me.

I messed up the number twice and then it rang.

Please, pick up.

Suite dreams.

I must've done something right on laundry day. If I kept my eyes closed, I was lying in a lavender field. Or maybe in a pool of lavender oil. This was too soft to be ground with gravity. It was also too soft to be anything I could afford…

Opening my eyes was a mistake.

As soon as I let the sun knife its way in, a million things started registering as *wrong* in my body. I slapped myself in the face trying to block out the light but that helped nothing. My skull was gnawing on my brain and my tongue felt like a furry animal and both were shaken into a death rattle with a good whack on the nose.

Water. I needed water. My tongue was stuck now.

This wasn't my bed. I couldn't afford this many pillows, nor these silk, satin, whatever-the-heck sheets. I also definitely couldn't afford the view out that window. But why would I sleep in a bed that wasn't mine? Was this a dream? No, I felt far too sick to be dreaming.

DigitAlive. That was why I was so dehydrated. All the screaming. Should've listened to Ilsung. He told me to be more careful this time. Hopefully I didn't have any recordings coming up. No, no, there was more. Minchi under the stage. The guards. Mino. Saichi's art in the dressing room. Hyejin driving me to the club. I went to a *club*.

Ooh, and at some point during that long neon nightmare, I got very, very drunk. That was why I couldn't sit up. I wasn't sick. I was hungover. A first for me. My head felt like a bowling ball. So did my arms. So did my body in general. I was made of bowling balls.

If I slept more, would I wake up feeling better? *Could* I sleep, considering I had no idea where I was? Yeah. Except that there was a cat noise behind me and that demanded my attention.

I rolled my thousand-pound body over and then I was face to face with *Oh Saichi*. Silvery bangs askew, dark lashes in sweet, peaceful curves, bottom lip out for the taking. The leader of the K-Pop world had his angel head on the same pillow as me. Nope. Even if I got completely plastered last night, there was *no way...*

I shut my eyes.

He was still there when I opened them.

Oh Saichi mewed again and a stubby hand skimmed up his chest. His bare, naked chest, oh god, oh god. Wait. *Whose hand was that?!*

Kim Mino.

Was the big spoon.

I screamed my way out of bed and landed with an excruciating crash. My stomach burst like a water balloon. I barely shut my mouth in time to keep the burn down.

"What the fuck?" Mino peered over the edge of the bed, and I screamed again because it really was him. "Excuse me, can you not?! What am I, a fucking monster?! Shut up!"

He was *also* shirtless. I had to get out of here *now*. Fighting a blanket tangle every four-legged step of the way, I scrambled for the door, but Mino wasn't having it. He stepped on my blanket tail and I faceplanted.

"What's your deal?"

I moaned into the carpet. "My life is over..."

"Oh stop. Get up, drama queen." He hauled my body up and squeezed a set of tears loose. To my horror, they splotched black onto the white blanket.

"Min! You made her cry!"

"Hey, hey, hey. You're fine! What're you crying for?"

"I'm in a hotel with Vortex! I'm gonna get fired! My life is *over!*"

Mino giggled and petted my hair. "Pshh nah, you're not gonna get fired over a little thing like this. Nobody even knows you're here! Chill, will ya? This hotel is just as hush-hush as Sevens."

Saichi was up there on the bed in nothing but boxers and I was supposed to be chill?! My lipstick was all over his neck and my name was autographed across his chest *and I was supposed to be chill?!*

"Sunbaenim, I did that to you?!"

"Did what?"

"This can't be right! What happened last night?! Did I really sleep with both of you? I can't have! I *can't* have! That's *impossible!*"

I could've slapped Mino when he burst out laughing.

"First threesome, huh?"

"Oh *god!*"

"Shut your dirty mouth, Min! That's not what happened!"

"Kit, I'm just kidding, ya moron. We didn't fuck. Now shush! Somebody's gonna call the cops on us." I crammed my fingers in my mouth to slow the hyperventilation but nothing could help me stomach the sobs or the hiccups.

"If we didn't… do anything, then why is everybody naked?"

"You call this naked? You're more churchy than I thought."

"I'm in a robe! Where are my clothes?!"

"You puked on your clothes, remember? What, did you black out? I guess that's no surprise. We got fucked *up* last night. I think *I* even feel a little bit of a hangover today. You, Satch?"

I didn't hear Saichi's response. I threw up in front of Minchi? I got blackout drunk in front of Minchi? And came to a hotel and slept in a robe in a bed with two men who also happened to be Minchi?!

"You swear to god we really didn't…?"

Saichi's eyes flashed with tears and I wasn't sure if that made me more or less inclined to believe him, but it was a terrible thing to see. "No, of course not, Kit, I would never—" Maybe I believed *Saichi*, but I seemed to recall something about Mino and a gang of sequined women last night…

"Nuh-uh, no way, Kit. You were out like a light by the time we got you up here. I only fuck chicks that can call my name."

I gagged.

"Min, can you please watch your mouth? That's *graphic*."

Mino however was more occupied with my gagging. "You're not gonna puke again, are you? Do me a favor and don't."

"So n-nothing happened? For sure?"

"Nah, all we did was babysit. Made sure you didn't choke in your sleep or something. Just like, let this be a lesson, yeah? Alcohol's fun. I get that. But you gotta know your limits, baby girl."

He ruffled my hair with disquieting affection, like I was a kid who'd made a forgivable mistake. Saichi slapped his hand off me. "Don't lecture her. You're the one that was pushing drinks on her."

"S-sorry to overreact. It's just… for all I know, I might already be fired. I can't get fired. I knew I shouldn't have gone to a club, I knew I was crossing lines and—" Again, Mino's laughing interrupted me.

"Here I thought you were worried about your virtue! But nope, work-obsessed as ever. You were blubbering about your career last night too. Like, who gets drunk and wants to talk about work? You're even worse than Jae."

Every hiccup made the vise around my head tighter. "Where's my phone? I gotta make sure Ilsung-shi hasn't called."

"And who the fuck's this Ilsung? He the one that brutalized the fuck out of your neck last night?"

"What? He's my manager! What about my neck?"

"The manager again. Ughh." He tossed me his phone, already ringing. "Talk to Jae. He probably has your phone and stuff. But just so you know, he's a total monster before noon."

"Wha—? Why do *I* have to call him then?"

"Because he'll bite my head off."

Sure enough, a feral growl ripped through the speaker. Breathe. Don't cry. Greet the man. "Good morning, Jaeyoon-shi."

"Like hell it is, Mino."

I didn't sound like Mino, did I? "This is Kit Allister." There was a long pause and a lot of rustling. "I was wondering if you happened to know the whereabouts of my purse, because—"

"Excuse me? Why are you calling from Mino's phone?!"

"Um, because mine is in my purse?"

"How did he manage to…?! Never mind. I'm coming. Just give me a minute. Where are you?"

"I don't actually know."

He bit off a curse. "May I please speak with Mino?" He sounded much more awake now, and somehow even scarier. I tried to mouth a warning to Mino but he was already giggling.

"What's cooking, crabass?" He strolled happily out of the room with the phone a good two feet from his head. Jaeyoon's response was so loud he could've been on speakerphone.

The second we were alone, Saichi was on the floor in front of me with a glass of water. Lifegiving water. In just a few minutes, I'd cried out every last drop of liquid in me and seared my throat with acid. Water never tasted so divine. But could I maybe not dwell on the way our fingers touched on the glass? Could I maybe not choke over the way he tugged my robe tighter around me when it slipped?

"Kit, I'm so sorry. Things got out of hand last night. As our guest, we should've taken better care of you and… I never meant for, for… the… um, I didn't mean to…"

He was wiggling with words, turning red with them, trying to force them out. I almost reached for him because he looked so distraught, but then my eyes found the lipstick on his collarbone and I shuddered to imagine my mouth on him. Nope, I was absolutely not allowed to touch him anymore. Words worked just fine for me.

"You're not responsible for my bad decisions, Sunbaenim."

It exploded out of him. "I'm the one making all the bad decisions, not you! Kit, I'm really sorry. I shouldn't have kissed you when we were drunk, and I wish I'd thought about how scared you might be to wake up with us—"

"*Kissed…?*"

We kissed? What kind of sick trick of fate was this? Oh Saichi kissed me and I couldn't remember it?! My lips tingled under my fingers, but the touch brought back only the silhouette of a memory, void of any real detail. We *did* kiss… with my song as a soundtrack?

"Kit?"

How could my brain rob me of clarity in that memory? A once in a lifetime kiss with my idol and I had to scrounge around my woolly head for details? Give me *something*, brain. That was probably the peak of my existence!

"Kit, really, I'm so sorry. Please, please don't come away from this hating me. I promise I'm not usually like this. I don't know what got into me last night. I just… I'm sorry. It was a mistake."

A mistake? No. A *miracle*.

"I didn't mind," I mumbled.

"Oh."

I peeked through my fingers and he was suddenly much closer. My heart lurched again but he wasn't looking at my lips. He was inspecting my throat like he'd found a bug on it.

"But that mark on your neck, I didn't do *that*, did I? I would never—! Ahh, or would I?! I don't even know anymore!"

"What's on my neck?" If there was something gross on my skin, I didn't want him to see it. As if I had any shred of pride left after throwing up in front of him. Still, I rushed for the bathroom.

My reflection was a horror show. Ratty hair, blurry lipstick, mascara tracks down my cheeks… and there was an unfamiliar oval of red on the side of my neck. I wetted my fingers and tried to rub it off but that made it worse. A bruise. A red bruise.

"So who bit you?" Mino startled me. I found his eyes piercing the mirror, accusatory onyx.

"Huh? Why would someone bite me?"

"I dunno. To get a taste? I'd bite you…"

"Ew? This isn't a bite!"

Smugness soaked his voice. "Um, yeah it is. Biting is kinda my thing, baby girl. I know a hickey when I see one."

A *hickey?!* No. "It's just a weird bruise," I insisted, but my voice came out empty of conviction.

"Oh yeah? Wanna see a mark just like that one? Go check the back of Satch's neck. You can compare samples."

"*What?* Did I—?"

"Nah. It's *my* thing."

"Then was it you that bit me?"

"You really don't remember?" He yanked my body back against his and spoke against my neck, "Someone coming this close to you?" I shuddered. My head throbbed. I was *never* drinking again. The more I tried to remember, the more the night kaleidoscoped into chaos, every piece sharp-edged and unmatching. My knuckles grinding into the wall. Hair tickling my jaw. Teeth scraping. And cinnamon.

Cinnamon... gum? *Ryo?!*

No. What? Shut up, brain. Not a chance in hell. Right? Well, but could I maybe just ask Mino if Ryo was also the biting type? No. Nope. Not worth it over a faulty memory.

There was silence while Mino dug around in my eyes, and then, "Fine," he decided. "You can have one secret. *One*. But no more from now on, mkay? Now out. I wanna shower and Satch took the other bathroom. Order some room service or something, would ya?"

"Wait, but—"

"What? You wanna join me?" His lips crooked into that feline grin that now triggered odd déjà vu. "Don't tempt me, baby girl."

"No! I just want to wash my face!"

"The panda look is cute. Keep it." He shoved me out and slammed the door. Dammit, how could I face Saichi again knowing that this was what I looked like? And Jaeyoon was coming! I already felt judged and he wasn't even here yet.

I was at the vanity trying to make do with hot water and tissues when a series of sporadic knocks came at the door. It sounded like he was trying to be polite at first, but then got stressed out. I was reluctant to answer it but he was my best ticket out at this point.

He immediately took my face in his hands and studied every smear of makeup, every etch of anxiety like it was a map to an explanation. "Are you alright? What happened?"

"Nothing."

Saichi peeked into the room and cooed, "G'morning, Jaeyoon." Wrapped in a fluffy towel and a fluffy robe, he looked more stuffed animal than human, and he was all pink and flowery from his shower. Jaeyoon, on the other hand, drained of all color.

"Hyung, you too? You *both...?!*"

"We both what?" Saichi was still smiling.

"No, no, no. Jaeyoon-shi, that's not what happened."

But Jaeyoon's map led him to the mark on my neck and he roared, "*Kim Mino!* You absolute moral contaminant, get out here *now!*"

Mino's giggles preceded him. "Listen, Jae baby, I know what this looks like but—"

Jaeyoon's hands moved up to cover my ears but that did little to staunch his volume. "Do you have to screw everything that moves?! What part of 'off-limits' do you not understand? And to involve Hyung as well! Hyung, god almighty, are *you* okay?"

Mino shouted with laughter. "Will you shut up, man? We didn't double-team her, ya fucking idiot!"

I touched Jaeyoon's hand. "I was too sick to go home! That's all!"

So much air exploded out of Jaeyoon that he looked deflated afterward. He took a few moments to breathe, then he smoothed my hair and nodded. "So the situation is bad, but it's not a complete catastrophe. Still, Mino, how dare you leave a mark on an idol."

"Wasn't me."

"Says the rabid dog."

"It's toothpaste!"

"Just keep your jaws away from her from now on, you little mongrel. And if that's really the story, if she needed care last night, then you should've contacted me for help instead of dragging her up here into your favorite love nest." Jaeyoon turned and my stomach did too because the door to the hall was still wide open. If even Jaeyoon was throwing caution to the wind, the 'hush-hush' factor of this hotel had to be outstanding.

Then I spotted the heaps of bags and boxes stacked outside in Christmas proportions. "Mino enlightened me to your situation on the phone, Kit-shi. I brought you something to wear."

Mino pushed past me to gather some of the boxes in his arms, still laughing. "Um no? You clearly brought her a whole new wardrobe.

What, is she moving in to SK Suites?"

"Close your mouth, Mino. You know I don't do mornings. I was in a *rush*, I was *upset*, I couldn't think what her size was—"

"But Jaeyoon-shi, my purse? My phone? And would you happen to know if there's anything in the tabloids today about… this?"

Mino snorted. "And Little Miss Goody-Two-Shoes strikes again." To my satisfaction, Saichi stabbed a finger in his side and he went down with boxes hurricaning from his arms.

"Stop making a mess!" Jaeyoon scolded.

"Haha, who's shoes now?" Mino tried to scowl at Saichi from his shoebox burrow but he couldn't maintain it for long. "And look, Min, she's not goody-two-shoes. She's much goodier than that. She's goody-*eight*-shoes."

"Oh my god, stop. You're not funny."

"This is no time for messing around, you two. Kit-shi, pick something and change please. I'm taking you home."

Mino stuck out his tongue. "*Lame ass.*"

Jaeyoon's car smelled stiflingly brand new, and as we drove, it also gradually stunk up with his disappointment. Hoping to help me with my hangover, he'd commissioned a smoothie from the hotel chef before we left, but I was having a hard time drinking it, especially in his fancy, dustless, spotless car. Even if stains supposedly excited him, I wasn't about to risk it.

While I may have muted Jaeyoon with my mistakes, Mino was not so silent. I didn't know how he got my number, but he apparently felt it was perfectly acceptable to text me now.

—he's so fucking dramatic smh
>*—he's right to be mad*
>*—we could really get in trouble over this*
—tell him I only have threesomes with two girls
—ooobviously
>*—ugh I absolutely will not tell him that*
—well see you around bb girl it's been real xo

I also found a perfunctory text from Ilsung that had arrived earlier that morning—just the usual well-wishing, a reminder of my schedule, and reassurance that the DigitAlive Twitter blow-up was being handled. Nothing about Sevens. Nothing about SK Suites.

I flinched when Jaeyoon finally spoke up, "Kit-shi, I apologize for not keeping closer tabs on you last night. I should have known that Mino would make a mess of things."

"You don't need to apologize. I share responsibility. Also, I think I remember running away from you when you tried to help out anyway, so I'm sorry that I acted so childishly. I didn't realize what an effect alcohol could have on me."

He was quiet a moment, thinking loudly. I was distracted by how much his profile looked like some kind of luxury advertisement while he was driving, so I almost dropped my phone in my smoothie when he asked, "Are you romantically interested in Saichi-hyung?"

"*What?*"

"I won't tell anyone. You can be honest." He stopped at a light and turned his dark shades on me. I saw myself frozen in his lenses, a stiff deer in the headlights of a semi. He was reading me again. Rather than 'you *can* be honest,' he meant 'I will know if you're not.'

"I've never really thought about it before?" Until he kissed me.

"It's time to think about it, Kit-shi. If you can't see him in a romantic way, then please make that clear to him as soon as possible. He's been very badly hurt before and I'm sure you wouldn't want to open up that wound again, correct?"

"Correct." Oh man. That got heavy fast.

"Also, about the collaboration—"

I gasped. "You're still interested? Even after what just happened?"

"Of course I am. We both know this incident was an exception, and it doesn't diminish the respect I have for you and your work. Furthermore, I've stumbled across a good proposal. Last night, I ran across Saichi-hyung in a karaoke room and he mentioned that he liked your 'just hold me' as a duet. Personally, I feel that would sell extremely well with our audiences, and it could be a tame way to exploit the Kitchi narrative. However, I leave the choice up to you."

Singing with Saichi again. Not drunk this time. Maybe it would clear up my memories and my feelings. And even without all that, good god, it was the opportunity of a lifetime. A collaboration with K-Pop's finest. "If Saichi-shi is okay with it, then yes, I'd love to."

"Wonderful."

"Um, you really think things will be okay after last night?"

"Lucky Sevens doesn't leak. It's Mino I'm most worried about."

"Mino-shi leaks…?"

Jaeyoon had been deadly serious ever since we got in the car but that broke him a little bit. He had to cover his face and breathe a moment to subdue the smile. "No, but I'm sure you've come to understand what a bad influence he is. He's risky to associate with as a rookie idol and I'm concerned now that you've caught his eye. Especially if you and Saichi-hyung start dating—"

"Whether I like Saichi-shi romantically or not, I still intend to obey our agency's dating ban."

"Of course. But should you ever change your mind and decide to make another exception, I just want to warn you not to let Mino get caught up in the mix."

"Um?" What a strange thing to warn me about. Was he actually warning me not to have a threesome with Minchi? "Okay, I won't?" Embarrassed, I found myself looking down at my borrowed skirt and I just got even more flustered because Jaeyoon had to put together fashion's most classy walk of shame for me. "Also, these clothes…"

"Keep them. You'll do my brand good wearing them around. And if you want your tour t-shirt back, I'll make sure—"

"*Please* don't bother." I *vomited* on it, Jaeyoon. Please have some standards with your stain loving. "Oh, but what about Pac-Man?"

His lips jumped into a triumphant smirk. "Took care of him first thing when I got home last night. That stain was no match for me. Now Pac-Man can rest in peace."

"Um, please don't throw him away?"

That bothered him quite a bit but he nodded. "Fine. Only for you. Get home safe, Kit-shi." I glanced out the window. We were maybe thirty feet from my door, but I appreciated the sentiment anyway.

Soup or salad?

The next day, Ilsung and I were in a conference room being actively ignored by three choreographers, a producer, a stylist, and a videographer, all 'elites' who agreed on only one thing—Kit Allister should just sit pretty and hush. When my phone started flashing and buzzing in my bag, I normally would've silenced it and then quietly apologized, because I value professionalism. But these clowns didn't want a professional. They wanted vapid spineless opinionless InstaKit, so what did it matter if I checked my phone or not?

I had to check because it had to be Mino. The only other person who had my number was Ilsung, and Ilsung knew that. He watched with silent sky-high eyebrows as I reached for my bag. I had the decency to wait until the producer and the videographer started arguing about their visions and then I peeked.

—*recovered from our threesome yet?*

God, Mino! What if someone saw?! I shoved my purse off my lap. It flopped deadweight to the floor and the room quieted into a staring contest. I just shrugged and smiled. "Bug." And apparently violence toward bugs could really bring people together because the meeting wrapped up soon after with smiles all around.

I started getting texts from Mino almost every day.

At first, I deleted them on sight because I was terrified Ilsung might see them, but Mino learned pretty quickly that all his stupid dirty talk wasn't landing with me, so he decided to change tack. And just like that, his texts became utterly *precious*.

Updates on his day, anecdotes about the others, and so, so many pictures. Weird selfies. Jaeyoon wearing dorky glasses and a fake mustache. Ryo flipping off the camera with his cheeks full of food. Videos of Namgi doing semi-dangerous stunts. And lots and lots of pictures of Saichi. Saichi in laughing tears, Saichi standing on his head, Saichi shirtless trying to flex, Saichi sleeping at the table with his cheek in kimchi…

I couldn't delete stuff like that. And dammit, Mino got me trained. I started to look forward to my breaks between jobs because there was always something waiting for me on my phone. It was a nice change from a year of nothing but work texts and emails.

Before I knew it, I was replying more often than not, but only after I convinced myself that Ilsung and Ryo wouldn't be upset if they found out.

—we're in the same building today. I heard you're in studio X
—but Jae is playing prison guard so I can't come visit
—he still doesn't know I have your number and I. love. it.
—I think Satch is getting jealous tho lol he keeps asking who I'm texting

There was a picture of Saichi glowering through his silver bangs. I laughed and found myself replying yet again.

—you're keeping it a secret from him?
—yeah he's just as protective of you as Jae is
—we're breaking for lunch soon. meet in the cafeteria?
—will anyone else be there?
—it's a company cafeteria bb girl I'm pretty sure there'll be other people
—I meant other Vortex members
—I can't meet with you alone it'd be weird

—looool so what you're trying to say is you want me to bring Satch

> *—um no actually can you definitely NOT bring him?*

> *—how about Jaeyoon-shi or Namgi-shi?*

—you got something against my Satch? I thought you liked him

> *—nothing against him. I just promised a lot of people that*
> *I wouldn't make the rumors about him and me any worse*

—goody goody goody goody eight shoes

—wait so you're actually gonna come?

> *—maybe*

—FINALLY

—see you in five

Coworkers could eat lunch together in the company cafeteria without it being scandalous, right? It was hardly something anyone could get mad about. It was just socializing. Maybe even networking. And the whole DigitAlive mess was being 'handled' by our social media team, so hopefully, soon I'd be no worse for wear.

I knew I still needed to apologize to Ryo at some point for mishandling our little deal, but as long as I didn't further exacerbate the situation, he probably wasn't *that* mad, right? I sent out a thumbs-up to Mino just as Ilsung walked in.

"Great work today, Kit-shi! You must be starving! Would you like me to order something in for you?"

"Actually…" Ilsung was always my gauge, my scandal-o-meter. His reaction would tell me everything I needed to know, and it'd feel good to be honest with him after all the lies last week. "I heard that Vortex is working in this building today. Can I go eat with them in the cafeteria?"

"Oh!" He stopped up short. Surprised? Scandalized?

"Is it… no good?"

"No! That's wonderful! See if you can get a read on that collaboration Jaeyoon-shi was interested in!"

"Rumors won't start if we're seen eating together, right?"

His face took on a fatherly shade of affection and guilt started splashing around in my stomach. "Ahh, there's our Miss Perfect!

Always so conscientious! So professional! Don't worry, I'm sure it'll be just fine! Although, please don't be disappointed if Vortex doesn't show up, okay? I believe they usually have a catering service deliver meals to their dressing rooms."

"Ah. Right, of course."

"But it doesn't hurt to try! Go on! Off you go!"

I still felt guilty. I guess being honest in the moment didn't mean anything if I wasn't honest about everything leading up to that moment. Maybe it'd get easier as time went on and I distanced myself from everything that happened at Sevens. As long as I avoided doing anything else that stupid…

At least this lunch was Ilsung-approved. I felt like I needed it to set things straight. Most of my interactions with Vortex so far had been under stressful circumstances, so I really wanted a normal, decent, friendly lunch with them. I knew that was a big ask, and sort of greedy as a fan, but maybe little non-stressful meetings like this could form a foundation to build an actual friendship on…

Yeah, even if Mino was the only one that showed up in the cafeteria, I would still probably risk a rumor to sit and eat with him.

Mino wasn't alone. Should've known he would totally ignore my request to not bring Saichi, dammit. I almost turned and left, but Saichi spotted me the second I set foot in the cafeteria.

I waved. He dropped his spoon into his bowl and soup splashed all over everything, including his shirt of course. Evidently, we can't hang out without ruining at least one article of clothing. Mino just laughed and thumped him on the back, which was only making the mess worse, so I scanned for Ryo and then rushed to the rescue.

"I'm sorry! Did I surprise you, Saichi-nim?"

He grimaced. Mino laughed harder. "Jesus, she's still at it with the 'nim,' Satch! You better do something about that fast or you'll never make oppa status!"

Not that again. I amended, "Sorry, Saichi-shi." I forgot he asked me to stop using honorifics with him. Mino's path crossed with mine during a quest for napkins and I hissed, "Thanks a lot, *Sunbaenim*."

"Op-*pa*."

Okay, I wasn't supposed to see Saichi but I couldn't just unsee him now. Well, it was semi-difficult to look straight at him because his bangs were extra floppy and cute today, but I made valiant efforts. I didn't have to leave. This was *fine*. I'd already decided this wasn't a scandalous thing to do. If Ilsung thought this was safe, then surely Ryo would agree. So I grabbed a salad and sat myself down with Minchi, trying not to notice the surrounding eyes.

"*Now* do you understand why I wanted to come to the cafeteria?"

"But how'd you know Kit would be here?"

Mino ignored the question. Instead, he stuck his hand up Saichi's shirt and yanked the stain into his mouth. I was *astonished*. Saichi just whined and smacked him away.

"What? You wanna pay for this shirt?"

"No, but—"

"Then don't be such a klutz, messy boy." He leaned back down and started loudly sucking the soup out. I now knew that they didn't bat an eye at sleeping naked in the same bed, but seriously, wow, Minchi knew no bounds.

"Miiin, would you stop? I'm not a kid!" Saichi turned his eyes to the ceiling. "We're in public! And Kit is here! You're being rude!"

I glanced around. As soon as I looked up, the table next to us burst into unnaturally loud conversation. Yeah, they'd been watching. Minchi was such a gift.

Mino giggled and poked Saichi's nose. "When has an audience ever stopped me? Look, I got it out. You should be thanking me, boo. Now you won't have to deal with Jae."

"Glad to see Minchi is still doing well," I murmured.

"Speaking of Minchi, have you seen the latest ship war on Twitter?" Mino's expression was exultant. "Minchi fans are battling two camps at once—Kitchi shippers and Kit-Mino shippers. You should check it out. It's *super* entertaining."

"K-kitchi…" Could we not utter that word right in front of Saichi? "My team assured me that the situation was being handled…"

"Oh hell no. It's outta control, baby girl. Actually, I might venture a guess that the higher-ups are jumping on the bandwagon."

Okay. So one, Ryo was probably going to be mad after all. And two, I had good reason to fear for my life because if my publicist didn't kill me, the Vortexans would. Three, Mino was absolutely right: Kyungsoon had in fact admitted she was cultivating Kitchi... So was my team fighting a doomed battle against the CEO? Did they even know who they were up against?

"I'm gonna get mugged on the streets..."

"You'll be fiiine. You've got good security."

I flinched when he patted my head. No touching allowed! Especially now! "That doesn't make me feel any better! I don't want to be hated by Vortexans! I *am* Vortexan!"

"Oh, hush. Ship wars are harmless publicity. We need a better name for our ship though. Kitchi versus Mint?"

No, no. This was a dangerous game. Mino's foul unfiltered mouth was always a goldmine of memes, as well as the bank that coined half of Korea's Twitter trends. If he started interfering, I was screwed.

Saichi's frown deepened. "More like Kitchi versus Kit*no*."

Mino and I both exploded into laughter. "Brilliant, Satch. Always so goddamn brilliant." I liked how Mino's praise turned Saichi pink. But he shouldn't be allowed to get any cuter. "Ooh, and I've got more for ya, Kit. So Sevens is supposed to be leak-proof but—"

"Dear god, what? What leaked?!" I leaned close and whispered, "Was it the bite?"

Mino's eyes narrowed. "Nope. Still no leads on that one."

"See! I told you no one bit me! Now tell me what leaked!"

"First of all, calm yourself. It's not a leak to the public. *Jesus*."

"Okay? Go on?"

"All of KJ is gossiping about one, you and Jae, and two, you and Namgi. So like, what the hell were you doing before you came up to the birdcage? It wasn't Babo that bit you, was it? Because like—"

"There's no way it was him!" I put down my fork. My salad didn't really look like food anymore. "I used to only get Twitter speculation involving Saichi-shi and now there are rumors about me with practically every member?"

"Yup! Kudos, baby girl! You've conquered Vortex!"

"Just kill me now…" Because you'll probably be gentler than Ryo.

Saichi sloshed zigzags with his spoon. His voice came out soft, "I'm sorry about what I did at the concert, Kit. I didn't mean to make trouble for you. I was just really excited to see you…"

I sighed. "No, don't be sorry. I was really excited too."

"Aww, what a loving fan," Mino crooned into his tea. "Jae says to keep publicly insisting that we're all just good friends, but me, I think we should sell the narrative like we sell Minchi."

"I decline. And don't talk about Minchi like it's a product."

"Hate to tell ya, baby girl, but queerbait is a *hot* product." Saichi and I both frowned. I was glad when he hit Mino, but of course, the brat was unfazed. "And Minchi knows how to sell out."

The question slipped out before I could stop it, "What started Minchi anyway?" The two exchanged a look. I got flustered and edited, "I mean, if you're gonna talk about Minchi like it's a product, I agree that you two do a great job marketing it, but where did you even get the idea?"

Mino's lips curled into that wicked feline grin of his. "I'm the original Satch fanboy. I've been after this stud since we were trainees. And he *acts* like he just barely puts up with me, but secretly he loves the attention…" The cafeteria went through another brief hush when he tried to worm his cotton candy head under Saichi's arm. I dug my nails into my thighs to keep calm.

Saichi went from pink to red. "Min, you're being embarrassing."

"No, I'm being *cute*. Pet me."

"We're in public."

Such a gift. They were such a gift. I felt healed inside, like I'd just scrolled through a bunch of kittens on Instagram. "One of these days, you guys are gonna give me a heart attack," I told them happily and dug into my salad. Worry about Ryo and #Kitchi later. Consume Minchi content in the moment.

"Min. She said you're gonna give her a heart attack."

"She's fiiine. You should eat some more. Sandwich?" Mino held it up to his mouth but Saichi pulled away.

"I don't like mayo."

"And you say you're not a kid."

"Feel free to have some of my salad," I chimed in. "It's huge and I don't have that much time until my next job."

Mino speared some spinach and stuck it under Saichi's nose. "C'mon, you. It's Kit-nim salad. You know you want it."

Saichi sighed, but he was smiling when he chomped onto the fork. I wished I could somehow share the magic of all this with the rest of the Minchi fandom. They were so freaking cute.

Wrecker.

I left the cafeteria feeling oddly optimistic, maybe because the last time I'd had lunch with friends was back in New York.

Shea, Marie-Louise, and Dawson made it a weekend ritual to drop by my coffee shop and study together. I had a coworker who always owed me for her vape breaks, so she'd take over the lunch hour and let me go hang out with them. Luckily, the owner always felt like he owed me something too because of all the hours I worked. He didn't bat an eye at granting me unlimited drinks and muffins, even when some of my employee benefits inevitably found their way to my friends' table. Somewhere along the line, I distracted Shea out of her biology textbook and into a video of Minchi and soon she was a Vortexan convert. Dawson learned to earbud up at the first hint of a caffeinated squeal, and Marie-Louise was eventually inspired to write an article about queerbaiting for her journalism class.

Shea was actually the one who razzed me into that fateful performance of 'Delusion' at open mic night. She probably wouldn't have done it if she'd known it would lead to my ditching America, but what was done was done. Now I really wished I could talk to her about real-life Minchi, but I hadn't heard from any of them in months. More my fault than theirs. Since moving here, I'd worked pretty much all day every day, and even if I did find the time to Skype, the thirteen-hour time difference wasn't exactly accommodating.

And what did we have in common now anyway? The three of them had probably forgotten all about me. They'd probably moved on to new friends. Me, I wasn't so lucky in my new life friend-wise. With all of the industry's restrictions, it was near impossible to make friends outside the idol world, and until now, I'd always been too intimidated to befriend another artist. Sometimes, the isolation brought back dark memories of nursing school, but I always shut those thoughts down. This was so much better. I was being paid to have fun. And I had Ilsung. He was my family now.

Besides, things were changing.

I was maybe friends with *Vortex* now.

What had I ever done to deserve that? Maybe the universe was finally balancing things out for me. Maybe all the misery I went through in America finally tipped the scales in my favor.

Things were *perfect* now. Almost too perfect.

I was so wrapped up in my thoughts that I didn't hear footsteps until I stopped at my dressing room door. Of course, my paranoid mind went immediately to Ryo, but when I turned, it was just Mino, laughing and waving at me.

I pointed behind him. Another artist was coming down the hall, a grungy-looking kid with bleached hair. Mino went from laughing to shouting in a matter of seconds, "*Jesus*, will you quit fucking following me?! I know your game, asshole. Back off!" To my surprise, the kid immediately took off running.

"What was that all about?"

Mino shrugged. "This group of goddamn trainees has been tailing me for like a week now, always fucking spying on me and shit. They're not even supposed to be in this wing!"

"What do they want? Are they fans of yours or something?"

"Who knows? Don't worry about it." He pointed at my dressing room door. "Anybody in there?" It was dark inside. I shook my head. "Then can we have a chat in private?"

That sounded a little risky. What if Ilsung walked in? Would Mino know what to say? "Um, I don't know if we should…"

"Pretty please? I'm sick of texting. Let's talk in person."

He knew exactly how cute he was, pulling a Saichi pout and batting his unfair eyelashes. Someday, someone would put their foot down and tell him 'no' anyway, but I knew it wasn't going to be me. Besides, if we were going to be friends, then I needed to stop looking at Mino like he was nothing but a liability. Why did my mind always race to worst-case scenarios? If Ilsung asked, I'd tell him the truth. We were just friends 'having a chat.'

"Okay, but just for a second."

"Goody-*nine*-shoes." He flipped on the light and made a noise of displeasure. "Small," he muttered. "What the fuck, KJ?"

I shrugged. "I'm a rookie."

"Not anymore. You're an elite now. I heard it from the jaws of the head witch herself."

"You mean President Kyungsoon-nim?"

"Who else?"

"That's not a very polite way to talk about the president."

"Goody-*ten*."

"I'm just saying."

"You don't know her like I do, Kit-nim. You gotta be cutthroat to run an empire as huge as KJ."

"Well, I like her. It's not easy to climb the company ladder as a woman, you know. I think she's incredible."

"Yeah, well, I'm sure you'll change your tune soon."

I checked up and down the hall for Ilsung before I shut the door. When I turned back around, Mino was right behind me. *Way* too close. I froze. He reached under my arm and the lock clicked shut.

"So. Pretty sure Satch likes you. You like him back?"

"W-what?"

"Are you gonna ask him out? I think you'll have to take the initiative with him. We tried to help him meet you for like a year, but Shy Boy was happy just with a handshake at a fan meet."

"He was at one of my fan meets and I didn't see him?!"

"Not like you were expecting him. Plus he's pretty good at

disguising himself, which is another reason why he'd make a good idol date. So you gonna ask him out or not?"

First Jaeyoon, now Mino. What was the big rush? Also, did we need to have this conversation standing a foot apart? I sighed and shook my head, "I don't plan on asking him out."

"Why not?"

"Mino, there's a dating ban."

"*That?* It's just a formality."

"Maybe to you. You're Vortex. You're invincible. I, on the other hand, am not, so I'm gonna stick to the rules as much as I can."

He eyed me just long enough to make me uncomfortable and then he shrugged. "Hm. Well, we'll work on that."

"And another thing, I don't think Saichi-shi is interested in me like that anyway. We're both just… fans of each other, I guess, and fans don't necessarily want to… to um, do things with the people they're fans of."

"*You* do."

"I do?"

"Don't you?"

"I thought we established that I'm a soft stan."

"Let's test that."

All week, I tried over and over to remember my kiss with Saichi, but the more I searched for details, the more certain I became that nothing had happened after all. But with my back against the cold door and Mino's breath on my face, I was flooded with the sights and sounds of the karaoke room.

Up close, Mino's eyes weren't onyx after all. They were dark, dark chocolate, just melted enough to shine. He blurred as the distance between us disappeared and he caught my lips firmly with his. My world paused in the confusion, then it tried to make up for lost time and suddenly everything was spinning too quickly.

Yeah, I remembered now. The way Saichi nibbled my lip. The feel of his fingers in my hair, on my skin. The taste of something citrus on his tongue. But also how quickly he stopped up short. If I'd grabbed him and held on tight, if I'd tried harder to kiss him back, would he have kept going?

Mino's teeth slid off my ear and clicked. "Atta girl." The words were hot in my ear, but I shivered.

"Mino…" I said it aloud to remind myself who he was.

His upper lip vanished into the curve of his trademark smirk and I wanted to go looking for it. What an alien thought. He leaned into my hand like a pleased cat, his pastel hair like warm down between my fingers. When had I reached out to him?

"C'mon now, you know you wanna." His chin lifted, beckoning. The small dark beauty mark there caught my eyes. I already felt a hint of his smile against my lips when I realized what I was doing.

"*Whoa.*"

I jerked my head backward and banged it loudly on the door. Mino frowned, disappointed. "What."

The little bang to my skull woke up my brain and it imploded, vacuuming coherent thought back in. Scattered reality reassembled itself and I blurted it out, "Sorry. I can't."

"If you bring up the damn dating ban again, I swear…"

"I like Saichi."

I what? Where did that come from?! Since when was my mouth ahead of my head? Ahead of my heart?

Mino's nose wrinkled like my words stunk. "You *just* said—"

"I know. But I think I realize now—"

I was willing to let my mouth go because I was interested in what it had to say, but Mino wasn't. "You realized that you like him after kissing *me*? What the fuck?"

"Sorry."

His body went slack in surprise, but only for a second, and then he almost choked with laughter. I tried to laugh along but I was more than a little confused, both with him and with myself. "*Dayum*, girl! I can't believe this! This has literally never happened to me before!"

"What… is happening?"

"Like, am I losing my touch or what?" Our eyes met and his filled with devilish glitter. "Nah, actually, hang on a minute." His hands thudded loudly on either side of my head and I jumped. "You sure it's not *me* you hard stan? I'm the one you made out with. I know lots of chicks who soft stan their bias and hard stan their bias wrecker."

I ignored his question entirely. "Go bother *them* then, playboy. And who says you're my bias wrecker?"

"*Salty* fangirl! Don't you feel this chemistry?" His fingers played through my hair and flicked my earring. "Don't you wanna see where this could take us?"

"Mino, stop. You have no idea how difficult it is to… to…"

He giggled. "Resist me? I'm well aware, baby girl. Why do you think I'm trying so hard? But alright, alright, I know the 'stop' word. I respect that."

"Thank you."

"I've still got game though, yeah?"

"Yes, Mino. You've still got it." He grinned and planted a sloppy kiss on my cheek. I immediately wiped it off and smeared it on his shirt. "But even if I accidentally kissed you back a little, and even if I maybe like Saichi a little, I'm *definitely* still a soft Vortexan, so I'm not playing that game, got it?"

He cackled and nudged me aside. "We'll call it a truce. And you'll call me if you ever change your mind, yeah? In the meantime, I'll keep working on wrecking your bias."

"Don't you dare wreck him!" I shouted down the hall after him.

"All mine to wreck until you claim him, Kit-nim! Catch ya later!"

So… I like Saichi?

Did I say that just to get Mino off my back? As much fun as Mino was to hang out with, I was undeniably scared of his player side. He basically admitted to the fact that all of this was a big game for him, and that game had no consequences for him, only for me. If we were caught together, I could get sent back to America. My new life here would be over.

And dammit, those same consequences applied with Saichi too, so no more kissing *him* anymore either. Did I want to? Apparently yes…? I thought about him the whole time Mino was kissing me. That was *so* messed up.

But still, did I like Saichi romantically, or did I just idolize him?

Whatever. I could think about it later. I was going to be late for my next job. As my dressing room door swung shut, I found that grungy kid from earlier leaning on the wall behind it.

"How long were you there?"

He looked up and smiled. "Hi Noona. I'm a big fan." He had the voice memo app open on his phone, and I pride myself on the speed with which I snatched that thing right out of his hand.

"Were you recording my conversation with him?!"

"You can delete it. I already sent it out."

"To who?! Where is your respect?! Don't you know who he is?! You're trying to debut under this agency and you have the nerve to leak the private conversations of your sunbaes? This isn't how KJ works! You're definitely going to get fired!"

He shook his head. "This *is* my debut, Noona. And yes, this *is* how KJ works. I'm not gonna get fired. It's the president who wanted that audio."

"W-what? Why?" I was too stupefied to stop him from snatching the phone back again. Was this what Kyungsoon meant by being 'held to a higher standard' as an elite?

"I'm guessing you'll find out soon enough." He waved and ambled off with a jaunt in his step. "Bye Noona. Stay pretty!"

Harmony.

"Kit-shi?" My photographer, Siwoo, lowered his camera and laughed. "Your mind is elsewhere. Your eyes are empty."

"Ah. Pardon me."

Ilsung looked up from his newspaper, surprised. Focus wasn't usually a problem for me, but Siwoo was right. My mind was definitely elsewhere. At any given moment, I was expecting to get hauled off by the president, confronted by Ryo, hounded by a trainee, seduced by Mino, or swarmed by angry Vortexans… and how was I supposed to focus on an InstaKit photoshoot when today was the day I was scheduled to record my duet with Saichi?! My nerves were frying themselves for breakfast.

Siwoo laughed louder this time. "You just broke again, Kit-shi! I've never seen you like this. Is something wrong?"

"No, sorry, sorry. I'm here." Dammit. How unprofessional.

"Easy now. Don't get flushed."

Finally done, I emerged from the changing room and found Jaeyoon in conversation with Ilsung. He inclined his head in a relaxed greeting, but I was trying to suck up, so I bowed deeply in response.

"Well done, Kit! Don't worry about being distracted! I know

you're just excited today! I'm excited too! But I'm sorry to tell you that I just learned I can't accompany you to the studio as planned. I've been called into the president's office—"

"Oh *god*."

"Kit! What kind of reaction is that? You've been doing so well lately that I'm sure she's got something wonderful in store for you, like a raise or a tour or maybe your own radio show!"

"Um, I hope so…?"

"Not to worry! Jaeyoon-shi is going to escort you to the studio! I've cleared your schedule for the rest of the day so take your time and have fun, okay? I'll be in touch."

"Yes, sir." He shot me a quizzical look. The awkward formality wasn't lost on him, but he must've chalked it up to my being 'excited' again because with a quick bouncy bow, he was gone and I was left alone with Jaeyoon.

"Shall we, Kit-shi? The studio I booked is on the twenty-fifth floor. Hyung is likely up there waiting." He led the way off the set through the fluttery hush of staff in rightful awe of him. Like always, I felt woefully underdressed beside him. I wished I could've just kept my photoshoot outfit on, but nope, couldn't afford it. If only Ilsung was right about that raise. I was almost certainly getting a pay cut instead. Hopefully not fired… What exactly was the punishment for fraternizing with other idols?

My shoulders jumped up to my ears at the pound of the elevator doors. A ridiculously familiar sound to jump at, but I wound up even tighter when Jaeyoon laid a set of rings on me. "Are you nervous about recording with him?"

"Among other things, yes."

"I guarantee it'll be the most effortless recording you ever make. He's very easy to work with. Kind, patient, forgiving, selfless, thoughtful, loyal…" What did any of that have to do with recording? "And he'll be ecstatic over any little thing you do, so you shouldn't worry. Also, have you thought about what I said at all?"

"About what?"

He laughed. "About your feelings for Saichi-hyung."

The elevator was either running out of oxygen or it was shrinking in on us. And either way, it was definitely moving too slow. "Oh. Yes. Among... other things. Do you think the president will approve of this collaboration?"

"That hardly matters. I don't answer to her when it comes to Vortex. I'll be obligated to present this recording to our teams, and she'll act as though she has the final say on it for appearance's sake, but the bottom line is, what I want will be." Jeez, Jaeyoon. She's still the CEO! "But yes, she'll approve without a doubt."

"Um, good."

The doors opened and I gasped for breath. Absolutely unbearable to be stuck in such a small enclosed space with such a massive commanding personality.

Jaeyoon guided me quietly into the studio and pressed a warm mug of tea into my hands. I wasn't usually allowed on this side of a recording, so I couldn't help staring as the sound engineer's fingers fiddled up and down the mixing board, sound etching itself into mesmerizing rainbow bricks across the screen. Then Jaeyoon touched my shoulder and pointed through the glass.

Saichi was already in the booth.

Every fiber of him was tuned to the microphone, long fingers clenched around his headphones. His face was torn with emotion, and I almost averted my eyes, because god, what had I ever done to deserve a glimpse into his private galaxy? To watch him weaving miracles into music right before my eyes?

"Here, this is sure to turn your day around." Jaeyoon stretched a pair of headphones over my ears and suddenly, I was submerged headfirst in the cool bottomless ocean of his voice, falling upward through his mind. And he was singing the second verse of my song.

This was life at its completion. I could've died right then and I wouldn't have been upset. Well, almost. I couldn't die until I'd sung with him again.

The engineer cut the music when the song moved into the next chorus. Blinking, Saichi returned to Earth, and I felt like I'd been shaken out of a pleasant dream.

"He really is something, isn't he?" Jaeyoon murmured fondly. For a moment, neither of us could move, and then he found himself. "Alright, come on. Let's get your part recorded too."

Saichi pulled on an adorable droopy smile when I came in and my heartstrings knotted in my chest. He had a bit of a bedhead look to him and I wondered if it was the headphones or if he'd been napping between jobs. Cheeks peachy, he took a small step closer, like he was testing the temperature between us.

"Saichi-shi, long time no see…"

Having just heard him sing, I felt vaguely as though I was in the presence of a deity. Our eyes met and he paused to let that moment happen, then he spoke, soft as fur, "Thank you for agreeing to this. You know how much I like this song." Some tuft of a memory curled through the air around us. He bit his lip, and I had to look away.

"It's an honor," I managed.

Jaeyoon spoke up, "As you may have noticed, Hyung was just recording the second verse. We'd like you to sing the first verse, then harmonize on the choruses, and we've divided up the lines in the bridge." Now in producer mode, he was quick to move things forward, illustrating his vision with a color-coded lyric sheet. Saichi's lines were highlighted in blue, mine in pink. I thought of Mino's hair and heard Marie-Louise in my head carping on gender stereotypes. "If the harmony doesn't come naturally, Mino's put together some sheet music for your reference. Do you read music?" I nodded. "Any objections? No? Alright. Kit-shi, you're up first."

"Can I please stay in here while she records?" Saichi *batted his eyes*. Did he learn that from Mino or was he innately that cute?

Jaeyoon chuckled and threw up his hands. "You and Mino always do this. Yes, you can stay if you must, but you know the drill, Hyung. No funny business." Pleased, Saichi scuttled over to a chair in the corner, but how was I supposed to sing with him sitting right there?!

"Are you nervous?" he asked. "You look nervous."

"I am," I admitted readily. I half-hoped he'd take the hint and go somewhere that I couldn't stare at him. Instead, he grinned at me.

"You won't be once the song starts. I've seen you. You get lost in it, just like I do. All this…" He waved his hands, headphones rattling on his arm. "It'll disappear. And you know it."

"*You* won't," I breathed.

"Hm?"

"It's you I go looking for."

I was startled by what had just come out of my mouth. That was too honest, too revealing. What would he think if he knew that I only sang because of him? That I was talentless. That I was just an imitator. That my current life was all just a reaction to him.

I checked his face. He was unruffled, but he looked thoughtful and that was bad. I had to say something before he could theorize, but at the worst possible moment, my confession to Mino flashed like a meteor as it pierced my mind's atmosphere… I like Saichi.

"Kit, I—"

"I meant, I just meant—"

"Okay, lovebirds. Time to get some work done." Jaeyoon's voice crackled overhead. Lovebirds?! Now I *really* couldn't look at Saichi. "Kit-shi, please put your headphones on so we can begin."

I like Saichi?

The intro threaded through my thoughts and doubts and they dissolved. I waded into the music, wandering, *trying* to get lost, trying to find him. He'd be there when I truly let go, standing on some edge of the universe, singing into whatever was beyond it.

He wasn't so hard to find when he was in the same space, breathing the same air as me. I pitched into the deep with ease, and soon the chorus began to build. I could feel him, almost touch him. Somewhere far away, Jaeyoon murmured, "He's getting up. Unmute his mic." My eyes sprang open and Saichi's voice encircled mine.

Our voices remembered each other. Mine rushed out to greet his, and they fit together more perfectly than two interlocking puzzle pieces. The harmony was less of a jigsaw and more of a drop of dye in clear water—one swirl and I flushed with his color.

I glanced to the window and Jaeyoon was nodding, waving us on. Saichi launched into the second verse alone, his eyes falling into mine.

But he seemed to be looking through me, out into desolate emptiness. The pain in his voice made my skin prickle.

I joined him in the second chorus with my eyes flooding, pushing through a thousand memories of this hue of sound. I'd risen from the lows of my life by blending my voice into the musical mirage of him piped through cheap electronics, but no, this sound was organic, unfiltered. It immersed me in the far sweeter memory of citrus syllables and warm woven breath. I could almost feel his lips on mine again. Our voices shivered together as the song spiraled into its bridge, and then, he grabbed my hand. A tear splashed onto my chest. Our fingers locked tight with each other.

"*So please.*"

"*Please.*"

"*Just hold me…*" The notes could only whisper past our lips. "*Let me pretend for one lonely moment that I'm yours.*"

As if it had heard us, the moment was long and slow to fade.

I felt I was fighting a natural pull toward him. I wanted to hold, to be held… but his eyes lost their veneer and my feet hit the floor, and then I was hyper-conscious of my fingers gripping his.

Jaeyoon's voice filtered into our ears, "I should've known you two would nail this in one take." Our fingers fell away from each other. I was grateful that Jaeyoon didn't say anything disparaging. "That was positively… unearthly. Well done. Truly. I'm rather certain our work here is finished."

"Did you get chills too? I always do when I listen to you sing…" Smiling, Saichi skimmed his hands over my forearms and my skin tingled under his touch. I was glad to have his touch back. Without it, the chills wouldn't stop. And now without his voice around mine, I felt like a mere half of a whole. Reality was rocky outside the space we'd shared in the song.

Good god. I had to get my head back on straight. Any other day, with any other person, I would've made a joke about my voice being bone-chilling, or maybe I would've told him that he needed to learn the difference between chills and cringes, but he spoke with such sincerity that I couldn't find the heart to insult myself.

Instead, I snuck another searching look at him.

The pain that inspired 'just hold me' came from the sudden loss of the woman who raised me, my Aunt Caroline. She and I never got to say a true goodbye, and I'd never stopped wanting one last hug. She always gave the warmest, tightest, safest hugs. They were what used to set everything right-side-up in my world.

After Ilsung helped me shoot down all the other candidates for my debut single, 'just hold me' did face one last line of criticism before recording. At that point, I was more than happy to honor my producer's suggestion to tweak a few lines and turn it into a love song. Tweaked or not, the original emotions remained powerfully embedded in the song and coursed through me every time I sang it. And even though I'd obviously written the song in Korean, I always got the sense that my aunt was listening nearby, maybe even holding me in some stellular embrace. After all, there were no language barriers in the afterlife, right?

And yet, Saichi...

When he sang my lyrics, I recognized my own wounds in him. The unending pursuit of what's gone, the grayscale of grief, the pained and hopeless supplication... I knew that broken ache in his voice, felt it unsettle my frame. You couldn't fake that.

What did he see over that edge when he sang?

'He's been very badly hurt before...'

Who had he lost?

Dissonance.

Jaeyoon expounded on his plans for the release as the three of us walked, but my mind still pulsed with withdrawal symptoms and didn't register a thing he said. Did Saichi feel that too? He was quiet, but that wasn't really out of the ordinary. Me, I knew my life had peaked. The high was stratospheric and it was all downhill from here. I would never top a duet with Oh Saichi.

Jaeyoon glided to a halt and I thought he might call me out for not listening. Instead, he bent into an elegant apologetic angle. "Pardon me, but this is where I leave you two. I have another engagement to attend to."

"Thank you for all your help today, Jaeyoon."

"No, thank *you*, Saichi-hyung, for coming up with such a fitting collaboration. I believe you're free to go enjoy the rest of the day off. Oh, and come to think of it, Kit-shi, your manager cleared your schedule too, didn't he? You two should go get dinner to celebrate. Just wish I could join you. Perhaps another time. Thank you again for your hard work today, Kit-shi. See you at the meeting."

As a parting gift, he offered a clue in his eyes that I wasn't present enough to read, and then he was gone. Another engagement, huh? Thank god Ilsung cleared my plate because I was *useless* right now.

Sure, I'd been scatterbrained all day, but that was nothing compared to the bizarre, buzzing numbness in my skull now.

"Kit…"

I turned, a little dizzily. Saichi scuffed at the carpet and made a gallant attempt to raise his head, then our eyes locked and I heard an echo of our voices. My hope was that we could buff out the intensity between us with some small talk and a few jokes, and then part on common ground that wasn't such tricky territory. Jaeyoon's breezy formalities caught a crosswind through my own awkward attempts at formulating 'thank you and goodbye' in my mind. If I had even half his social grace, I could've easily sidestepped the trap of Saichi's eyes, but Saichi didn't want out of the woods yet. He went deeper.

Finally he spoke, "I hope I wasn't out of line today."

"Out of line?" Since when did Oh Saichi walk in line with the rest of humanity? Why was he worried? Because I cried? Because he held my hand? It was all just the passion of the performance, wasn't it?

"I'm very grateful for the chance to sing together, but I didn't mean for things to go this way. Whenever our paths cross, I screw something up and… and then Vortex comes out unscathed and you have to face the fallout by yourself. I feel like I should stay away from you as much as I can, and yet, here I am asking you for a collaboration with all the clout of Vortex—"

Okay, I couldn't afford to be drunk on our duet anymore.

"What? Yes, but by all means, clout me." I would've laughed but again, he was being so sincere. "I promise you that I very happily accepted the opportunity to collaborate. Why would I not want to record with you? You're *Oh Saichi*. And I'm your fan!"

"You're still my fan? Even after everything I've done? Even after getting up close and personal with my complete mess of a life?"

"The way things have been going, I should be asking *you* that. You've done nothing wrong, and you're definitely not a mess. Why would I like you any less now that I've met you in person?"

He looked drained of words after his speech, but after a search, he found more. "Because idols are perfect and humans aren't."

"But you're an amazing human."

"No, I'm bad at living real life." His eyes broke away and he wilted. Or rather he seemed to unbloom, drawing into himself, binding his arms tight across his chest. "Even when I'm trying my hardest, all I do is cause problems for you. I got caught at your concert and then I was stupid enough to get you caught at *our* concert, and then I got drunk and... and..."

I couldn't listen anymore. I dropped everything I was holding and pushed into his world. Or maybe I pulled him into mine.

"You're hugging me, Kit."

"Yeah, I wasn't sure words would cut it. I can stop if you want."

"No, that's okay."

"Saichi-shi, don't worry about the hashtags or the tabloids or what happened at Sevens. None of that changes how I look at you as a person. You've done so much good in my life that, at this point, there's honestly nothing you could do bad."

"But you act like you hate me..."

I pulled back to study his face, and then I realized we were inches apart, and we were standing in the middle of a hallway where anyone from our industry could see us. *God.* Wake up, Kit. I stepped back and replanted myself in reality, but I still doubted what my ears were repeating to my brain. "What are you talking about?"

"You won't even look at me sometimes. You and Min are so friendly and comfortable with each other and then there's me, sitting there like an idiot with my spilled soup—"

"Mino's just louder and pushier than you, that's all! I didn't mean to make you feel ignored or overlooked. I just—"

"There. See? You call him Mino. And I'm still Saichi-shi."

"Ah." Hmm, true. "You have a point. But I don't call you that because I'm trying to push you away! It's just that you and your vocals and your dancing and your choreography are all so incredible, and I really..." Don't say like. Don't make it weird. "I can't help feeling so much respect and admiration for you." And I just like you in general. I might even want to try kissing you again when I'm not so stupid drunk. "So please don't ever think that I hate you because I will always... not hate you, um, Saichi." Shi. No, shut up.

"You mean it?"

This man was the bedrock my current life was built on. The one person who gave me hope when I was alone and horrified by life. The light that helped me out of my tunnel vision. In short, I was semi-obsessed with him, and yet, he thought I hated him... This was much more than a lack of social grace; my people skills just *sucked*.

"I mean it. I'm a huge fan and that will never change."

Why did that make him pout? Did he still not believe me?

Suddenly, he sank down onto his heels to address the purse situation. My phone, my wallet, a compact mirror, an old script... everything was flung out onto the floor. He addressed his question at a tube of vanilla lip balm I hadn't seen in weeks, "I don't wanna keep bothering you, but can I ask you one more thing?"

"I think so."

"Are you dating Min?"

"Heck no," I answered immediately.

Again, I almost laughed, but I was scared to hurt his feelings. Apparently I'd already hurt him quite a bit. He looked up with glassy doubtful eyes, unreasonably cute. Even cuter when he asked in Japanese, "Promise?"

"Why would I lie to you?"

"I don't know." He bowed his head and sighed so violently that heat sprayed on my toes. "Because everybody lies. I lie all the time. It's just part of the job." The zipper of my purse growled shut and then he reached up and squeezed my hand. From down there, his hand felt so heavy. "Please don't date him."

I held my breath, startled by how serious he'd become. He didn't elaborate either. He just pressed my knuckles to his forehead, like a message might seep through our skin.

"Okay, I wasn't planning on it but, wait, *wait*—!" It was almost reflex to snatch at his fingers as they slipped away. I missed, but he caught my hand and pressed the handle of my purse into my palm. If he didn't hold it there, I would've dropped it all over again.

"Sorry, I'm out of line again."

"You can't be out of line when you're at the front."

Finally, he smiled, just a little. "I'm not the leader."

"Listen um, Saichi, I'm bad at real life too. I'm terrible at turning off my work brain, and worse at turning off my fan brain, so when it comes to you... I have no idea how to act. But I'd really like to work on that, if you don't mind. Maybe we could take this outside of work? Maybe we could be more than fans?"

"Y-you mean—?"

"Can we be friends? Like normal people?"

First, his eyebrow crooked a little, then his nose scrunched up, and then he started to giggle. "Yes, please. But what do normal friends do? Do you remember what it was like to be normal?"

"Back in the day, my friends and I always got coffee together. We'd go window-shopping in Manhattan, bike through the park, sneak into a movie, get froyo in the summer..."

"I like that. Let's try being normal."

"Right now?"

"Why not?"

Grandkid

For normalcy's sake, we decided to take the metro, but *nothing* felt normal about standing next to the nation's top idol in public. Also maybe he'd forgotten that normal friends don't exactly hold hands on the train? With Mino as his closest friend, I guess I couldn't fault him for being confused. I didn't really mind either way. His thumb bounced along my knuckles to a rhythm I thought I recognized and my fangirl heart was all too eager to play along to the beat of his drum. Besides, his fingers were starting to feel familiar in mine.

Suspicion was painfully tangible in the air around us, but there was no way the other passengers could tell who we were. Sunglasses, masks, hats, hoods—the two of us looked more like a terror threat than idols in disguise. We had to avoid looking at each other because the giggles were difficult to recover from.

Once, the train jolted around a bit and he caught me to his chest. Did I almost squeal? Yes, but I also made the interesting realization that his smell was also familiar now. I was still trying to put my finger on it, but he always seemed to smell like he'd just come in out of the wind on a brisk day.

Adrenalized by getting away with it all, we took the station stairs by twos up into the hordes out enjoying a warm evening in Seoul.

Saichi's confidence evaporated in the sunlight of a frenetic street lined with restaurants. "Normal friends go out to eat, right? Are you hungry? Jaeyoon mentioned dinner…"

I shook my head. How could I think about food when I was with Oh Saichi? "Are you?"

"Not really." His eyebrows worried together. "Should I take you to a movie then? Or… a theme park? You said coffee earlier? Maybe we should—"

Those activities all sounded a little like date activities… What was the differentiating factor between coffee with a friend and a coffee date? At my coffee shop, I could always tell right away just by looking at the couple. But what was it exactly? Intent? Atmosphere? Holding hands between sips? *This* wasn't a date, right? Should we be doing this? Mino's voice rang in my head, *'It's not about what you should do. It's about what you're gonna do 'cuz you wanna.'*

Yeah, I was hearing a lot of shoulds. Not a lot of wannas.

"Saichi, I'd rather do what you actually want to do."

"But shouldn't I take you somewhere fancy?"

After my last VIP experience? Nuh-uh. "No, if we're going to be normal, let's be real middle-class normal, not rich. The fancy stuff just makes me nervous."

"Are you sure? I have plenty of money?"

"It's okay! I like the incognito thing we're doing right now… Low-cost, low-key, good old-fashioned sort of thing?"

My phone buzzed in my purse and I already knew it was Ilsung, my lifeline to reality. God, I'd forgotten all about him, all about the meeting with the president, the recording, *Ryo's deal*—!

"Kit? Are you still in the studio? I didn't want to interrupt anything so I wasn't sure if I should call!"

"You're fine! We already finished! I'm sorry, it went so well and it was all just so exciting that I forgot to text you! What did the president say? Am I in trouble?"

"What? Oh! No, no! Actually, I don't know what that was all about so I unfortunately don't have anything useful to report back. I'm just sorry I missed out on the recording! I can't wait to hear it!

Are you still in the building? Do you need me to pick you up?"

He had a meeting with the president and he had nothing to say about it? That wasn't like him. "It's okay! I took the metro!"

"Oh! Well then, please keep a mask on and get home safe, alright? I'm proud of you for being so independent lately!"

"Yessir!" The *guilt*. But I didn't have time to dwell on it. People were muttering and pointing at Saichi. And no wonder! I'd never seen anyone try to attract a taxi by doing jumping jacks on the curb…

"Saichi! Act casual!" I wasn't really concerned. I think I was drunk on him. I couldn't stop giggling.

"And how does one act casual?" Over his mask and under his hat brim, his eyes were joking with me. I wanted his whole smile.

"Watch me."

I shoved my hands into imaginary pockets and tried to whistle through my mask. To my surprise, Saichi gasped and scrambled to put his hands over my face. "Don't whistle! It's almost nighttime!"

I burst into laughter. "What's that got to do with anything?"

"Ah, um, snakes will come out…? Or ghosts. I don't remember." He shoved his hands into actual pockets and his blush almost made it through his mask. "Sorry, it's just something my grandma always told me. I guess I never realized how strange—"

"Oh! A superstition? We have a lot of weird ones in America too. 'Step on a crack, break your mother's back.' And we bless people when they sneeze so the demons don't steal their souls."

His eyes went round. "What crack? Step on what crack?"

"Sidewalk cracks."

He looked around in alarm. "But those are *everywhere!* And what did you say about sneezing demons?!"

"It's just superstition!" Still laughing, I flagged down an approaching taxi and he gave me a slight stink-eye for making it look easy. "I was sort of a New Yorker for a little while," I reminded him.

Inside the taxi, Saichi rattled off some perplexing directions to the driver and then spun to face me, shedding layers of his disguise as he spoke. "I'll tell you all the Japanese and Korean ones I know, and you tell me all the American ones, and then we'll be the safest luckiest people on Earth. Okay? Now tell me more. I gotta protect my mother's back."

"You owe me another one first."

"Four is unlucky because it sounds like death. And so is nine, because it sounds like suffering. That's another reason why I don't like being called Saichi-shi. It sounds like Saichi-death to me."

"Oh *god*. I'm sorry! I didn't mean to be so creepy—"

"No, no. Don't worry about it."

"Why are all superstitions so morbid?"

That made him grin. I was glad I could see all of his face now. "Not all of them! My favorite one is 'if you see a cat washing its face, it'll rain tomorrow!'"

"What? That's so cute! I seriously can't think of any cute ones… Seven years of bad luck for breaking a mirror."

"Oooh, for us, it's breaking a comb!"

"Are brushes safe? I break a lot of those. My hair is kinda thick."

"It *is* thick. And so soft! Ah, sorry, do you mind if I—?"

My face got hot. "G-go right ahead." Of course I didn't mind, but carrying on our conversation got significantly more difficult with his fingers winding through my hair. I could barely keep my eyes open. Was he *braiding* it? This was ridiculous. I got my hair done almost every day. How could his fingers feel so different from my stylist's? To distract myself, I went on, "D-don't walk under ladders."

"Well, that's just common sense, right?" He smiled at his fingers, fast at work. Would it be bad to lean closer? The longer he touched me, the less I cared about literally everything besides him. "But then again, 'don't cut your nails at night' is sorta common sense too."

I had to laugh. "What'll happen if you do?"

"Summons evil spirits, I think. Pretty much everything does, according to Grandma. They're all over the place." Finished, he plucked up my baseball cap and popped it backward on my head. "So cute…"

Nope. Ignoring that. "Are these all Japanese superstitions so far, or is this your Korean grandmother we're talking about?"

"I think there are overlaps, but I learned most of these growing up in Japan. My parents worked a lot, so I stayed with my grandma out in the countryside, and she used to tell me folktales every night. Remember how we were talking about rice paddies? Same era."

"The era of chasing…" C'mon, drunken memory. "Medaka?"

"You do remember! You really do have a knack for languages."

"No, I have a knack for remembering everything you say," I admitted. "I asked my manager to start correcting me when I say words in Japanese, but he says it's part of my charm…"

"I like it. Don't change it. But also, maybe don't learn Korean by listening to us talk anymore because Min's dirty mouth is catchy. That's how Ryo got so profane, you know."

"Mino corrupted Ryo? Wow, Mino."

The taxi driver interrupted our laugh for clarification, which reminded Saichi that he was uneasy. "Kit, you're sure you don't wanna go to a fancy restaurant?"

"I'm secretly a small-town girl, remember? I'd be happy just to hang out with you in a cornfield." I couldn't stop myself. I was already doing it, poking his lip in because it was pouting. And I was shocked at myself, but it worked. He stopped pouting and laughed.

"Me too. Someday let's do that, okay?"

The taxi slid to a halt, the sudden quiet muted by languid jazz that had tiptoed unnoticed from the radio. Saichi's voice capered in perfect time with a teasing clarinet, making even a friendly thank you to a cabbie into music. He batted my wallet away so I sketched through my breath on the window, tracing the swaying thicket of sailboats as he laughed through an autograph. Sailboats. We'd come to the river? A marina?

"I like to come here on my days off," he murmured to my thoughts and then threw open the door.

Cool air burst into the backseat with flare and tang as Saichi stepped out, smelling more like him than he did. The breeze battered his silvery hair like an old friend, and I felt inexplicable nostalgia as it encased us in his color scheme. This place was part of him.

"So, you wanna see my boat?"

"You have your own boat?"

"I sure do!"

With a cheerful greeting to the guard nearby, the sprawling gates rattled open. The guard seemed to be the only one around, so we didn't bother masking up, even when Saichi took my hand again. Grinning, he tugged me through the breeze and through nodding ranks of boats that seemed to smack their lips at us as we went by. Then he stopped and pointed, and I burst into laughter.

"That's the same reaction Min had."

"That's not a boat, Saichi! That's a ship!"

A giant blue fishing boat lurked at the end of the row, streaky beards of orange rust drizzling down its steel sides. It looked hilariously out of place between two gleaming yachts. Only Vortex's Oh Saichi could get away with keeping that in such a fancy marina.

"They had to add onto the dock to give her the space she needs." He laughed in delight. "Isn't she gorgeous?"

"Yes. I *love* her. Where on earth did you get her?"

"I rent her from a nice old Chinese fisherman from Weihai, just west of here. He sailed all the way across the Yellow Sea to bring me this beauty! And the Coast Guard was so mad about it. They thought he came to steal Korean fish."

"Wait, what? What's the story there? How'd you make friends with a fisherman from China?"

"Well, you know how the Bae family runs a Chinese restaurant back in Namgi-ya's hometown? After one of our concerts down there in Daegu, we all went home with him to try his mom's famous potstickers. And while we were eating, they had Chinese television on… to create atmosphere maybe? I think it was a documentary on small fishing villages, and Grandpa Zhang was in it." He giggled. "Min made some comment saying his hair looked just like mine."

"So you found the fisherman guy in a documentary…?"

"Yeah! I didn't know for sure what he was saying, but I kinda recognized some of the words in the subtitles. He kept saying he was tired, but he couldn't stop working or his wife would go hungry.

They never had kids, so there was no one to take care of them when they got older. And I thought, my grandma won't let me support her, so why not try helping out Grandpa Zhang instead?"

"But how'd you actually find him though?"

"Oh, I got their address from the filmmaker and sent them a letter. I don't know if you know this, but Japanese borrowed symbols from China a long time ago, so I can kinda—"

"You mean like *kanji?*"

He covered a smile. "You learned that word from me, didn't you? That's the Japanese word for them. In Korean, they're actually called *hanja.* And in Mandarin, I think they're called *hanzi?* Anyway, the borrowed words usually mean the same thing, mostly look the same, and they can even *sound* the same… which is why I get confused sometimes. I'm sorry I spread my confusion to you too…"

"I don't mind. So Grandpa Zhang could understand your letter?"

"Sort of! Ryo knows some Cantonese because his father does business in Hong Kong, and Namgi knows a lot of Chinese food words from his parents' menu, so they helped me a bit. Lately, I get cards from Grandma Zhang too on all the Chinese holidays."

"So you're still in touch?"

"Yup! We're pen pals! I told Grandpa Zhang that I wanted to be a supportive grandson, but he's a very proud man and doesn't want 'charity,' so I'm 'renting' Noriko—, I mean the boat. One of these days, if I ever get enough time off, I wanna sail her back over there and take the Zhangs out on a little cruise or something."

"Jeez, that filmmaker should follow *you* around."

"Oh, I dunno about that."

Saichi had painted 'NORIKO' on the side of the boat, which he told me was his grandma's name, and he painted over all the Chinese symbols with cute little fish so the Coast Guard wouldn't bother him anymore. I had to ask, "So do you ever actually fish?"

"I always meant to, but I don't know how to work all the rigging. I don't have any fishing poles either." He shrugged and let the waves trouble him for a moment. Then he admitted, "And I'm not sure what I'd do with a fish if I caught one. I think I'd probably let it go again?"

"That's sort of what I thought."

"Which is another reason why Min thinks I'm crazy wasting my money on her. But the way I see it..." He grinned a little rakishly. "You're not planning on letting me take you out to fancy places so..."

"I will gladly forgo all fancy things from now until forever if it means that Grandpa Zhang can take Grandma Zhang out to said fancy places instead."

"And there's where you're a lot nicer than Min, Kit." We laughed at that. He slapped Noriko's metal sides with affection and she clanged like a giant bell in response. "I mean, I still get a boat out of the deal, right? So I'm happy. Plus, I have Chinese grandparents now!"

"*And* Korean grandparents *and* Japanese grandparents. What a cosmopolitan you are, Saichi."

"Sure am. I even hang around with cool ladies from New York." The way I snorted at that wasn't very cool, but whatever. "Um, also, just so you know, I appreciate you... talking about it like it's a good thing that I'm... um, half and half. Before I became an idol, it wasn't so great being... both. Not belonging."

"But it *is* a good thing. You're the best of both worlds."

His eyes lowered. "I'm glad you think that. Most people didn't."

"I'm sorry..."

He shook his head into a sad little smirk. "Wanna know a secret? I actually used different names in each country. Growing up in Japan, I took my grandma's last name: Ayukawa. And then in high school over here, I used the Korean reading of my name to live as Chaeji."

"Ayukawa Saichi. Oh Chaeji." Both were musical, but tragic.

"Our little secret?"

I nodded. "I'm glad you can just be *you* now, Oh Saichi. It's always a good goal to live closer to who you really are. I'll work on that too."

He seemed to see something in my eyes, then he looked around and started sparkling with excitement. "C'mon, Kit! There's something else I wanna show you!"

Tangerine

He towed me along the docks until he found the perfect spot, then he plopped down, yanked his shoes off, and plunged his feet in the water. I laughed uneasily because New York had given me a lot of mistrust for any city river. But then he grinned up at me, murmured, "Highly recommend," and I wasn't about to turn down the invitation when he patted the dock next to him. "This is the best place to watch the sunset. Even better out on Noriko, but I didn't bring her keys."

I hadn't even noticed that the sun was setting. The colors were shocking, and intensifying by the minute, but Saichi was just that distracting. "Looks like we got here just in time for the show."

"Is this normal enough for you?"

"This is way better than normal, Saichi."

The water was icy and ticklish on my ankles and the wind had decided to pester us again, a little more belligerently than before. Saichi noticed when I shivered. He asked very politely, "May I keep you warm?" and then scooted a little closer.

"Um, yes, please, thank you." My eyes caught a smile forming on his lips and I started to curl in closer to his chest… until I realized what I was doing. This was *the Oh Saichi.*

"Why do you keep pulling back?"

"Sorry, I just... Do you mind if I...? May I...?" No, what an awkward thing to ask. May I cuddle you? May I hold your hand? May I lay my head on your shoulder? Not a single one of those was physically possible to say. But he *had* asked if he could keep me warm. Maybe it was fine to be blunt with him?

Like it was effortless, he read my mind. "Always assume my answer will be 'yes' to questions like that," he told me and he tucked me tightly against him. I was paralyzed. The atmosphere suddenly felt different. Was it the tropical filter of the sunset? If I saw us in my coffee shop right now, I might make different assumptions than before. He even squeezed me a little. "See? It's fine. Anything you want to do with me, do it. Anything you want out of me, take it."

"Be careful what you say, Saichi. That's... easy to misinterpret. You wouldn't want me to take those words and run with them."

"That sounds like exactly what I want."

I giggled and my thoughts slipped loose, "This feels like a date." Crap. I sat up to apologize but his arm stayed tight around me.

"So?" I couldn't tell if he was blushing or if it was the sunset on his face, but I knew for sure that my own cheeks had gotten hot. "What if this *was* a date?"

Oh man, I *knew* the atmosphere had changed. Just like that, one vague shift in the air, and boom, I was violating company policy again. Last time I did that, I woke up hungover in bed with two men. I lowered my eyes, but not before I saw rejection register on his face. It wasn't a look I liked on him, and it was worse that I'd put it there.

"You don't want that..." He sighed his arm off of my waist. "Okay. I understand. I'm sorry, I'm always crossing lines with you."

"No, hold on—" Hold on? It just slipped out, because I wanted that arm to stay around me. But no, I couldn't just sit here and enjoy close contact with him without thinking of the implications.

'I like Saichi.' That was what I told Mino, but was that the truth? I was definitely attracted to Saichi, but that was because he was attractive. I liked him, but that was because he was an idol and I was his fan. Did I like him as a person? Also, yes. Okay, but did I like him romantically? If this was a date, I guess I'd be happy...?

And I'd be scared. "I um, I guess I didn't know that was on the table today." He snuck a glance at me. I had the sudden urge to slide forward into the water and just disappear. I shook myself serious. "But also, we're idols."

"So?"

"We're *idols*. We have company policy to follow. And we have a responsibility to our fans." Since meeting Vortex, I had parroted those lines so many times that I felt like I'd been programmed. Maybe I had. I was a product. And if I didn't sell, life as I knew it would be over. So I had to be responsible. Logical. Robotic.

"We won't be idols forever?"

"Don't say that…" I shuddered to think Vortex might ever end. And I shuddered to think of going back to America.

"What if I got permission?"

"From who? The fans? My manager? Yours? Kyungsoon-nim?"

"Whoever you want. Would that make you feel better?"

"It doesn't change that we belong to our fans. No matter how careful we are, eventually they'll find out and they'll be hurt."

He huffed. "If you belong to your fans and I belong to mine, then we belong to each other anyway. And besides, our fans want us to be happy, don't they?" His lip was sticking out, but this time I didn't poke it back in. "If I weren't an idol, would you date me then?"

That was a dangerous road to go down. I couldn't swallow. "Saichi, if you weren't an idol, I'd still be living thousands of miles away right now, and I wouldn't even know that you exist. We're from different worlds…"

"You're avoiding the question. I mean if I sat here beside you as a regular person, just me, and you were just you, would you mind being my girlfriend? Do you like me that way?"

I was honest, "I don't know." But probably yes.

"Did you like it when we kissed?"

Oh god. I had to cover my face before I spoke. "I know this sounds really terrible, but I don't actually remember it all that well."

"*Oh.*"

Nervous, I peeked through my fingers.

Half ablaze with color, half bathed in shadow, he looked like an eclipse of the sun. I stopped believing he was real until I reached out and felt his hair. Even silver silk could gleam gold.

"Kit, do you maybe want a reminder?"

More than a want. More of a need. "Maybe."

The touch of his lips brought the orange glitter in off the water and told me exactly where my heart was. A shroud of fog burned off for just a flash of memory, but I didn't care about that anymore. I had this. I had now. I had him again, and somehow he meant even more now than he ever had before.

When he pulled back, I was confused. Because his lips naturally fit with mine and they weren't supposed to be apart. I left my eyes closed. I didn't want to come back. I preferred the tangerine world behind my eyelids where we had kissed.

"Did that help? Do you remember?"

"No. Maybe if you do that a little more—" He snuffled a laugh and bumped his shoulder into mine. I only opened my eyes because I missed his face. The air around him glowed like iced tea in the sun.

"So you liked it?"

I nodded. It was difficult to keep my fingers away from my lips. They felt different now. There was no taking back the realization that without his lips, mine were only half of what they were meant to be. I'd felt the same way about my voice after singing with him.

"Then I'll kiss you again on our next date."

I bumped him back. "You're getting ahead of yourself."

"Or maybe you're a little bit behind?"

That surprised a laugh out of me. "Maybe. Sorry I'm slow."

"I'm just kidding." He put a warm hand over mine and suddenly my hand felt like a half too. This wasn't fair. I was losing everything to him. As the sunset reached its final encore, his eyes went molten. "I'm not going anywhere, Kit. I'm waiting right here. And if you get to where I am, we can move forward together as slowly or quickly as you want. You set the pace. Okay?"

I nodded again. He smiled and the sun melted into the water, leaving only fiery banners painted across the sky.

Mocha

—What are you up to today?

           *—just finishing morning dance practice ^^*

—Me too!

—I have a little time before my next job. Can I see you? (ᴵ◡ᴵ)♡

           —yeah! I'll head to the vending machines afterward

           —to "get a drink" lol meet you there?

—Sounds like a second date to me~♪

        —♡♡

I was passing one of the larger dance studios on my way there and raucous shouts and laughter netted me into taking a peek, mainly because I recognized Namgi's maniacal cackle outpacing every other sound. Inside, Vortex was wrapping up a DigitAlive rehearsal with a troop of backup dancers. Being an 'elite' now and frequenting headquarters really had its perks. Just catching this glimpse meant the world to me.

"Ryooo, c'mon. Come with me. Pretty please?" I flinched. Mino's whining was close, right by the doorway. "They're gonna bother me. You're big and muscly. Tell 'em to fuck off."

"*You* fuck off, Mino. Leave me alone! Go ask your boyfriend!"

"He's not my boyfriend, dumbass. He's Kit's. And he says he's gotta go somewhere, so I need you to—"

"Hold up. *What?*"

And that was my cue to run.

I knew I couldn't hide it from Ryo forever, but that really wasn't the way I wanted him to find out. Although, maybe if we were discreet about it, he wouldn't care after all? It was only the hashtag that pissed him off, right? So we just had to make sure we didn't get caught, which was obviously our plan anyway. I was a lot more scared of the dating ban than I was of Ryo.

I'd always intended to wholeheartedly obey that ban, but the way things were going, I was definitely trying to have my cake and eat it too. I either had to stop seeing Saichi like this or accept that I was dating him and breaking the rule. Plus, Jaeyoon told me I needed to be clear with Saichi about my feelings, and yet our little talk on the dock had definitely ended on a wishy-washy note. Did a kiss count as a confession?

Saichi poked his head around the corner and I burst into giggles. His hair was pushed up in a sweatband and rehearsal was still fresh on his face. I held my hands out to him because it felt like the right way to greet such a cute man, and because I missed his touch. To my gratification, he shuffled right up and squeezed my fingers.

"I'm supposed to be showering," he admitted. "Do I stink?"

I stifled another laugh. "No?"

"Promise?" It was no wonder I'd picked up that word from him. He used it a lot. I leaned in to sniff his shirt. He squirmed and giggled something about tickles.

"Yup! Promise! You smell like you always do."

"What do I always smell like?"

"A beach, I think. Or maybe just wind. And oil paint?" That made him giggle more. I pulled some wipes from my bag. "Here, I don't want your makeup artist to yell at you."

"Thanks." We took little cat baths together and then he waved excitedly at the machines. "Want a drink? My treat! I can buy you a coffee? That was on our list, right? Of normal people things?"

We both froze at the sound of yelling in the men's locker room.

"What the heck is that?"

I mapped out an escape to my own locker room a little farther down the hall, and I didn't realize how tense I'd gotten until Saichi's hand patted my shoulder.

"Don't worry about it. The guys always get a bit rowdy in the showers. What would you like?" He slid a few coins into my hand and nodded toward the machines.

"Hmm, what's *your* favorite, Saichi?"

His finger found an empty slot for a canned mocha. "That one, but I drank the last one last month. They never restock this thing."

"I've got an idea then." Two cans tumbled out of the machine—black coffee and hot chocolate. I pressed the hot chocolate into his hands. "We can make our own mocha."

His mouth made an 'oh' as adorable as his name. "I forgot you worked at a coffee shop! You know the ingredients! Next time we hang out, can we go to a real coffee shop? And then you can tell me what all that Italian is on the menu?"

"Of course! Cheers to that!" I expected canned coffee to be unbearable, but it wasn't terrible. I held it out to him so we could switch, but there was this funny grin working its way across his face. He didn't take the can. His fingers pushed into my hair instead.

"I've got an idea too, Kit." I caught his drift but couldn't quite believe it. Our mouths moved together like magnets. His tongue tasted like chocolate and I swear sparklers went off in my veins. Mouth mochas. Who knew?

He always pulled away too soon, and inevitably I was standing there with my eyes glued shut to make the moment longer. Maybe if I stood really still and waited really patiently, he'd kiss me again?

"*That.*" His whisper tickled my face. "Was the best mocha I've ever had. If we make it that way, is it French instead of Italian?"

Dad joke. I had to laugh. "Definitely neither."

"Let's claim it for our own country then."

"Korea?"

"Mhm. The Korean Kitchi Mocha."

Him using our couple name definitely just made me ship us. Which maybe should've been a given because I was kissing him. Dammit, we were kissing again and I still hadn't—

My chin tipped back at the request of his fingers and I felt him kiss away a runaway drop escaping along my jaw. I would've given anything for him to continue that thought, but his touch disappeared. When I opened my eyes, he'd stepped back and he looked a little gray.

"Min…"

What?

"*Min*, you're gonna catch a cold! You're soaking wet!"

Mino stood at the mouth of the hall. His clothes were patterned with water stains and his hair had dimmed into dripping jewel tones. When he came closer, there was a strange wintery bleakness in his eyes. His face had none of its vibrancy, its expressiveness. He looked like carved marble, but only if stone could shiver. "Don't mind me," he muttered. "Just getting something hot to drink." I held out my coffee. His fingers were ice on mine.

"Mino, are you okay? What happened to you?"

"Nothing. Got in a little tussle in the showers." He jerked away from Saichi's outstretched hand. "It's fine. Fuck off."

Tussle? As in a fight? Was that common in the men's locker room? In the *showers?* Was that what Saichi meant by rowdy? I turned to him in disbelief. He was thunderstruck. So no, not common, right?

Mino shuddered the coffee down his throat and then turned to leave. I'd never seen him look so severe. It didn't suit him. His back told us, "Glad you two… got things figured out. See ya in a bit, Satch. Go shower. You stink."

Neither of us could move.

"Saichi, what was that all about?"

He shook his head. "No idea. Something was very off."

"He was limping. Do you think he's hurt?"

"He better not be hurt." A shadow passed through his eyes and his knuckles crackled. "A bunch of kids have been following him around lately. Our backup dancers were bothering him today too. Maybe he finally snapped."

That fit with what I'd overheard him saying to Ryo. Why didn't Ryo just go with him to the locker room? Then maybe there wouldn't have been a fight!

"I should go after him."

"Yeah. Go. Talk to him."

His eyes returned to me and his face honeyed over. "Sorry to interrupt our date, Kit." I smiled and gave him a push.

"It couldn't have gone on much longer anyway." I glanced down to find the hot chocolate back in my hands. The heat of it provided a stark contrast for how cold Mino's fingers had been.

"Finish that for me, okay? See you on a third date soon maybe? Hopefully?" My face steamed over, partially with frustration at myself because I still hadn't made anything clear, but I let myself nod.

—hope the rest of your day went well
—is Mino okay?
—I'm not sure. He was really mad and wouldn't talk about it…
—Jaeyoon told me to let you know he's presenting our duet tomorrow.
—oh!
—He had Ilsung-shi work the meeting into your schedule.
—okay! are you going to be there?
—I wouldn't miss it.
—Sweet dreams, Kit~

Red light.

The conference room was full of debating suits that looked at me like I was made of plastic and talked about me like I wasn't there at all. A few other KJ talents sat muttering nearby in a cluster of lounge chairs. One kept sneaking disparaging looks at me.

But where the heck were the people that mattered? I could understand Vortex arriving fashionably late, but it was out of character for Ilsung. He'd taught me that ten minutes early was five minutes late, especially for a meeting this important.

The door swung open. I prayed for a familiar face, and it *was* familiar, but it was Ryo's face... a poker face rapidly turning overcast. Definitely not an improvement for the room's atmosphere. But he didn't bother to come in. He stabbed a finger at me and then pointed to his feet. 'Come,' he mouthed.

What was I, a dog to him? Was that how they beckoned people in Japan? No way. I'd never seen Saichi do anything like that. Because it was just plain rude and Saichi would never be rude.

'Now.' He went from overcast to stormy in seconds. But did we really have to do this 'now' of all times? Did I have to get the Ryo scolding I'd been dreading right before arguably the most important meeting of my career?

All eyes followed me as far as they could, but they could only protect me so long. As soon as I was out of sight, Ryo seized my wrist and dragged me into another conference room. For one dumb second, I thought I'd gone to the wrong meeting and Ryo was actually helping me out, but then the room turned out to be empty and the door banged shut behind me.

"You've got a lot of nerve putting together this collaboration after I specifically told you to fuck off. And what the hell's all this bullshit I hear about you being Hyung's girlfriend? What part of no more Kitchi did you not fucking get?!"

I was floored. I had no words. I knew he was gonna be mad, but did he have to be so violent about it? "Um, I beg your pardon?"

"What? Do you need me to say it in fucking English? Still haven't bothered to learn Korean, huh?"

"No, I—"

"I said, *fuck you!* Stay the living fuck away from Hyung, do you hear me? He doesn't need some foreign bitch nipping at his heels everywhere he goes. Unless you *want* to ruin his reputation?!"

He wasn't going to listen, so I reached up and put my hand over his mouth, and he was so shocked that it actually worked for a second. "Excuse me, but what is your problem? I am sorry about DigitAlive, but it didn't actually end up being that bad on Twitter. Our publicists worked really hard to alter the narrative—"

I lost my words and my grip because he had my wrist again, an uncomfortably familiar sensation. I tried to back away, but my body hit the door and three memories overlapped. Saichi in the karaoke room, Mino in my dressing room, and Ryo... holding my hands over my head? His eyes looked like they could burn right through mine. But thank god he didn't pin me this time. Instead, he tossed my wrist away like garbage.

"Oh, so you think there are no consequences for your behavior? You're wrong. Cancel this collaboration or I'm leaking the picture."

My voice came out faint, "What picture? I don't remember—"

"Are you fucking kidding me? Jesus Christ, who blacks out anymore? How fucking drunk were you?"

"Your mouth is worse than Mino's."

"*Shi*. Mino-*shi*, you disrespectful—"

Déjà vu. Dizzying déjà vu swept in on that cinnamon smell.

"No," I told him firmly. "I call him Mino because we're friends. Now what's this picture you keep talking about? Refresh my memory, please." It was coming back to me. But if he really had that picture, why hadn't he leaked it already? Had he lost it? Was he bluffing?

Rolling his eyes, he yanked his phone out, scrolled a bit, then held it out. Right away, I tried to snatch it from him, but his grip was white-knuckle tight and he snarled at me. "How dumb do you think I am? Hands off."

Ah. Yup, the picture was familiar. I'd seen it before. It was worse than I remembered though. Dammit, how *did* I forget something like that? My brain could remember medaka and Pac-Man and a sequined harem but it couldn't remember this jerk biting my neck and blackmailing me?! Did I repress it or something?

"I can't believe you *bit* me. Do you know how hard that was to hide? I had to wear concealer there for a week! And I was terrified because I didn't know who or what did that to me!"

"Maybe don't be such a sloppy drunk then."

"Why did you bite me?"

"To end your career."

"Why am I still here then?"

"Because I woke up the next morning and decided to be nice. Thought maybe you'd learn your lesson and fuck off. How was I supposed to know you'd sink this fucking low? Either call off the collaboration or consider yourself totally fucked. And stop spreading bullshit rumors that you're dating Hyung. It's pathetic, even for you."

It was a struggle not to shake with anger, but I needed to keep my composure. He'd think I was shaking out of fear, and I wasn't about to give him that satisfaction. "I *am* dating him." Little white lie. We'd been on two sort of dates, and I was still quibbling with myself over making things official, but Ryo didn't need to know that. It wasn't his freaking business.

"Shut the fuck up. You are not."

"How about you ask *him?*"

"You bet your ass I will! He's got more self-respect than to fuck around with someone like you. And unlike you, he knows better than to violate his contract—"

"You're insulting his decisions now and I don't appreciate it."

"How *noble* of his fake girlfriend. Good luck selling that narrative after I plaster this picture all over the internet."

"You really wanna publicize evidence of you attacking me?"

"We both know the world won't take it that way. The internet will crucify you. You'll never be able to show your face in public again. Or you can march into that meeting and shut this stupid-ass idea down. Come on, Miss Perfect. Be a good girl for me."

"For your information, this collaboration was *Saichi's* idea and Jaeyoon organized it, so don't you dare call it stupid." I left off the honorifics just to piss him off. "You're the one being stupid. Media exposure isn't a pie. Collaborating doesn't mean any less of a slice for Vortex. It's mutually beneficial. I'm surprised you don't know that."

"Mutual, my ass. You're the only one who will benefit, leech."

"What is your problem with me?! What did I ever do to you?"

"This discussion is over."

He pushed me out of the way and slammed the door behind him again. Outside, I heard Namgi wail, "Ryo-chan, there you are! Coming to the meeting? Wanna go get a snack instead?"

The feeling in my stomach was bringing back more unwanted memories, only this time I didn't have a bucket handy to throw up into. Nor did I have time to cry. The meeting was about to start.

"Stop trying to weasel out of it, Babo. Let's get inside." Mino was out there too. What if I told him that Ryo was the mystery biter all this time? How would Ryo like that?

"I heard it wasn't mandatory. I don't wannaaa."

"C'mon, Nam-ah." Ryo's voice completely sugared over for Namgi, and it made me so mad that the tears boiled right off my face. Did Namgi have any clue what a jerk Ryo was? The guy wanted to end my career just because he could. And like hell was I gonna wait quietly in here when I had the chance to humiliate him right now.

I threw the door open. All three were shocked.

Then Mino frowned. "Ryo, didn't you just come outta there?"

I wanted to scream, but more people were coming down the hall. So I stuck a finger in his face and growled, "Screw you, Ryo," and then I stormed past.

He hissed after me, "*Shi!*" and I swear I could've turned around and punched him, but instead, I walked into that meeting ready to stand at the front of the room and announce to them all that Kasugai Ryo had assaulted me and was trying to blackmail me.

But then I saw Ilsung. And Saichi. They were chatting with sunny looks on their faces and an open seat was waiting for me between them. Ilsung was the closest thing I'd ever had to a father. Saichi was what got me out of bed in the morning. If the two of them saw that picture, they'd be crushed. I couldn't do that to them. I wished I could just tell Saichi what was going on, but I'd be asking him to believe me over someone he'd known and trusted for years. Vortex's group harmony would be at stake.

I couldn't do it.

That said, I absolutely would not dump Saichi just to placate Ryo. Maybe he could manipulate my career, but not my love life.

Jaeyoon waved to me from the head of the table. My heart sank because he was going to be so disappointed. I started toward him, trying to find the words to apologize, to beg him not to present the recording… but before I could get far, Ilsung spotted me.

"Kit! Come sit! Where were you? Ten minutes early—"

"Is five minutes late." I tried to smile. "I know. I'm sorry to worry you, Ilsung-shi." He smiled and patted me into my seat, then scurried over to flutter around one of Vortex's managers.

"Hi." Saichi's knee nudged mine. His eyes caught what even Ilsung had missed and turned his voice velvet. "Is everything alright?"

"Well—"

The door bumped open and the remaining three Vortex members filed into a brief hush. I locked eyes with Ryo and he scowled. Asshole. Beside him, Mino's eyes sought out the empty seat next to Saichi, but no expression registered, not even when we called out to him and tried to wave him over. His face was solid cold marble again as he took a seat across the table instead.

"Saichi," I whispered. "What was that? Did you two fight?"

"No, but he's been avoiding me and acting weird ever since that day at the vending machines. He won't even talk to me."

"Does it have anything to do with the locker room fight?"

"But that wasn't *my* fault…"

"Yeah, you're right. Did anything else happen that day?"

"No? We went on the news that morning and he was hugging me and hanging off me and stuff, just like always. And he was normal during rehearsal too. But now he won't talk to me, won't sit by me… Kit, um, do you think he's pouting because we're dating?"

"What? Why?" Pouting over us? If that was true, then he wasn't the only one. Ryo wouldn't stop glaring at me across the table.

"So you don't think that Min might maybe…? You know…?"

"Hmm?"

"Never mind. Min's just weird."

"Know who else is weird? *Ryo.*"

"Oh? Yeah, sometimes, I guess."

What could I possibly say to everyone to convince them all that this collaboration was no longer a good idea? Or was there something I could do to fight Ryo on this? "Saichi, do you think—"

The door flung itself open and an arresting voice curled like smoke over the top of the room. "I am short on time."

The suits froze, terrorized. Ilsung was the first to break the spell. He came zipping to his seat in a panic, and then Lee Kyungsoon glided into the room on pointed heels. No way. This nightmare of a meeting just somehow got worse? My role model was here for this doomed presentation and I was going to be the one to waste her time.

"Am I understood? Let's get straight to business."

There was a general murmur of assent. Ilsung hissed, "Since when does the president come to exploratory meetings? My bad, Kit, I guess I should've known anything with Vortex would involve her."

"So this collaboration really is a big deal…"

"Shh!"

She patted my head as she went by with a "Hello pet," and a teasing tail of jasmine followed her. I flustered straight in my seat and found myself facing Mino.

The venom on his face was so chilling that my hair stood on end. For a moment, I was sure he wanted to murder me. But he wasn't looking at me, thank god. He was looking at Kyungsoon? Why though? I remembered Mino calling her 'head witch' but jeez, what the hell did she ever do to him to deserve such a filthy look? That lethal of hatred was all the more obscene on his babyface.

She addressed the room, "To be frank, my mind is already made up on this matter. However, just for the sake of it, let's hear this song, Jaeyoon. I've been listening to your team rant about it all week and I've quite had it with the hysteria."

"Certainly." Jaeyoon bowed briskly, and then he somehow managed to make even the simple operation of a remote control look graceful. He had a bit of a smug smile on and I thought about what he'd said in the elevator, how this was all for appearance's sake. Kyungsoon had almost just admitted the same. *'What I want will be,'* Jaeyoon repeated in my head. Then to heck with this charade of a meeting. Ultimately, I just had to survive the presentation and then privately persuade Jaeyoon afterward that I was too shy to go forward with the project.

But would Ryo be willing to wait that long? I found him the focus of Namgi's fun across the table. Bless that man, who with little to no regard for his own safety was attempting to poke the scowl off of Ryo's face. It wasn't going anywhere. His glare dragged my eyes in and I witnessed consequences already in motion there.

The strategic phone lay dark and still on the table, but the message it sent was loud and clear. It was a loaded gun within reach and he drummed ready trigger fingers beside it.

The song began to play over the room's speakers. To borrow some of Ryo's eloquence, I considered myself totally fucked.

Yellow light.

A year ago, when I originally recorded the song, I was still in that nervy, overenthusiastic, fledgling phase. I was new to the country, new to the industry, new to the process. I tried to put as much heart into the recording as I had into the writing, but I was tense. Too scared to really lose myself in the music.

But this time around, I had Saichi in the room with me, pushing me deeper, further into the song with every note. The result was a raw, impassioned tangle of emotions that burned in my throat like alcohol, a performance so personal that I felt stripped naked in front of all these people.

I flinched when Saichi's fingers found their way into mine under the table. I'd never been so honest in a song before, so connected to the message, but for him, this was just another day's work. And that was why his performances were always so powerful. He poured everything he had into each and every one of them.

At first glance, he was unaffected, but then I saw it—a faint fret in the back of his eyes, a slight tightness to his mouth. I wanted to ask him, does it ever get easier? Aren't you exhausted? Do you ever run out of pieces of yourself to lay bare? Do you keep any part of your soul for yourself?

'The world sees enough of me. They don't need my art too.'

He kept his art. His boat. And little pieces of his past. But he gave away all of his heart in every single song and that brought tears burning to my eyes when I heard his verse. He sounded so desolate, alone even though I'd been standing right next to him.

I wanted to hold him.

I didn't care about the people around us. Didn't care about the picture Ryo had. Didn't care about my career. I just wanted to hold Saichi and coax that loneliness out of him, quench it somehow…

But dammit, maybe I was delusional. *I* couldn't fake that level of emotion in my voice, but maybe he could. He was a professional, the world's best singer.

I had to calm down or I'd cry in front of everyone. He squeezed my hand, telling me he understood. And with his grip as a distraction, soon the rattling experience was over.

The room was swathed in silence for a few moments too long. What? Did they hate it? Maybe Saichi's part was perfect, but *mine*—

Jaeyoon piped up, "I prepared a presentation on how our joint appearance on Tick Tock Talk broke viewership records for the show, and I collected samples of all the positive press that followed, but I'm not sure any additional argument is necessary for this song. I believe it speaks for itself."

"Or rather it *sings* for itself," Saichi whispered. I tried not to snort. Ilsung giggled because they shared a love for dad jokes.

Kyungsoon smiled as if she'd heard. "Yes, it most certainly does. That will sell. Unmistakably."

Ryo launched to his feet and my stomach turned to lead. "President Kyungsoon-nim, with all due respect, this is not a matter of sales! This is a *crisis*. Vortex's immaculate image is being dragged through the mud left and right at the hand of this woman."

"I think you mean 'young lady,' Ryo-gun," Kyungsoon rectified. "And you needn't voice your opinions here. You've made them known to me on multiple occasions and I resent having to repeat myself. And yet, I remind you once more: it's a boon, not a crisis."

"If I may, I have *evidence*—"

"I repeat yet again, a *boon*. Might I also remind you Kit Allister is, like you, a representative of KJ Global Entertainment? She is your colleague and her success is your success. Just as she is honored to have your name lent to her, you should be grateful that she has lent her name to yours, whether through Twitter trends or talk show appearances or tabloid attention."

"Vortex doesn't need to be lent anything. We're strong enough on our own. This is beneficial only on her end."

"And are you so stingy with your influence?"

"We made it with our own strength. As should she."

Her voice took on a menacing note. "You made it with the strength of KJ Global Entertainment, Ryo-gun. This clearly isn't about Vortex at all. This is a matter of your own arrogance."

"Arrogance?!" Ryo waved an arm at me and I knew it was time for my execution. "Fine then. Shall we ask Kit herself what she thinks of this collaboration?"

"*Shi*," I whispered. "It's Kit-shi to you." All eyes fell on me, Ryo's like razors on my skin. Kyungsoon laughed.

"And why would she object to this masterpiece going public?"

I really had to oppose the wishes of the president just because of Ryo's stupid inexplicable grudge against me? What could I even say? I stood up to give myself some courage. "Perhaps Ryo-shi has a point. I dislike Vortex getting negative exposure because of me. If this collaboration would in any way make Vortex fans uncomfortable, then perhaps I'm unsure… whether it's best to go forward with it."

Kyungsoon looked enormously entertained. I could already tell I'd ruined my chance to shut down the collaboration. I was doomed.

"Thank you for your input, love." She smiled and waved for me to sit back down. "I know you are a fan of this rude young man, so it must be difficult to contradict him, but it's time you accept that you cannot please every human on this planet."

"Yes, ma'am."

"This collaboration is a golden opportunity for you and your brand and it would be deeply unprofessional for you to squander it because of personal interests."

The room went so quiet that I heard Ryo's teeth grit. I could feel his cutting eyes trained on me, just waiting for me to look up, but I didn't need eye contact to know the picture would be sent out the second the meeting was over.

Jaeyoon's voice shocked the silence. "Complacency is the enemy of excellence," he declared, with all the theatrical confidence of a politician. "That's one of my mottos. It's a constant challenge to stay relevant during such fast-changing times, and in such, Vortex must continue to innovate and diversify, or we risk losing our place on top. This is a golden opportunity, not just for Kit-shi, but for Vortex as well—a chance to surprise our fans, to reach new audiences, and to cause a favorable media stir."

Kyungsoon applauded. So did a few suited suck-ups. "And my motto," she announced, "is that there is no bad publicity. Ryo-gun, you are overruled. I grant Jaeyoon full rein over this project and any further collaborations with Kit Allister. Meeting adjourned."

I couldn't breathe. Was there anything I could've said to save myself? I accidentally met Ilsung's eyes and wasn't surprised to see him stunned. "What on earth was that?!" he whispered. "Is it just me or was Ryo-shi trying to start a vendetta against you?"

"It's not just you," Saichi spoke for me, a fight gathering in his voice. "But no worries, Ilsung-shi. The rest of us have our heads on straight and are eager to move forward." I didn't like that tone of voice, and I didn't like to see him glare, not even at Ryo. A frown was as misfitted on his face as murder had been on Mino's.

"I should hope so…" Ilsung shot uneasy eyes at Ryo. Namgi was distracting him again but how long until he picked up his phone and ended my career? "That aside, the song was just outstanding! Congratulations to you both—"

As predicted, Jaeyoon was in charge, and he was the one I had to convince to call it off. But what could possibly persuade him to shelf something he was so proud of? He was pushing his way upstream through the suits, eager to join us and celebrate. There wasn't a shred of resentment on his face for what I'd said, nor any kind of anger directed at Ryo. Just wholehearted excitement. That made it harder.

Saichi tugged on my arm and nodded across the room. Mino was hemmed in by a tightening ring of leering faces. I recognized one bleachy head and realized these were probably the same upstarts that had been annoying him lately. Maybe even the same kids that had fought with him in the locker room? Mino was holding his ground, but his hackles were definitely up. It looked bad. Ryo could wait for a second, couldn't he?

"C'mon, Saichi. Let's go act normal and see if he does the same."

The circle shushed when we approached. It took a nudge but Saichi accepted my challenge and sidled up to Mino. In true Minchi fashion, he ignored every single other person in the room and put on the cutest fluffiest smile just for Mino, spoke in the cutest fluffiest voice only to Mino, "Um, did you like it?"

And what did Mino do? The little bastard smacked Saichi's hand off his arm and snapped, "Gross. What the fuck, Satch? Can you not be all clingy? It's not like we're onstage."

Like, *what?* What a load of absolute bull. They weren't onstage when they mashed faces *under* the stage post-concert?! They weren't onstage when they couldn't keep their hands of each other in their dressing room?! They weren't onstage when they were spooning half-naked in the same bed?! I had all the ammo in the world to call him out, but I didn't have time for this. My career was on the line.

"What the hell's your problem, Mino? He just asked—"

"The duet? It was cute." He turned to the rest of the group with a grimy smirk, jerking a thumb at me. "But just for the record, I tapped that first."

"Wh-what? No?! Saichi—"

The shock on Saichi's face wrenched on my guts. And I guess all the stress shortened my fuse because I accidentally slapped the smirk right off Mino's mouth.

The room iced over and held its breath. And then Kyungsoon lightly cleared her throat. I was startled to see her still lounging at the head of the table, eyes trained on us. A small smile bent her lipstick.

Ohhh god, what did I just do?! How in the hell had I managed to make things even worse?! Kit *Allister!*

"All of you apart from Kit are dismissed. Immediately."

The room drained in perfect silence. I watched helplessly as Saichi shambled out of the room, unable to take his eyes from the floor. Then Ilsung with his jaw hanging loose, and Ryo, the utter jackass, grinning his way out the door. Had he pulled the trigger when I was already dead? Was I double fired?

Mino stood in the doorway, the last to leave and reluctant to close the door. Kyungsoon waved him off but he ignored her, shooting me this strange worried look that I couldn't read. I had to hand it to him. It was really sweet to show any concern for someone who just hit him, but also, I was still mad at him.

The sound of the door shutting was fittingly foreboding. Alone with me now, Kyungsoon coasted across the room and motioned for me to follow. "Join me in my office, Kit dear."

"Yes, ma'am."

Green light.

Her office was three or four times bigger than my apartment, and it was in dramatic motion when we entered—clouds racing between buildings outside, underlings skating through proud errands, and a flurry of paper cascading off her desk.

Kyungsoon clapped at a passing clipboard, pointing to the unfurling mess. "Why has that not been addressed?" I wondered if that was my contract, unworthy of a paperweight, destined for the trash, but she offered me a laugh and melodic English consolation. "Don't pay that any mind. Mino was in here before the meeting, wasting my time with his whining. That boy is really something else. Come. Let's have a seat somewhere more comfortable."

More comfortable? In every movie I'd seen, the CEO used their gargantuan desk to reinforce power dynamics in scenes like these. Kyungsoon, however, led me over to an alcove of white leather chairs near the windows. The view was suitably spectacular to complement walls coated with glinting awards.

Sitting down while I was this stressed out wasn't gonna happen. I also couldn't think of an apology that was formal enough in English, so I sought out Korean instead. "Speaking of Mino-shi, I apologize for such flagrant misconduct while in your company."

"I found it amusing. And I assume he deserved it."

But violence is never the answer? That slap alone should've been enough to get me fired on the spot. Mino was KJ royalty and I'd just committed treason in front of everyone...

She floated down into a seat with the deliberation of a ballet dancer, and at the wave of her hand, a suited young man swooped in with a tray sporting an assortment of teas. "Sit, won't you?"

The china jangled like bells as he arranged it on the glass coffee table and she shot him an exasperated look. Still nothing but smiles for me though. The contrast was unnerving.

"If you see anything you like, help yourself."

"Thank you..." Again, what English could reflect the deference of Korean honorifics? How was I supposed to address her without being rude? "...Madam President? But I—"

"Kyungsoon will do just fine. I like to fancy myself still a young woman like yourself."

"Yes, ma'am." Couldn't we just speak in Korean? Even in English, the thought of calling the president without her title had my brain blaring alarms. I plucked up a sachet of chamomile hoping it might soothe my nerves, but in the meantime, everything I touched clattered. True to brand, I also spilled, but Kyungsoon graciously ignored it. With a brandish of her vermillion nails, she elected for the same tea as me and I felt an interesting camaraderie. Her eyes didn't leave mine as she poured.

"So tell me, Kit. Which one are you dating?"

I sputtered in my tea and burned my upper lip.

"*Which*—?!" I hurried to set down my cup before I could spill again. "I am not dating anyone, K-kyungsoon. I will never violate the KJ Global Entertainment dating ban." Even to my own ears, my English sounded stilted, rusty, and full of lies.

"Oh, enough of that. It's *me*. I wrote that ban. It's total nonsense, and it doesn't apply to any elite who has half a brain. As a top artist, you earn yourself the right to certain freedoms. All I ask is that you exercise good judgment, love. So, now that we've got that out of the way, tell me. Which one?"

I was aghast. Was this a trick? "Truly, I—"

"Don't play coy, Kit. Which one is it? I know I can rule out *Ryo*." Her eyes tried to share the joke with me but I shivered. "Unless the tension between you two is some convoluted ploy to throw us all off, of course. Have you any idea what you've done to offend him?"

I shook my head. Her smile widened.

"Well, then it's almost funny, really, how much he despises you. Would you believe he's been in my office complaining about you since the day you set foot in Korea? And you should have seen the idiotic photo he brought me the other day!"

"A photo?!" *The* photo?

"Yes, the man is just ridiculous sometimes."

That son of a bitch! He was trying to blackmail me with a photo that he already tried and failed to leak?! Unbelievable! I was gonna hunt him down and just *scream* at him—

Kyungsoon seemed to read my face and she smiled and patted my hand. Her lips remained a flawless matte crimson even on her fifth sip of tea. "Love, that photo will never see the light of day."

"It won't?"

"Of course not! I'm invested in you. Why would I let Ryo tarnish your image over some imagined slight?" Maybe because you're *more* invested in Vortex? Your top group? "Don't you worry your pretty head about Ryo. I have my ways to shut him up. I'm a very powerful woman, you know."

"Yes, ma'am."

"And with me backing you, Kit Allister, so are you. So stand up for yourself. Am I clear? I expect there to be no repeat of today's events. Don't let Ryo push you around again. And certainly don't let him near your throat. Use your new-found slapping skills."

"Yes, ma'am."

I couldn't believe my ears. It was that easy? I won without even trying? Kyungsoon was my hero all over again. She'd just sided with *me* over Kasugai Ryo, and just like that, all my worries were over.

"I know it doesn't mean much coming from me, but I am sorry about his behavior. Between you and me, Ryo has a lot on his plate right now and I think it's had some effect on his judgment."

"I can only guess how much stress he's under." I was too giddy to even focus on what she was saying. "Vortex has been especially busy this year and there's the world tour—"

"No, no, it's personal matters. Want me to dish?"

What? "I hardly... I couldn't..."

"Oh, let me gossip." She was offering me dirt on the man who had dirt on me. How could I refuse?

"Yes, ma'am."

"What with your extensive knowledge of our language, I'm sure you know Kasugai Ryo isn't a Korean name, hmm? And what with your extensive knowledge of your beloved Vortex, I'm sure you know that Ryo wasn't born here in Korea."

That all came off strangely condescending, but it *was* common knowledge for any Vortexan, so I droned, "Yes, he was a rap artist in Japan before joined up." I felt like a circus monkey when she clapped.

"Indeed. But he's also from quite a reputable family. His father is a prominent politician, his mother a celebrated professor, and the Kasugai name is old and distinguished in Tokyo, so all eyes were on Ryo as the eldest son. He wasn't raised just to be some rap artist, love. He was *cultivated* to uphold and elevate the esteem of the family."

"They don't approve of what he's doing with his life?"

"No, dear, they're disgusted to see him wasting his education and they're absolutely appalled by his choice of residence. They have rather nationalist views toward Korea, you see, so in their eyes, our Ryo is a disgrace to his family. A complete failure."

Dammit, I didn't wanna feel bad for him! He tried to ruin my life! But of course, once a Vortexan, always a Vortexan. I was still a fan and I was enraged to hear his career insulted. "Ryo is anything but a failure! He's world-famous and extremely talented! Why can't they be supportive of that?"

"Not only are they not supportive, they're also *constantly* getting in the way. Every few weeks, they issue me some kind of ultimatum. Withdraw his visa, fire him, send him home, ad nauseam. A grown man and they just refuse to let him go. Even more pathetic, they have no leverage whatsoever in Korea, so all of their threats are backless anyway." She set down her teacup with a bit more noise than before, a china-on-china gavel, and then her atmosphere changed. "Alright, I dished. Now *you* dish, Kit. Which member are you dating?"

So it was an eye for an eye she was going for. I shook my head and scrounged for more lies, but she was quick to cut off my rambling.

"Love, do you honestly think I don't already know? I've heard it from a good ten different reliable sources, and I've seen the evidence with my own eyes. Now I just want to hear you confirm it."

Well, shit. She knew all along?! Of course she did. Whether I told her or not, I was fired, so out with it, "I'm currently considering a relationship with Saichi."

She applauded again. "That is truly just delightful to hear, Kit! You know, I never took him for the type, but he's shown such remarkable interest in you since that viral video—"

I tried to smile. "Mino has said much the same."

"How predictable of Mino to insert himself in the matter." Again, she exulted in a joke, but this time, she only shared it with herself and my smile got heavy on my cheeks. Then suddenly, she cut off her laugh. Her eyebrows met ever so slightly, a lone line on her porcelain face. "About Mino: you've been associating with him as well, yes?"

I'd never seen her lose even a molecule of her composure before, so it alarmed me. "We're on friendly terms?"

Her eyes narrowed. "Kit, love, really, when I ask you a question, assume I already know the answer. Mino has been making advances on you. Has that stopped recently?"

She was talking about Mino's little foray into my dressing room— an incident she was privy to via that scoundrel trainee with the voice memo. It was semi-comforting to at least understand how she knew, but that made me wonder what else she'd been recording that she knew about Saichi and me as well. There was never anyone around when we talked about us... But at least now the voice memo was out in open air and I could breathe easy. "Now that I'm with Saichi, yes, Mino is leaving us alone."

"Lovely! That's just what I wanted to hear. It would appear my anti-Mino measures are finally starting to take effect." Wait, what?

"Would you believe I've got a whole team of trainees following him around and he still manages to get into trouble? I've even moved him back into the dorms to keep a closer eye on him."

I couldn't bite my tongue any longer. "Um, is everything okay?"

"Oh, all will be well in the long run. He just needs to be taken down a notch or two. And love, I'm quite bored with the subject of him. I'd much rather hear what the devil you mean by 'currently considering' a relationship with Saichi. That's meaningless."

A moment ago, I'd been on top of the world, but now my stomach was burning a hole in itself and the chamomile wasn't helping at all. What the hell was going on with Mino? And why did I have to sit here and talk about my love life with the president of my company? "He's asked me how I feel. I am considering it."

"My information would have me believe that you've been a massive fan of Saichi for years. Given the opportunity, why would you not immediately enter into a relationship with him?"

A jellied paisley of light quivered in my teacup, faster and faster. I couldn't lift my eyes from it. "Because of the dating ban?"

"Oh, *darling*…"

She burst into startling laughter, wiping away nonexistent tears. I had no idea where I stood with the woman. Did she like me? Disdain me? Was I fired? I didn't think so, but all of this could've been some complex scheme to get a confession out of me—

"Listen closely. You must go find him immediately and inform him that you are one hundred percent in. I give you the green light. Really, Kit, how ridiculous. I knew you were well-behaved, but this is just too much."

"I only wanted to uphold the standards of—"

"Hush, hush." I watched as she designed an elegant lady-like version of a facepalm. "Kit. Pet. *Please*. Next time I have you to tea, promise me you won't be leading such a boring existence."

And with that, she stood and shooed me away, but just before the door closed, she fired off one final parting shot, "Love, you should read some of the tabloids. And while you do, bear in mind that fact is supposed to be stranger than fiction, not duller."

Triggered

So, I was on with my day, with the green light to collaborate with Vortex and the green light to date Saichi. And again, I found myself thinking 'never meet your heroes.'

My opinion of Kyungsoon had changed a little. Why did she even bother writing the code of conduct if she didn't care how we conducted ourselves? I had *every line* of company policy memorized, and I'd just spent a year of my life panicking over every little inadvertent mistake, terrified of derailing my career or losing my visa. And yet, now that I was an 'elite,' Kyungsoon was encouraging me to run around like a lawless yahoo for her personal entertainment?

Also, what was this baloney about me being boring? I didn't know any other ex-nurse ex-barista who crossed the planet to become a popstar! I didn't know any other Midwestern bumpkin who could top a music chart! And since I met Vortex, they'd crammed every hour of every day with chaos. I'd been bitten, bullied, blacked out, and in bed with multiple men. My tongue had touched other tongues. I slapped someone. I harmonized with divinity.

If my life was 'boring' right now, then I never, ever wanted to be interesting. And why shame me for keeping out of trouble anyway? What was so bad about being Miss Perfect Goody-Eight-Shoes?

I stopped dead in the middle of the hall… because I barely recognized my own inner voice.

Day one in Korea, Ilsung declared a doomed war on my low self-esteem. It began at the Incheon airport when he commended me for studying my way to Korean proficiency. I shook my head and told him 'no, I just consumed so much Korean media that I absorbed the language by accident.' Then in rehearsal, when he ranted about my dancing, I told him 'no, there are millions of K-Pop fans out there with way better moves.' And every time he lost his mind over my voice in the studio, I told him 'no, I'm not a real singer. I'm just a karaoke copycat.'

But now that Mino was constantly calling me a goody-goody, and Ryo was calling me a parasite, and the president of my agency was calling me duller than fiction…

Now the gloves were off.

> —Saichi, I'm sorry about what happened at the meeting
> —Can we talk about it? Meet in my dressing room?

—Of course, Kit

Sorry, Kit-Kats. Sorry, Vortexans. If Saichi forgave me for being a violent psycho to his best friend, then I was going to be honest with him about my feelings and I was going to ask him out on a real date. And not just because Kyungsoon said I should. Because I wanted to. Because idols were allowed to be human sometimes. Right?

"Kit!"

I jumped so high I felt like I grazed the ceiling. A frantic Ilsung bounded down the hall toward me, eyes wild.

"What was *that* all about?"

"Wh-what?"

"President Kyungsoon! And Mino-shi! Is everything alright? You're not being penalized, are you? Did we keep our jobs?"

For a moment, I couldn't find words. So far, my time among KJ's elites had been tainted with slimy politics, double standards, and corruption. It wasn't the world that Ilsung had prepared me for, because it wasn't the world Ilsung was from. The dear sweet man was KJ's final vestige of propriety and he'd been sheltering me in his gentler reality all this time.

I patted his arm, loving him all the more. "We're still employed."

"Thank goodness! I knew she liked you too much to punish you!"

I bent at the waist deeper than I'd ever had reason to go before. "Ilsung-shi, I'm very sorry that I acted that way in front of everyone. I never want my behavior to reflect poorly on you when you've done so much for me."

"Oh, don't trouble yourself over me. I'm more worried about *you*. This was very out of character! All I can think is that Mino-shi must have said or done something truly awful for you to react that way. Do I need to speak to Vortex management about him?"

"No, he was just being really rude to Saichi-shi and—"

"*Kit…*" The hand on my shoulder was stern. "I would not recommend that you involve yourself in Vortex's intergroup relations. Particularly between those two. I know you have strong feelings for Saichi-shi, but I've heard worrying things about him and Mino-shi."

I couldn't help sighing. "I know. It's no excuse, but I think my nerves were a little frayed from the confrontation with Ryo-shi."

"Of course. That *was* upsetting, wasn't it? But as someone who cares about you, there's one more thing I feel duty-bound to say…"

"Yes, sir?"

"I'm sure this was a one-time incident and I don't mean to beat a dead horse, but in the future, if someone upsets you, let's try not to come to blows, okay? That's not how we treat our fellow idols, nor our fellow human beings."

"You're absolutely right, Ilsung-shi. I'm just lucky I wasn't fired."

He let out a little laugh. "You *are* lucky. Of all things, to hit a Vortex member's face! Lately, you're full of surprises. Anyway, what did the president have to say then?"

"Oddly enough, I think she was trying to… get to know me?"

"*Really.*" His eyebrows disappeared into his bangs, and for a second, I thought he was calling my bluff. But of course, he was just brimming over with enthusiasm, as always. "That is astonishing! She's paying you a lot of special attention, Kit. Between her goodwill and the Vortex collaboration, you're really moving up in the world! We should celebrate—the recording was a big hit *and* we didn't get fired today. How about your favorite hot-pot restaurant? My treat!"

Crap. Saichi could be here any second.

"Um, actually…" Ilsung would never believe I already had plans. "My nerves… from the meeting… my stomach is still a little upset."

"Oh!" He rifled through his bag until he found a rattle of pills. "Here! These worked for you last time! And listen, this weekend might be your last weekend off. I'm *certain* that things are about to take off! So rest up and get ready to work hard, okay?"

"O-okay. Thank you, Ilsung-shi."

The lies left a sour taste on my tongue. He was the one person who was proud of my goody shoes and just wanted the best for me. We worked so hard together to maintain my public image, and here I was sneaking around behind his back putting everything at risk.

'I knew you were well-behaved, but this is too much,' Kyungsoon taunted in my head. Actually, now that I had her permission, maybe I could just tell Ilsung the truth about Saichi and me?

"Now that you mention it, you don't look so good, Kit. Do you want me to take you home? I know it's been a very eventful week…"

I swallowed the nausea and lied yet again, "No, don't worry, Ilsung-shi! I'm gonna go dance it off in the rehearsal room! I'm sure I'll feel better in no time and then I'll metro home!"

"Your work ethic is the best in the agency, Kit! You make my job too easy sometimes!"

Ouch. That stung.

Saichi didn't knock, and I didn't hear his footsteps approach. But I was standing right by the door, lightheaded, light on my feet, focusing all my energy on the other side, so I heard him when he sighed outside. I flung the door open before I could falter.

"Saichi, I'm so sorry—"

"I still like you."

The rest of my words tangled in my throat. Saichi had his chin on his chest and wouldn't look up from his fists on the hem of his shirt.

"A lot. I like you a lot. Who you slept with before me doesn't change a thing because of course it doesn't. And Min was very disrespectful to you in mixed company, so I'm not speaking with him and I don't blame you for hitting him either. And that's all."

"I like you too."

His head shot up. But again, words weren't gonna cut it. I threw my arms around him because he looked too small, too unprotected. Together we were just a little sturdier. Together nothing else mattered. A soft note of relief breezed through my hair as so much strain thawed out of his body.

"Also, I absolutely did not sleep with Mino. He kissed me once, and it meant nothing compared to… to when you do it." He broke my hold and I felt a kiss start to whisper into existence and I had to stop him. I felt like somehow Kyungsoon was watching. "Not here. Can we go somewhere together or something? I want to talk more about… us and… things like that."

His eyes lit up. "A third date?"

"Yes, please. And a fourth and a fifth and sixth, but let's start with a third. What's your ideal date, Saichi?"

The wheels in his head turned a moment, churned out a small smile at what I'd implied, and then he answered, "An outing with Noriko… but not today. See? A cat must've licked its face last night."

I looked to the window. Rain drizzled in crystal veins down the pane, webbing off the cityscape outside. What a strange bit of reprieve. Seoul's clouds were washing down KJ's headquarters, and maybe just for today, maybe just while it was raining, my mind could clean itself of all the caustic disquiet and relax with Saichi.

"Don't you love a city in the rain?" He spoke softly, much closer again. "It takes away some of the abrasiveness. Softens the edges, dulls the noise, slows people down…" I turned to read those words in his eyes but he flushed and cut himself off.

"That's lovely, Saichi…"

"I'll tell Min to write a song about it. Or maybe *you* should."

It was my turn to flush. "I'm no Kim Mino, but I can try."

"I'll look for it on your next album then."

"Oh, um, no, sorry, I don't really get to pick my album tracklists... or write the songs, for that matter. My pitches usually get shot down."

"What? Why? All your best songs are *your* songs!"

"My producers prefer songs about love, hope, happy endings... The stuff I write is too dark and dreary to be on-brand with InstaKit. They'll all definitely tease me if I come in with a rain song because I'm supposedly such a downer."

He glared at the door of my dressing room like maybe one of my team members might come through it, or maybe he was considering going out to find them. And he spoke up louder, like they could hear him, "Your songs aren't dreary! They're real. And they make me feel better about being real."

Wow. "Can I quote you on that?"

"Yes, you can." I poked his pout back in, but it refused to be tamed. "Tell them that I said to shut up and cut you loose. No one ever tells *Min* what to write. How come they're ordering *you* around?"

"I don't know, because I'm a foreigner? And a rookie? And a girl? And they don't want me to mess up KJ's perfect little InstaKit. A lot of time and money goes into manufacturing my image, you know."

"I don't like the Instagram Kit," he huffed. "The pictures make me feel further away from you instead of closer. I became a fan because of 'just hold me,' not because of all that nonsense a bunch of strangers post for you."

I shook my head. "InstaKit is who I aspire to be. I'm trying to become more like her, so it won't all be lies. And as for my next album, my head producer gave me a bunch of romance novels to read, so I'm gonna try and write something fluffy and sweet to fit the bill—"

"*No.*"

I jumped a little when he grabbed my hand.

"Write *your* story how *you* see it, Kit."

"Um, okay?"

"Maybe we're supposed to look and act perfect, but our art is how we let our true selves out, and talk about real life and real problems. Real life isn't a fluffy sweet romance. Not every life has a happy ending. Life is pushing through when it's hard and making things work when you can't get what you want. Life is ugly and difficult and painful, and I like it when you're honest about that in your songs. Like I said, it makes me feel better."

"Oh."

"Kit, you're not just some product manufactured by KJ. You're more than that. You're an artist. So protect your art, okay?"

But InstaKit was perfect. She was fashionable and wealthy and had her life together. And Saichi was perfect. Didn't I need to be perfect too to deserve him?

'Idols are perfect and humans aren't.'

What about artists? Saichi taught me what art was with our duet. He stripped away everything protecting us, everything disguising us, and gave the world a window into our naked emotions. He was right. Art was sharing your humanity. Sharing your real life. That was what he wanted me to be. Human, real, not perfect.

For over a year now, I'd lived everybody else's lies without questioning it, and now for the first time, I had permission to be me.

I didn't know what to say except "Thanks for believing in me."

"You're easy to believe in. Besides, I think your fans would love the real you. Look at me. I know you, and I can't get enough of you." He buckled my hands around his neck and our bodies picked up the beat where we'd left off, swaying to echoes that never seemed to fade. I'd hear that song until we sang a new one together.

And with his eyes glowing amber sunlight from under those raincloud bangs, I was losing my resolve not to kiss him. "If we can't go boating, where can we go, Saichi? What do you do on rainy days?"

"Paint," he answered right away. "But that's not a date. Something indoors… We could go see a movie? Is there anything out you've been wanting to see?"

"You tell me. Have you acted in anything lately?"

We both laughed. "Not lately, no. DigitAlive prep is top priority. What do *you* usually do on a rainy day?"

"I just curl up at home," I admitted. "But that's not a date either."

He giggled. "Well, that *is* sort of a date, but it's a little soon for us to do the at-home date thing."

I thought about it, and I could hear Kyungsoon calling me a 'boring existence' and Mino calling me 'goody-eight-shoes' and even my own brain insisting I was doomed to die alone in Ohio.

Dammit. Fine.

"No," I said firmly. "Let's do it." He was astounded. Ah, because that sounded a little questionable. Oops. I revised, "We're both adults. Would you like to come over? Actually, no, can I come over to your place and um, watch you paint? I'd really like to see more of your art, if you don't mind."

His eyes flew wide open. "*Ehh?*"

It'd been so long since I'd heard him do that. The last time was on a variety show. He'd lost a game and had to try standing on his hands as punishment, so he put on a big show of giggly jitters and Mino teased him mercilessly for his Japanese '*ehh.*' Revenge came swift. Saichi tipped into a perfect handstand and chased after Mino on his hands, terrifying Mino into a laughing blue streak.

Ugh. Right. Mino. Think about that later.

"It's okay if you'd rather not?"

"No, no, it's just no one's ever watched me paint before! I don't think it's very interesting…? But, but I'd be glad to have you over…? I mean, I've never actually had people over before but—"

"You haven't? Not even Vortex?"

Him stumbling through words was so cute it pained me. I kinda liked being capable of surprising him. This was a good new personal policy: don't be boring.

"Well, yeah, they used to barge in sometimes, but Ryo's place is the biggest, so we usually meet up there. But, but this is different. You're not Vortex. You're Kit… and this is a date…" He was actually fanning himself. How could he be so cute?!

Oh hell. Oh shit. Oh God. Oh Jesus. What was I *doing?*

Oh *Saichi.* I was going to Oh Saichi's apartment. I, Kit Allister, was going to Vortex's Oh Saichi's apartment.

And who was the driver Saichi found? It was Hyejin, of course. Our eyes met multiple times during the drive and hers were always filled with concerned questions. She'd seen me go from a flighty naïve bundle of nerves to whatever reckless rule-breaker I was now. But how it looked didn't matter. The fans, the policies, every other thing and person in the world didn't matter when it was just the two of us, and I was committed to my new brave life, so I did my best to meet Hyejin's eyes with confidence.

Boring, my foot, Kyungsoon. Would a boring Ohioan church girl be going over to her celebrity boyfriend's apartment? No, she wouldn't. I wasn't her anymore. That girl was gone. So was the depressed college student flunking all her courses, and the no-name barista slogging through twenty-hour workdays split between multiple jobs. There wasn't a single damn thing boring about me anymore. I was Kit Allister, American K-Pop idol, and I was dating Oh Saichi, leader of Vortex.

We probably had a bit more on our plate than a normal couple— two demanding careers, millions of loving but possessive fans, an entire network of bloodthirsty netizens salivating over our every mistake, tabloid journalists and paparazzi constantly circling overhead—but so what? We couldn't date like normal people, because we *weren't* normal people, and that was fine. We'd make it work. We'd find our own way. Our very own not-boring way.

Gallery.

All of the furniture in Saichi's living room was shoved against the walls and the floor was completely canvased over with roll after giant roll of paint-smattered paper.

And every surface I saw was patchworked with Saichi's art.

Pencil, ink, oil, watercolor. Bitten apples, yawning cats, hillside flowers, windy beaches, sailboat sunsets. His coffee table was littered with its own little world of clay beings who all paused their activities when we turned on the lights. Easels stood aloof among cups of brushes and palettes muddy with color. *Color*. Color seeped from every pore of the room and the air tasted alive. I was in a sacred place. It was a place to worship creation.

"Oh, *Saichi*," I breathed, like a prayer. He shuffled up behind me.

"Shit," he whispered.

He stepped into the puzzle of paint and waffled on his feet, moving for the sheet on the couch, then for the stack of canvases, then he looked lost. "Shit, I'm sorry, I haven't really been home a lot lately, and I just, I never have guests, so I guess I forgot this is how I live…? Ahh, I'm sorry, there's nowhere to sit! *Shit*."

"Leave it," I blurted. "Don't mess everything up on my account."

He offered a sheepish smile. "But it's already a mess?"

"No, it's *perfect*." I pointed to the border where paper met hardwood. "May I come in and explore the gallery? Or do I need a ticket?" He laughed at my word choice until he saw I was serious.

"Come on in! If you really want to? I hope the paint's all dry…"

I peeked at his face and saw a mixture of apprehension and excitement, like he was watching a child take its first steps. In a way, he was. How much of this had yet to be seen by another set of eyes? I could feel his gaze follow me as I navigated through the easels, past the ladder, all along the mosaic of work on the walls, around the world of miniatures. I pointed up the wall at a watercolor.

"I know that sunset."

Grinning, he hopped his way over to me. "Yes, you do."

"And that's Tokyo Tower, right? The Eiffel isn't orange…"

"Yeah, no, you're right. I haven't been to Paris yet. Soon though! World tour and all." I was used to feeling a pang of loneliness whenever I thought about Vortex leaving Korea, but now it was almost debilitating. "Ryo still has his old apartment in Tokyo, so we go to visit now and again. This is his neighborhood during the winter. The trees are so covered in lights that the glow is almost a fog, sometimes white, sometimes red, and the hill makes them look like they're hugging Tokyo Tower… Ryo ditched me because I had to sit down right there and draw it."

"It looks *beautiful*." Considering it's where Ryo lives. "I'd love to visit Japan someday. Maybe I'll go when Vortex goes for DigitAlive." Besides the China venues, Japan was the closest appearance they'd make. If I really scrimped and saved, maybe I could make it happen.

I pointed again. "That's the back of Jaeyoon's head. But like, from a year or so ago." There was affection in the painting, the feeling of watching over someone you love. And the angle of his head, just starting to turn, his ear peeking out… it was Jaeyoon right as you called out to him.

Saichi was startled but pleased. "You're *good*."

"No, *you're* good." I reached for the calico curled up in a coil of thick rope. She made several appearances all around the room. "Who's the kitty?"

"I call him Yuji. He started hanging around the marina when I first brought Noriko home, I think because Noriko still kinda stunk of fish back then? But now she's squeaky clean and Yuji's still around, so I like to think we're friends. He even boats with me sometimes."

Now Saichi really was perfect. He had a cat. I was so starved for a cat's affection here in Korea that I once chased after a stray during an outdoor photoshoot and got myself scolded by the staff. They told me to go to a cat café like a normal person, but I'm not a normal person, so the last cats I'd cuddled were back in Ohio resting in peace with my aunt. Spick and Span, the twin tabbies.

"I think he's a she, Saichi. Calicos are usually girls."

He giggled. "Oh. Oops. Maybe I'll call her Yujin instead?"

"I'm sure she doesn't mind either way. Where was she the other day when we were at the marina? I wanna meet her! She's *adorable*."

"You like cats? I always thought you were maybe a dog person. You know, because of Bitna."

"Right. Bitna." I laughed. "She's great. Love her lots, but fun fact: she's not actually mine. She belongs to one of the photographers that I work with for my Instagram."

"You have a fake pet? Your producers are *weird*, Kit."

"Yeah, again, it's all part of the cultivated persona that is InstaKit." I rounded an easel and found a sketch stained with anxiety. I knew those stubby fingers. "Mino's hands," I labeled without thinking. Folded up stiff on a table beneath an uncomfortable conversation. There was a knot in the wood that looked like an eye.

"I like these hands better." Saichi sighed quietly and reached around me to scoot it over on the easel. "They're happier. Right?"

Watercolor. Intimate. Two hands interlaced on a pillow, the sun just starting to creep across. Minchi's hands, no doubt. My heart squirreled around in my chest, because not only did they hold hands in their sleep, but Saichi had felt the need to paint the image? I *couldn't*. To quiet the chest squirrel, I glossed into a new subject. "You said you aren't painting lately. How come?"

His eyes slid away from mine. "Um, I've been staying at Jaeyoon's a lot this year. It gets kinda quiet around here…"

"Oh." Unexpected… "What's the most recent then?"

His eyes flicked back to mine a little too quickly, and he flushed. I knew before he even opened his mouth that he was going to lie. "Most recent? Dunno. Can't keep track." His eyes darted to the far corner and then back. I started to laugh.

"What are you hiding? Or rather, why?"

"I hide nothing."

"Is there something you don't want me to see?"

"*No?*" he scoffed. "I just think that maybe *you* wouldn't want to see it. It's still unfinished, and I haven't done it justice, and, and I—" I was already moving toward the corner. Each of his works seemed like a diary entry. I wanted to know what his latest state of mind was. He hadn't told me expressly *not* to look.

"Oh."

On the other side of the easel was a woman, light streaming from behind her, clinging to her silhouette. She was ablaze, star-studded, a mic in her hand, and she glanced down, blowing a kiss into the shadows below her.

I recognized that outfit. My face stung with heat. I stared at the sharp curving brushstrokes and I could almost feel them on my own skin. *Oh Saichi* painted this. Of *me*.

"You looked right at me," he murmured, much nearer now than I'd realized. "My heart stopped."

"I know the feeling," I whispered. "You sang to me at DigitAlive. My world's been upside down since then. You were so close…"

"So close I almost could've reached out and touched you. Could've, but couldn't." He laughed softly, and suddenly he was close enough to feel. His words brushed my neck, "And now I can. Isn't that amazing?" My body wanted to melt against him, but my nerves tensed up. He noticed. "Sorry. Too fast?"

"Saichi-shi, I—"

He immediately laughed. "I scared a 'Saichi-shi' out of you."

"Sorry. *Saichi*. It's just that being around your artwork… is sort of a constant reminder of who you are… and how much I respect you."

"Stop that. Stop respecting me."

"Vortex's leader, Oh Saichi. Top idol. Main vocalist. Main dancer. Choreographer—"

"Boat owner," he objected. "*Baker*. And I'm not the leader!"

I could see him turning pink so I went on, "Artist. Actor. Model. KJ Global Entertainment's pride and joy. One of Korea's, no, the world's, the *galaxy's* five brightest stars—"

"Donnn't," he moaned and we both burst into laughter.

I turned and put my arms around him. "Mocha drinker. Medaka chaser. Patron of Chinese grandpas. Friend of marina cats."

"That's better. I like those better." He was quiet for a moment and his fingers painted a train of thought up and down my back. I was thoroughly distracted from our conversation by the time he spoke up. "I don't wanna be Vortex's Oh Saichi when we're alone, okay?"

"What?"

"All those big labels are heavy to carry around all the time, and when it's just us, I don't want them to come between us."

"Saichi, I'm sorry if I—"

He pressed a finger to my lips and my heart beat so violently that my whole body shivered. "It's okay. I'm not upset. I'm my own to give away, right? I give myself to KJ, to Korea, to the fans, to Vortex... But sometimes I just want to be yours alone."

Mine alone? I couldn't move. Couldn't breathe. Couldn't blink. My body buzzed for air, then screamed for it, but who had time for breathing when Saichi wanted to be *mine alone?* Vortex's Oh Saichi wanted to be *my* Oh Saichi. His hands caught me when I swayed.

"Hey. You're all white. What's wrong? Kit, breathe..."

I had no oxygen to speak but I tried anyway, "Sorry, but that was a lot for my heart to handle—"

He laughed in relief. "Oh! Sorry! I said some heavy things too, didn't I? I hope I didn't—" A familiar jingle corded through the air and the two of us stilled. His arms slid away. "Maybe it's Ilsung-shi."

"Hm? No, that's not my phone." I couldn't afford that ringtone.

"Oh. Me then?" He frowned and we picked our way over to the small table in the front hall. His phone was there next to my purse. The screen read 'Min.'

Presence

I returned the courtesy. "You can get it."

"Don't wanna." He thumbed 'ignore' and walked away.

"Don't you think you two should talk?"

"No, I think I should cook you some dinner."

The phone started ringing again and Saichi called from the kitchen, "Ignore him for me, would you?" I complied reluctantly. Right away, the screen filled with messages. I tried hard not to read them, but my brain was too slow to ignore my eyes.

—Satchiii wtfff pick upp
—listen I was kidding I didn't fuck Goody8 okay?
—Dinner at Jae's? let's make him cook us some Italy food

Saichi reappeared with a mug of tea for me. He pulled on a weak smile when he saw the texts. "No surprises there. He never says he's sorry because he never is."

"If you explain why you're upset, maybe he'll apologize?"

"Even if he says the word 'sorry,' he doesn't mean it. And it's annoying that he doesn't even know why I'm upset. I don't care if he slept with you or not. I care that he told all those trainees that he did!"

"The rumors are gonna suck, yes. But also, can we talk about how rude he was to you? First of all, how completely hypocritical of him to call *you* clingy. Second of all, who talks to their best friend like that?"

His smile diluted even more. "Well, he wasn't wrong. I am gross and clingy. But hearing it from him was a first."

"You are *not*. We're gonna have a talk with that little—" For a moment, I thought I was being censored by a higher power, but it was just the oven summoning us to the kitchen. Saichi lured me into a seat at the table using the steaming mug of tea as bait. Ordered not to move, I sipped at earthy green tea and watched him dance around the kitchen, chopping vegetables, clattering pans, dripping oils, spraying spices. He made cooking into choreography.

"So it would be a big deal if he said sorry and meant it?"

"Let's not talk about him anymore, Kit. I'm yours alone right now, remember? Now tell me funny stories while I cook."

"Not more corn stories!"

"Ah! Corn!" His spatula spasmed in excitement. "Can you get my bag from the front hall? There's something I want you to see!"

I was crossing the living room when the sun found a window between the rainclouds and the horizon. It soaked the room in orange, repainting every canvas, and I basked in my new favorite color— Saichi's kiss. But there was always something tragic about the lurid display of a sunset, like the sun was flavoring the air with its desperation as Earth turned her face away.

"Kit?"

"Got it!" Saichi's phone buzzed when I picked up the bag and dammit, I accidentally read the screen again. Such an ingrained habit.

—look outside there's a rainbow

Tucked away from the sunset, gray clouds outside the kitchen window glowed like raging coals, but as promised, a faint ribbon endured the inferno. Saichi's voice came soft and fond over my shoulder, "Rainbows are so hopeful, don't you think?"

"I'm thinking the city rain song should end with a rainbow."

"Yes, that'd be perfect." The rainbow bleached away and our eyes landed on the bag I'd retrieved. "So, there's a piece in my sketchbook that I want your approval on." Intriguing…

I found the well-loved sketchbook tucked in among a neat array of art supplies. Like the rest of his work, it felt personal, like a diary. I was nervous to even touch it, let alone flip through the pages, but Saichi only laughed at my apprehension.

The first page was Mino.

Even in graphite, his clear, straight gaze made me shy away. And even in graphite, he had more life than the marble Mino that came to the meeting earlier. I waited for the annoyance to come, but it was next to impossible to stay angry at this smile. It had none of that teasing, impish filter I was used to, none of the felinity. This was the unadulterated, uncomplicated smile he showed only to Saichi when he thought the world wasn't looking. Whatever was going on with him, I hoped he'd get this smile back soon.

"I know it's just because it's a pencil sketch, but still, I've never seen Mino with black hair before. It surprised me."

Saichi looked up in surprise, then he too seemed to soften at the image. "He had black hair when we met. When debut came around, we couldn't decide between pink and blue for him, and we always tie at rock-paper-scissors, so…" He sighed. "Anyway, keep going. You'll know it when you see it!"

Namgi and Ryo rehearsing together—hair spiked up in all directions, shirts like sweat atlases, oversized laughter on their faces.

Then a grid of stage lights with their gazes knocked into disarray, searching everywhere but forward. Beams slicing gloom with razor precision, hot through the paper.

Jaeyoon intent over a table scribbling notes, teeth sunk into a pillowy lip, rings in jagged detail. A touchable sweep of two-tone hair cupped sculpted cheeks like a curling barcode.

The view out a window barred by blinds, scarred by a bough stretching bony fingers through the air. I could see their movement in the wind, and hear two pearly sparrows telling stories.

Namgi flat on his back lathered with a roly-poly tussle of pompon puppies, one aloft in his hands wriggling. Saichi absorbed the euphoria in the moment, pushed it through his pencil, and now I got to feel it burbling up out of my stomach.

And then I found it—the entrance to a corn maze. I burst into much louder laughter. "This is the last thing I expected to find in here! What the heck? When did you find time to go explore Ohio?"

"I only explored in spirit... via Instagram hashtags. Have you ever made one of those pumpkin faces? Is it hard?"

"Yup, we do that for Halloween! It's hard work! The inside is really slimy, but it's full of big seeds you can roast in the oven. With a little salt or cinnamon sugar, they're *delicious*."

"That settles it then! We're gonna cook pumpkin together this fall! The pumpkins around here, the green ones? *Kabocha?* They're too small and tough to cut shapes into, but I can simmer them all soft and yummy and you can roast the seeds for me!"

"Sounds like a plan!" I had holiday plans. It'd been a long time since I shared any kind of tradition with someone. My eyes returned to the sketch and I let my fingers stroke over the familiar shapes. "Thanks for showing me this."

It was a portal back to simpler times. Back to bugs on the windowsill, squeaky stairs, a rocking chair on the porch, raindrops slapping the bottom of the bucket by my bed. Clutching at the sun during endless summers and clutching at each other during merciless winters. Always some little predicament that my aunt kept tucked out of sight—the car payment, the medical debt, utility bills, an unfriendly letter, a broken pipe. Until the bitter end, she never did learn to rely on me, but between us and our friendly posse of critters, we found happiness for a while. While she was in my life, she always made sure the future seemed bright.

"Kit?" His eyes were studying me. "Did I make you homesick?"

I dug up a smile. "No, not homesick. Just reminiscent."

"But you look so sad... Is there something sad at home?"

It was a grief I shared with no one, a grief I hid so deep, and yet he'd found it in mere seconds, like I had it painted all over my face. "I just miss my aunt. That's all."

"Your aunt?"

"She raised me."

"Have you been back to visit since you came to Korea?"

"No, she passed on while I was away at college."

"Oh." He set down his spatula in a matter-of-fact way, like it was written in the recipe, and then he bent over the back of my chair and draped warm, heavy arms around my shoulders. "I'm sorry," he whispered into my hair.

Why couldn't my family have done this? Why didn't anyone just hold me like this? Or tell me they were sorry when I lost the most important person in my life? How come none of them knew how to act about death? Did they just not care?

Imposter syndrome made my brief stint in nursing school a dry spell for friendship, so I was already long out of practice with people when my aunt died. Then at the funeral, none of my family would even look me in the eye. Their words were choppy, insincere. All I'd needed was a bit of human warmth, and yet they taught me humans were supposed to shut each other out in difficult situations.

That mindset took forever to fix. I was just starting to open up to the friends that orbited my coffee shop in Brooklyn when I got dragged off to Korea… and then once I got here, Ilsung and I kept 'Kit' in a protective snow globe devoid of human warmth. The most affection I got came from brief snuggle sessions with a dog that wasn't even mine.

But now, everything had changed. Vortex brought my snow globe to a boil and broke me out. Ever since the concert, there was always someone hugging me, tapping my shoulder, holding my hand, kissing me. Human warmth was such a miracle, meant to be shared.

I leaned back into the chair and let Saichi's arms tighten around me, fastening me to Seoul. "Thank you, Saichi. I've always, always wanted to thank you. From the second you debuted."

"Why's that?"

"You were my rainbow. You got me through the rain." I was glad we couldn't see each other's faces. It made it easier to be honest. "That night at Sevens, you were asking about my life before Korea, before KJ… but America stopped being a happy place for me a long time ago. There's really nothing there for me to go back to anymore."

"Your aunt was your home, hm?"

That was exactly it, but I'd never thought of it that way before. "She was. In all senses of the word. When she died, my cousins ripped up the will and sold the house, the land, the animals—"

"What? How could they get away with that?"

"They blamed me for her death."

"*What?*"

"I should've known she was sick. I came home from New York that Christmas between semesters. And she was so happy, so proud of how I was doing in school. She told me I was following in my mom's footsteps, and that my mom was smiling down from heaven. I was her hero, studying to save other people's lives... *Other* people. I totally missed the symptoms of my own aunt right under my nose—" My voice broke under the weight of the words. My voice had never said any of this aloud before. "She sent me back to school with a smile, and then a few weeks later, she was gone. No goodbye. Just gone."

"Oh, Kit..."

"So I dropped out and exiled myself from Ohio."

"You can't blame yourself for what happened. You don't deserve that on your conscience, okay?" His arms laced a little tighter, squeezed the memory away, reminded me I was here now in a new life with him. Thanks to him.

"I was so alone after that, no future, no direction, no hope... and then I heard your voice. That's why I want to thank you, Saichi. Thank you for being you and doing your thing because you pulled me out of a life that wasn't working for me. And I'm sorry that I kept you at a distance at first, but I'm just so scared of getting sent back. All I want is to stay here with you and Vortex and Ilsung..."

I felt him shake his head. "You don't have to be scared anymore. Okay? I promise I won't let you get sent back. You belong here with us now. Seoul is your home now." That was exactly what I needed most to hear. "And Kit? Thank *you.*"

"For what?"

"You were my rainbow too." He turned his lips to my cheek, and then we smelled something burning.

Merlot.

Saichi's home cooking only cooked his home a little bit. Besides that, it was the best meal I'd had since I left Ohio, and a few hours later, we sat spilling wine all over the papered floor, each splash more abstract than the last. I liked wine better than everything I'd tried at Sevens. Every laugh made me feel lighter than air. My joints, my bones, my muscles were all inflatable, carbonated with laughter.

Saichi's eyes were trained on my mouth and he was fighting to look serious, but his body was all wobbly. I could've breathed on him and he would've fallen over. "Why you pouting, Saichi?"

He took his thumb and started wiping my bottom lip, over and over again until I stuck my tongue out and licked him. I got him to giggle, but then he told me begrudgingly, "I never knew I was a jealous person. I don't think it's a good trait."

"What are you jealous about?"

"Min kissed you here… I know how he kisses. It's really, *really* upsetting to think of him doing anything like that to your mouth."

"You don't gotta be jealous. You kissed me first. And the whole time he was kissing me, I was imagining it was you." His eyes blew open and they were such a bright, sticky honey brown that I was transfixed. "Sorry, did I make it worse? Don't think about it too hard. The point is, there's nothing between Mino and me. I promise."

"You *promise*, huh?"

The cute Japanese word made us both laugh more, float more, and then suddenly, I was much closer to him. He was very easy to push down, so I crawled over him and let gravity bring my lips to his. Who said I had to wait for him to kiss me on every date? A sugary sound of surprise caught in his throat, but then his fingers curled in my hair and pulled me closer.

"Mhm, I like *you* and you only."

He turned his head before I could kiss him again. "Wait. Just to make sure. When you say 'like,' are you saying that as a fan or—"

I laughed. "No, fans don't kiss their idols, Saichi."

"They might if you let them."

"Don't worry, I like you yourself as me myself. And I'm done worrying about the dating ban and the fans. Because you're right. This is just between us. And I wanna belong to only you too."

"Can we keep doing this then? Can we keep seeing each other and going on dates and holding hands and being like… this?"

"You want me to keep sitting on you?"

We broke into laughter, but then he touched my cheek and told me semi-seriously, "Yes. Forever. Just keep me right here forever."

"Anything you want," I murmured. "I'm all yours." He flushed as dark as the wine next to his ear. Was that weird to say? It just slipped out. Wine soaked up the worries and made my mouth loose. I tipped back another mouthful just because I could.

"One more time?" he whispered.

I repeated with conviction, "I'm up for anything you want, Saichi. I'm yours as long as you want me."

He cast an arm over his eyes and took a breath so deep that I felt myself rise and fall. "I should not b-be this happy when you're saying sorta p-problematic things. It's not like I, um, wanna *own* you but—"

"I like making you happy. What else can I do to make you happy?"

He peeked out from under his arm. Being adorable was so effortless to him. "It also makes me happy when you kiss me?"

I bent and immediately obliged.

For a moment, I thought the room had flipped but no, we'd rolled.

The woody parch of wine stuck between our tongues. I locked my legs around him, snatched for fistfuls of his shirt, rucking it up his chest. I wanted his skin against mine.

The kiss snapped loudly and Saichi sat back, panting raggedly. My mouth scorched even dryer watching his stomach contort with each breath. I wanted to run my fingers through those divots, bump along the grid, trace those lines angling from his hips, down, down, down… My heart lodged itself into my throat and beat like a speaker. I didn't even hear him at first telling me, "Okay, okay. N-no more, Kit. We can't, we can't."

"Why not?" My voice was unrecognizable.

"We're drunk."

"So? I feel *immortal* right now. Drink some more, Saichi."

I doused my fingers in the wine that hadn't spilled and swiped it across my lips. It started to dribble down my chin, but it didn't make it far. Saichi made a weak, frustrated sound that stirred my stomach, and he kissed the drip away. I think I moaned when his tongue slid across my lips.

Here too. And here. I drew streaks down my neck, across my collarbone, speckled my chest, and he chased after the stains, his nose tickling my ribs, his lips nibbling goosebumps. Every touch went straight down my spine and into an electric pool in my hips. The edges of my mind blurred and my thoughts were satiny and sunbathed when he dragged himself away from me again.

"No. We're drunk. The, um, your inhibitions."

"Huh?"

"You can't… consent."

My heart staggered against my rib cage. Consent. That was a wake-up word. The alcohol seemed to evaporate right out of me.

Church taught me sex was shameful and dirty, a matter of duty alone. Its only purpose was to provide children, and the goal was to keep my uterus pure and clear until I could fulfill that purpose in marriage. Not that I ever paid much attention to the sex sermons. They weren't relevant to me. My aunt and I were ostracized from town, so all my friends were library books and animals. I never bothered with boys…

But I had a boyfriend now, and all of a sudden, sex was an actual possibility. Maybe even expected. I mean, look at me, I sat on him, and I kissed him, and I unbuttoned my shirt, and I got wine all over the place—! At-home date, drunk, half-naked! You knew what this could turn into, Kit Allister, you dumb bumpkin!

"*Kit.*"

So what? None of the stuff I learned as a kid was true. Sex was normal, natural, not shameful at all. There was no such thing as sin, and there was no such thing as virginity either.

But was I supposed to tell him that it was my first time? Or could I just follow his lead and act like I knew what I was doing? There had to be some instincts in there somewhere. Otherwise, humans would be extinct. Right? Instinct right now was telling me to rip the rest of my clothes off but that seemed rash.

"Kit? Please, are you okay?"

"I consent."

He shook his head. "I won't do it. You're drunk."

"So? I feel like I *gotta* be drunk to do this. I consent. Do you?"

He snorted. "That's silly." I frowned.

"No, it's not?"

"But I'm a man…"

"So? You and Mino are both men and that doesn't mean that it's not important for—" His face startled white, and I stopped.

"Um, what about Min…?"

"Well, I was just gonna say that fans wouldn't cheer for Minchi if it wasn't consensual."

"But we're not having sex onstage?"

"No, of course not, but it's *your* body he's touching all the time." His frown was bothering me. For all that talk about giving himself to KJ, to the fans, to Vortex, did he give himself to Minchi too or did Mino just take that from him? "You do consent… to all that, right?"

"Um, Min's never asked. It's just something we do."

"Jeez, maybe he *should* ask, don't you think?"

"I guess he should. Huh." He vanished backward into his brain, suddenly a whole galaxy away.

"Saichi?"

He held out a hand and tugged me to my feet, then started to lead me down the hall. To his *bedroom*. Did he change his mind? The door clicked shut behind us and he pulled me into a lamplit nest of blues. I watched in disbelief as he unbuttoned his jeans and pushed them to the floor. Good *god*, the more I saw of him, the more I wanted him… He took a step toward me and I crashed into the pillows.

"Kit. Look at me."

I felt the bed contort as he crawled over me. I hadn't realized that I'd covered my face. I peeked through my fingers to find his eyes searching for mine, amber in the lamplight. Ensnaring amber.

"Are you okay?"

"Yeah. You're just… gorgeous."

He smiled and the amber flashed. "I've got your attention then?"

"Absolutely. Full attention."

"Just… no more bringing up Min, okay? And don't cheer for Minchi anymore either. Don't cheer for me being with him. If I gotta be jealous, then you should too."

"O-okay?"

"Besides… um, to tell you the truth, if I had any spine at all, then I would've told him to stop a long time ago."

I dropped in free fall right through the bed. Not only did Saichi not consent to Minchi, he also wanted it to stop. *Minchi*. The one and only adorable Minchi. How much of it did he hate? Were they even friends? They had to be! They always seemed so happy together!

"Saichi, y-you don't like Minchi?"

"No, it's not that. It's… complicated. Please let's not talk about it anymore, okay?" His lips pressed briefly to mine, then he pulled back into another relaxed smile. "Maybe just… hold me?"

He whispered my lyrics in my hair as his arms wrapped around me, hummed my melody into our kiss, and soon I could think of nothing but him and the heat between our bodies.

Then he sighed all over my face. "But no sex tonight. We're drunk. And I want our first time to be special. I want you to be sure."

"I *am* sure."

"You might think that right now, but after what happened at SK Suites… I just can't. I don't ever want to wake up to you crying again. Also, I haven't really done this before, so I don't think I should try it for the first time when I'm drunk and—"

"Wait, what?"

I crabbed backward and hammered my skull into the headboard. He was alarmed. "I'm a quick learner, I promise!"

"No, it's okay! I'm just… surprised. It's your first time too?"

"Kit, it's *your* first time too?!"

I ignored that. "But… *how?* You're like, really, um, sexy?"

He sat back and laughed at the ceiling. "I don't mean to be rude, but how hard did you hit your head just now?" I giggled and pushed him over into the pillows. "No, but seriously, you're okay with me being your first? You don't mind…?"

Oh, please, Saichi. *Mind?* "Hmm, you know what? Now that you mention it, I must be crazy! Who the heck wants to have their first time with someone they freaking *love?*"

"*Ehh?!* Are you talking about me? *Love?* Kit, you—"

Aw jeez, crap. I launched myself at him and clapped my hands over his mouth. "Shhh, no, no, I'm drunk! And I have a concussion! We'll talk about that some other time!"

Gently, his fingers circled my wrists and he kissed my palms. "What if I have something I want to say in return?"

"I didn't officially say it yet! We only just started dating! I swear that I don't throw that word around—"

"Why? There's plenty of love in the world. People should throw it around more. It's not like you can ever run out, and it never gets any less powerful or any less important. But if you want that to be special the first time too, I'll wait."

Oh, Saichi. If I loved him, I loved him because he said things like that. I let him curl me into his arms and toss the blankets over our heads. In the dark, I kissed everything I could reach of him, trying to throw love at him. "Love, love, love, *love.*"

He giggled. "Night, Kit. Sweet dreams."

Palette

I dreamed of him onstage. His toes writing calligraphy in ice. Every movement so effortless, like physics just didn't apply to him. He knew no gravity, no strain, no friction. Liquid with edges, fluid into each beat, and then flashing with stillness, frozen until the next snap. And his voice... Prismatic, clear as a midwinter night.

Pale morning filtered through my eyelids and I felt wrapped in sunlight. How satisfying to wake up before any alarm, any call from Ilsung, any sound but the breeze, and to have the luxury of going back to sleep...

Then I smelled warm citrus and oil paint, and I remembered.

His face was so close that I had nowhere else to look, and that was all I ever wanted my world to look like. Memories washed around on his skin, hazy waifs of expressions, echoes of words. I could see him flushed, covering his face. Him laughing over dinner. Him kissing my stomach. Curious, watching me. Holding back.

Was yesterday only one day? Why did alcohol always turn my brain into meaningless soup? I had to stop drinking. It wasn't worth the loss of precious memories. Ugh. I'd told myself that before.

His voice slurred out of him. *"Mmnnn, too early..."*

"Good morning, Saichi." I couldn't believe I got to say those words. There had to be magic in them.

"Morning, Kit." He squeezed my body to his and nuzzled my hair. I was too happy to even breathe. "This is so nice. You're so warm. Can you just live here?"

I buried my face a little deeper in his neck. "Don't tempt me." Then he sat up and that particular spell was broken. But as long as the world kept turning, there would be more magical mornings of waking up next to him. For today, it was on to the next spell.

He smiled down at me, a tawny miracle in the sun. That was a spell in itself. "Want some coffee? I can't make anything fancy but…"

"That sounds wonderful, yes." I tried to get up, but the morning took a power tool to my skull. I'd forgotten the other thing I hated about alcohol.

Saichi grabbed my hand. "Kit?"

"F-fine. I'm fine. Headache."

"Coffee will help, I promise. Cream? Sugar?"

"Just black, thanks."

I stared at the wine stains on the papered floor and listened to frayed strings of thought come ringing back to me. I was proud of myself. Last night, I was brave. Cavalier. I'd known what I wanted, and I went after it, regardless of consequences or shame or sin.

Saichi came to find me, a rumor of coffee following him.

"I wouldn't have regretted it," I told him.

"Huh?"

"If we had slept together, I wouldn't have regretted it. But you were probably right to make sure we didn't do anything while we were drunk, so thank you."

He didn't react. He was frozen, like he'd glitched, so I leaned and kissed him on the cheek. He was my boyfriend now, after all. I could do that now. He sparked back to life and grinned.

"That's good to hear. To be honest, I fully expected you to wake up and punch me this morning."

I laughed. "Why would I do that?"

"Well, I wasn't sure how much the alcohol was affecting you and… um, yesterday seemed kinda too good to be true? You changed your mind so suddenly."

"About that… Kyungsoon-nim told me it's okay if I date you."

He broke into a coughing fit and had to grab my shoulder for balance. "*President* Kyungsoon? The president told you that?"

"Yeah, after the meeting yesterday, she said—"

"You, you actually went and asked for her permission?"

"She sort of brought it up on her own…"

He laughed and shook off the shock. "Wow, you really don't mess around, Kit. I didn't know you were so high up on the food chain."

"I'm not! But yeah, she was fine with it, so I decided to stop being such a coward all the time and just go for it."

"You're not a coward. Nothing scares you."

"Social media backlash scares me. Scandals scare me. Upsetting my fans, disappointing my manager, losing my job, all that scares me. But I'm not going to let that stop me anymore."

"None of that makes you a coward. You're a conscientious professional. And I think you're very strong. You came to Korea all by yourself to chase your dreams. You're amazing, Kit."

"It's not a big deal." It was mortifying to be praised by him of all people. I didn't come here chasing dreams. I came here chasing *him*. "I'm just a crazy fan. I just wanted to be close to you somehow."

He reached out and my face was so hot that his fingers felt cool on my cheek. "Well, here I am. Is this close enough?"

"Almost."

"Don't call my girlfriend crazy. Or a coward," he told me softly.

I could feel the pull of his lips. I wanted to get back the memory of his mouth. I wanted to capture those hazy remnants of last night and bring them to the here and now.

"Hey Kit?"

"Hm?"

"You're completely sober now, right?"

I knew what he was asking me. My heart started to race.

"I consent."

Inch by inch, he freed my skin, printing desperation into it with his lips. It felt like a dance, our bodies moving and bending, fighting to escape our clothes. He drew me into his choreography, built something around us that overpowered hesitation, shyness, innocence.

Then I bumped into his ladder and my back was splattered with cold, slippery wet. I froze, confused, and Saichi laughed as a plastic jar clattered to our feet, slopping paint all over his shirt on the floor… I cringed to feel it still oozing down my back. "Why do I always wreck your clothes? I need to—" His hands slicked a blue shiver up my back and smeared sleeves down his arms. "*Oh.*"

"Who needs clothes? Paint me, Kit."

Could I really? He took my hand and stamped a wing on his chest. The paint made my skin skate over his and a laugh bubbled past his lips as the wing stroked into a stripe. He kissed a daub off my wrist, and then trailed blue kisses up my arm until there was only a shadow of it left on his bottom lip. I tried to thumb it away but he was busy inscribing the curve of my collarbone.

"It's been so long since I last painted…"

He spun and grabbed for more containers, lids popping loudly into the air, and then two chilly fingers swirled purple and red across my chest. I felt flowers bloom in my stomach, and somehow, he found them and he peppered them with little violet butterflies.

Zebra stripes down my arms.

Curling rosettes over my heart.

A galaxy of constellations along my neck.

Coils of white-hot yellow like lit filaments, burning red claw marks, hazy lavender clouds raining merlot. He caught drumbeats in his hands, found the frantic throbbing under my skin, and the world melted into a vibrant vortex around us. Then he held a brush in his teeth and I was breathless under its power. Under *his* power as he feathered torture over the tip of my breast, dripped cerulean ice onto my ribs. My skin sparkled almost painfully like my nerves were reawakening after a stretch of numbness. There was no escape, and nothing left but him. I was hypnotized.

"Saichi…"

When had I made it to the floor?

When did his silver hair go from monochrome to opalescent?

I was covered in a carnal tango of paint. Every part of me churned with color. I looked like a mythical creature, and I felt as powerful as one as I climbed over top of him.

"Hmm?"

"*Love.*"

My thumbs smudged sunshine yellow up his cheekbones and then I bent and pushed into his mouth. He groaned and I could feel the frosty track of paint his hands left as they slid down my back and pulled my hips to his.

Down the hall, Saichi's phone was ringing. How long had it been ringing? Or was it just my ears? I didn't know. I'd lost my mind. Saichi pushed down his boxers and started to slide up inside me.

"Oh!"

He stilled, worried.

The empty room gave sharp edges to our breathing.

But he'd done it again. Shown me how I could be more complete with him. It was tight, but I knew we were two halves meant to fit perfectly together, so I let myself sink. We were connected, closer than we'd ever been. I had Saichi inside me and it was so *powerful*.

"Are you okay?" He pushed my hair back from my face, tugged my lip out of my teeth. I nodded. I wanted more of him. I wanted more of the delicious sound he made when I landed on him. I wanted more of that delirium on his face.

His hands locked around my hips and he rocked my body forward, pulling, pushing. My hands splashed two new prints on his chest and he moaned, "Call my name, Kit."

"*Saichi.*" His name was a battle cry. I didn't care if the whole world heard me. He was glorious and I was an Amazon and I rode him with all the strength he'd painted into my skin. He was lightning inside me and I radiated energy, invincible. "*Saichi!*"

But then I neared the edge, and suddenly just existing was impossible. I fell apart, lost my rhythm and stuttered to a halt.

Saichi moaned and I found his nails digging tracks in the paper. Why wasn't I strong enough to keep going? I couldn't even hold my head up. He caught me when my body started to teeter off of him. Every touch, every movement dragged sounds out of my vocal cords, but I just wanted to cover my mouth and listen again for the sound of that angel voice drenched in sex.

"Saichi. *Saichi.*" For a moment, I forgot all other words.

I barely understood him trying to tell me, "You, you're amazing," and I could barely breathe to tell him, "No, I'm sorry I… I c-can't… keep going… I'm no good at this…" I couldn't even move anymore. Not while he was still inside me. It was all too intense. Too tight. But dammit, I wasn't done yet! And neither was Saichi… I wanted to hear him when we lost control.

I fell forward and clung to him, distracted by the tense landscape of his back. My mythical powers blurred into an intoxicating haze. Then he petted my hair and murmured, "You don't have to top, silly. I think I can manage it."

"I j-just wanted to make you feel good."

"Every little thing you do feels good, Kit."

He rolled me onto my back and the motion zapped through my entire body. Electrified. My thighs buzzed when he pulled them apart. My body was going to buzz for the rest of my life.

My heart picked up, both panicked and also desperate to have him inside me again, but he stayed still for a moment. He just knelt there, looking at my body, and I was too far gone to even care. I felt powerless and weak, but I sort of liked it.

"Promise you're okay?"

"Promise."

Then he struck forward and the shock of it went from my fingertips to my toes. His body lit mine up into something blinding from the inside out. He struck again. Our voices rebounded around us. My head fell back and he nosed my neck, dragged his lips, breath scorching my skin. I grabbed knots of his hair. *Again.*

Then the tempo broke into a chaotic sprint, and the room filled with our sounds, our voices finding harmony again.

If this was all I did for the rest of my life, I'd be happy. I'd just stay here in Saichi's artsy love nest and have sex all day and all night… This was what humans were made to do. I didn't need food, or water, or anything. Just Oh Saichi.

Just Saichi.

His hips wrenched forward one last time and hot paint spilled into me. Every inch of me was his art, inside and out. We were locked together in that one endless moment, and then we crashed to the floor, remembering oxygen, remembering time, remembering limitation.

"Mine," he gasped. His fingers slipped into my hair, pulled my face to his chest. I swallowed, dug for courage. Wrapped my arms around what of him I could reach. And I squeezed.

"Mine," I whispered back.

Not Korea's. Not KJ's. Not Vortex's.

"*Mine.*"

Fresh start.

A lot of perfectly good clothes were drowned in puddles of paint and we both badly needed a shower, but I balked when I caught sight of myself in the mirror. I'm not always on the best terms with my reflection. We greet each other briefly, check in only when necessary, and we usually avoid eye contact. But today, I twisted and turned to see every angle. I was so moved that my voice shook, "Thank you for making me into art, Saichi."

"What are you talking about? You've always been art. Everything you do, everything about you is art." I actually saw his words leave a pink trail across my face.

"Oh, shush." My eyes combed the designs almost violently, trying to commit every inch to memory. The paint gave me power. I just hoped I'd be able to picture this mythical me next time I had to acknowledge a mirror. "I hate that we can't show this to anybody else. I wish I was a sculpture. Then you could put me in a museum like this and the whole world could see what a genius you are."

He burst into laughter. "*That* would make me very jealous."

"How long do you think I can make it last? I could leave it on under my clothes? I'm serious! Don't laugh! I really might cry if I have to wash it off…"

"I promise I'll paint you again some other time, okay? But let's not leave that on your skin too long. You might get sick from it or something. C'mon, what if it's poisoning you?"

"Then I'll make the most sensational corpse ever. Make sure you tell the mortician not to change a thing. Tell him this is how I looked in life. And turn my funeral into a photoshoot."

He doubled over the sink. "Kit, *noo*."

"Hey, Saichi. What if we… you know?"

Could I say it? It was bold. It was sort of naughty. Was I brave enough? He looked up at me and grinned, completing my thought, "Turned right now into a photoshoot?"

"It'd be *so* bad, right?"

"If it'll make you feel better, let's do it!"

I always wondered why people were stupid enough to take pictures of themselves in compromising settings—naked in bed with their lover or posing in risqué underwear. *Especially* celebrities. That was just asking for a scandal. I never thought I'd be the sort to do that. Never, *ever*. But this was different. I let Saichi tease me out of nerves and into laughter and we ended up running all over his apartment playing photo tag.

Before we got in the shower, I took just one selfie of the two of us. We had each other's touch painted on our faces and Saichi pressed a kiss-turned-giggle to my cheek. Maybe we'd run across that selfie years down the road and smile at our magical messy beginning.

Saichi's kitchen table was paradise, complete with one pajamaed Saichi, one fuzzy robe, and two mugs of reheated coffee. His shower had been paradise too, complete with steam, tangled bodies, and colors melting around our feet. I reveled in the bitter coffee and the sweet soreness and forgot anything else existed outside his apartment. I think we both did for a while, grinning and poking each other, until his phone reminded us we weren't alone in the world, and then our eyes met and we giggled through the guilt. What time was it anyway? I had the weekend off so Ilsung probably wasn't worried, but still, probably best to find my phone.

Before either of us could move, the front door opened.

"Saaatch! God damn, boy!"

Mino was here. Saichi's shoulders scrunched up like a cornered cat and he flashed to his feet. It was my first time hearing Saichi growl. He rushed to tuck my robe tighter around me, but that quickly frustrated him and he raced for the living room, hauling a tarp back with him. For a second, I thought he might use it to hide me, but instead, he swaddled me in the world's bulkiest toga.

Then Mino appeared in the kitchen doorway, startling dark stains under his eyes. His jaw fell. "*Whoa!* Kit? 'The fuck are you doing here?"

"No, what are *you* doing here, Min?"

"This is historic, Satch! You never have people over!"

"No, I don't. So why are you here?"

"You wouldn't answer your phone. I thought you were dead."

"Keep your eyes off her!" Saichi mirrored every one of Mino's movements, trying to block me from view, even though I was *extremely* covered at this point. Mino found it all very funny.

"Were you modeling for him, Kit? Did he paint your picture?"

"It's none of your business, Min."

Mino ignored him. "You *naked* under that thing or what?"

"No?!" I wormed up out of the tarp and tugged on Saichi's arm. "Hey, it's okay, Saichi. This is a good chance to talk, don't you think?"

Mino's eyebrows shot up. "Damn. No 'shi' for Satch anymore." And then he was suddenly perfectly still. His eyes latched onto mine over Saichi's shoulder. "Wait, hang on..."

"As you can see, I'm not dead, Min. So you can leave now."

"Did... did you two *fuck?!*"

My face burst into flames. What a dirty word to describe a miracle that transcended all other human experiences. Saichi growled again, "So what if we did?"

I covered my face. "*Saichi...*" Why did he have to admit to it? Now Mino would never shut up about it! I peeked through my fingers, sure that I'd see that dirty little feline grin on his face.

But Mino had gone grayscale, and utterly motionless, like he'd been snapped up in an old photograph.

"So you two, you really are a thing now, huh? I mean, I should've guessed from the—"

"Yes," Saichi insisted. "We're serious about each other."

"Well, damn." Mino twisted his mouth into something that was probably supposed to be a smile, but his eyes stayed flat and dark. "Congrats, Satch. You finally got yourself a real girlfriend."

"Yes, *my* girlfriend. Mine. Not yours. So you stay away from her from now on, and you keep your mouth shut about her in front of random trainees. In fact, you're gonna track down every single one of them and tell them what you said was a bad joke—"

I almost smiled. "Saichi, it's really okay."

"No, it's not. You hear me, Min? You are responsible for whatever rumors come out of what you said."

"Nah, I ain't going anywhere near those fuckers. Sorry, Kit, but I'm gonna stand by my words 'cuz dealing with the side effects of Minchi has been a real bitch lately. Goes without saying that it's way better people think I'm fucking *you* rather than fucking Satch, yeah?"

"What?"

"Yup yup. Some asshole's spreading shit around about me and Satch again. And I mean, come on, you guys both know how fucking ridiculous that is. I'm literally the furthest thing from a fag."

Oh, absolutely *not*. "Excuse me, Mino, before you go on, can you do me a favor and never say that word again?"

"Bitch? Fucker? Asshole? When did you get so thin-skinned?"

"No, you idiot, you used a homophobic slur."

"Oh, fag? What's the big deal? You got a better word for them? How about fairy then? Queer? Gay? Homo? What do *you* care anyway? Clearly *you're* not gay."

Saichi was shaking. I curled my arm a little tighter around him. I'd never really heard him yell before, but there was an eruption building under his skin, something loud and hot and infuriated, so I spoke fast, "Mino, just shut up if you can't stop being so offensive."

"So Min, you dragged Kit in front of all those kids just so you could maintain your reputation as a ladies man? Do you realize how pathetic that sounds?"

Mino sighed loud enough to hurt. "That's not the *whole* story—"

"I'm not interested in hearing the rest."

"Saichi. Mino. Can we forget about me for a second and focus on you two? Vortex members can't fight. Mino, I think you owe Saichi an apology for the way you treated him."

"What'd I do to Satch?"

"You've got some nerve slapping him around—"

"If I recall, *you're* the slappy one."

"—and acting like you're only friends when you're onstage."

"That? C'mon, that was just for show. We do shit like that for show all the time. That's what Minchi *is*."

"Well, Min, maybe if you quit making a show out of me, then the trainees will leave you alone and you can go back to all your lady friends in peace."

"Wait. Satch, wait. Chill, will ya? What are you saying right now?"

Oh god. I couldn't say anything. As much as I wanted to scream and cry, I couldn't. If Saichi really didn't like Minchi, then this was his chance to put a stop to it, and it wasn't my place to interrupt. So I curled tight into his chest to hide. His voice was even louder there, "I'm saying if it's such a big deal that a couple kids think we're gay, then maybe you should stop pretending to like me onstage."

"*Satch*. Come *on*. You can't be serious."

"You should leave, Min. Just get out."

"Yeah, whatever."

The front door slammed and I burst into tears. The magma washed right out of Saichi. "Kit, no, no, why are you crying?"

"You two *can't fight!*"

"Please don't cry. It's okay. Really, it's okay." He stumbled back and lowered himself into his chair like his bones ached. "I'm sorry you had to see that though…"

"Saichi, I really d-don't care about what he said to the trainees. You don't have to get s-so mad about it."

"Didn't you see his reaction when he came in? He likes you, Kit. And that's definitely why he said something so stupid to those—"

"But it doesn't *matter* if he likes me or not."

"Um, let me just… give you some context or something? Okay? Please don't cry. Is it too early for a beer?"

I found one sulking in the back of the fridge, cracked it open, and slid it across the table to him. I didn't recognize the 'thank you' he muttered, so I assume it wasn't in Korean. I waited. He took a long crackling sip and sighed.

"Min and I have fought like this before," he said from far away.

"Over a girl? Is that why you're so worried?"

"No, a year ago… we fought about Minchi. A really bad fight. And it was almost the end of Vortex. It *should've* been the end of Minchi, but Min drank so much that night… I don't know, he doesn't seem to remember anything about what happened, so Minchi just picked right back up again afterward but… but I remember every second of it… I'd never seen him like that. We were both screaming at each other and… and we ended up in the hospital…"

"*What?* Why the hospital?! Did you hurt each other?"

"No, Min had to have his stomach pumped and… I'm sorry, Kit, it's really hard for me to talk about this. It was… really, really awful. What I'm trying to say is that now is as good a time as any to just… stop Minchi. I don't want things to get out of control again."

"But what about your friendship offstage? Please, Saichi, even if there are other things at play here, I really can't stand to think that I'm the catalyst for this. Even if you stop Minchi, shouldn't you make sure to protect your relationship with him?"

"We're not as close as you think we are, Kit. We've always been a little… superficial. He's got this buffer zone around him and he never lets anyone into it." A buffer zone? The king of invading personal bubbles kept a buffer zone around himself? Saichi left only a moment's silence, but it was so dense that I could hear the froth whispering in his beer. I wished he wouldn't bite dents into his lip.

"Have you ever had that happen with someone? Every day you both try to get your point across with sarcasm and hypotheticals and jokes, and then you laugh it all off until you don't even know what's real anymore. You build this false reality together, and then it gets so complicated that you're trapped in it."

I struggled to keep my voice level, "Well, if you're constantly bumping up against a buffer zone, then I can see how that might happen. But then maybe this fight is a good sign, Saichi. Maybe it means you're finally being more honest with each other. You can establish healthy boundaries and—"

"I... I don't know about that, Kit..."

The light in his eyes turned liquid and his fingers skated blindly along the grain of the table to a familiar knot. The varnish was worn there from his touch, but I still recognized it as the little unblinking eye from that sketch of Mino's hands. Now I felt like I could better understand the tension Saichi had penciled in. His best friend kept him at an arm's length emotionally even though the two of them were plastered to each other every day.

His voice grew impossibly soft. "Imagine a mess that's such a lost cause that you just toss a match in it. Sure, some of your stuff gets destroyed, but at least you don't have to think about it anymore."

"Saichi, don't you think it's worth fixing?"

"No, I think I want to just... start fresh," the words were more of an exhale than a declaration. "Erase everything up until now."

"It's been that terrible up until now?"

An unhappy answer fell from his eyes. I crooked a finger and shaved it from his cheekbone, and then he told me, "He's not the only one with a buffer zone. There are parts of me that I hide too."

He tugged me to my feet and led me into the living room. I could see where he'd gotten the tarp. A stack of dark canvases that was hidden before sat bare in the back corner. He stepped over a wall of paint buckets to reach an easel veiled with a sheet.

"This is also me," he told me, and then he yanked the sheet off.

Canvas boards of all sizes tumbled to the floor. The few that remained on the easel shocked me as drastically different from the rest of his work. These paintings had clotted veins and burnt edges. They were grotesque. Distorted. Paint thrown, spattered, smeared. Cracks, tangles, scratches. Black red dribbling from gaping canvas wounds... I was speechless, and I was scared for him. I had to fight to get the words up my throat, "Saichi, what are all these?"

"Parts of me that I have to hide..." He kicked the pile and the canvases flipped and scattered, laying bare more horror at his feet. "This is what the inside of my mind looks like... Only sometimes. Not all the time. I was trying to get it out, put it on a canvas instead, but it didn't really work. I just ended up painting all this... trash."

"It's not trash. It's pain."

This was the pain I heard in his voice when he sang. I hadn't imagined it. He was hurting and he was hiding it. But *why?* What was hurting him? Was it his own mind? Was it Mino?

He surveyed the array with sullen disgust and then threw the sheet over everything again. "No, it's trash. More mess that I just wanna throw a match in."

"Please, Saichi, can I please help somehow?"

He shook his head. "Things are different now."

"Are they?"

"Yes." He reached out and I picked my way through the mess into his arms. I felt a sigh gust through my hair. "You're here now, Kit... You're my fresh start."

"I'm here," I agreed. "Whatever you need to say, whatever you need to talk about, I'm here, okay?" I squeezed a little tighter and he coughed up a laugh.

"I was a little worried you'd run away after seeing all that."

"Never. You don't have to hide anything anymore, okay?"

"Thanks, Kit."

Blindside.

The next day, Vortex had an interview on an entertainment news channel. They were discussing the plans for their world tour when a question came up about what fans were calling the 'Kiss Blackout.' Was Minchi waiting to have their first kiss in Paris instead?

Mino immediately hooked an arm around Saichi's waist and started on some raunchy rant, cut short when Saichi shoved him off. "I'm sure our fans know that Minchi is all just for show, right?"

Mino's mouth popped wide open and a quake went through Vortex. Jaeyoon moved forward to cover for them, but Mino recovered quickly with a hoarse laugh, "That blackout? That was the day Minchi died, y'all. Minchi is *dead*."

The studio audience broke into such hysterics that the interview quickly became unsalvageable. Post-commercial break, Jaeyoon stood alone on the stage, addressing logistical questions with subzero solemnity. I called Saichi.

"Hey, are you okay?"

"I'm fine, Kit. Just tossed the match in, that's all. It's for the best."

"I'm not sure that this was the best way—"

"I gotta go, okay? A bunch of reporters want some kind of statement and I'm not really sure what to say."

That was neither the first nor the last time that Saichi stonewalled me on the subject of Mino. There was no way that brief isolated incident at the meeting was enough to stir them up to this extent. Some far bigger puzzle piece was lurking in the dark of their buffer zones—the fight they had a year ago that ended in the hospital. Having such an ominous gap in my knowledge about my own boyfriend scared me, but worse was the feeling that the other shoe hadn't dropped yet. As bad as it already seemed, the two of them were somehow still dancing around that titanic unknown.

A month went by.

If I didn't think about it too hard, I was happy. If I didn't think about the fans, or my job, or the policies, or Mino, or Vortex, or Ilsung, or Kyungsoon… and if I also ignored the filthy rumor going around that Saichi, Mino and I were having three-way sex, I was happy.

We couldn't meet much outside of work because Ilsung was spot on about my 'last weekend off.' More work poured in every day, so Saichi and I snuck around headquarters and met in rehearsal rooms, in offices, in conference rooms, anywhere that we could be alone and chat and cuddle.

I loved every second I spent with him. They were maybe some of the happiest weeks in my recent life. I was really happy, dammit, and I hoped he was happy too. While I still didn't know what had brought them about in the first place, I hoped his paintings weren't red anymore. I hoped that the next time I heard him sing, his voice wouldn't sound so hurt. I hoped he liked his fresh start.

But I hated what our relationship did to Vortex. The closer I got to Saichi, the harder he pushed Mino away. The two of them seemed dead set on blowing up the 'Minchi Quarrel' into a media sensation. Onstage, they altered choreography to avoid touching. During interviews, Mino stood as far away as possible and made snarky comments whenever Saichi spoke. I watched a heartbreaking clip on Twitter of Mino refusing to sing a line he would normally harmonize on with Saichi.

At this rate, they were going to kill Vortex too.

And then there was Ryo, definitely plotting *my* death. If he ever caught me coming down the hall to visit Saichi, he chased me off like vermin. That stupid picture of us never leaked, but I knew I had Kyungsoon to thank for that, not Ryo.

So it was the best month I had in years, but it was bittersweet. Guiltysweet. Stressfulsweet.

And then it all came to a head. Saichi and I talked about a fourth date for weeks until, finally, the stars and our schedules aligned and we were set to go out on Noriko after work.

—I'll be done soon! I'll give really short answers in this interview!

—so excited!!!

—but do the interview properly, Mr. Saichi

—I'm sure they're very important questions

—Indeed. The world simply must know my favorite animal.

—which is…?

—Yujin

—good answer ♡ see you soon!

Maybe a little overeager, I decided to go surprise him in his dressing room. That way we wouldn't waste a second. I wanted to see the entire plot of the sunset: beginning, middle, end, and epilogue.

And I had another important agenda. I'd made up my mind about this date. Once we were out on the boat, he couldn't run away from my questions. I was going to find out what happened between Minchi a year ago and I was going to fix it, no matter what.

But when I got to his dressing room, I walked into a slightly hostile environment that held Jaeyoon, Namgi, and Mino, all staring me down. "Ah. Um. Hi. Just came for Saichi, but he's not here, so I—"

"*Kittie!*" Namgi vaulted over the coffee table and roped his arms around me. "Oh my gosh, I missed you, Kittie! I heard you're going out with Minchi now! And like, I totally support you! Like, get it, girl! But still, you're so busy with them now that I never get to see you anymore! Don't forget about us little guys now that you're like, the hottest girl idol on the block!"

"Namgi, how many times have I told you that's open slander?" Jaeyoon offered me a smile that poorly veiled stress. The magazine on his lap was equally stressed by his terse page turning.

"*I* think it's totally hip!"

"Oppa, please don't tell me you believe those rumors."

"Well, Minmin told me all about—"

"*Mino!* You're supposed to deny it, not spread it more!" I couldn't go on. My stomach almost fell out of my body when I looked at him. He was a lot smaller than the last time I'd seen him, and without makeup, his face was dropping hints that he hadn't slept in a week.

"What's up, murderer?"

I gasped.

Jaeyoon cleared his throat over the snap of another page. "Uncalled for. Exercise some command over your mouth, please. And Kit-shi, I'm sorry. I've been spending every free moment working to prevent anything defamatory from escaping the agency and going public." Mino managed a laugh, but it looked like it hurt.

Namgi harbored me a little deeper in his arms and whined at him, "Minmin, why would you lie to me? I was so happy for you guys! And also, the dead Minchi thing is really getting old…"

But I didn't need protection. I pulled out of Namgi's shelter ready to fight. "Excuse me, Mino, but do you have any idea how disconcerting it is to walk the halls these days with everyone in headquarters leering at me?! Stop spreading gross rumors about me! Oh, and another thing, I'm no murderer. I didn't kill Minchi. You did. Don't you dare try to blame all this on me."

"Oh, so it's entirely coincifuckingdental that the moment *you* came along, my best friend started hating me?"

"You're the one that picked a fight with him at that meeting. You're the one that alienated said best friend just to save face in front of a bunch of random trainees you don't even know!"

"Save face?! You *hit* my face. My idol face that my whole damn career depends on. You, a supposed fan, slapped it!"

"Maybe you wouldn't need your face so much if you made more of an effort with your personality."

"Maybe if you just played it cool at the meeting, then Satch wouldn't have even batted an eye at what happened! But no, you had to get all offended over nothing, ya fucking *prude*. And it's the same shit now! What do you care about a rumor or two? Fuck, I'm doing you a favor! Everybody knows I only fuck the hottest chicks—"

Jaeyoon's voice rose above ours, "This is not how adults communicate. Adjust." Namgi, on the other hand, was egging me on, whispering encouragement, patting me on the back.

"It amazes me that you think the meeting is the only thing Saichi is upset about, Mino. You don't know anything."

"'The fuck are you on? He's my best friend! I know him miles better than *you* do?! You just met! You think that just because you two are fucking you've got some special connection now?"

Jaeyoon hissed, "*Kim Mino*, I am *seconds* from losing my patience."

But I had one final punch to land. "You need to take a closer look at the way you treat Saichi onstage, offstage, whatever, and consider the possibility that you've been hurting him for a *very* long time."

Jaeyoon slapped his magazine shut. I thought he was going to inform us that he'd officially lost his patience, but instead, his eyes silently dissected my face, dark brows conferring with one another. Then he turned a scorching glare on Mino and his tone grew acidic, "She's right, Mino. I told you a thousand times to stop taking him for granted. Did you listen? Do you *ever* listen? No. And now look, what a surprise. He's had it with you."

"So we're just gonna pretend Vortex isn't about to fall apart because of this chick?"

Those words hit my gut like a blade. That could never happen. Vortex couldn't fall apart. This was just a little tiny fight, so much smaller than the enormity of Vortex.

"You really think—?"

Namgi tugged on Jaeyoon's sleeve, pointing at us. With a vexed sigh, Jaeyoon stood and tossed aside the magazine. "I am not listening to this. This is not how conflicts get resolved. Both of you are deepening the rift. And Kit-shi, for the record, you bear no responsibility for Vortex's problems."

Problems. There were Vortex problems. "Oh god."

Namgi made an exasperated sound. "Everyone is blowing this up way too much. Minmin, Kittie, you both know Vortex can't ever end. Now let's just stop fighting so much, okay?"

"Namgi, *come*. I think they need to have a private discussion." Jaeyoon shot me a loaded look that made absolutely no sense, and then they were gone before I could find the words to question him.

Mino compacted into something surly and frigid. I touched his arm, desperate to get the knife out of my stomach. "Mino, please, why did you say that? Is Vortex okay?"

"Some relationship y'all got if Satch hasn't told you anything."

"Mino, what? What's going on?"

He wrenched my wrist off of him and tried to crush it in his fist. "Jae was just being nice, Kit. Hate to be the one to break it to ya, but shit's rough right now, and if Vortex disbands, it's *your fault*."

Is there any parallel universe out there in which that *wouldn't* be the moment Saichi walked in? Of course not. Stupid damn universe. The worst possible time for him to walk in... and that was when he walked in. Murphy's Law.

"What the hell, Mino."

"Oh, hi there, asshole. How's it hangin'?"

I'd never seen Saichi so infuriated. Two fists shook at his sides, ready. My surge toward him was automatic, but Mino's grip was unforgiving and my body jerked back. "Saichi, don't be mad. We're fine. Nothing's going on. Everything's good and—" Saichi took a threatening step toward us and Mino pulled me closer like a shield.

"Hands to yourself," Saichi snarled and Mino's hands sprang open. "This issue is between you and me, Mino. Leave Kit out of it."

"What absolute bullshit. Kit is literally the *center* of the issue. You're throwing away Vortex because of her."

"I am not throwing away Vortex. I broke up a subunit."

"So that's all we ever were, huh? Fuck, and here I thought we were actually friends!"

"We could still be friends if you stop trashing Kit all the time."

"Why the fuck is she so important to you? *I'm* your best friend, not her! I never ditched *you* over any of the chicks I fucked over the years, but you toss me to the curb over your first piece of tail?"

"She's not just someone I sleep with, Mino. And I'm not tossing you to the curb. You said you were tired of people assuming that we're gay, so I gave you an out and ended Minchi. But instead of letting it go, you're making up *more* rumors and I'm supposed to just roll with the punches?"

I was stunned when Mino nudged past me and started pawing at Saichi's chest. "I didn't wanna kill Minchi."

Saichi started vibrating in anger under Mino's touch, but he kept his voice in check behind his teeth, "So you wanna fake it with me onstage and fake it with my girlfriend offstage? Why don't you just try being real for once? I'm tired of bending over backward so you can play your little harassment game during concerts!"

Mino's jaw dropped. "You did *not* just call Minchi harassment."

"Oh? When did I ever consent to what you do to me?"

"*Consent?* What the fucking fuck, Satch? It's not like I'm putting my dick in you onstage?! Where you coming up with this crazy shit?"

"I just—"

"If you've got some kinda fucking problem with us doing Minchi, why didn't you speak up like a million years ago?! Like, fuck, we've been planning the Minchi Kiss since we were trainees!"

Saichi stepped back and took a long rattling breath, but it didn't help. If anything, it fueled the flames. He was reaching a boiling point, seething under his skin, just like he had in the kitchen. I wanted to take his arm, to whisper calming words, to avoid another explosion… but it didn't feel right for me to interfere right now. The best I could do was try keep them at an arm's length from each other.

"Screw the Minchi Kiss. You threw Kit and I under the bus over one little rumor that you're gay, but you think you can handle kissing me in front of the whole world?"

Stupidly brave, Mino put his arms around Saichi's neck and brought their faces close. Saichi was outright shaking now, like he might fall apart entirely. How could Mino just stand there hugging a ticking time bomb?

"We just gotta get rid of those trainees, Satch. The Ice Bitch laughed me out of her office when I tried to get them fired, but *you*… She'd do anything for you. She'll get rid of them and then we can just go about our business. Nobody *else* thinks we're actually gay. Everybody else knows I fuck around and you've got Kit and—"

"*Min.*" Something broke deep inside him and let all the steam out. "I'm sorry, but no. I can't do Minchi anymore, okay?"

"Why not?!"

"I just don't want to."

"'The hell kinda reason is that?"

"I want… to belong to Kit. So I can't share so much with you."

"Satch, what the actual fuck are you talking about? Why can't Kitchi and Minchi coexist? We don't have to fucking take sides in the stupid-ass ship war, you idiot. This is real life, not Twitter!"

"Exactly. It's real life and it really hurts."

"Hah? What hurts?"

"The fact that you're faking it and I'm not."

There was one last soft peaceful moment in my life as they searched each other's eyes, and then the echo of his words ripped through. My hand reached blindly through a reality incinerating around me, but Saichi's sleeve slipped through my fingertips as he reached up and took Mino's face in his hands.

And kissed him.

Wake-up call

I waited, but it made less sense every second, and every second seemed slower than the last. I watched Saichi's thumb stroke over the beauty mark on Mino's chin and thought of the knot in his kitchen table. He knew where it was without looking.

This was the kiss I'd been waiting for all this time, but it was all wrong. It wasn't two idols onstage doing fluffy fanservice. It was my boyfriend kissing someone else right in front of me. Those were lips that fit with mine. *Mine*. Wasn't Saichi mine?

Stubby fingers twisted in Saichi's hair and he lost the upper hand. They spun, Saichi's back thudded against the door, and suddenly violent, breathless, furious, Mino pushed deeper when Saichi gasped, eyes wide open, onyx blazing into amber.

Then their mouths snapped apart and Saichi moaned. The sound shuddered through Mino's body. He clapped a hand over Saichi's mouth and something vicious guttered out of him, "You gotta be fucking kidding me, Satch."

Saichi just shook his head, tears bumping over Mino's fingers.

"You're fucking disgusting." His hand slid off only to wrench on the door handle. The door exploded open into the hall and dumped Saichi into a crumple on the ground. No, no. Not disgusting. Never.

I knelt down in spirals of nausea, wishing I could help him up, but I couldn't touch him. He wasn't mine anymore. Was he ever mine?

He'd gone brittle. Shocked. He wouldn't blink, wouldn't breathe, but he still tried to speak, "Min, *please*—"

"Don't call me that! Who the fuck *are* you?!"

The tears tripled. "D-do you get it now, Min? Why I just c-can't—" He fought to say more but his mouth was out of sync with his throat.

"Yeah, I get it. Now take your fake girlfriend and get the fuck out of my sight. Just looking at you makes me fucking sick, *faggot*."

My voice sounded foreign to my own ears, "Mino, shut your stupid mouth!" and it was far too little far too late. Saichi was already up, stumbling away down the hall.

"I'm sorry," he mumbled, and then the door slammed, shut us out.

'Fall. Fall. Fall into delusion.' That was my favorite line of Saichi's in their debut single, but I'd never let myself fall *too* far. Whenever Minchi got too cute, I dug my nails into reality and tried to keep myself in check. But that reality was a carefully crafted delusion all along, and now bigger heavier puzzle pieces repaved the way forward. The red paintings, the tear I'd taken from his cheek, the loneliness in his voice when he sang…

It all fit together now.

KJ always rolled their eyes at them. *'Yes, yes, they're very good friends. We have no official stance on them.'* Netizens would snap at all the hashtags on Twitter, *'Shut up, it's just fanservice. Don't be nasty. You're all perverts.'* The other Vortex members always just smiled and ruffled their hair. *'Ahh, they're at it again. Look, aren't they cute?'* And millions of fangirls, myself included, squealed over and over again, *'Let Minchi kiss!'*

Did believing in something have power? Could visualizing something make it materialize? No, it was there all along. The other shoe had finally dropped. Saichi was in love with Mino and he'd never been mine.

I should've known it was too good to be true, but I'd let my guard down. I let myself start to dream about what we'd become, about the memories we had yet to make, about the things we'd create together.

The fans, the policies, the media, the tabloids—there were so many things I was willing to overcome so we could be together. But this... There wasn't anything I could do about this. I'd lost. Lost him, and lost half of myself.

I had to find him. I could mute the pain a little longer. He had it so much worse than me, and he didn't deserve to suffer somewhere alone. I was going to strangle Mino, but first, I had to find Saichi and hold him and talk him through this.

Where was he going?

Did he know I was chasing him? Every turn I rounded, I only caught a glimpse of him disappearing again. I was moving too fast to see but too slow to catch him. I had no breath to call out.

Saichi?

I ran for the steely blast of a door slam. A stairwell, the slaps of his feet cascading down to me. Flight after flight, I couldn't keep up. I stopped to kick off my stupid damn heels. Why was he running? And where the hell was he going? What was up there?

Another resounding slam.

The weight of the world glued the door shut. I didn't realize that was strange until I threw my weight into it and plunged into a gale of wind. We were outside. He'd led me to the roof.

My heart iced over.

"*Saichi, no!*" The breath of the city whipped my voice from me. "*Don't jump!*" But I couldn't find him, couldn't see through the burn, so I hurtled for the edge. The plunge beyond the railing swelled and rippled, the buildings melting down each other. He was already gone. I caught a snatch of laughter and turned. Nothing. He was nowhere in a maze of rumbling metal.

"Saichi?!"

"Up here," he called.

Another flight of stairs up. A helipad. Saichi was sprawled in the middle of it, staring up into the stewing sky. Relief blew my knees out from under me.

"That's not how I would do it," he told the clouds. They crowded me down onto all fours, but no matter how low I got, there was no escaping the sky. It bit at our clothes, snatched at his voice, threatened to whisk us up into the air.

"Do what?"

"Die. I have nightmares about falling, so I think I'd rather it be quick if I got to pick." If it weren't for the tears turning mercurial in his hair, he could've been talking about the weather.

"Let's not think about that anymore, okay?"

"I'm fine, Kit. I'm not gonna jump. I just come up here to think."

"Aren't there safer places to think?"

"Maybe. But I like this big H."

"But what if a helicopter comes?"

"What? Why would a helicopter come?"

"Never mind."

"In Japanese, we say 'H' to mean sex."

"Oh...?"

"Because the word 'hentai' starts with an h. It means... perversion. That's why I like to lie here. It's like I can be honest for a moment and show the whole world that I'm depraved, deviant, defective."

"Saichi, please—"

"Don't yell at me yet. 'Hentai' has another meaning if you change up the kanji... Transformation. Metamorphosis. I was holding out hope for that one." With years beyond his age, he sat up and tried to smile at me. "I'm sorry, Kit. I'm really sorry. I was trying to change."

Oh.

Oh god.

"You love Mino."

He didn't deny it. The uneven smile melted off and he hid his face. "I was trying not to. I was serious about you..."

I didn't want him to hear me whisper, "I was serious too."

"I'm sorry, Kit, I'm so sorry," he kept repeating into his fingers. He looked smaller with every sob, like the tears were what he was made of.

I couldn't. I couldn't be mad at him. I could be sad for myself later, but I could never yell at this man. A man who painted his pain because he was afraid to show it to anyone. A man who had been forcing himself for years, and finally just snapped under the pressure. I choked the words out, "You never needed to change anything. There's nothing wrong with you. Not a thing. You're perfect."

"How can you say that after what I just did? I just attacked my best friend right in front of my girlfriend!"

"Everyone makes mistakes. And... I'm not even sure this was a mistake. Maybe this is how it was supposed to be all along?"

"No, I'm supposed to be over him. I already gave up on him!

Because he *told* me to! This is exactly what happened a year ago…"

"This was what you fought about?"

"Yeah… and then I fell in love with you, Kit."

Oh, please, god, no. Don't tell me that right now.

"You're everything I ever wanted. You do what's right, you chase what you love, you're honest and selfless and careful with the people around you. Kit, I really, truly love—"

"*Don't*. Stop there. Don't say it. You can't say that to me right now. And I can't hear that from you right now. Not until everything is fixed. Not until you talk this out and solve things with everyone. For a month, you and I have been living in our own little bubble and it's been so perfect and I was so happy during every second with you… But Saichi, ever since you tossed that match, the whole world has been on fire around us. I'm sorry, I know it's been so painful for you, but this isn't the solution. *I'm* not the solution."

"No, Kit, you *are*."

"Then why did you kiss Mino?"

"I… don't know. I just… lost control for one second…"

"And what's to say you won't lose control again?"

"Well, if he would just leave me alone—?! The more I push him away, the more he gets in my face! Every second of every day, he's lying all over me, hugging me, touching me, driving me *insane!*"

His knuckles turned bone white in his hair, and I felt it when he yanked, twice, three times, trying to pluck feelings out. I moved to stop him, but he grabbed my hands and pressed them to his face, tears trickling down my fingers and beading on my nails. Trying to send me messages through his skin again. I'd misread them all along.

"You two really need to have a talk about boundaries. A talk, not a fight like today. Don't you think there's a reason he's always on you? Maybe you don't need to fight your feelings for him…"

"W-what do you mean? You saw what happened! He hates me!"

He still shook, and no matter how tight I held him, I couldn't pull him back together. All I could do was run my fingers through his hair, again and again, hoping to smooth the panic away, feeling tear after tear scald its way through my shirt.

"I think he was just surprised. Give him a little time."

"No, Kit. Min's never going to let me anywhere near him again. If I were him, I wouldn't either. I'm a freak. Like he says, a f-faggot. And I have been for all these years, just sitting there letting him throw himself at me when he had no idea that I actually—"

"Stop saying mean words." I squeezed a little tighter to quiet him. Words like that hurt to hear. I couldn't imagine how much they hurt Saichi coming from his own head.

"It's fine. Mean is good. Distance is good. I deserve it."

"*No.*"

"Really, it's better this way. It'll be so much easier for me to move on if he stays away from me…"

"Saichi, please, let's not give up quite yet. I know it might seem complicated or hopeless to you, but let's stop tossing matches in things and try to clean up the mess instead, okay? Otherwise, don't you think it's just going to keep coming back to burn you?"

"Hi there…"

We jerked away from each other in horror, but it was just Jaeyoon. The wind lashed his clothing into knots around him as he came carefully up the stairs. Judging by the rueful knit behind his bangs, he'd overheard something he didn't approve of.

"Kit-shi, I'll take it from here." There was veiled steel in his voice, an unspoken order to leave. I wanted so much to protest, to hold on tighter to Saichi, but Jaeyoon's eyes burned on my face.

What if I made Mino apologize?

What if I dragged him up here by his damn unicorn hair?

What if I locked them on the roof until they talked things out?

Jaeyoon shook his head. Saichi was crying again and Jaeyoon pulled him from my arms. I asked him with my eyes, *'What can I do?'* *'How can I help?'* but he just nodded me away. I left him rubbing the sobs out of Saichi's back.

Denial

I didn't make it down three stairs before I crashed.

This exact pitch of alone was familiar. This was the void of losing a person who had become everything. The acute lack of a person who had become a need.

Before him, I'd gotten good at being alone. Just a short time ago, Ilsung was all I needed. I let my career occupy such a colossal slice of my life that I didn't have space for anything or anyone else. I lived convinced that a full schedule was fulfillment, and I was strong, focused, driven. Too busy to even notice I was alone.

And then Saichi came along and carved himself into my calendar, reminded me how warm and sweet it was to love because, all of a sudden, I had someone giggly and cuddly who held my hand and pulled me through days I hadn't known were hard. Someone who dad-joked and burned food and painted the world prettier. Someone who loved my art and thought the real me mattered.

He came in and took over every thought, every moment, every beat of my pulse, and now he was ripping himself back out again and I was left emptier than ever. But nothing he could say or do at this point would convince me that he belonged in my life. However much he loved me, he loved Mino more.

Didn't I learn my lesson when Aunt Caroline died? Love led to pain and relying on others was a trap. I never meant to love anyone like that again, never meant to make myself vulnerable to anyone again. But here I was…

Everything he brought into my life was going to leave with him. The human warmth, the bright colors, the laughter, the secrets, and everything else that was waiting somewhere down the road. Gone.

I stared at the tears on my palms and suddenly wished they were paint instead. But even on my plain, bland, naked skin, I could still clearly picture the pattern he'd painted. And while that memory was ruined for me now, I retained my Amazon status. I was still strong, powerful, brave. I could handle this. I'd handled worse. I'd gotten the feels to fuck off before and I could do it again.

Fuck off, feelings. Stairs are for going up or down. Not for crying. Not now. Not here. I had to find Mino.

I didn't go in right away, because what could I even say to him? All I wanted was to beat him up. I wanted to call him every name he called Saichi and more, make him feel the damage he'd done…

But punching him wasn't going to erase him from Saichi's heart, and today didn't need to see any more violence or name-calling or pain. I had to be calm and reason with him. He probably felt terrible for saying those kinds of things to his best friend, so it would probably be easy to convince him to go apologize and talk things out.

I was still wiping my face and untangling my brain when voices came trickling under the door, and I knew it was wrong and rude but whatever, I cracked the door open. Maybe Mino was sorry, and crying, and confessing that he actually liked Saichi, and then I could play cupid and pretend that my heart wasn't broken.

It was Namgi mid-rant. "—which is why I'm totally confused. Shouldn't we be celebrating right now? It's the Minchi Kiss! You two have been foreplaying for like, *ever* now—"

"That's not how I wanted it to happen! That fucking weirdo attacked me and stuck his tongue down my throat!"

"That sounds *sexy*—"

"Shut up, Babo!"

"Both of you shut up for a second." Crap, Ryo was in there too... If he caught me eavesdropping, I was as good as dead. "Am I missing something? Mino, you mean to tell me you're *not* fucking Hyung?"

"*What?!* Jesus, *fuck no!* I'm no fucking fag?!"

"*You watch your bitch mouth.*"

For once, I was happy to hear Ryo all scary and pissed off. I never thought I'd hear words like that outside of Ohio, but Mino apparently had yet to join the rest of us in the 21st century. No wonder Saichi hadn't come out until now.

"God damn it, Mino. You've been whoring yourself all over him for years and *you mean to tell me you're not fucking him?* What the fuck is wrong with you? Why aren't you fucking him?!"

"We're just friends, you sick-ass! Or we *were* friends."

Namgi broke into a whine, "You and I are friends too, aren't we? You never touch *my* butt, or hold *my* hand, or kiss *me*. You and *I* don't have a couple name that everybody knows—"

"Oh fuck off, Babo."

"No, Mino. He's exactly right. Friends don't do what you and Hyung do. Far as I know, you have no goddamn right to get this pissy over a little kiss when you've been leading him on for actual years."

"Like hell I have!"

"Well, you sure led *me* on. Christ, you're so unbelievably selfish, you know that? First, you stage a breakup in public, and now you're bitching and bickering in private too? Over *nothing!* You're not even fucking! I can't believe you're dragging the whole group down with this stupid shit!"

"Yeah? Well, fuck this gay-ass group!"

Mino shoved the door and rammed me in the forehead. I didn't even feel it, and I hardly heard Ryo roar, "*How long were you there?!*" I wasn't scared of him anymore. I glared at Mino through the stars.

"Move," he growled through his teeth. He was splotchy-faced, glassy-eyed, and blinking a little too fast. He'd either been crying or was about to start, and if he was going to cry, I was absolutely going to be there for it.

"You know what? Fuck all of you for calling me paranoid all the time! I was right! Look at her! She's blatantly spying!"

"Ryo-chan, you stop that right now. She's one of us now so just give it up. And cut her some slack. Her boyfriends just uhh…"

"Why are you *never* wearing shoes?! Fucking barbaric—"

"I said move, Kit!"

Mino pushed past me, but I'd already chased down one crying man today, and Mino was much easier to follow because he refused to run. He just kept spitting curses and walking faster. His best attempt at evasion was an abrupt turn through a random door, and it was easy enough to duck in before he could lock it.

Triple-edged

"What the fuck, Kit?! This is a men's bathroom! And you're not wearing any fucking shoes! Don't be fucking nasty! Get out! *Now!*"

I didn't have the energy to yell back. "No, I'd like you to come with me. You and Saichi need to talk."

"What are you, Vortex's mom? Fuck off!"

"You owe Saichi an apology."

"I fucking do *not!* He should apologize to *me!*"

"Take it from me, he's sorry. And he would tell you as much if you'd have a civilized conversation with him instead of hitting him and calling him names."

"Yeah? Well, he threw civility out the window when he put his tongue in my mouth! I'm not going anywhere *near* him." He turned petulantly away, but the Mino in the mirror had his guard down and scrubbed at his eyes. His voice was cautious. "Did you uh, catch up with him?"

"Yes. I found him on the roof."

He spun so fast that he knocked a soap dispenser off the wall and stumbled into the sink. "And you *left him there?!*"

"He's with Jaeyoon-shi."

I saw the blood rush from his head and try to drag him down.

"Don't fucking scare me like that," he croaked.

"Oh, so you *do* care about him."

"Obviously I don't want my best fucking friend to jump off a fucking building, dammit! Just because I hate him now doesn't mean I want him to fucking die!" He wobbled over to the wall and let it lead him into a ball on the tile. Beside him, soap spooled off the counter in pearlescent ribbons, a growing puddle creeping sluggishly toward his toes. "What did he say about... what happened?"

"I'm not going to spoon-feed you information from our private conversation. You want answers then go talk to him yourself, and I'd advise sooner rather than later, because the longer you avoid it, the harder it's going to get."

"Easier to never talk to him again."

"Do you really want that though?"

"I don't know? Maybe?!" He shriveled a little under my glare. "*No*. I mean, no. Because this is all a stupid misunderstanding, right?"

"Mino, it's not my place to be his voice in something so private... If you value your... friendship with him, then you need to show him that by being open and honest and vulnerable and helping him feel that it's okay to—"

"*Ugghhh*, girl, stop. You're giving me fucking goosebumps with all this pansy-ass girl talk. Why are you being so dramatic about this? It's not like he actually... He's definitely not... This is just stupid. There's no way he actually meant it like *that*, ya know? Like, c'mon, he's dating *you*. You're a chick! So he can't be... He can't wanna... *Fuckkk*, god dammit, Kit! Throw me a bone here! He's not fucking gay and you know it!"

Idiot. What an absolute idiot. Reality wasn't going to change just to make him more comfortable. Reality didn't give a shit about anybody's feelings.

"If you're so sure about that, then come talk to him. Absolutely nothing to be afraid of."

"Who the fuck says I'm afraid?!"

"You're a textbook homophobe right now."

"I'm not homo-*anything*, you hear me?!"

"You're a homo sapiens, aren't you? You have *that* in common, don't you? If you can't treat him like a friend, then at least treat him like a human! I'm sure he's still up there—"

"No means nope, Kit."

"Please? For the good of the group?"

"Don't even start with the Vortex shit right now. I'm sick of hearing about how I'm gonna be the doom of the damn group 'cuz apparently I'm KJ's fucking dumpster fire idol. I bust my nuts for Vortex for *years* and I get no fucking respect! Got fucking trainees up my ass all day long, the Ice Bitch pissing all over me, and now my own best friend fucking attacking me! Like, fuck, if I'm such disrespectable shit, just fucking fire me and get yourself a new Mino! And Vortex? Vortex can go to hell if y'all expect me to kiss and make up with that bastard after he *assaulted* me. Gimme a fucking break!"

Assault. The accusation sent ice through my veins. I didn't want to get behind an 'assault,' but somehow, his tone made it sound like just another word he was trying to weaponize.

"Assault isn't a word to throw around, Mino. And I'm sorry about all the other stuff that's going on, but as far as Saichi goes, *assault?* Seriously? It looked to me like he was very gentle and sweet and *you're* the one that pinned him and started sticking tongues places—"

"Oh, so just because he was gentle about doing something totally against my will, all the sudden that makes it fucking okay?!"

"No! Of course not! But you did kiss him back?!"

"I did not! I was just—! It was self-defense! I was getting him off me, that's all! Jesus fuck, Kit, you gotta lay off the punch with the Minchi cult, okay? He's your *boyfriend!* You're fucking delusional!"

"You're fucking in denial! Whether you like him or not, and whether he likes you or not, you two need to work this out *now!*"

"Fuck off!"

Kit Allister, you can't fight fire with fire. Chill out.

"Mino, just listen for a second..." I crouched down next to him and tried to put out a hand, feeling a little like I was reaching toward a wild animal. The second he caught a softer note in my voice, he bristled over and swiped my hand away. "He feels harassed and you feel assaulted. You're hurt, he's hurt... That's not great grounds for friends to be on. You care about how he feels, right? And he cares about you, so shouldn't you just—"

"Shut up! I've had enough of this bullshit." He surged to his feet. And fell almost as quickly, bowling us both over in a soap slick. I tried to grab him, but his hand slithered right out of mine and latched onto the sink, hauling him up. He might've run for the door, but his feet kept squirting out from under him, so he went crashing through a stall door instead. The other stalls all juddered when he banged it shut again. "Fuck you, fuck him, fuck the group, fuck all of it!"

"Mino, come on—"

"Not interested. Too big of a mess. Too fucked up to fix. Too much goddamn work. Just cut your losses and give it up, Kit."

"Why are you both so quick to toss a match in a friendship you've had for *years*? You're willing to sacrifice that much?"

"Yup. Give it up. Sorry your boyfriend's an asshole, but just throw the whole man out 'cuz I don't want him either."

"God, I cannot *believe* you're able to talk about Saichi like that. You're kidding yourself. You better stay locked in there because if you come out here, this soap is going in your mouth."

"Whatever, *mom*."

He wheezed, trying to muffle something more honest. I *knew* it. Loud, belligerent, and foul-mouthed, but just like everything else in his life, it was all for show. And why? Why bother trying to fool me? This was that stupid buffer zone Saichi told me about. Mino would rather throw out every person in his life than admit he had emotions and cared about people?

"Just get out of here, Kit."

"Sure, Mino. You both clearly need to talk but sure, go ahead and cry alone in a bathroom. See where that gets you."

I wasn't done with him. I definitely wasn't done. They were going to fix this whether they liked it or not. All I'd seen out of them so far was denial, avoidance, and suppression. Their friendship didn't have to end like this. *Vortex* didn't have to end like this. All they needed was a little bit of communication.

And consent. Without it, little things that had seemed loving and cute suddenly became harassment, assault. Consent needed to be part of the conversation, but I really just wanted to drag them somewhere and force them to talk... Could I be hypocritical for a second to fix the hypocrisy of Mino's homophobia?

Then again, was he upset because he was internalizing something, or did he really feel like he'd be assaulted? I couldn't in good conscience question the justification of that. No matter what Saichi had hoped the kiss to mean, if Mino felt wronged, his feelings were valid and no one could say otherwise.

If only Mino would extend that same understanding to Saichi. Couldn't he think for a second how conflicted and confused Saichi must've felt all these years with Mino all over him? Saichi hadn't even thought a man *could* consent. That made me want to vomit.

When my aunt was a teenager, an older man who was a friend of the family forced himself on her. She got pregnant and the entire town turned against her for it. To them, it didn't matter that she'd been forced, because she must have propositioned him, or she must have been wearing something indecent at the time.

When she miscarried, some called it an act of God and claimed that it was for the best. Others accused her of finding a way to abort the baby. They gave her hell on earth when none of it was her fault.

After that, she never married and never had any children of her own. And the people in town? Even decades later, they gossiped about her for staying single her whole life.

She never acted resentful and never fought back against them, but the older I got, the more I understood how lonely her forced exile made her. Even at her *funeral*, the in-towners had the nerve to whisper in the pews. They wouldn't let her rest even after they'd lowered her into the ground. They were probably still talking about her now, and no doubt, they were trashing me too.

I couldn't be like them. I couldn't stand on the wrong side of consent. But this time, I was in a position where I could see both sides and neither was wrong nor right. What the hell would I have to do to get them to see that for themselves?

When I left the bathroom, Ryo was leaning against the wall right outside. He muttered "Nice try" right in my ear and I almost jumped out of my skin.

"You were listening?!"

"Just returning the favor, spy. What would you have done if someone walked in? You'd have been in deep shit. I guarded the door. You're welcome."

"Wouldn't it make you happy if I got in trouble?"

He rolled his eyes. Then he dangled a pair of shoes in my face. "Here. Present. From Jaeyoon, not me. Want them?"

"You're not gonna tell me to butt out of your business?"

"Not this time. I figured I'd find you throwing a tantrum way worse than Mino's, but instead, you're trying to help." I stifled a gasp. This was not the reaction I expected out of him. Did I finally win him over? By *not* freaking out when my boyfriend kissed another guy? Great, I guess. One less thing to worry about. "You're still being nosy and irritating, but your heart's in the right place, and it's also gotta genuinely suck to be you today, so I'll let this one slide. I also sort of owe you an apology."

"Do you now?"

The prospect of admitting he was wrong looked like it was physically sickening him, but I refused to say anything to ease his distress. He *did* owe me an apology. It wasn't exactly my biggest concern right now, but still, thanks?

"Sorry for giving you shit about Hyung. I thought he was with Mino, but clearly they're not as fucking legit as they put on. I don't think I need dirt on you anymore, so I'll delete the picture and we can call it a truce, yeah?"

"Truce, huh? You tried unsuccessfully to end my career and now you're being oh-so-generous by deleting an entirely staged photo. Thanks a bunch, Ryo. *Definitely* feels like we're even now."

I heard two deep thuds and thought my heartbeat was finally returning, but no, I was still numb. It was the sound of his fists slamming into the wall. And he hissed but the hiss didn't turn into 'shi' this time. I think it was 'shit' instead.

Unfortunately, the little triumph was too short-lived to gloat over because a traumatic puff of cinnamon arrived in my face. It was entirely involuntary to cuff a hand over my neck, but it still triggered this sick, satisfied smirk on Ryo's face.

"Fine then. I'll keep the picture. Consider it an incentive to leave Hyung alone from now on. You forced him to act straight long enough. Now let him swing the way he's meant to."

"*Excuse me?* I didn't force *anything*—"

"Not that I think he's gonna come crawling back to you anyway, but if he does, forget about it. This picture might not work on tabloid writers, but you can bet your ass it'll work on him."

"You're being unbelievably petty."

"Well, next time show some gratitude when I apologize, you fucking American spitfire. Need I remind you that you're *nobody?*"

"God, you really test a fangirl, Ryo…"

"Just put these damn shoes on and get the hell out of here before someone sees us together." The shoes clattered loudly to the floor, and then his eyes found the soap stains spiderwebbing my clothes. "Also, do you *always* have to be so disgusting? As usual, you're an embarrassment to KJ. Go home and change."

"I'll do as I please, thank you. I'm going back to find Saichi."

"What did I *just* say about that picture? Your services as a beard are no longer required. Stay away from him."

"I don't answer to you. I answer to the president."

His fingers shackled my wrist when I turned to go. I was triggered again and lost my nerve. "I'm serious, Kit. Go the fuck home. Hyung already left with Jaeyoon anyway. Just let it be."

Deep in the night, my phone mushroomed with notifications and I woke to a heartbreaking screenful of missed calls and texts, a time-stamped archive of panic and deteriorating willpower. The most recent entry had arrived ridden with typos, three minutes prior to my alarm. Somewhere in Seoul, Saichi was still awake, still upset, still ashamed. I felt guilty for sleeping when he hadn't. I'd only managed it because I dug up some expired sleeping meds left over from that first fateful transpacific flight.

> *—Saichi, you don't need to apologize anymore. It's okay.*
> *I promise. Please get some rest.*

I hoped to god he had an easy schedule today. In the wall of Saichi notifications, one message from an unknown number stood out:

—This is Mahn Jaeyoon. We need to have a conversation. Please call this number as soon as you see this message, regardless of the hour. Thank you.

It wasn't even six yet. Not-a-morning-person Jaeyoon couldn't possibly want me to call him so early, and I didn't really want to talk to him in monster-mode anyway. I saved the number and moved on.

I meant to call him between jobs a little later in the day, but that didn't cut it for him. He was waiting for me outside the studio after my morning dance practice, eyes dented purple with exhaustion. "Come with me" was all he said before he set off down the hall without a backward glance.

"I have to—"

"Clearly I'm aware of your schedule."

He led me into the costume department, the hallways flashing awake as he went. At a door marked only 'MJ,' he pulled a jingle of keys from his pocket.

"Um, I'm supposed to—"

"I know. I'll do your makeup. Sit down." He flicked a switch and the room telescoped with bank after bank of lights, layer after layer in a tableau of fashion design.

If not parallel, then perpendicular—there was obsessive order to each drawing board, most unblemished by ink, others blessed by the certain strokes of inspiration. The glaring white of parchment and the gleaming floors would've edged toward hospital-level sterility if not for the scattered lurk of mannequins drenched in loud chaotic color. I'd half-expected Jaeyoon to lead me to Saichi, but none of the mannequins moved. Their bored stares unsettled my stomach.

Jaeyoon pressed some products into my hands and waved me over to the kitchenette. "Wash and moisturize. Quickly." The ongoing austerity had my mind racing for reasons I could be at fault for what happened. Unsatisfactory performance as Saichi's girlfriend? Poor peacekeeping and failure to defuse the situation in a timely manner?

"Jaeyoon-shi, it's an honor to have you do my makeup but…" Thankfully, the sink blurred the anxiety in my voice. "Does my manager know I'm here?"

"It's fine." A dishtowel slid down the counter. Nearby, a coffee machine started to gurgle. "Prime." Another product slammed down next to the sink and I heard a chair scrape up behind me.

I still held out some hope that all this was just his daily scheduled monster-mode, but I had to ask, "Did I do something wrong?"

The cupboard bumped shut and two mugs clinked in his hands.

"Sit. Coffee?" The coffee smelled tempting, but my stomach was in anxious turmoil now.

"No, thank you."

Sitting in front of him with a light angled at my face... I was about to be interrogated, for sure. I flinched at first when he came at me with a brush, but none of his abrasive mood made it through the fibers. If I closed my eyes, the familiar route across my skin almost persuaded me to relax. Almost. It was impossible to shut out the man behind the brush.

He took a breath. I held mine.

"Is it possible for you to give Hyung another chance?"

I flinched again. Gentle but insistent, he pinched my chin to steady me. He was looking at my brows, not at my eyes, but I avoided his gaze anyway. How was I supposed to answer that?

The wounds were still gaping, and my nightmares had ensured that I bled through the night. All morning, I'd been avoiding prodding around in there, which was easy enough while immersed in routine. But now Jaeyoon's little poke confirmed for me that shock still had me anesthetized. There was even some clueless part of me that was still waiting to go out on Noriko with Saichi. I had everything one day, nothing the next, and apparently that hadn't fully registered yet.

"I don't really know where I stand with him right now, but I have a feeling that he and I should no longer... associate in that way."

"Look up." I nearly winced the mascara into an utter disaster. "What is your reasoning behind that?"

My reasoning? He had to know already, so why did I have to say it out loud? I didn't want to put it in words. "He loves someone else."

He was just applying concealer, but he conveniently blended away a rogue tear before I could be embarrassed about it. When my throat got too tight to speak, he blended foundation down my neck.

"Did Hyung explicitly tell you he loves someone else?"

"I don't think I read him wrong."

"Maybe he does love Mino, but what does that have to do with his feelings for you?" A brush tickled my cheeks and I closed my eyes again. I couldn't tell if not being able to see made the conversation easier or more difficult.

"I don't think he should waste time with me if he loves Mino."

"Loving you is not a waste of time, Kit-shi. Loving Mino, however, is likely the worst possible way for Hyung to kill time."

My jaw dropped. He used the moment to gloss my lips.

"That's a little harsh?"

"Mino thinks only of his own gratification. He denies that his attentions have any underlying meaning, and he stubbornly refuses to believe that he's causing any kind of psychological damage to Hyung in the process."

"His attentions, as in Minchi."

"Yes. Mino uses it as an easy excuse to touch Hyung whenever and wherever he pleases, and Hyung has been tolerating it to his own detriment for years."

"I always thought the two of them looked so happy together... We *all* did. I can't believe how wrong I was."

"You weren't necessarily wrong." I heard the sink. Was he done? He stood washing his brushes and I tried not to think of Saichi doing the same. "Kit-shi, think of something that's rewarding in the moment but does long-term damage. Something that gives you false confidence, false strength, false happiness, but only temporarily. Something that's good the first time, better the second, but then it's not enough the third time, and it never will be again. Does that sound familiar at all?"

"Addiction."

"Exactly. Mino is toxic to Hyung but he's addicted all the same."

"But don't you think that if they sat down and talked things out that maybe they could heal? Maybe they might both—"

"No, I don't. Kit-shi, I hadn't planned on telling you any of this, but at this point, it's vital you understand the gravity of the situation. So I have something of a confession to make." He took a deep breath and turned to face me. "I may have had some significant involvement in your recruitment."

"My recruitment? You mean, *you* scouted me?!"

"Yes, but as for the details of that… I'm in a bit of a predicament. This really isn't my story to tell. Has Hyung spoken to you at all about what happened a year ago?"

"The Minchi Incident? I know that they fought and drank and ended up in the hospital? And Saichi said something about how yesterday's fight was a lot like what happened back then? Did they kiss back then too and—?"

"So you do know *something* about it. That makes me feel marginally better, I suppose… The incident took place at our first-anniversary party. I don't know how much champagne those two consumed, but it was altogether too much. Hyung confessed to Mino, something physical took place, then Mino had a sudden change of heart and things went downhill fast. And yes, both were hospitalized. Mino for alcohol poisoning, and Hyung… for an overdose."

No.

No.

Please, no.

Scalding horror clawed up my throat, but Jaeyoon went on.

"He said his heart hurt, so he kept taking painkillers…"

"Oh, Saichi, *no*…"

I wished I could go find him and hold him. I thought reality couldn't get any heavier. The reality of twisted paintings, lit matches, lonely eyes. The reality that Saichi hated himself for his own feelings.

Now it was heavier than my chest could handle.

"So there you have it. Mino almost killed Hyung, and he woke up with no memory of it whatsoever. Furthermore, since the president believes in tough love and values profit above all else, Minchi continues, despite my best efforts to stop it."

"The Blackout."

"Was me, yes. But that did little to discourage them. Only one of my methods has ever succeeded, which is where you come in…"

"I don't understand."

One by one, Jaeyoon twisted each of his rings as he made his way through the memory. "In the hospital, Hyung was alive but… lifeless. He wouldn't let me tell anyone, wouldn't let me call in any family to keep him company. I brought him flowers, sweets, art supplies… but he just sat there scraping a red crayon back and forth, back and forth. I didn't know what to do for him. Then I found your video. It was the only thing that got him to smile… You were the only thing he showed any interest in whatsoever."

Tears seared down my cheeks at the images Jaeyoon was showing me, and at the thought that my singing had helped Saichi up from rock bottom, just like his had helped me.

"I wanted to fly you in to meet him, but the president got wind of my plan and one-upped me. She wanted you here accessible, within reach of Hyung… a happy distraction to keep him out of the hospital and on the stage."

Another punch to the stomach. How long until I just vomited all over everything? "So my career… wasn't founded in talent or skill… I was just a stupid pawn for you and the president? A toy for Saichi? I'm here right now just because I made him smile once?"

"The fact is that video was a clear display of your talent, and it wouldn't have caught my attention otherwise. What's more, you've proved yourself again and again over the past year. You're extremely talented, and more than capable of sustained success, so don't let this provoke any self-doubt in your abilities. You're more than a pawn."

But a pawn, nonetheless.

He picked himself up off the counter and started brushing out my hair, but my nerves were actively splitting, fraying. Brushing them wasn't helping anything. The dry shampoo sent me into shivers.

"Likewise, I'm sure you know how very real your relationship with Hyung was, regardless of how or why it began."

"It wasn't real though."

"Yes, Kit-shi. It was, and it still could be. He cried the entire night. Not just over Mino. Over *you*. He loves you too. And I think he has a real chance at happiness with you."

"He's gay."

"Don't be ignorant. He's clearly bisexual."

Oh.

I should've thought of that.

Oh, thank god. So he *was* attracted to me? Half my nightmares last night had circled the miserable idea that Saichi had been forcing himself when we had sex.

Jaeyoon's hand pulled me from my thoughts and over to a drawing table. The table tipped flat and two steaming mugs knocked down in front of me.

"You don't have to drink it. Just humor me."

Across from me, he didn't drink his either. He held it to his cheek, a sight distantly recognizable from DigitAlive. I couldn't smell the coffee, and if I drank it, I knew I wouldn't taste it. The black hole of liquid was strangely disquieting, so I closed my eyes again and studied the warm neon static of my eyelids. Some of Saichi's paintings had looked like that, but the world behind his eyes was so much crueler than mine, with words like 'defective' and 'perversion' sailing around. He said he tried to paint it out. But it didn't work.

Why couldn't Mino take Saichi as he was? There was nothing at all wrong with him. He was perfect in every way.

"Kit-shi. You love him, don't you?"

I nodded.

"So can't you take him back?"

If I took him back, we'd be avoiding the problem, and then the next time Saichi broke, it would be even worse. Jaeyoon and Kyungsoon wanted Saichi and me together as some kind of fairytale cookie-cutter solution, but I was just a band-aid they slapped over an emotional cancer. The real solution was going to be much more complicated.

"I'll talk to him."

I'll talk to them both. And they're gonna talk to each other.

"Thank you, Kit-shi."

Take no prisoners.

—I've got the goods! Headed your way~
> *—Thank you, Namgi-oppa*
> *—How did you convince him??*
—You'll see~

That sounded a bit ominous, but I just didn't have it in me to care. Too much else on my mind. I knew I scarcely had the right to meddle in something so pivotal to other people's paths, so if I messed up and made the situation worse, I'd never forgive myself.

Saichi was already here waiting.

—Text me when you get to the marina. I'm out getting Noriko ready.

I screenshotted it and sent it to Namgi.

Coming back to the marina was demoralizing. Tonight's evening was insisting on another spectacular sunset, and the scene was a paradoxical downpour on my already damp spirits. Behind my eyelids, I could still see the sun lining his lips, and I could feel the simmer of our sweet tangerine memory acidifying.

Something nudged my shin. A familiar calico with almond jade eyes and a forever-kitten voice pawed at my shoelace.

"Oh, hi there. You must be Yuji Yujin."

Feeling fur between my fingers brought tears to my eyes, but she purred on unperturbed. I missed Spick and Span so much. Once all this wrapped up, maybe it was time for me to get a real pet. Screw the apartment policies prohibiting it. Far as I knew, they were just a formality too. And sure, feeding another mouth would eat into my slim grocery budget, but whatever. A pet was a safer bet than a boyfriend. Less scandal, less heartbreak.

Yujin bolted at the scream of tires. Beyond the gate, some sassy little sports car darted into the parking lot and jerked to a halt. The headlights flashed once and my phone began to buzz.

–we are go for launch! tell Leader you're here!
–we'll tail you guys to the boat!
–this is SO FUN I feel like James Bond!
–lol the name's Bond. Bond Namgi

–Saichi, I'm here at the gate
–I'll be right there.

His silhouette flared up like a phantom on the docks, the boats lunging for him as he slipped past. Even on dry land, he brought waves under my feet. I was desperate to read his face, but the backlight of the setting sun robbed me of details until he stepped into the pooling floodlights. He didn't quite manage a smile.

"Hi Kit. I missed you."

I wanted to grab hold of his clothes and look for the amber in his eyes, feel the heat of his skin, search for the details that were so quick to fade. But I couldn't do that anymore, so I dodged his eyes entirely. For all I knew, my heart was written all over my face.

"Hi. Shall we go then?"

My brevity pricked him. "Y-yeah." He started to reach for my hand, but he stopped himself in time. "Be careful on the docks, okay? It's a little windy today."

He slid back into shadow and I followed him out onto the docks. The sky was rampant with color around us, but the wrinkled river shattered daylight and remained mulishly gray. It was all a little more menacing than I remembered. I half-wished I could hold onto him after all, because the wind kept lashing my hair into a blinding web, and the folding water seemed hungry.

Behind us, Namgi was very poor at sneaking. He also looked alone. Where was Mino?

Climbing onto Noriko made me mourn the dead possibilities all over again. Saichi's atmosphere assumed confidence onboard, almost like he'd stepped onstage. He moved sturdily across the rocking deck, his hands deft on the ropes.

"Alright Kit, we're casting off."

The engine buzzed under our toes and anxiety buzzed in my ears. I went to the window and scoured the dock for Namgi. He stood waving as we pulled away.

–Minmin's on the back of the boat
–go out and get him when you guys are ready to talk!

Mino was just… waiting back there? Really, how in the heck had Namgi convinced him to do this? He must've cooled down quite a bit since our talk in the bathroom. Which was good; one willing party was better than none. This was maybe the stupidest thing I'd ever done. What if I triggered Saichi? What if I made the two of them fight even more?

Saichi was watching me. "Are you nervous?"

Yes. "No, I trust you." I stepped away from the window and tried not to watch him at the helm. Couldn't I look and not stare? Couldn't I stare and not imagine? Not miss? Not want?

"Good. I promise you don't have to worry. I'm a good captain. How far out do you want to go?"

"Just far enough for some privacy."

"Okay…" I caught his glance, felt his confidence quiver.

I tried to soften the blow, "Um, far enough to watch the sunset?"

and immediately regretted it. When I asked him to come out here with me, I tried so hard not to give him any false hope. I didn't say anything about fixing things or trying again. I told him I wanted to talk, and that was it.

The engine quieted and so did his voice, "I think this should do. I don't wanna take you too far." We slowed and the boat grew heavy in the water. The commitment I'd made sunk in as I watched the keys plunge into his pocket. "I'll drop the anchor. Be right back, okay?"

I panicked thinking of Mino, but Saichi returned uneventfully. Then he didn't know what to do with himself, so he sat on a crate and made it easy to elude eye contact. I appreciated the cushion of space he kept between us, but as the night hungered after the windows, the cabin felt smaller and smaller and the pressure of 'talking' seemed to grow physical on Saichi's body. I meant to speak up first. I failed.

"Kit, first and foremost, I want you to know how sorry I am for what I did. I can offer no excuse for my behavior that day. I can only apologize. I never, ever meant to hurt you like that."

"I forgave you the second it happened."

He was so close so quickly, his fingers warm and sure on mine. The touch made me ache. Where did the cushion of space go?

"I don't know what came over me that day, but I'm not going to lose control like that again... because I'm not going to let him anywhere near me outside of work. He'll probably be keeping his distance from me anyway, so we really have nothing to worry about. Please, if you could just give me one more chance, I promise I won't hurt you again. I *promise*, Kit. *Please.*"

I made the mistake of meeting his eyes. Bright earnest amber, with a sunset pooling along his lash line. The draw of his lips felt inevitable. I wanted so bad to fall back into his world. To forget that I'd ever found out—

"Saichi..." He shrank away from the minor key in my voice. Immediately, the temperature plummeted again. Anxiety. Nausea. Claustrophobia. All came surging back. I had to force the rest of the words up and out, "That's not why I asked to see you today."

His chest heaved and his eyes and fingers fluttered off of me. "Sorry, I had to try or I'd always wonder, and I don't have room in me for any more regrets. If I could go back to that day, I swear I'd—"

"I wouldn't have you change a thing," I cut him off. My words shocked him. "Maybe that wasn't the best way for Mino to find out, but it's good that it's all out in the open now, right?"

He shook his head vigorously. "It was cruel to you both."

"Well, what's done is done." I'd spent all last night lying awake drafting mini speeches. I had this in the bag. "Saichi, the actions you take without thinking don't determine who you are. What matters is what you do next. And you have to know that getting back together with me—and just trying to avoid him—won't really help anything. You'll never heal that way."

"Yes, I will. You heal me."

"No. Even when we were together, your feelings for him were so strong that you had to act on them. Shouldn't you respect that? I don't want you to push those feelings aside because I'm in the way."

"It's not like that, Kit." A sigh blew him off his feet and he slid down the control board to the deck. He spoke into his hands, "I don't even know what I feel toward Min anymore. After so many years of being around him and putting up with everything he does, I can't tell if I still like him or if I'm just trained to smile for the cameras every time he touches me."

Pavlov's dog? Or was it Stockholm syndrome? When he looked up at me, I saw straight into the exasperating maze he'd been chasing himself through. Whatever it was, it was eating him alive.

"And even if I do like him, so what? He's not interested."

"No, you can't be sure how he feels. You didn't exactly confess? When I talked to him, he was completely deluding himself about the whole thing. So if you really explain to him…?"

"I think we were both pretty clear about our feelings. I kissed him and he called me a—"

"*Don't* say it. No more of that damned word, please. And no, you both still need to actually talk things out. Not yell, or fight, or kiss. Whether it's frustration, attraction, romantic feelings, *whatever*, you gotta stop keeping it pent up inside you. You lost control that day because you kept it in too long."

"I've tried to get it out. I've tried to kill it off…"

"Saichi, that's what I'm trying to tell you. You can't kill feelings. You can't force them out, can't paint them out. You need to experience them, and talk about them, and try to understand them. You need to let Mino in on what you've been going through for all these years…"

What was it that I told myself yesterday on the stairs to the roof? 'Fuck off, feelings?' I believed in everything I was saying to him, but still, could I really stand here giving Saichi advice about listening to his feelings while I was still actively trying to discount my own?

Yes, because I wanted better for him than I wanted for myself.

"I *can't*, Kit…" He grabbed his sides and squeezed. He needed someone to hold him, but it couldn't be me. "If he thinks that kiss didn't mean anything, that's fine. Or even if he knows exactly what it meant but he's in denial about it, that's fine too… That's the reality I wanna live in. I've already lost you. I don't wanna lose him too."

"It's gonna be alright. We're gonna talk it all out tonight, okay? And I'll be right there with you to help."

"What?"

I hurried for the door before I could lose my nerve. Twilight had deepened and my heart was crashing in my chest.

"Mino? Are you out here?"

Oh, good god.

An odd-looking bundle sat up against the back railing. I could make out the glitter of two eyes, but everything else was confusing. He was all rolled up in a blanket. Cinched with a belt? And he had a rag in his mouth?!

He was already growling at me.

Namgi had *kidnapped* him.

No return.

"Oh my god, oh my god. Mino, listen, I am so sorry."

I tripped and smashed into the deck in my hurry. And as soon as I wrestled the rag out of his mouth, he exploded, "Kit, *you* did this?! You and Babo—" The wind snatched away most of his screaming.

"He wasn't supposed to kidnap you!"

Behind me, a loud gasp. "Kit, why is Min on my boat?!"

"Satch?! *What the fuck is going on?*"

They both probably thought I was some kind of sociopath now. Maybe I was. But dammit, it wasn't supposed to happen this way! "Everyone just calm down!"

"How the fuck am I supposed to be calm?!"

"Please just hold still so I can get you out of this thing, okay?"

"Why? So you can fucking murder me or some shit?!"

"No! I just brought you out here to talk to Saichi."

The concept shocked them both into stillness, so I managed to get the belt off of Mino, but when I started untangling the blanket, he snarled and thrashed away from me. I almost got kicked in the face. "Kit Allister, you're literally fucking insane!"

He scrambled to his feet the second he was free, whipping off his shirt just as another cold blast jetted across the water. The fabric snapped like a flag in his hand, spattering us with sweat, then it seemed to vanish up into the night. My eyes were still searching for it when Saichi gave a shout of alarm. He tried to catch Mino as he reeled toward the railing, but Mino shoved him roughly aside and hurled his body half-overboard to retch into the river.

Saichi subdued the urge to help and turned to tell me very softly, "I don't think this is going to work…" I stayed down on my knees, appropriately apologetic, but also prepared to plead with them.

"I'm sorry about this, Mino." I pressed my forehead to the deck in formal apology. "I am really very sorry, but—"

"And I'm really very fucking pissed." Half his words gurgled with bile, the other half were spat into the water. "Like, Jesus fucking Christ, Kit, you're crossing into serious sasaeng territory here."

"I didn't mean it to be like this. Namgi was just supposed to *convince* you; not kidnap you!"

"Yeah, well, all three of you are shit human beings!" He spotted the belt on the deck and tried to kick it, but he almost fell into Saichi. Saichi still clearly wasn't sure whether to help him or give him space. "You." Mino jabbed a finger at him. "Take me back *now*."

"Um, I *am* sorry and all, Mino, but can we wait a bit before we—?"

Mino spun, skin flashing silver with sweat, and he looked ready to rip me limb from limb, but he only made it three stomps before his legs jellied and dragged him into a crumple on the deck. "*Dammit!* Piss on fucking pins and needles! And piss on boats and piss on Babo and piss on your stupid fucking scheme, Kit!" He latched onto my shirt and dragged me close enough to burn my face with his breath. "If you think I'm gonna stay out here and talk to you backstabbing pieces of shit, you've got another think coming."

Saichi jerked back to life. "Get your hands off Kit!"

The hit was audible. Saichi looked more offended than hurt, but that didn't change the fact that Mino had hit him. My nails bit the deck to quell the reciprocal violence that simmered up in my stomach.

"Don't fucking touch me, creepy-ass. I said take me back *now*."

Saichi grimaced and his body deflated. It was the words that got him, not the hit. It was always the words. "Yeah sure," he mumbled. I grabbed his pant leg when he turned to head inside.

Even under the best circumstances, this was more or less what I'd expected to happen during my little intervention. It was time to put my foot down. No turning back now.

"Saichi, *no*." Before I could think twice, I reached up and dug into his pocket, yanking out a fishing bobber with cat ears and two chiming keys. "We're staying out here until this is fixed. Why do you think we're on a boat? It's so nobody can run away."

Both were shocked again.

"Unbefuckinglievable."

"And *you*. Stop calling Saichi names. And if you lay a finger on him again, I'm throwing these keys in the river. I'm sorry Namgi manhandled you and I'm sorry that I have to do something this crazy, but it's time you two had a talk!"

Saichi shook his head. "I'm sorry, Kit. Thank you for trying, but we're not going to be able to talk when he's this... mad."

"He's just gonna have to get un-mad."

Mino crossed his arms and legs and wiggled himself into a stubborn ball. "Nope. We can stay out here all fucking night if you want, but I'm not talking to either of you fucking psychos."

"Is it so much to ask for you to have an adult conversation?"

"What part of this hostage situation is adult conversation?!"

"Why do I gotta go this far to make you talk to your best friend?"

"That fucker isn't my best friend anymore. He's dead to me."

Saichi flinched and my palm jerked into the air, ready to smack Mino again. But then Ilsung's voice echoed back to me, *'In the future, if someone upsets you, let's try not to come to blows, okay?'* Dammit.

"You listen here, Kim Mino. You gotta learn to just shut your mouth when you've got nothing but toxic things to say. That's what you're gonna do tonight. You're gonna shut up and listen to Saichi."

Saichi gently took my hand from the air and patted it between his. "At least come inside, Min. It's cold out here and you lost your shirt."

"I refuse," Mino spat. "Take me back."

"Mino, the sooner you come sit down and work out some kind of ceasefire, the sooner I'll let him drive us home. Now come on."

Pressurized

Mino found a booth in the back of the cabin and sat at the table looking defiant, like a spoiled child impatient for dinner. I brought him a beer from the mini-fridge as a peace offering.

"No thanks. I'm drunk enough." Grumbling instead of yelling was definitely an improvement.

"You're drunk?"

"How else do you think Babo got me rolled up in a damn blanket? The fucking bastard." He eyed me for a moment and then laughed. "Did you think I just vomited out of anger or something?"

"I figured you were seasick."

"Ah, right. Either way, no more beer for me tonight, baby girl." Calling me that was another good sign. Reading those signs, Saichi crept carefully closer.

"Min, are you cold? Do you want me to go get Namgi-ya's blanket from the deck? Maybe I can find a spare shirt…"

All friendliness evaporated. "Aw fuck, I probably *should* cover up. Kit, help me, I'm stuck on a boat and some nasty creep won't stop eye-fucking me." My blood bubbled as Saichi shrunk backward again.

"Dammit, Mino! What did I *just* say about calling Saichi names?" I stood up and ripped my shirt off, because what the hell did anything matter anymore? I'd abducted someone tonight. If this ended badly, I was probably headed for jail. "Here, brat. Wear mine if you're so worried, but if I catch you eye-fucking *me*, you're gonna catch my hands." I threw the wad at his hanging jaw.

"Seriously, Kit, were you always this fucking crazy?"

Before I could answer, Saichi nudged his body in front of mine, fingers tripping over his buttons. "Min, I don't care if you call me names. I deserve it. But stop talking to Kit that way. She did this because she cares about us."

My heart gave an unwelcome wobble when Saichi shrugged off his shirt and turned to ease it gently up my arms. Mino just laughed. "Topless Kitchi colludes in kinky kidnapping. You're really not helping the threesome rumors right now, guys."

Saichi and I both shuddered. "Min, don't."

"That is *not* what this is about, Mino!"

"I'd almost forgive you if it was."

"*Ew.*"

"What's the big deal, Kit? You've already been with both of us. Why not both at the same time?"

Muttering angry Japanese, Saichi's fingers pushed a little faster up the buttons and I tried very hard to ignore the tickle of his touch, the red on his cheeks, the intimacy of having his bare body so close to mine… I could *not* focus on that right now. Especially not with Mino trying to turn this into a weird sex thing.

"Mino, stop making it sound like you and I were ever anything. You're not fooling anyone. Saichi knows the truth. I know the truth. Now can we talk about something that actually matters, please?"

"Sure, baby girl. Let's hear it. What do *you* think actually matters? 'Cuz all I can figure out is all the crazy shit you don't give a flying fuck about. Assault. Abduction. Flashing your tits—"

"I'm wearing a bra, you idiot."

"—and the fact that your boyfriend made out with someone else right in your face. Didn't even bat an eye, did ya? Was that just another Minchi moment for ya? Did ya get off on watching him—"

"Mino, I *swear*…"

Saichi's chin hit his chest and sent tears splashing to our shoes. His fingers fell off my top button and into my hands, giving me a squeeze. "It's only because we've got him cornered," he whispered. "I promise he's not really this mean. This is just what he does when anyone pushes into the buffer zone. He pushes back. So can we stop? I don't like this. I don't want him saying these things to you."

"It's fine, Saichi. I know exactly what he's doing." I squeezed his hands back, but he still wouldn't lift his eyes so I told Mino instead, "Fortunately, I really *don't* give a flying fuck."

"But I do." That all-too-familiar sensation of breaking a whole in half struck again as his hands left mine. And how pathetic. We were never meant to fit together. Maybe we'd only fit because we tried so hard to mold ourselves to each other's broken edges. But we could only hold a false shape for so long before we broke again.

He leaned over the table to soak in Mino's attention. When he spoke, his voice held no anger, no evidence of tears, no emotion at all. For a voice that could hold so much and move so many hearts, the emptiness was chilling.

"Your fight is with me, Mino. I'm the thing you hate. The f—, freak. The supposed friend who violated your trust all these years. The sick, defective, twisted freak. That's me."

Hearing his own hate in Saichi's voice seemed to sink teeth into Mino, folding him smaller. "Satch, don't. Stop—"

"I was wrong to force myself on you. I'm sorry for my actions. But there's nothing I can do about who I am. I was born messed up."

"I said *stop*. No, you weren't."

"It's okay, Min. It doesn't have to ruin everything. Nothing has to change between us. I promise I'm very good at fighting it. Just… every now and then, I lose control."

"Lose control of what?!"

"*Myself*. Me, myself, and the things I wish I didn't want."

Like anything compressed a little too much, Mino finally blew up. "Just *shut up!* Shut the fucking fuck up!" One swat and the beer can flew across the cabin and burst against the far wall. Both ignored it. I watched it gush froth in all directions, feeling the same fizz spilling through my stomach. It took every muscle in my throat to swallow another scream bubbling up. Mino was the one who needed to shut up and listen. But things were moving forward now, and if I said anything, Mino's vitriol would refract through me and send the conversation into a million idiot directions again. All I could do was press a supportive hand against Saichi's back.

"Whether or not I say things out loud doesn't change what *is*."

"Bullshit. I can't believe you can spout all this absolute *bullshit* with your girlfriend standing right there! Like, god dammit, Satch! Stop being so fucking stupid! You're not fucking gay!"

Saichi's back rippled beneath my fingers. Jaeyoon clicked his tongue in my ears. *'Don't be ignorant. He's clearly bisexual.'* He started to tremble again, like he had in the kitchen, in the dressing room, on the roof… the tremble of him fighting to contain, control, compress. Mino was constantly exploding, constantly spewing every thought that crossed his head, but Saichi so rarely let anything out. He *was* good at 'fighting it,' but how unfair that he even felt that necessary.

Saichi's voice tore itself into a faint, tormented whisper meant for no one's ears, "I'm sorry, Min, but… I really do love you."

Mino fell back into the booth with a painful thud, and then there was endless silence. No sound but the sigh of wind, the hopeless slap of waves against steel. Whatever flowered on Mino's face was unreadable to me. For one second, I let myself really, really hate him for taking Saichi from me.

Then finally, the tension scared up a laugh.

"Well, fuck. Now ya said it."

"Please don't be afraid of me, don't avoid me, don't hate me…"

"I'm not afraid of you, stupid. You're just a little confused. No shit you like me. We're best fucking friends, remember? And like, *hello?* I'm Kim Mino? Lots of people like me! I'm cute or whatever."

You gaslighting little—

"Min…"

"You think just 'cuz you kissed me once now you're gay? I was in on that kiss too. So what? Am I magically gay now too? Nah, Satch. You're just confused. You don't gotta make it all weird."

"Min, I wanna kiss you a lot more than once. Does that answer your question?" Two bright berries rose into Mino's cheeks. Something wafted through the cabin, the faintest whiff of the slimmest possibility that things were heating up. I had a sudden overwhelming *need* to be elsewhere. I could wait outside while they worked out whatever ideas were wandering between their minds.

"Okay, so tell me, Satch…"

I inched toward the door as Mino rounded the table, but Saichi clutched at my hand the second I moved. The distance between the three of us closed too quickly for comfort. I didn't know if I could handle another Minchi kiss right in front of me. This wasn't exactly how I saw my intervention going. I thought best-case scenario was them leaving as friends, not boyfriends. I mean, great for them if they got together, but please don't make me watch. My fucks were slowly but surely flying back to me.

But Mino merely pressed close enough to get a better look into Saichi's eyes before he asked, "So you wanna fuck me then? That's what 'gay' is, Satch. Do you even know how two dudes fuck?"

Saichi and I made the same agonized sound. He still wouldn't let me go so I ducked behind him to hide. "Min, can we *please* not talk about this? Especially in front of Kit? I promise you I'm not… imagining stuff about you without your permission, okay?"

"Satch, c'mon, you've got it all fucking wrong. You're so not gay. Let me just ask you something: if you took a shoe and rubbed my dick with it, would you say I'm attracted to shoes if I got hard?"

I couldn't believe my ears. But when I peeked out from behind Saichi, there was not even a figment of a joke on Mino's face.

"Min, what the hell are you talking about?"

He shrugged and smiled with maddening indifference. "All I'm saying is you're not gay just because I'm objectively hot and good at getting you hard onstage. It's just the physicality of things, dummy."

Saichi was speechless so I took over. "Do you even hear yourself?! I honestly can't believe the depth of your denial! You're just outing yourself more and more, you know that?"

"Oh, stop. You're both so fucking naïve."

"*Be quiet, Min.*" Saichi's voice was soft but potent, and the cabin shivered into silence. "You really think I'm that stupid? That I don't know what's going on in my own head, my own body? Why would I put myself through all this if I wasn't sure?!"

Step by step, he drove Mino backward across the cabin. Would I be able to stop a fight if I had to? They weren't *that* much bigger than me, but I was outnumbered.

"If I could change, if I could stop... I would've done it years ago! I would've done it way before I fell in love with Kit! Don't you get it?! Loving you is torture! I don't *want* to love you. All I want is to get over you, but you won't leave me the hell alone!"

Mino's mind was absent from his words as he digested, but he still managed to be an asshole, "So all the years I thought we were friends, you were just—"

"Maybe Kit's right. Maybe it's not my feelings you're afraid of. Maybe you're denying your own. Honestly, Min. *Shoes?* What kind of logic is that? You're a train wreck."

I was so proud of him I could've applauded, but I was afraid to fan the flames. It took Mino another minute to generate more venom, "Fuck you. I don't swing your way, sicko."

"Is that right? Are you *sure?*" Saichi took another aggressive step. Mino sat with a plop onto the table. Then Saichi's fingers spread on his bare chest and pushed, and Mino plunged backward. Was this where I was supposed to jump in and mediate? I couldn't. My bones melted as he crawled over top of a muted Mino and sat on him.

"What about a year ago, Min? When you pushed me into bed—"

"Hah?!"

"—and started riding me? What was that all about?"

"You, you fucking *liar!* I d-did not—?! Get off me!"

Saichi sat back on Mino's hips and crossed his arms, a harsh laugh breaking out of him. "Yeah, that's what I thought. You know, I drank twice as much as you that night. I tried *everything I could* to forget, and I still remember it like it was yesterday. But okay, Min, if you're that scared, *fine.* We'll keep living in your little fantasy world and pretending nothing happened."

The anniversary party... Mino went that far with Saichi and then turned on him?! And then they both just ignored the incident and went back to normal after they got discharged?!

As shocking and awful as it was to imagine, it was definitely believable. But whether or not Mino actually remembered it was a different story. I knew from experience that the human brain was capable of tossing out massive chunks of crucial information with just a little alcohol in the mix, but it only took *me* a couple tiny reminders to piece reality back together again... so how did Mino manage to muffle such a life-altering memory for an entire year? Was he lying? Saichi was a saint to give him the benefit of the doubt all this time, but either way, they were skating around a huge breach of trust on exceptionally thin ice.

Helpless, Mino laid back and hid his face behind a cross of fists, a nightmare rendition of one of Vortex's signature moves. "S-satch..."

"I don't care anymore if you ever remember. I *will* get over you. Because I fell in love with a complete lie. You're not the person you pretend to be in front of the fans, and I promise you: if you ever throw yourself at me onstage again, I'm gonna call you on it."

When he spoke, it was more like he was running a program, and less like he had any control over his words. "Y-you're the one lying and making up shit! And you know M-minchi's not—"

"If my words mean nothing to you, then just stop talking to me." He climbed off of Mino and thrust a hand at me, his face striped with conflict. "Kit. Keys, please? I'm pulling the anchor. We're going home." I'd never heard him sound so cold, but his fingers lingered on mine a moment longer than necessary, sparking some glimmer of a message I couldn't quite read.

Mino was shaking, tightening on the table. His teeth creaked under the words, "No. Hang on."

Twin beads of blood snaked elegantly down his wrists. I gagged in revulsion, could barely scream, "Mino, *stop!*" His fists pounded down on either side of him and then he sprang up, wild-eyed.

"All this stupid bullshit stays on here on this boat, ya hear me?! Don't you two go spreading that fake-ass story around or I swear—!"

"Mino, please! Calm down!" I snatched up his hands, peeling finger after finger open. My stomach convulsed at the bloody crescents his nails had carved into his palms, but I kept him firmly shackled where he was. He didn't even seem to notice me, his voice pushing into ever higher hysterics.

"Whatever happened that night, you're wrong about me, okay?! I am *not like you! I fuck women!*"

"So do I." Saichi was a wall of bland dispassion in the face of Mino's frenzy. Emotion had vacated his voice again, and somehow, the contrast helped me home in on everything Mino's voice was trying to tell us... It held much more fear than anger, and not an internalized phobia kind of fear either. Legitimate terror.

"Then stick with that! You stick with Kit and I'll stick with my bitches and you just keep your stupid gay mouth shut! I'm sick of taking all the flack just because I'm the one with the pink hair!"

"What flack?"

"These rumors about us go around and you just breeze right through them like they're nothing! Meanwhile I'm getting fucking hunted in my own goddamn agency!"

"What do you mean *hunted?*"

"Those trainees!" The emptied beer can gave an innocent rattle as Noriko bumped over a wave and Mino's eyes shot to it. Seized by some sadistic, primordial urge, he wrenched free from me and smashed the can under his heel, splattering my face with icy spray. "They've been making my life a living *hell!*"

Breaking point.

The peculiar light in his eyes, the way he ground his shoe into the can carcass, the blood dripping from his fingers… Who was he?

Saichi and I passed silent speculation back and forth across the cabin. Mino was a lot of things—whiny, moody, outspoken, touchy-feely—but that kind of meatheaded violence was a little odd for him. And yet, he'd been doing so many things out of character lately that I wasn't sure I'd gotten to know the right character at all. The Mino that I knew wouldn't get in fights in the locker room, or tell all the fans that Minchi is dead, or play hot-and-cold with Saichi.

I tugged his wrist again, trying not to feel the tackiness of blood. "Can we maybe talk about whatever's going on with those trainees?"

His trance fractured. "Fuck no?"

"Mino, when you say you're getting hunted, I can't help but wonder what exactly went down a month ago… in the locker room?" His eyes snapped up and scorched mine. I'd hit close to the mark.

"That? That was nothing. Nothing happened. Fuck off."

Saichi backed me up. "That *was* when everything took a turn for the worse. You've been… off ever since then."

"Mino, were you hurt?"

"Do I fucking look hurt to you?!" I couldn't tell. His face had shelled over into mean marble again.

"Um, actually, Kyungsoon-nim might have told me a little about the situation—"

"*What did she fucking tell you?*" Mino scared me right off my feet and into the beer slick, the can biting into my thigh. "Whatever she said to you, it's all a fucking lie!"

Saichi shoved Mino aside and lifted me back up, murmuring in my ear, "It's all a lie? Nothing happened? Sounds familiar."

"Jeez, Mino. Can you calm down please?" I flung the beer off my fingers but there was nothing I could do about the sticky situation on the seat of my jeans. Why did this *always* happen? At least I kept Saichi's shirt relatively clean this time, but still…

"*I am calm!* What the fuck did she tell you? No, wait—" He jerked me away from Saichi and pointed into his pastel mop. "Whisper it."

"You're acting really sketchy over 'nothing,' Mino. I'm not whispering anything. I'm sick of secrets. She told me—" Expecting it, I ducked under his attempt to cover my mouth. "She's having you monitored to keep you out of trouble. And she said she moved you back into the dorms. Now what's *actually* going on?"

His face dimmed to a bloodless pallor, and the anger seemed to wash away, leaving him and his voice shaky. "You mean to tell me they've got her fucking mandate? Jesus fuck, real nice, Kyungsoon. Real fucking nice. I can't wait to watch that frosty bitch melt in hell. Like, no wonder those twerpy little pieces of fuck are so cocky—"

Saichi's fingers found Mino's sleeve, only to be elbowed away. "Min, you're living in the dorms again?"

"Yeah, so? No fucking big deal." He paced back to the booth and slammed into his seat again, going for nonchalance.

"But you're Vortex."

"Not to the Ice Bitch, I'm not."

"I don't understand."

"Don't worry about it. I'm doing fucking great in the dorms. Except for those little shits. I thought we were going home? Let's go."

"Min, whatever's going on, can I please help somehow?"

"I already told you what you could do to help. You shat on me."

"I'm sorry. I didn't know the issue was so serious."

"You wanna help? Storm the Ice Bitch's office, remind her that you're responsible for over half of KJ's revenue, then bat your eyes and get those little fuckers fired. She's not gonna ask you for a reason. She knows what they fucking did."

"Min, what…? What did they do?!"

"You don't gotta know the nitty-gritty to help me out."

I had *no* patience for this. I was across the cabin in seconds, slamming open palms on the table. "What is really going on?!"

"Drop it, Kit. Step off."

"No! What are you hiding?"

"Fucking. *Nothing.*" The threat in Mino's voice summoned a nervous hand to my shoulder, a wordless request from Saichi to leave things where they were. His fingers were trembling again, but what was the worst Mino could do? He wasn't gonna hit me. Even if he did, I wouldn't care. We'd made it this far. Like hell was I going to back out of the buffer zone now.

"Mino, the more you push back, the worse I think it is, and the more I desperately want to help. What is it? Are they breaking the law? Is it drugs? Prostitutes? A fight ring? Or are they just trashing your dorm? Why won't you talk to us about it? You're scaring me—"

He caught my wrist in an iron squeeze and yanked me across the table, almost knocking our foreheads together. He spoke low, fast, and poisonous straight into my ear, "When are you gonna be fucking satisfied? You stole my best friend and totally ruined him for me, and now you wanna embarrass me in front of him too? Listen, I'll kill the threesome rumor, so how about you just back the fuck off?"

Great. So, from the sounds of it, I'd accomplished nothing tonight. No apologies, no sympathy, no self-reflection, no *humanity* out of Mino whatsoever, regardless of Saichi's honesty. Only a saint like Saichi could fall for someone so impossible.

No, no, no. I had to believe he cared more about Saichi than he was showing, and if Saichi loved him so much, then there had to be a good person hiding in there somewhere.

"Let *go.*" Saichi worked frantically to pry Mino's fingers off of me. The smear of crimson he left on my wrist riled up my stomach again.

I needed to air out my head. I tried to get down, tried to ground myself, but my eyes glued to the starbursts where Mino had brought his fists down on the table like blooded hammers.

What a joke: a would-be nurse with hemophobia. Was I really gonna pass out over a couple spots of unicorn blood? There wasn't time for that. Even if Mino was rapidly ascending my shit list, I still cared about him, still wanted to help... so I still had to fend off any and every flying fuck.

"Whatever your problem is, stop taking it out on Kit."

"Tell her to quit pushing my fucking buttons then."

I grabbed Mino's wrist right back. "You think you can scare me? *Nothing* scares me anymore. I'm not letting this go just because you tell me to. If it's embarrassing or private or whatever, I can step out, but *he* deserves to know what's going on. He's the one you're asking to storm the president's office."

"I'll do it," Saichi spoke up, his fingers folding over top of mine. "I owe that to my best friend. If he wants my help, I'll give it. Especially since I brushed him off before..."

"Aren't you concerned about facing off with the president when you don't even know what's really going on?"

Saichi took my hand into his, stroked his thumb over my knuckles, smoothed the frustration out of my fingers. Half of an uneasy smile found its way onto his face, and he shook his head. The utter saint...

"No, if he says those trainees did something worth getting fired over, then I believe him. He wouldn't ask for help if he didn't really need it... um, so maybe should just leave it alone at this point? Because it seems like maybe—"

I turned to Mino. "You hear that? He sees you're uncomfortable, and he wants to help you out. No judgment, no conditions, no questions asked. He tells *you* he's uncomfortable and you gaslight the hell out of him and deny his sexuality."

Mino cringed a little, shrugged a little, did everything physical that he could to keep my words out of his brain, but such a barefaced double standard was hard for even him to deny.

Finally, he growled, "I don't know what more you want, Kit.

Minchi's already dead, isn't it? I'm sure as hell not gonna be playing subunit with a guy calling himself gay—"

"Can't you even attempt to sound nice about it?"

"What? Do you expect me to wave a rainbow flag or something?! He can believe whatever he wants about himself as long as he stays the hell away from me!"

"You're so unbelievably annoying, Mino."

"You're just salty your boyfriend quit your whole gender for me."

"Oh my god, he's bisexual, you asshole."

"He buys what now?"

"Bisexual. He likes both. Is that so unfathomable?"

There was a single blessed moment of quiet as Mino gave my words some thought. Then Saichi yelped, "There's a name for that?"

"What? You didn't know?"

Mino recovered. "That's not a real thing. Satch, just quit with this bullshit and take Kit back already, would ya? This is pathetic."

"*You're* pathetic, Mino! It's so ridiculous to me that you can sit here and talk like such a homophobic jerk when we all know you just want Saichi for yourself!"

Saichi put a hand on both of us and brought us hurtling back to Earth. How was he so calm? I almost wished he would push Mino down again and finish the job.

Whoa. Easy there, Kit. Consent. *Consent*.

Saichi's face was stony with gravity as he quietly reminded us, "We were discussing something important."

"Yeah." Mino let out an endless sigh that snuffed out the heat. "Just please talk to the fucking president for me? The fact that she sent those kids to… do what they did is really fucking sick."

"I'll do everything I can. Do you have some names for me?"

"You don't need names. The Ice Bitch knows who they are."

"But maybe I want to have my own conversation with them first."

"I remember a few faces from the meeting," I told him eagerly. "Plus I had a run-in with one a little while back. Let's hunt them down, Saichi. They have *no right* to mess with Mino."

Mino smirked. "Getting whiplash here, Kit. You hate me or not?"

"Of course I don't hate you. Bottom-rung trainees… no, even KJ's top-rung talents should be kissing Vortex's feet. I'll fight any one of those stupid punks."

He scoffed. "It's easy to fight off *one*. It's when they come in a group that things get gnarly."

A chill spidered down my spine and tore its way through Saichi. We shared a look of sheer horror because suddenly it was all too easy to put two and two together: Mino trapped in a locker room shower with a gang of bullies who had nothing to lose and everything to gain. Maybe the only reason we hadn't seen it before was that it seemed too terrible to be true.

I should've listened to Saichi's warning. Should've left it alone.

"Mino, I'm sorry. I didn't realize…" A specter of something haunting ran across his face and all words fell right back down my throat. He just shook his head, mute.

Saichi reached across the table and touched Mino like his skin was glass. I held my breath, fully expecting Mino to pull back or swear or slap him away, but instead, he just stared down at their overlapping fingers. For all the times I failed to read the messages Saichi sent through his skin, the two of them seemed to exchange a whole conversation in one touch. The moment inflated, stretched itself thin, then snapped.

Mino blinked a single tear out of his eyelashes, and Saichi bowed his head into Mino's hands. The ferocity in his voice ripped through the tabletop. "I *will* be speaking with the president, and she *will* listen. If she doesn't, I'm resigning and I'm taking you and Vortex with me."

Mino and I both flinched. Saichi looked up with murder in his eyes and Mino was quick to clear away any more tears.

"Fuck, Satch. Chill out, will ya?"

"My anger is warranted. You deserve to feel safe in your place of work, and you deserve respect from your employer. From now on, please don't hide things this serious from me, okay? Promise me."

"Nah, I take care of my own damn problems. It's just this once. Help me out. Get those kids fired. But don't do anything stupid and fuck up Vortex."

"Your health and safety come first. For that same reason, you're moving out of the dorms *tonight*. You can have my apartment. Between Room O, Jaeyoon's guest suite, and Noriko, I've got plenty of places to stay until I can—"

"Stop being so dramatic!"

Saichi patted Mino's hands and shook his head. His eyes and his jaw were set, and while he'd hate to hear me even think it, he looked and sounded like a leader. "Min, the situation is out of hand. I'm just putting it back in your hands. Now, for real this time, I think we should call it a night."

I didn't know whether to feel guilty for putting them through this, or relieved that they'd finally communicated, but either way, definitely plenty for one night.

"Agreed."

No foul

Saichi brought a water bucket to the table and started scrubbing Mino's blood from the wood. As satisfied as I was to see the biohazard go, each stain disappeared with unsettling ease, like it was all too simple to wipe away everything that had happened tonight. I'd let those same hands wash all colorful evidence of us from my skin, and I still regretted it.

"Better?" he asked. I nodded. Was my aversion that obvious?

His smile made me want to cry. I'd dragged secrets out of him tonight that he might've preferred to take to his grave, and in doing so, I'd inadvertently given Mino more ammunition to hurt him with. Even Mino would be disembarking Noriko traumatized by whatever ordeal I'd forced him to relive. Talk about opening Pandora's Box…

The only good thing to come out of tonight was the imminent termination of those trainees. And hopefully Saichi had a little less of a burden to carry around now?

Apparently, my grief was also very obvious. Saichi tossed away the rag and pressed his fingers over mine, his voice painfully sweet, "It's okay, Kit. I'm okay. Thank you for this."

How was this okay? "But—"

"All in good time. Or maybe not. Either way, I'm okay. I promise."

He set a little white box on the table and then eased himself up, muttering something about the anchor. My heart ached to see his movements so leaden. This was a man whose body could break physics. It had all finally caught up to him.

I sighed at the sight of the white box, recognizable in any country. "*First-aid Kit.*" Aunt Caroline always liked to joke that my mom, having been a nurse, must've named me after these boxes. Maybe today I'd finally live up to the name.

"Don't mumble random English, weirdo." Mino watched me warily from across the table, emptied and exhausted. I ignored him and ripped open an alcohol wipe with my teeth, hating every association attached to the smell.

"Give me your hands."

"Nurse Kit strikes again." He sandwiched his hands together. "Leave 'em. No biggie."

"Don't be dumb. You got blood all over everything and you're still bleeding. Do you have a coagulation disorder or what?"

"Hah? A what? Making up words left and right today, aren't we?"

"Look it up." Annoyed, I snatched up his hands and broke them open like an egg on the table. His palms were a Rorschach test hosting four dancing pairs of gory shoes. The cabin gave a fascinating half-spin and sent my stomach tumbling inside me, but these were Kim Mino's hands—important hands that wrote lyrics, played guitar, piano—and these were just tiny, tiny cuts. Red paint had been no problem. Why was blood so different? I could handle this.

He shrugged. "Can't. Babo's got my phone."

"Well, you need to update your inner dictionary. You're behind on the times. I didn't insult *you* when you were acting over-the-top heterosexual with all those women at Sevens. But you call Saichi the f-word for kissing you and then totally deny his orientation exists just because it makes you nervous?"

"Why are you on my case again? Weren't we talking about blood?"

"Sure. Blood." I dabbed another cut and he hissed. "Humans all bleed the same, no matter who they love. You think it doesn't hurt Saichi when you say that stuff? How would you like it if he called you names every time you touched him?"

Saichi stepped back into the cabin, wiping his hands on his jeans. I was a little ashamed of how little control I had over my reactions to him and his unreasonable body. My stupid mouth was watering.

"I don't get what your end game is, Kit. Look at you. You worked hard to hit that. Don't you want him back?"

I choked on my Saichi drool. "I want him to be happy."

"Well, *I* can't give him that. Whatever happened between us was a fluke. Not gonna happen again, got it? I fuck women."

"As we've established, it's perfectly possible to want both."

"Nuh-uh. That airy-fairy bullshit is only ever one of two things: a convenience clause for threesomes or a gateway to real gay."

I aborted bandaging halfway through and threw the roll of gauze at him. The kit's medical tape was a tempting solution to his mouth. "One of my friends in New York is bisexual. And that screwed up way of thinking is what ruined all her relationships. Her partners were all so insecure it was pathetic. All dead *certain* she was gonna run to the other gender at any second."

He shrugged. "Well? Odds of cheating are doubled, aren't they?"

"No, you *idiot*. People only cheat if they're a lying asshole. Bisexuality doesn't magically make you an asshole. And just because you *can* like more than one gender doesn't mean you're drooling over every single human that walks by. She was completely capable of committing to one person and being loyal to them."

"I dunno why you're telling me this shit. You know me. I sure as fuck don't commit to one person. Monogamy's fucking outdated."

"Just… try and empathize for a second with someone who *does* want a committed relationship. My friend's heart got broken so many times she's given up on dating, and she got so much hate from straight people and LGBTQ people alike that she's back in the closet. Is that what you want for Saichi? You want him to give up on love? To feel like he's not allowed to be attracted to anybody? You want him to be happy too, don't you? I'm not saying you need to date him. I'm saying he needs your support as his friend."

The engine roared to life and Mino studied Saichi's back in silence.

I couldn't believe I'd actually shut him up. We were moving again, headed back to reality. To a better place? Was the fight over or not?

"It suits him," Mino murmured. "He's always stuck in the middle, always between two worlds. You wanna know the real reason he moved here to Korea? Because back in Japan, they were merciless when they found out he's half-Korean. These were kids he'd known his whole life, and the second they found out his dad was Korean, they turned on him. So he left his precious grandma and came over here to start over, and then how does Korea welcome him to his new home? By bullying him right out of high school for the same shit..." Old, dull anger glinted in his eyes. "And look at me. I'm no fucking better. I'm even worse because I'm supposed to be his best friend."

Bullied for being biracial, bicultural, bisexual. So that was the dark truth behind the need for Oh Saichi to live as Ayukawa Saichi and Oh Chaeji. He was just trying to fit in.

I took Mino's hand to stop him from clawing into the fresh gauze. There *was* still hope for him. There *was* a good person buried in all the bluster. "It's never too late to choose kindness."

"I'll work on it." He pulled his hand free with a smirk and collapsed forward onto the gory table, heaving with some sweet and sour sound. "After all, I won't have this face forever. Gotta work on my personality, like you said, or I'll end up a lonely old fuck someday."

I found my shirt on the floor and draped it over the goosebumps peppering his arms. He looked up and managed to giggle a little, tugging it on over his floofy head. It wasn't the best fit on him, but it was somehow emblematic of a white flag, minus a few bloodstains.

The engine sputtered quiet.

I looked up in surprise to see Saichi standing over us.

"Hm? What's up, captain?" Mino reached out across the table and poked his stomach, leaving a bloodstain there too. Disgusted, I licked my thumb and rubbed it off of him. Saichi's face and his whole upper body flushed and Mino found a giggle with a lot more life in it.

"I just thought I heard—"

Saichi was interrupted by a long wail sailing across the water.

Insidious.

"There's someone waiting for us." At the helm again, Saichi pointed ahead through the windows. Mino and I scrambled out onto the deck. My first thought was paparazzi, but it didn't take me long to recognize Namgi's neon tracksuit smeared across the dock.

"Ballsy of him to come back here," Mino snarled.

"*Oppa?*" He didn't look up. "What's wrong with him? Is he injured or something? Why does he look all squished?"

"Nah. He's blubbering about something. Happens all the time." The engine cut again and we glided closer into ever louder sobbing. Saichi slipped past us and leapt onto the dock.

"Stay there until I—"

I ignored him and jumped. "Oppa, why are you crying?"

"*You.*" Mino bowled us both over and took Namgi by the collar. "Blanket burrito, huh? You lawless piece of crap! You think it's funny to abduct people?! If I weren't fucking exhausted, I'd strangle you and throw you in the river!"

"*Do it!* Just throw me in! I don't wanna live anymore!"

Saichi and I exchanged a look and he chuckled. "Namgi-ya, was the store out of your favorite chocolate again?"

"*No! You don't understannnd!*"

"Shh, Oppa, take a deep breath. You're okay…"

He pulled his head out of his knees and looked up at us, but seeing our faces pulled out that same long loud billowing wail. Some kind of maternal instinct kicked in and I knelt down to rub his back. "Kittie, I'm sorry I'm like this! Leader, I'm trying *all* your calm down strategies and none of them are working! I'm just so *mad!* And you know *I cry when I'm mad!*"

"Do you wanna talk about it, Oppa?"

"No, I don't! I don't wanna say it. I don't want it to be real."

"Hey, hey, you're alright…"

"I am not alright!" I smoothed his hair out of his face and he latched onto my hands and shook them. "Oh, Kittie, but I gotta say it or it's gonna be really bad. Leader, Minmin, we gotta stop him—"

"Mhm?"

"Ryo-chan told me he's quitting!"

Quitting.

Quitting… Vortex?

No, he couldn't mean that.

But all three of them were powerfully quiet, like that was exactly what Namgi meant. But he *couldn't* mean that. Vortex couldn't be quit. Vortex members couldn't stop being Vortex. Vortex was just the five of them existing together. That couldn't stop, end, or change.

Finally, Mino spoke, "That's not something to joke about."

"That's what *I* said! And I just got so *mad!*"

"Where is he?" Saichi asked softly.

"I tried to call Jaejae too from my phone *and* Minmin's but he still hasn't unblocked us from last month."

"Gimme back my phone, you boob."

"Here. Call from mine. Honestly, you both need to stop pestering Jaeyoon so much. You know it makes him sad to have to block you. Can we just make it a Vortex policy not to prank call each other?"

"Declare it as leader."

"*No.*"

"Leader, you'll talk to Ryo-chan, right? You can make him stay with us, right? I came straight here to get you—"

"Straight here from where?"

"From Ryo-chan's place. He called me saying he wanted to talk, and he was being all serious and scary, and—"

"Shh, let's head back over there and talk to him. Up, up." Saichi helped him to his feet and fluffed his hair. "Namgi-ya, we're gonna need a ride. Can you manage it?"

"No answer, Satch."

"It's fine. Call again in a bit. Let's go."

Um, no. Me going along probably wasn't the best idea. The stakes were way too high. I'd just spent most of my evening mixed up in the politics of Minchi, and I still wasn't convinced that I hadn't made things worse. If there was even the slightest chance I could jinx things and screw up Vortex for the whole world, then I wanted nothing to do with whatever conversation was about to take place. And it wasn't all that slight of a chance, because if I showed up on Ryo's doorstep during a time like this, he'd go ballistic.

Yeah, they needed to talk this out alone among themselves, without a sixth wheel clogging up the works. Just watching their backs disappear down the dock, that much was clear. They looked better without me, and they'd be much better off.

But could I really go home and go to bed still uncertain if my world was ending or not? Maybe if I knocked myself out with sleeping meds again…

"You're still in a mountain of shit, Babo Namgi, but apparently we've got bigger fish to fry tonight, so rain check, yeah? I'm still gonna fight you, but like, next week."

"Minmin, you know I win when we fight. I'm bigger."

"I'm gonna roll you in a damn blanket and *then* we'll fight." Mino turned and saw me lagging behind. "Hey." He stomped back and grabbed my arm. "Don't fuck around out here in the dark. You're gonna fall in or some dumb shit like that."

"Please focus on the road," Saichi begged. He had his hands dug into Namgi's shoulders, partially because our seat belts were unable to keep us from being thrown violently all over the back seat, and partially to try and massage the bawling to a halt.

"I wouldn't even be in Vortex without him! And now he's ditching me? We had a pact!"

Mino was making sure there was always a third hand on the wheel but it wasn't helping. "Look, can you not melt down while we're on the fucking highway? I don't wanna die tonight, dickhead."

"I'd be back in Daegu washing dishes!"

"Satch, Kit, you guys be the judge. Am I sober enough to take the wheel from this lunatic? Fucking hell."

I was critically close to vomiting. One more veer might do it. "Oppa, we need to not cry while we're driving, okay?"

"I'm *sorry*. I cry when I'm *mad*."

"Then let's work on not being mad, Namgi-ya. It's going to be alright, but first, we have to make it back to Ryo's apartment alive."

I tugged Saichi close and murmured in his ear, "Can't *you* drive? You didn't drink tonight."

"Sorry, I don't have a license."

"You have a boat license…?"

"We'd die, Kit."

"We might die anyway."

"I don't think so. I'm being careful about Korean, Japanese, *and* American superstitions now. My luck is good. We'll be fine."

More turbulence. I moaned and took shelter between my knees. Someone told me that was a way to stop dizziness. Maybe it did help my head stop spinning, but it also made it easier for bile to climb up my throat. I really didn't want to vomit all over Namgi's fancy car. Saichi was kind enough to stroke my back, but that brought back some distant unwelcome memory of being hunched over a toilet regurgitating glittery acid. Looking for some kind of sick bag, my fingers found a wad of fabric under the seat. Denim. A jean jacket?

"Here, Saichi. Better than nothing."

"Oh, thanks." The tires shrilled. I dove back between my knees.

"Better?" I nodded, uncoiled, and let Saichi help me up out of the back seat. Namgi's car was whole, undefiled, and safe, and somehow so were we. But crap. We were here. Was it too late to run?

Maybe Namgi's driving had knocked me right out of my body, but I felt more like I was swimming through a dream than walking through a parking garage. And what a bizarre parking garage. I knew parking garages as dank caves stinking of crime, but this one seemed more like a dystopian temple honoring luxury cars.

Mino got Jaeyoon's answering machine again and launched into another tirade, "Fucking hell, Jae! Pick the fuck up, ya rat bastard! You *always* answer when I call from Satch's phone! How the fuck can you tell it's me?! You got some kinda sixth sense?!"

"Min…"

"Get your fancy ass over to Ryo's *now!* You're fucking late!"

Namgi giggled a little. "That'll get him. You called him 'late.'"

"Damn straight that'll get him. I can't believe that asshole—"

Saichi patted Mino's back. "Let's not waste energy getting angry. For all we know, Jaeyoon's already upstairs with Ryo."

"Well, then let's get the fuck up there."

Even in the shared public space of a parking garage, I already felt like I was trespassing on Ryo's private property, and I knew Ryo himself would agree. So I balked. "Um, guys, I should go. This isn't my place. Please just give me a call when things are resolved and—"

Mino whirled like he'd been waiting for an excuse to yell.

"You're gonna go home *now?*" His voice boomed out behind us and set off a car alarm. "Nuh-uh! Kick off the goody shoes and get in the fucking elevator! Ain't *nobody* got time for this right now!"

I had to raise my voice over the noise. "I can't be a part of this!"

Saichi turned and frowned. "What makes you say that?"

A security guard came slinking out of a booth and tried to comfort the car in distress. He approached with righteous purpose in his stride, but only until he got close enough to recognize us.

"For starters, Ryo-shi *hates* me. And I really don't think I should stick my nose into this when—" Namgi started crying again, and Mino's face was turning impossible colors, so I shut up.

"What the fuck are you talking about?!"

The guard jumped a foot in the air and scurried back into his booth. Mino was gonna set off more alarms if he didn't calm down.

"You're such a nosy-ass busybody that you had me fucking *kidnapped* so you could fuck with my life but *this* is where you draw the line?!"

"That was different! It was a personal issue! And that barely even worked! I don't wanna risk screwing this up! This is a big deal!"

"Yeah? It's a big deal, huh? Then why don't we just waste some more time fucking around in the parking garage? That should help things a whole bunch, right? By all means, Kit, keep wasting time!"

"I just don't think I should be there! It's private!"

"We're idols! There's no fucking such thing as private!"

"Stop yelling! And stop taking this out on me!"

"I'll stop yelling when you stop being so damn stupid all the time! Whatever! Go ahead and fuck off, Kit! Some friend you are, ditching us in a fucking crisis!"

Was that how I came off? I half-reached for him as he stamped off toward the elevator, and Saichi half-reached for me but changed his mind and jerked around his collar instead. The jean jacket lent him an outlandish quality, and somehow he seemed colder than he had shirtless, but he also looked like a summer month on a dirty calendar.

"Please stay? We're just going to go talk to him and find out what's going on, and then I promise I'll get you safely home. Please, I'll worry otherwise..." There was a palpable difference between how he spoke to me and how he spoke to the others. I clearly sapped his confidence, and that was yet another reason for me to get the hell out of here. He needed to be the leader right now more than ever.

"Don't you think it'd be better if I stayed out of this? You need to talk some sense into Ryo-shi, and I don't wanna get in the way."

Saichi shook his head. A growl and a curse echoed across the garage to us. Mino was picking a fight with the elevator door, ramming it with his shoulder every time it tried to close. The anxious guard stood nearby, trying to coax him out of the doorway.

"Kittie," Namgi pleaded. "Please? You're one of us."

"Jesus fuck, can we just go already?! All y'all get your jackasses over here before this janky piece of shit snaps me in half!"

4-letter word

Why did an elevator need a table? That meant there was someone in this building who was paid to water that orchid, polish that vase, and dust that table. For an arbitrary elevator decoration. Had Saichi's elevator been like this? *My* elevator didn't look like this. My elevator reminded me a bit of the filthy walk-in fridge at my old coffee shop.

Of course, Ryo lived on one of the highest floors. So high that my ears popped in the elevator, and when my hearing came surging back full volume, I was startled by how loud silence could be.

"What if I wait in the hall?"

"Shut *up*, Kit."

"I can't just stroll into his apartment in the middle of the night!" A soft touch silenced me.

"It might be better if you're there," Saichi murmured. "If he's serious about quitting, then it'll be good for him to look a fan in the eye and think of the consequences."

That made me shiver. It felt too real. It couldn't be real. It had to be a misunderstanding. I might have whimpered because Namgi turned to me and patted my head.

"Kittie, you don't gotta worry about Ryo-chan. He's all bark and no bite. Like, he might yell a lot, but he's just a big butter ball."

"To you, maybe…" Kasugai Ryo, a butter ball. Yeah, right.

But through Namgi's eyes, it was the truth. Every fan knew that Ryo had a soft spot for Namgi. I'd seen it for myself on Tick Tock Talk. And it was rare, but we'd *all* seen when Vortex turned into an utter goat rodeo onstage because of said soft spot. Some fated planets would align during a dance segment and then boom, an unknown force would compel Namgi to start galloping spirals around Ryo until the man collapsed in laughter. With Ryo down, chaos reigned. Saichi was free to swing on a vocal playground in his private galaxy and Mino was free to grind on anyone and anything that caught his eye. And then, as Vortex's final bastion of sanity, Jaeyoon would be the only one left following choreography, and he alone had to wrangle them back into a presentable group.

Even if only out of pity for Jaeyoon, Ryo always tried hard to regain his composure as quickly as possible, but once Namgi launched into his loose interpretation of yodeling, not even a state-of-the-art industrial sound system could stand up to him, so a certain butter ball never stood a chance. During their one-year anniversary concert, the softie had the hiccups for a good fifteen minutes after Namgi tried to do the worm. It ruined one of my favorite raps live but I didn't mind.

Post-rodeo, Jaeyoon always scolded them mercilessly for throwing off his carefully perfected production, and the media would have a field day speculating about Vortex's downfall. But in the audience, we never minded the turmoil. It was the goat rodeo moments that reminded us how Vortex was young and goofy and human, and we cherished that. During those moments, it was easy to see that all five members had really good relationships with each other… Soft spots all around.

How could Ryo want to leave that? He couldn't. If anyone loved Vortex more than us fans, it was the Vortex members themselves. That was something that gave us all comfort, because we were certain that they would never split up. We knew Vortex would always, always be together, all five of them.

There had to be a misunderstanding. Ryo couldn't mean it.

The doors slid open and I followed the three of them down the long carpeted hall, feeling like I was headed to my own execution. There was *another* table. A table that's only purpose was to hold a fancy lamp. A fancy lamp that had *no* purpose because there was plenty of lighting overhead.

Saichi raised a hand to knock, but Namgi handed him the key. "I'm so mad," he muttered and sprayed another tear. "But he's in for it now. I brought reinforcements."

Mino punted the door over and over, making it impossible for Saichi to thread the key in. "I wish I'd gotten a hold of Jae. That guy would never stand for this fucking bullshit."

The door swung open and the hall was dark. Namgi quailed at the gloom. "Ryo-chan? Did you go to bed? You're in big trouble!"

Silence.

Mino took off raving down the hall. "Where in the fuck'd he go?! He can't just announce he's quitting and then parade off into the fucking night, that godless piece of *shit!*"

"He was already kinda drunk when I came over. Maybe he went back out to drink more? Sometimes I worry about Ryo-chan's liver."

"We'll wait." Saichi waved us in. "He'll be back."

"Oh, *oh*, but what if he *doesn't* come back?! Leader, what if he already left? What if he's already on a plane to Japan?"

"Shh, shh. You know he's not that impulsive. He's probably out on an errand or something. Maybe he's at the gym downstairs—"

I laughed. "In the middle of the night?"

"He's funny like that."

"No, I bet I know exactly what bar he's at. I bet he's at Skeletons. Leader, do you know how to get into Skeletons? You do, right?"

Mino snorted. "The speakeasy? Isn't that urban legend?"

"We can't go running all over Seoul looking for him, Namgi-ya. He'll be back. Just hurry and come inside. We've already got security all stressed out about us."

"Um?" It was worth one last try. "Being that he's not here—"

Mino shot me a savage look and snapped a finger down the ominous hall. "Nah, girlie. At this point, I'm feeling petty. Get the fuck in here. And make sure you boohoo like a brokenhearted fangirl when he starts firehosing horseshit about quitting. Consider it payback for kidnapping me."

I wanted to say that it was *Namgi* who kidnapped him, not me, but Namgi was already having a pretty rough night, so I just let Mino steer me through the door.

Ryo's apartment was *huge*, but tastefully minimalist. Clean, sleek, cool to the touch, and two stories…? I guess I didn't even know that was possible for an apartment.

As fancy as everything was, the real centerpiece of the apartment was the view—a whole wall open to the jewelry box of lights that was nighttime Seoul. Out there, the city was still alight and alive, only the low clouds and the mountains cradling swathes of shadow.

I knew this nightscape from my first descent into the country… I'll never forget the moment when I broke the cloudline and burst upon a glittering spectacle that had seemed so exotic and alien back then. Now it was familiar. Home.

Saichi surprised me with a soft laugh. "Recognize the view at all? I live right over there. See? Ryo and I sorta share a slice of skyline." He pointed at another twinkling tower looming nearby.

"Oh! You're neighbors!" I knew I'd never find his window, but I searched anyway, just out of desperation to feel connected to him still. His gallery, his home cooking, and his view were all sealed off to me now. Nothing but memories I was better off forgetting.

Saichi felt me ice up and he leaned against the window to see into my eyes. I knew the only thing that could make the view more beautiful was seeing it studded in his amber eyes, but I couldn't look or I'd cry. When I turned away, he laced his fingers into mine on the cool glass and the tears came anyway.

"My ma taught me that you never say the d-word in a marriage." Namgi stomped circles around the coffee table and Mino tried to trip him every time he went by. And he somehow could still crack jokes.

"Dick? Dipshit? Dumbass? Dammit?"

"*Divorce*, dummy. You can't even *whisper* the word, because marriage is a forever promise and you have to trust each other!"

"Babo, what the honest fuck are you talking about?"

"And that's what this is like! He's really gonna have to work hard to earn my trust again! He said the q-word in our, in our—"

"Marriage?"

"No! Our pact!"

Mino was not doing a good job handling him, and Namgi and I both needed a distraction to keep from crying, so I spoke up, "What's this pact you keep talking about, Oppa?"

"Oh *Kittie*, I'm gonna tell you all about it, and then you'll see how great Ryo-chan is, and maybe you won't be scared of him anymore!"

I took slight offense. "I'm not scared of him. I'm just trying to respect his boundaries. But I'd love to hear about your pact, Oppa."

"So like, I joined KJ in high school and all, but once I got done with school, I was supposed to go back to Daegu and take over my family's restaurant. I was kinda really sad about it, but it was taking forever to debut and Seoul is super expensive so I didn't know what else to do. I was working all these part-time jobs and my pops was just like, son, ya goofball, if you're not gonna be an idol and you're just gonna work at a restaurant, come back home and work at *our* restaurant! And he had a point, so I was like, welp, time to call it quits, and I booked a ticket home for after graduation!"

Mino rolled his eyes. "Even though you'd been an honorary Kim for years and my old man was totally fine with you staying—"

That tripped me up. "Huh?"

"Our dads were childhood friends. Babo lived with my family for a while so he could go to school in Seoul."

"What? I didn't know you two knew each other before Vortex!"

"Yeahh, all of us have got hella history, baby girl."

"Still, Min, I was gonna go home out of respect for my pops, but then I met Ryo-chan and he was like, naw, screw that. It's your life, Nam-ah, he said, and you're the one who's gotta live it every day, so you gotta do what makes your own self happy! And that's the pact: work hard and make your own self happy, not your parents! There was a word he used... Fill, Phillup? It's like respect for your folks?"

"Filial piety," Saichi murmured.

"That! Ryo-chan said screw filial pie. It's gotta be mutual respect or nothing at all! And *yeah!* But like, my folks are super awesome and cool, so we didn't fight on it. It's the Ryo-chans that suck, not the Baes."

I nodded. "I heard a bit about his parents. It's a shame. I don't get why they won't support his career choices when he's obviously been so successful." Mino and Saichi exchanged a glance and eyed me with curiosity. Right. It was weird that I knew about his private life. Blame Kyungsoon's gossip problem.

"It's a *total* shame. But anyway, I told my pops, sorry, a restaurant isn't my dream right now and I gotta make my own self happy. And he was like, awesome, do it, but I can't afford to help. So I was gonna find even more jobs, but then! Kittie, it's like Ryo-chan *knew*, because literally *a week later*, Vortex came together, and now I'm the one sending money to them! And they can afford to hire another son!"

Mino snorted. "A part-timer. They hired a *part-timer* for the restaurant. They didn't hire another son, you moron."

"Wow." I felt myself smile a little bit, which was a welcome change from the resting funeral face I'd had on since getting dumped. "A week later… Really, thank god Ryo-shi talked you out of leaving. Vortex wouldn't be the same without you, Oppa."

"Exactly! And Vortex can't be the same without Ryo-chan either! Like, what was the point of him fighting his parents all this time if he was just gonna ditch us in the end? Vortex is *five*. Vortex can't be four! He can't just leave! We need him! *I* need him!" He plunked down on the rug to cry again. "Stupid mean *jerk!*"

Saichi sat down beside him and started fluffing his blonde head again. "Did he give you any kind of reason for wanting to quit?"

"I dunno, he said the q-word and then I didn't wanna listen…"

"Namgi-ya, I'm sure there's an explanation for this. We're all very invested in Vortex, and we take care of Vortex together. We're a team. I don't think Ryo would throw that away so easily."

Namgi buried his head in Saichi's shoulder. "Thanks, Leader."

"I'm not the leader. No one leads in Vortex, and no one follows. We walk together, right?"

"T-together five-ever."

Written off.

I told him not to, and Mino agreed, but when Namgi got sleepy, he crawled under the glass coffee table, saying he always wanted a canopy bed. We could hear him getting upset again under there, but he 'wanted to be alone' and his fortress of pillows was supposed to be impenetrable. Before long, he cried himself to sleep.

"Fuck, what about the world tour? DigitAlive is booked two *years* in advance. Is that all just fucking canceled now?" Mino whispered. "Man, I really did not need this tonight."

"Or any night," Saichi agreed. "But it's not over yet."

Mino had long since checked out. His eyes had stopped seeing a good hour ago and he wasn't blinking nearly enough. "Satch," he croaked. "Sorry but can I just…?" He keeled over onto Saichi's lap. Saichi froze.

Dammit. Textbook problematic Minchi. Glaring evidence that I'd solved absolutely nothing tonight. Minchi was going to live on and Saichi was going to waste away like the monk saint he was.

"Min, you sure you wanna lie on… on some… f-faggot's lap?"

Mino sighed. "Do you gotta make everything weird now?"

"It's always been weird."

"Sorry I called you that. I won't do it again, mkay? But like, don't get all hung up on it. It's just a word."

I could hear Saichi in my head talking about 'H' and calling himself defective, and I could hear him telling me labels were heavy. "No, it's much more than just a word, Mino. It's a weapon. And I told you before it's very offensive."

"Fuck, you're such a nag. I said I'll work on it! I'll start calling our lil captain of both teams '*bisexual*.' What's up, bi-boy? Sure hope it ain't your dick! Can I lie on your lap a sec or am I gonna tent your pants? There. Ya happy now, Kit?"

"No, I'm not. Why call him anything at all besides his real name? And why are you so *mean?!* I thought you reflected on this—"

Saichi reached out to quiet me, but he was anchored by Mino's thick skull. "It's fine. Joking is how he copes. That and yelling and—"

"Pff, whatever, Mr. Therapist."

"It's *not* fine. Bullying, teasing, joking, or whatever is not fine. Mino, seriously, stop tacking labels on Saichi and just focus on the human aspect of him for once! The best friend aspect!"

"Sure. I can do that, but you're wasting your time fighting labels, baby girl. Humans are *made* of labels. That's what society's all about. The worse the labels are, the more they erase the human."

Saichi's lip jutted out and I wished Mino could see what his words were doing. He was echoing Saichi's cruel inner monologue almost word for word. "*No.* You're more than the sum of your labels. And don't you dare imply that anything besides hetero is a bad label."

"Society rules that it's subjectively bad, so you gotta hide it or it'll erase you. Works the same in the other direction too. When you're too subjectively good, you lose your humanity. If you're too smart, too pretty, too ripped… Like, what the fuck do you think idols are? We gotta be perfect, gotta get all the best labels… We become humans completely erased."

"Fans are never asking you to be perfect." I hoped my words would reach both him and Saichi. "We love you because of the human that peeks through the perfection. And it's okay to have parts of you that are different from the norm. Societal norms can be really stupid and outdated and isn't it up to us to try and change things? That's what our voices are good for! We can help people not feel alone."

"Satch, we've got a fucking philosopher on our hands," he murmured, but his tone wasn't combative. He just sounded resigned. Carefully, Saichi put his fingers in Mino's hair and petted him into a purr. In moments, the smirk faded and he drifted away.

And Saichi cried in perfect silence.

"Saichi…"

"Why did I have to be like this?" he whispered. "I'm not trying to be bad. I don't wanna be erased…"

"You are *not bad*. There's nothing wrong with you, and there's nothing wrong with how you feel." I scooted over and put my arms around him. I didn't know what else to do.

"Then why did it have to be him?" He put his face in my neck and held his breath to quiet the tears. I could feel them working hot trails down my throat. They choked us both. The words gasped out of him, "Please take me back. *Please*. You're my only chance. I can just be good and normal with you—"

Everything burned. My throat, my stomach, my cheeks, my eyes. Burning, stinging, squeezing. This was hell. And why? What had I done so wrong? Even now I was gritting my teeth and trying to do the right thing. "You are good without me, Saichi." A sound caught in his throat and Namgi stirred in his fort. Saichi pulled away and sunk his teeth into his lip. "I don't want you… to hurt anymore, but I don't know if getting back together with me will really help you. Can we maybe give it a little bit of time? I'm not sure what's right."

"No, you're right. I need to get over him first. It's not fair to you. I'm sorry. I'm sorry I'm a f—"

"*Don't*. Please don't use that word anymore, Saichi."

He bowed his head and the tears fell into the glow of Mino's hair.

What a stupid, *stupid* label… but it was a label I was all too familiar with. I had my own guilty past. Sure, I never acted on my convictions, but my inner mind used to be toxic with intolerance. After all, I was raised in a bigoted church in a town so conservative that going out in a sleeveless top was considered risqué. And whatever, conservativism is fine. To each their own. But everyone in my town was dangerously close-minded about some key issues, and some of those mindsets stuck long after I left that church behind.

Even at the coffee shop, surrounded by eccentric liberals day in and day out, I never opened my ears to them. Certain prejudices were ingrained in me and didn't seem strange. I even managed to proofread a few of Marie-Louise's more woke essays without ever questioning my thinking. Then, ironically enough, it was Minchi that opened my mind. They were an odd paradox... pure yet obscene, wholesome yet crude, and supposedly unbothered by societal norms.

I don't know how they wormed their way through my narrow mind into my heart, but they fit together so well that it didn't matter whether they were a real couple or not. Just watching them smile at each other helped me see that any and all love could be beautiful.

And then all in one awful day, I found out that Minchi was somehow real, *too* real, but also agonizingly nowhere close to real. And they *could* be real, if not for the one brat in stubborn denial. Mino's homophobia was internalized so deep that if he sucked it in much more, he'd just implode into a sad little black hole.

Fanservice was supposed to be nothing but a silly public display put on for fans. Mino made Minchi much more than that. He could say it was all for show, but even award-winning actors needed breaks between scenes, and Mino never took a break. He glued himself to Saichi regardless of whether they were onstage or offstage, regardless of whether any fans were watching. He made Minchi so convincing in and out of the spotlight that he'd even had his own groupmates fooled. So all this hot air and bluster about getting hard over shoes and swinging only one way? I wasn't buying it. Some part of Mino was definitely attracted to Saichi.

All in all, maybe the two of them just needed to spend a little time getting to know each other again, learning to trust each other again. If only they could do that away from the judgmental world of labels, away from the shitty trainees and the domineering president, and especially, away from me...

Then maybe there'd be no more tears, no more buffer zones. And maybe they wouldn't end up happy together, but if they could both at least just *be happy*, that would be more than enough.

Centrifugal

Ryo came in falling-down drunk, and he definitely would've fallen down if Jaeyoon hadn't hauled him down the hall. "Got your message," he muttered to Saichi. "Found him. And tomorrow's tabloids aren't going to be pretty."

"Get *off*." Ryo shoved but lost his footing. "I'm *fine*."

Saichi dismantled part of Namgi's fort to get a pillow for Mino, and then he stood up. "So what's this quitting business?"

Jaeyoon raised his voice, "*No*, Hyung. I think we should talk about it in the morning. It's late, he's drunk, you're tired and… oh?" He'd spotted me. I was sort of hiding behind the couch.

Ryo slurred out some kind of "What."

"Nothing. Mino's here too…" His eyes asked Saichi frantic questions. Jaeyoon definitely agreed with my original assessment that I should not be here *ever*, let alone now.

"I *am* tired," Saichi agreed. "But I won't be able to sleep until I've heard an explanation. This affects all of us, Ryo. You know we can't and won't replace you. This will end Vortex."

"Yeah."

"That's all you're going to say?"

"Like Jae said, I'm drunk."

"Don't hide behind that," Saichi snapped. "I brought you to Korea so you could be yourself. So you could be free to do what you wanted with your life."

"Mhm. Thanks."

"So now that you've gotten to live how you wanted, you're just gonna throw us away? You're fine with ending our careers?"

"Yeah, sorry."

"Why are you going out of your way to be a jerk? It's *me*, Ryo. Can you please be serious and talk to me? What's going on?"

So it was real.

He really was leaving. But *why?!*

"I dunno what you want me to say, Hyung."

"How can you call me a brother when you're trying to destroy our relationship? What's the matter with you? You—" Suddenly, Saichi's voice jumped up half an octave and poured out of him in musical somersaults. In Japanese... I never knew he was physically capable of speaking that fast.

Ryo replied in another torrent and the cadence climbed higher and faster between them. Jaeyoon gave a loud sigh, rolling irritated eyes my way. He nodded subtly toward the door and I started to crawl around the back of the couch. "Excuse me," he spoke up to distract them. "May I please be included in this conversation?"

"It's nothing important," Saichi growled. "He says he's willing to put the four of us out of a job because he wants to run home and take up the family business like the dedicated son he is."

"But—"

"He says Vortex is over."

I couldn't help the noise I made. I was trying not to vomit, to sob, to scream, to swear. All at once. Luckily, Ryo didn't hear me.

"So you're going back to Japan then?" Jaeyoon asked. Mino's eyes blazed open at the mention of Japan.

"Yes." Ryo was miraculously sober now, and the lack of concern in his voice was frightening. He droned his reply with eerie robotic speed, "I'm going to finish my education there and pursue a more stable career with my degree."

"More *stable?*" Mino rose like a vengeful ghost. "Oh, I'm sorry, are we not making enough fucking money for you?!"

"What, Mino? Did you think we were gonna do this forever? There's no future in this! I'm ready to grow up and move on!"

"Grow up?!" Mino echoed again. I wished he wouldn't. I didn't want to hear any of this more than once. Once was one time too many.

"Yeah, it's time for me to quit screwing around and get a real job."

"A real job?" It was Jaeyoon's turn to echo. "Is this not real?"

"I'm wasting my education." That phrase was an echo too... Kyungsoon had said it sarcastically that day in her office. So Ryo was echoing his parents? He couldn't really believe that though...

"Who gives a fuck about your stupid education?" Mino stumbled over, ready to fight. "*Quit pulling shit outta your dumb ass!*"

The coffee table rang like a gong.

Namgi was awake. He bowled out through the pillows howling, mowing Mino down like a steamroller. And Ryo came bolting after him so I retreated to behind the armchair. "Nam-ah, why though? Why would you sleep under a table?"

There. There was some emotion.

"*Ryo-chann!* Did you change your m-mind? Are you still quitting? P-please tell me you were just making a *really bad, stupid, awful joke!*"

"I'm sorry, I... Jaeyoon, ice?"

"Wasn't this your p-passion, Ryo-chan? Weren't we, weren't we in this together? I thought we were... d-doing what we *loved*... and, and trying to make p-people *happy!*"

Come on, Butter Ball. Melt, dammit!

"I'm sorry, Nam-ah." Ryo stood up rigidly and walked away. When he spoke, he addressed the windows, and he ironed humanity right back out of his voice again. "I'm sorry, but I've grown out of Vortex. I belong in Japan. I have a future there."

"You sound like your dad!" Namgi burst out. Ryo flinched and butted his head against the glass. I knew it!

"Is that what this is about?"

I couldn't believe I'd spoken aloud. Ryo turned so fast that he fell back against the window. His eyes found mine in bloodshot fury.

"*You!* What the fuck are you doing on my property?!"

Well, shit.

But I was already discovered, so I was going to pursue my point. Everything Kyungsoon told me came crashing back. She told me she had his parents under control, and that they had no traction in Korea. But maybe she'd lost control of them. Maybe they'd finally found a way to blackmail Ryo into coming home. And if that was what was going on, he needed to be honest and quit 'firehosing horseshit.' Everyone had a right to know the real reason he was breaking up Vortex. So I stood up and squared off.

"You're quitting because of your parents, aren't you? Are they blackmailing you? Did they issue you some kind of ultimatum?"

He roared with anger and came thundering across the room. "*How the fuck do you know about that?*"

Saichi lunged to get between us, but I'd stopped being afraid of Ryo ages ago. Like Namgi said, all bark and no bite. Well, a little bite. I took a bit of a step back just in case, and my leg hit the coffee table. Ryo grabbed my arm. Maybe he'd smack me after all. No, he looked alarmed, not mad. He was catching me.

His knee shattered the table with a loud ugly crash.

"Ryo?! Your knee! Are you okay?" The table was everywhere around us in tiny shimmering pieces. I hurried to say, "Sorry I broke your coffee table…" I wished he would get off of me. Why was he looking at me like that? It seemed like his jeans had protected him from getting cut at least. And me, nothing hurt. I put my stupid ass right through his table, but I was fine. Namgi's pillow fort actually cushioned my fall. Why was everyone looking at me like that? Jaeyoon was already muttering into his phone.

My hand. I broke my fall with my hand. It was starting to blare like a siren. I lifted it and found it drenched in vibrant emergency red.

"Kit, I—" Ryo looked so scared. But it was just paint. I looked up at Saichi and caught a vivid memory of him smeared in color. He was frozen now and bleaching a minty gray. My hand felt hot.

"Saichi? I need help."

Black stole into the room and ate the light around him.

Reality check

Just as soon as I lost everything, I had it back. The black warmed to familiar pink and I knew I was safe behind my eyelids. If I was careful, maybe I could keep myself from thinking.

"—sorry, but that's out of the question."

A voice. Reality was still rolling. I'd ducked out for a second, but that only meant that I'd missed some things, not that they'd stopped. It was kind of nice to miss things. I didn't move, didn't open my eyes. I stayed as far away from life as my mind would let me.

"I think I'm being perfectly reasonable. This is standard practice. Don't expect special treatment because you're Vortex."

I could hear an edge in Ilsung's voice. He was upset, but trying to lid it because my eyes were still closed. If I closed them tighter, could I miss more things? Could the world just go on tiptoeing around me?

"Certainly. Go right ahead. Should the president exercise her authority, I will respect her wishes, but until then, I'll ask you to keep your distance, thank you. Goodbye." He sighed and muttered, "Sheesh. Thank you for getting her here, but I'm still mad, idiot."

I peeked through my eyelashes and saw the shape of him cut out in afternoon light. He tucked his phone away, and the mechanical chirping, the stench of sterility started drilling my senses. All familiar from a time I wanted long-forgotten… I was in a goddamned hospital.

"Get me out of here," I rasped. I had to go find Ryo. Where was everyone? Did Ryo already leave for Japan? Did someone stop him?

Ilsung spun faster than my eyes could keep up. "You're awake! Thank *goodness*. Oh, and you're *speaking!* In perfect Korean! Oh my, oh my. You gave me such a scare! You know who I am, right? Do you remember the year? Do you know your name? Your birthday?"

The only thing I didn't remember was, "Why am I here? How…?"

"You had a bit of an accident."

What, my little cut? I was in a hospital for *that?* What kind of idiot passes out over a little blood when a global crisis is underway?!

"Kit-shi. *Kit.*" Two of him wobbled into one man wiping his eyes. Oh, Ilsung. I closed him away, hid back behind my eyelids. I could feel warm arms there, frantically tight, the bump of a hurried walk. The slam of a car door, tense voices. I'd opened my eyes a few times, looking up at the shadows on his face. Who had held me like that? Saichi? Jaeyoon? Namgi? Where was he? How unnerving to surrender a slice of time like it never happened.

"Stay calm. Deep breaths. I'll call the doctor—"

"No doctor! I need to get out of here *now!*" Someone had to tell them it was all a lie. Ryo was lying. Someone had to stop him. He was going to destroy Vortex without even telling us why.

"Shh, shh, it's okay…"

A few unapologetic knocks penetrated the room and more voices flooded in. I could hear muffled sobs and I realized they were mine. Tears stung behind my eyelids. I couldn't escape there any longer. This nightmare was real.

Vortex.

What was there without Vortex?

"Miss Allister." English. My eyes flew open. A nurse was looking at me with dark, round eyes. I was glad it wasn't Kyungsoon. "I don't want to have to sedate you again, so I'm going to need you to calm yourself. Let's take a few deep breaths together, okay?"

A nurse. That could've been me. If I'd stuck with it, overcome the obstacles, then maybe I never would've gotten attached to Vortex, never would've had to see them splitting apart right before my eyes.

"Just sedate me. I'm not ready to wake up."

"That's not how life works, Miss Allister," she told me sternly, but I closed my eyes again. Away from her lack of sympathy, away from Ilsung wringing his hands, away from the unpleasant reminders of the world I'd run from in America.

What was Ryo hiding? Why was everyone in Vortex always hiding things from each other? They were supposed to know everything about each other!

Vortex.

What was there without Vortex?

I still had my job. My new life. That was more than I'd ever dreamed I'd have. Fuck off, feelings. Fuck off, self-pity.

But *Vortex…*

"What happened?" I wanted to know Ilsung's version.

The nurse switched to Korean to tell me very plainly, "You lost a lot of blood, but you're doing just fine. The theatrics are unnecessary." She shot Ilsung a look and my teeth gave an audible grit.

"Jaeyoon-shi told us that you fell through a glass coffee table in Ryo-shi's apartment?" The hurt on Ilsung's face was poorly hidden. I should've told him the truth when I had the chance. This was a terrible way for him to find out how much I'd been lying to him. "You're lucky Jaeyoon-shi acted quickly, and you're *very* lucky the table was tempered glass. The doctor said that you could've bled out if any of those pieces—"

The nurse clicked her tongue. "There's no sense in dwelling on what *could* have happened. Kit-nim is absolutely fine." I flinched thinking of Mino and they both surveyed my reaction with concern. "Anyhow, I'm Han Eunha, head nurse. I'll be taking care of you for the duration of your stay, Kit-nim." She bobbed in a peeved bow and then made for the door. "I'll return shortly. I've got some calls to make now that you're awake."

The second she was gone, I moved to tackle reality.

"Ilsung-shi, please forgive me for lying to you. I'm very sorry."

He shook his head. "Let's not talk about that right now, Kit. You're in a hospital bed. Don't stress yourself out."

No. I needed to be shaken awake. I needed reality to be shoved down my throat. Nurse Eunha was right. That's life. "Please go ahead and scold me. I've been irresponsible and stupid and I deserve a firm reprimand. Or to be fired. How bad is the damage? Has the public heard anything about this? Do my fans know I'm in the hospital?"

"For heaven's sake, your *health* is what's important right now! How could Vortex let you get so hurt?! You could've died! Those boys are lucky that Eunha-shi kicked them out before I got here. I would've put *them* in hospital beds too!"

"It's okay. I'm okay. I'll be okay."

"I just don't understand, Kit. I thought you were at home having an evening off. How much have you been hiding from me? I thought you knew how important it is that we're honest with each other."

"I'm very, very sorry, Ilsung-shi."

For the first time, he looked his age, and I was the one that did that to him. This was the man who met me at the airport, flagging me down with his handwritten sign, 'Welcome to Korea, Kit!' This was the man who told me from the start that I was going to be KJ's next top star. The man whose pep-talks never failed to pull my confidence out of a nosedive before and after every performance. He believed in me with such conviction that I had no choice but to believe in me too.

He'd never been anything but trusting and kind as my manager, and I betrayed him. Lied to him for months. I knew I'd probably be fired after this, but if I somehow kept my job, I hoped he would be stricter, colder with me from now on. I didn't deserve a second more of his kindness.

When he patted my head, I burst back into tears. "Ilsung-shi… I really am sorry. If I could get up, I would bow in the most formal apology and—"

"I don't want that, Kit." He shook his head, pressing a tissue into my hands. "I just want you to be safe. I'm just glad you're safe."

5 stages.

My apartment was quieter, chillier, lonelier than I remembered, and it was so empty that I spent hours every day contemplating getting a pet. I came close to getting a cat, then a rabbit, then a bird. Almost all three. Then I considered five. Five fuzzy little somethings that I could name after Vortex members. Meager replacements.

But I wasn't allowed pets in this apartment. Daydreaming about it was just a distraction to keep me from checking my news feed…

My reputation was in flames and I didn't want to watch it burn. Just once, I'd looked and read something about a brazen argument in a parking garage and mismatched clothes. The whole world knew that I was at Ryo's apartment in the middle of the night with all five Vortex members… and that someone had left in an ambulance.

I was just waiting to be fired and sent home. Any day now, I'd get the call from Ilsung, or from some stranger in upper management. You violated your contract. Your sales have dropped. You've taken too long off work. You're fired. Pack your bags.

And any day now, the news would drop: Vortex disbanded, Kasugai Ryo leaves for Japan, fans shattered, world tour canceled…

I hoped I was fired before that. It was going to get grisly here at ground zero once Korea found out Vortex's fate. Considering the scandal I'd just been involved in, Vortexans might actually blame me.

At least in America I could blend in, maybe even return to anonymity where I could wallow in peace. So go ahead, KJ. Exile me back to hell. Better to be lonely there than here where people were probably going to want my head on a spike.

What coffee shop would accept me now though? Lately, I couldn't even assemble a proper cup of instant coffee. Twice, I chewed powder. Once, I just drank boiling water.

I wasn't fired yet though. The last thing I'd heard from KJ was an order to lie low for a bit and recover from my injury. And the break from work was nice, but all the time alone with my worries was wearing on me. I needed a better distraction than imaginary pets, so I broke down and started watching old concert DVDs.

Every song was carved into my heart, and I knew every word of their banter during intermissions. Watching them dance pulled on my limbs, watching them laugh pulled out tears. Vortex was what propped my soul up. What was going to happen to me once they were gone? No more concerts, no more music, no more magazines, no more anything... If I'd known that during DigitAlive, I would've bought every single piece of merchandise they had on sale that day. Instead, I just had one measly poster hanging on my wall.

And the DigitAlive world tour... Two years of appearances were booked all over the globe. Maybe Ryo would agree to put off quitting just for the duration of the tour, but then Vortex would have to lug his betrayal all around the world with them. And if everyone knew it was their last tour before they split up, fans would go insane over the tickets and then cry through every concert.

Before, I'd always looked forward to watching Minchi flirt during these concert DVDs. Now, watching them lit up every inch of me with visceral pain. Seeing Saichi blush, seeing Jaeyoon's face tighten with worry, seeing Mino oblivious to the damage he was doing...

Forget me. What was going to happen to *Saichi* now?

The remaining four might join separate groups, or maybe they'd go solo, but I doubted it. Vortex was be-all and end-all. All five or nothing. No one wanted to see a four-man Vortex, and definitely no one wanted to see them scattered across the industry.

I didn't want to think about it anymore. I couldn't believe I'd been there hiding behind a couch, front-row seat in the VIP section, watching Vortex spiral apart. And just by being there, I'd made things worse for them. Now they had a scandal to worry about on top of their split-up. Ryo had been right to hate me. What a destructive parasite I was.

I went online and maxed out my credit card buying more goods. I didn't feel guilty using my insider knowledge to stock up. If I was going to blow money I didn't have, I figured I might as well do it before the prices skyrocketed. More bang for my nonexistent buck.

When I got through all my concert DVDs, I moved on to variety shows I'd recorded and let more familiarity wash over me. I had it all memorized. I knew every joke, every answer they gave during interviews, every shared smile…

This was how I first got to know Vortex.

Two years ago, after hearing 'Delusion' for the first time that morning in the gas station, I'd scrambled to find anything I could about Vortex on the internet, desperate to learn more about them, desperate to get closer to them…

And now, here I was, doing it all over again. It terrified me to think I was slipping further and further back in time.

I didn't want to go back to a time without them.

Final straw.

When a knock came at the door, I actually thought it was a package arriving—maybe a stack of back issue magazines, or a Saichi plushie, or last year's Vortex calendar. Either that or Ilsung was here to remind me that tomorrow it was time to come back to work.

I hadn't been fired. I almost wished I had. This industry was barren without Vortex, and I was dreading dealing with the fallout from my stupid scandal.

I set down my coffee and headed for the door, but before I could even reach the front hall, I heard the door open.

Didn't I lock it?! What kind of delivery man just walks in like they own the place? Ilsung certainly wouldn't. And I could hear that the intruder hadn't taken their shoes off. Ilsung would never be so rude. Okay, but a burglar wouldn't knock first before breaking in, right? Was it a disgruntled fan?

Anxious now, I retreated back into the kitchen. Then I heard a voice, "There's no way she's gone out. I heard she's been holed up in here for days. Maybe she's still in bed. Go check her bedroom."

"No. I told you I don't like this. You check her bedroom."

"I don't know where it is. I bet *you* do."

"I don't, damn you. I told you again and again—"

I was up all night. Maybe I was hallucinating. Or maybe the television was still on and I just hadn't noticed until now. I knew those voices, and it was just impossible that they were real.

I peeked around the corner into the living room and I looked straight into the eyes of Kasugai Ryo. He flinched. I flung myself back into the kitchen and banged my head on the wall.

What the fuck.

I was crazy. I was delusional. There was no way Ryo was here. Why would he be here? God, oh god, I had to call Ilsung. I needed help. I needed rehospitalization *now*.

"You gonna fucking hurt yourself again?!"

"Good morning," another apparition called in English, laughing. "I'd thank you to have a little more regard for that pretty head of yours, pet. You've been reckless lately!"

No, not even *my* brain could come up with something this strange. Why were Kyungsoon and Ryo here in my apartment?

Kyungsoon.

That Kyungsoon. The one who worked with Jaeyoon to uproot my entire life so I could come be the 'pet' of her top artist. The one who thought so little of Mino that she let him be tortured within the walls of her agency. I wasn't sure I liked her anymore.

That Kyungsoon was traipsing around my living room with her loud stilettos. Yes, I'd left magazines all over the floor, but did she have to step all over them? Ryo's eyes were on the stacks of CDs on my coffee table. I don't know why I felt embarrassed. I wouldn't be a true fan if I didn't have every CD.

But *why were they here?*

"Such a humble abode, isn't it, Ryo? Compared to *your* place." She scrutinized me and then she switched back to English, "Goodness, the past couple days have been hard on you, hmm?" Crap. I frenzied over my appearance, straightening my pajamas, raking fingers through my hair. "Anyway, I come bearing good news. Kit love, we're here to make you an offer you can't refuse—"

"She *can* refuse." Ryo looked up from a magazine near his feet. Unlike Kyungsoon, he'd taken his shoes off. I appreciated it.

Kyungsoon's spike heel was right in the middle of Mino's face. I felt like that was pretty damn symbolic.

Her smile widened. "She won't."

Were we just not going to address how weird it was for them to walk right into my apartment like they owned the place? Well, Kyungsoon probably did own the place...

Ryo avoided my eyes, looking tamer than I'd ever seen him, maybe even sheepish. *He* obviously knew it was weird to be here. Whatever. I could be hospitable even if this was bizarre.

"Um, I made some coffee?" Maybe. I think I got it right this time.

"Lovely. You sweet child. Let's chat over some coffee then."

"Can we chat in *Korean?*" Ryo grumbled.

"I think not. You should practice your English more often, Ryo. Come, come, into the tiny kitchen you go." And so I found myself with an idol and a CEO sitting at my shoddy kitchen table. I only had one mug though. Rushed and twitchy, I dumped my own coffee out and scrubbed the mug clean for Ryo. I served Kyungsoon coffee in a teacup and she definitely noticed.

"Aren't you going to have any, pet?" She knew I didn't have any more mugs, dammit! She tutted. "I know you were destitute in America, but you're an idol now, and one of *mine*, no less. You can absolutely afford a full set of dishes on your salary. Perhaps you shouldn't spend so much on Vortex paraphernalia, hmm? You're just funneling your money back into the company."

I didn't answer. I'd already taken her advice to heart once and it almost ruined my sanity.

"Kit dear, your coloring really is off. I do hope you'll be returning to work soon. All this indoor air clearly isn't agreeing with you. Come. Sit down before you collapse."

I did feel sick. She was here on some agenda obviously, and that was petrifying. What did she want from me now? Was she going to punish me for breaking up with Saichi?

"*Kit*. Are you listening to me? Come sit!"

I sloshed the rest of the coffee into a glass and I would've burned my hands bringing it to the table if it weren't for my bandages.

"I'm sorry about what happened with your boyfriend, love."

I flinched and coffee surged over the glass rim. And there, my bandages weren't white anymore and I'd burned my hands after all. But how did she always know *everything?!*

"I feel for you. I do. But I hope you can forgive the poor thing. He's been having such a hard time over the past few years. I really thought he might find some solace in you but…"

Was she openly admitting she'd known all along that Saichi loved Mino? And she still pushed me on him anyway? Her and Jaeyoon were two peas in a pod with this puppet master nonsense.

"Even if you're no longer in a relationship with him, I hope you'll still try to keep our dear Saichi comfortable during this difficult time. We wouldn't want him to do anything silly…"

I checked Ryo's face for any inkling of understanding, but it seemed like Jaeyoon and Kyungsoon were the only ones who knew about Saichi's overdose. Had Kyungsoon figured out that *I* knew? And what did she mean by keeping Saichi comfortable? What the hell was she asking me to do? If she wanted him comfortable, maybe we could start by *not* breaking up Vortex and throwing his whole life into turmoil? My quick glance at Ryo turned into a long reproachful glare. Did we have to talk about this in front of a traitor? Actually, did we have to talk about this at all? Was there nothing that Kyungsoon would let me keep private?

"To that same end, I'll also be putting Mino through sensitivity training, so that should help ease the situation a bit?"

Despite the circumstances, I almost smiled. "Yes, that should help. I think Mino could benefit from that."

"Yes, yes. At any rate, truly sorry for your loss, love, but try to keep your chin up and keep moving forward, hmm? And on that note, let's talk about why we're here, shall we? As you know, Ryo here is under some pressure to leave Vortex."

"I knew it," I hissed. "I knew there was more to it."

Ryo hid behind a sip of coffee. "You don't know shit."

Kyungsoon scoffed. "Oh, please. Don't irritate me right now, Ryo. Of course she knows! You *hospitalized* her with the news."

"I lied," Ryo ground the words past his teeth. "She doesn't know the specifics of why I'm quitting. No one does. I gave them all something easier to swallow."

She sighed and began a survey of her long red nails. "Lying to your own group… You really are something else, Ryo. Would you care to explain then, or shall I? What an absolute waste of my time."

"My parents are forcing me to get married," Ryo spat. So loudly that I almost knocked my glass over. And then his words set in.

Married. *Married.*

I gripped the table like that might keep my brain from floating out of my skull. These two wouldn't take kindly to me passing out.

"Married. You're getting *married?* Ryo…"

"Shi."

"Wait, *forcing* you to get married? Is that legal?"

"Like laws matter," Kyungsoon laughed happily and I shuddered. "The upper strata of society are rife with arranged marriages, Kit love. I know you can't be expected to understand, but it's actually rather run-of-the-mill. In fact, I'd venture a guess that Ryo's former social circles in Tokyo are comprised entirely of politically married couples and the unfortunate heirs they spawn out of necessity. If I recall correctly, Ryo's own parents—"

Ryo growled, "That's plenty, President."

"So they just… picked out a fiancée for you? W-when are you—?"

Ryo's eyes narrowed. I could see him getting ready to call me nosy and annoying, but then Kyungsoon waved her nails at him and he gave a bitter sigh. "I don't know when… Soon or else, basically. And yeah, they picked her out for me before I was even born. If my parents had anything to do with it, we'd already be married."

Kasugai Ryo was getting married.

A Vortex member *married*. First, Korea would combust, then the world would implode. Fans would swarm the ceremony. The woman would be razed on the altar. The wedding kiss of death.

No, it didn't matter anymore. Vortex was ending. He could do whatever he wanted now. The fans might not ever even find out.

So why did I have to find out? I didn't wanna know about this.

"Wait. Stop." I held up a hand. Kyungsoon boredly inspected her teacup. She hadn't bothered to drink any of the coffee. Just sniffed it and curled her lip a little. I waited for her to look up. I wanted to read her while I asked, "Why am I being told this? Why are you two here?"

Her eyes were flat as a shark's. Nothing to read there. She scoffed, "Don't you get all jittery, you funny little creature. We're here for a win-win situation. Everyone will be getting what they want today."

"*Hardly*," Ryo muttered.

She cuffed him on the shoulder. "This is taking too long, Ryo."

"They can't actually force you to get married though, right?"

His teeth grated and his knuckles whitened on my mug. Kyungsoon answered for him, "If he doesn't comply, his career—and Vortex's, for that matter—will be permanently over. They've assembled quite a juicy dossier, Kit love."

"Oh, so they're blackmailing their own son? What a shock." Apple Cinnamon here didn't fall far from his tree.

This time, Ryo's teeth ground so loud that it made my own ache. "It's nothing you need to know about." He scowled at Kyungsoon. "And thank you so very much for letting on about that. Now I'm never gonna hear the goddamn end of it."

"At present, I remain your president, Ryo. I ask that you conduct yourself accordingly and mind how you address me."

"Why do they want you to get married so much?"

"There's a lot of money in it for my parents. They won't see any of the Kasugai fortune if I don't start upholding the family name."

"Isn't Vortex enough for them? You're upholding plenty."

"None of that matters to my grandpa. I got on his bad side during my freshman year of college when I was out performing in clubs every night. And unfortunately, I'm the only male to carry on the name, so he wants me to settle down."

"Now for my counterstrategy!" Kyungsoon applauded herself. "Ryo can't marry that young lady in Japan if he's *already* married… The Christians just hate the idea of divorce after all, don't they?"

My skin crawled. But there was no way she was going where I thought she was going with this. Deep breaths. Deep breaths.

"Besides the fact that I'm a Vortex fan, I still don't see how this has anything to do with me."

"Oh yes, you do, pet. Use that pretty head. Ryo here has to get married. If he doesn't, Vortex is ruined. We don't want that, do we?"

"No, we don't."

"Of course not! So shouldn't we marry off our dear Ryo to someone… in the area? Someone who would understand and respect the demands of his career with Vortex. Someone who's a good little Christian girl that his parents will surely *adore* once they get to know her. Someone with a talent for picking up Asian languages. Someone who seems to favor… Japanese men. Have you caught my drift, love? I'm laying it on rather thick."

I gripped the table tighter, but my balance was unsalvageable now. The room seemed to pour to one side and empty away. I had to fight for the air in the words. "You want me to marry Kasugai Ryo."

Ryo groaned. "Would it kill you to use an honorific with my name just once in your life? *Fuck*."

Kyungsoon giggled. "Hush, Ryo-*san*." I started to tip. Ryo's hand snapped across the table to steady my head. His eyes burned me.

"Stay conscious, please. Breathe."

"Sorry…"

"Just say no. You can say no."

I tried to shake my head, but his hand was unforgiving. "No, no. If I say no, Vortex will—"

"No, she *can't* say no," Kyungsoon snapped. "I'm not losing my top group to some stuffy Japanese socialites."

"President—"

Her voice rolled over top of his, "What does she care anyway? What does she have to lose? She's just got to sign a paper and all our problems are solved. You get a wife, she gets Vortex, I get my money, and we all live happily ever after."

"I told you it's not going to be that simple. She's not Japanese. They're going to *hate* her—"

Again, she spoke over him, grabbing my hand. I shook her off. "Kit. Pet. Love. You know what's at stake. You simply can't say no."

"Yes, she can! And she should!"

"This is actually quite a bonus for you, Kit dear. After all, being an idol, it's not like you'll ever be able to marry otherwise. And this should help ease the pain of recent events, no? This way you still get to go home with a Vortex member of your very own!"

Saichi.

How could I do this to him? He was still holding out hope that I'd take him back. Marrying Ryo would be stabbing Saichi in the back when he was already down…

But once we explained the circumstances, he'd understand, wouldn't he? It was for the good of the group. For Vortex.

To his credit, Ryo looked as nauseated as I felt. "President, *please.*"

Steadier now, I pulled his hand off of my head and he quieted. Now that I broke up with Saichi, Kyungsoon was repurposing me. And if it meant protecting Vortex, I didn't even care. Far better to be a sentient puppet than the idiot I was before, running around thinking I had agency while every tiny thing in my life was completely orchestrated. Last time, she rearranged my life from the shadows, but this time around, I was present for the negotiations, and maybe I even had a few bargaining chips in my hand.

"Well, love? What's your decision?"

As if it was really my decision. I could've laughed, but I nodded. "Don't worry. I'll do it."

"*What?!*" Ryo exploded. His coffee came surging across the table and I watched it come, unconcerned. Kyungsoon applauded as it cascaded into my lap.

"There's my girl! I knew I could count on you!"

"I have one condition."

"What's wrong with you? What do you mean you'll do it?!"

I ignored him. I looked squarely into Kyungsoon's shark eyes. "I'll do it, provided that you fire those trainees you've been letting run wild." Take that, puppet master.

She stiffened and sucked all warmth from my kitchen. More coffee came curling off the table edge. It drilled icily down the side of my leg and then slowed to a trickle.

She burst into sudden laughter. "We don't have any wild trainees at my company, dear. They're *trained*. That's the point." Good god. That made it sound like they were acting on her orders. Did she know they were doing more than following Mino around? "Have some trainees been bothering you, Kit, dear? Boys will be boys, you know. You should take it as a compliment."

I crossed my arms, tightened the shakes out of my body, and pushed through her laughter. "Mino assured me that you would know exactly who and what I'm talking about."

Ryo sat back, confused. "Kit, what the hell?"

"Isn't she a funny thing, Ryo?"

"I'm not trying to be funny, President. I want your word that you'll put a stop to what's going on. This is about the safety of one of your top talents."

"Look at you driving a hard bargain! But think for a moment..." The laugh died unnaturally and her voice turned sinister, "Are you in any position to ask for favors after the scandal you caused?"

"I think I am. Because both of you need something out of me. And you're going to hear this same request from Saichi soon anyway, so you might as well just fire them. You shouldn't have brushed off Mino's complaints. From what I know of it, it's a serious issue."

Ryo was getting pissed off again. "Kit, seriously, what—?"

Annoyed, Kyungsoon swatted at him. "Shut up, you imbecile. I'm getting you a wife."

"Provided you meet my condition," I insisted. Time turned sticky as she studied my face. I didn't think I was asking that much, but she looked like she was about to threaten my immigration status.

"A top artist should never get too comfortable, love..." Definitely a threat. I'd officially gotten on her bad side. "It's a competitive industry, and our company puts out the best of the best exactly because our conditions can be severe. Mino should be able to handle a couple of rowdy trainees by himself. Sending you and Saichi on his errands, that's just pathetic."

"President, are you training artists or predators?"

Ryo growled, "Watch it, Kit."

"With all due respect, if you don't know what I'm talking about, then stay out of this, Ryo-shi."

He opened his mouth to bark back, but Kyungsoon clapped her hands again. "Very well, Kit dear." She didn't seem annoyed or angry. She seemed amused, and that was so disturbing. "If you really want to waste your one condition on something as trivial as the careers of some trainees—"

This time, I spoke over her, "I'm going to take that as your agreement to my condition."

"Hey. *Hey!*" Ryo had spotted the coffee. He ripped off his jacket and started sopping it up with the sleeves. "Doesn't that burn?!"

"I'm fine. Stop ruining your jacket."

"I've got plenty of jackets." He bent near to me and tried to catch my eyes. His voice got unnecessarily quiet, blistering with cinnamon. "Listen, screw what she says. You don't have to do this."

Did he really think I'd ever say no to something so important? Well, this would show him. I seemed to recall him calling me a parasite. A faker. A leech. I'd be damned if he ever called me anything like that again. Who was the leech now? I smiled. "If you didn't want me to accept, then you shouldn't have asked in the first place."

"*I* didn't ask anything. It's *her* idea."

"Then you'd rather not?"

"Are you seriously fucking asking me that? No shit I'd rather not! I don't even know you, let alone like you, and now I've gotta make you my fucking wife? I don't know why you're so calm about this, but I'm starting to think you're certifiably insane."

Kyungsoon dug her red talons into his arm and pulled him back into his seat. "Careful what you say to your future bride, Ryo."

"President, she's not of sound mind to make this decision."

"You're going to make a simply awful husband talking like that. Good thing you two won't be anywhere near each other."

"How many times do I have to say it? This isn't going to work! Kit, back me up, would you? Me, I'm only getting married because I fucking have to! *You* have a choice!" Not really, no, but I didn't care. "Just tell her you don't want to do this!"

"I don't really mind either way."

"*What?*"

"There you have it, Ryo. If you come up with some other solution to this problem, do let us know, but in the meantime, Kit will just have to do, won't she? Would you prefer to lose everything you've worked for? Would you prefer to disband Vortex?"

"No, damn it, but there's gotta be some other way! Can't I marry literally *any other woman* in this city?! Or can't we maybe work out some kind of compromise with my parents?! For the love of god—!"

"No." Kyungsoon stood and brushed herself off like my furniture had dirtied her. Her voice grew frigid, "KJ doesn't compromise. We're doing things *my* way, Ryo. End of discussion. Now *come.*"

"No!" Ryo's eyes turned to me, bright with panic. "Come on, Kit! Why the fuck are you okay with this?!"

I just didn't care.

I wasn't upset.

I wasn't nervous.

Everything was going to be okay now.

With those trainees out of the picture, maybe Mino and Saichi would have the chance to heal. They'd be able to reach a solution on their own time, and Jaeyoon would take care of Saichi through the ups and downs. Ryo would be able to honor his pact and stay with his group. Namgi wouldn't have to cry anymore.

Vortex wasn't going to split up. That was what mattered most. They were going to be okay. So I'd be okay too, no matter what.

"I'd do anything for Vortex."

Cast

Kit Allister – ex-Ohioan, ex-barista, college dropout

Vortex Members:

Oh Saichi – leader of Vortex

Kasugai Ryo – rap artist from Tokyo

Bae Namgi – your favorite oppa

Kim Mino – singer-songwriter, actor, brat

Mahn Jaeyoon – the mastermind maknae

KJ Global Entertainment:

Park Ilsung – Kit's manager

Lee Kyungsoon – CEO of KJ Global Entertainment

Shin Hyejin – Namgi's private driver

Lee Siwoo – photographer

Sun Woojin – chief of Vortex's personal security

Furry Friends:

Bitna – Kit's pet dog who actually belongs to Lee Siwoo

Choi Sangchul – the man pig host of Tick Tock Talk

Spick and Span – Aunt Caroline's two cats

Yuji / Yujin – Saichi's calico buddy that lives at the marina

Caroline Allister – Kit's late aunt

Ayukawa Noriko – Saichi's grandmother and boat

The Zhangs – Saichi's honorary grandparents in China

Han Eunha – head nurse at Seoul National Hospital

The Beer Can Brothers – R.I.P.

Honorific Suffixes

-ah: informal affectionate Korean suffix for names ending in consonants

-chan: informal affectionate Japanese suffix; usually used for females

-ie: informal affectionate Korean suffix for names ending in consonants

-gun: Korean suffix used by an adult to address young males

-san: polite neutral Japanese suffix

-shi: polite Korean suffix used among those of relatively equal standing

-nim: formal respectful Korean suffix; usually used with one's title rather than one's name to refer to superiors at work, teachers, customers, clients, guests, patients, or gods

-ya: informal affectionate Korean suffix for names ending in vowels

Korean Terms

babo: dummy, stupid; can be very offensive

hanja: written characters borrowed from the Chinese language; they are called *hanzi* in Mandarin, and *kanji* in Japanese

hyung: respectful term used by males to address older males; loosely means "big brother"

maknae: the youngest member in a group

noona: respectful term used by males to address older females; loosely means "big sister"

oppa: a friendly term used by females to address older males; loosely means "big brother"

sajin: photograph

sasaeng: an obsessive K-Pop 'fan' that stalks and harasses idols

sunbaenim: a formal and respectful way to refer to an individual who is one's senior at school or at work

yaksok: promise, plans

Japanese Terms

kabocha: a Japanese variety of winter squash

medaka: a small freshwater fish commonly found in rice paddies

shashin: photograph

yakusoku: promise, plans

K-Pop Terms and More

Anti: (anti-fan) a hater who dislikes something or someone but devotes time to mocking or criticizing it

Bae: (Before Anyone Else) an affectionate way to address one's significant other; like 'baby' or 'babe'; also Namgi's surname

Bias: one's favorite idol, or favorite member of an idol group

Bias wrecker: an idol who causes loyalty to one's bias to waver

DigitAlive: Vortex's latest global tour featuring augmented reality

Dalgona coffee: instant coffee powder, sugar, and hot water whipped and then added to cold or hot milk

Fanservice: giving fans what they are perceived to want

Fighting!: used for encouragement or support in the face of difficulty

Hard stan: a fan who views their idols in a sexual way

Idol: an entertainer marketed for image, attractiveness, and personality in Asian pop culture; usually singers and dancers, but also commonly trained in other roles, such as acting and modeling

Kit-Kat: a member of the Kit Allister fandom

Lightstick: customized LED wands sold for use during a concert

Minchi: a subunit in Vortex made up of Saichi and Mino

OTP: (One True Pairing) one's favorite fictional relationship

Netizen: (Internet citizen) an avid user of the internet, often actively involved on social media or in other various online communities

Queerbaiting: marketing or behavior that hints at an LGBTQ relationship without ever confirming or legitimizing it

Rookie: an idol who has debuted in the last year or so

Soft stan: a fan who views their idols in a pure or non-sexual way

Ship: to endorse a romantic relationship

Ship war: when groups of shippers fight over romantic pairings

Skinship: physical affection; often between group members

Stan: a devoted fan (of K-Pop, or a particular group or idol)

Subunit: a smaller group formed within an idol group

Tick Tock Talk: a Korean variety television talk show

Trainee: an artist at an entertainment agency who is still in training to debut as an idol

Vortexan: a member of the Vortex fandom

Acknowledgment.

Hey there, Vortexan.

Just acknowledging that was a major cliffhanger.
Wanna be the first to climb that cliff and *Face the Music?*
Or maybe you wanna come cliffhang out in the 34 St. Discord!
If you'd like to sign up for updates on the next book, or just
consume any and all content while you wait, here ya go:

Thanks for spending some time in our universe with us.

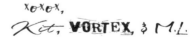

xoxox,
Kit, **VORTEX**, & M.L.

P.S. Don't forget to support the indie author with a review!